You Rolling River

BY
ARCHIE BINNS

YOU ROLLING RIVER

THE TIMBER BEAST

MIGHTY MOUNTAIN

THE LAND IS BRIGHT

THE LAURELS ARE CUT DOWN

BACKWATER VOYAGE

LIGHTSHIP

NORTHWEST GATEWAY

THE ROARING LAND

You Rolling River

BY
ARCHIE BINNS

CHARLES SCRIBNER'S SONS
NEW YORK
1947

For
JACQUELINE
AND GEORGIA

SHENANDOAH

Oh, Shenandoah, I long to hear you,
  Hoo-ray, you rolling river!
Oh, Shenandoah, I long to hear you,
  Ha-ha, we're bound away 'cross the wide Missouri!

Oh, Shenandoah, I love your daughter,
  Hoo-ray, you rolling river!
Oh, Shenandoah, I love your daughter,
  Ha-ha, we're bound away 'cross the wide Missouri!

Missouri she's a mighty river,
  Hoo-ray, you rolling river!
When she rolls down her topsails shiver,
  Ha-ha, we're bound away 'cross the wide Missouri!

Seven years I courted Sally,
  Hoo-ray, you rolling river!
Seven more I longed to have her,
  Ha-ha, we're bound away 'cross the wide Missouri!

Farewell, my dear, I'm bound to leave you,
  Hoo-ray, you rolling river!
Oh, Shenandoah, I'll not deceive you,
  Ha-ha, we're bound away 'cross the wide Missouri!

You Rolling River

1

ON THE STEAMER coming up to the Columbia River, John Fortune read aloud from Washington Irving's *Astoria*.

Marjorie, who was a good girl, listened attentively, and Dehlia listened because she was her husband's devout follower. Young John and Thomas were more interested in exploring the ship and talking to sailors. Once, when it was time for the reading aloud, Mr. Fortune had a long search before he found his sons, snugged down in a lifeboat, pretending to be castaways. Next time they were in the engine room, shouting questions at a man in greasy overalls while they watched the great, stamping dance of the engines. There were other derelictions, and the boys had to be disciplined sternly.

During his first days in Astoria, John Fortune was busy finding a home, and acquainting himself with his work at the custom house, but his mind returned to things in their proper order. On the afternoon when he bought the "old Prosser house," he asked the agent to show his family the historic places in town.

The real-estate agent was Edward Barton—"Just call me 'Ed'." He was a confident and coarsely good-looking young man, tireless in the interests of a client, and full of enterprises of his own. Willing gossips had informed Dehlia that the elder Barton operated a string of gambling houses in the section known as "Swilltown," but the son was anxious to make himself worthy of the better part of Astoria. He was honest as real-estate men go, and temperate in his habits,

[1]

patronizing the best bagnio unostentatiously, and never appearing in public with a prostitute. It was thought that marriage would reform him altogether—and he was already enamoured of a pretty and refined young woman who gave him no encouragement although her parents' hearts were set on the match.

Whatever else Ed Barton may have been, he was a practical businessman, startled by a serious-minded official asking after the ruins of the past. "Historic places, Mr. Fortune? I suppose you mean Fort Astoria. It's not much to look at, but I'll show you what there is."

The young man loaded the family into his carriage and rattled them east along a street terraced into the hillside that slanted down from the woods to the wide river. While he drove in search of the past, his mind went out to the future and to property on the other side of Youngs Bay, which he urged on the newcomers as a conservative investment. A bridge was about to be built and within a year property would double in value.

Dehlia knew that even honest optimism is not always justified and she felt uneasy, but her husband's voice reassured her. "Thank you, Mr. Barton. Buying a house I need is one thing; property I don't need is another. I never speculate," in the practiced voice of a teetotaler refusing a drink.

Barton said cheerfully, "It's such a sure thing that I hadn't thought of it as speculation, but I admire a man who knows his own mind. Cigar, Mr. Fortune?"

Mr. Fortune did not smoke, but he had no objection to the habit in another, provided it did not endanger his wife and children. "Shall I take the reins while you light your cigar?"

"Thanks, no." The young real-estate man lit his cigar while driving at a lively trot, and flicked the match into the road. "It's second nature to me." A minute later, he slowed the horses to a walk and turned the corner. "Whoa!" He stopped the carriage, with a cloud of cigar smoke drifting over the occupants of the back seat. Dehlia found it offensive to be bathed in smoke from the mouth of a young rake. She was about to object, when Barton pointed his whip toward the vacant lot across the sidewalk. "There's Fort Astoria."

The vacant lot was overgrown with brush and brambles, and strewn with rubbish at its edge. It was little enough to look at, but the history of the West had been touched off from that spot, and it had been worthy of a printed book. On the front seat, Mr. Fortune turned his square broadcloth shoulders and his square serious face, framed by a bowler hat and black mutton-chop whiskers. Catching the inattentive eyes of his older son, he asked, "Are you looking, John?"

"Yes, Papa."

"And you, Thomas?"

"Yes, Papa."

The father cleared his throat. "Well, boys, what do you see?"

Young John answered, "A vacant lot."

"With brush on it," Thomas said.

Ten-year-old Marjorie could have given a better answer, but John Fortune's pride was in his sons, and in them he also found his disappointments. "If you boys had paid more attention to what I read, you would see more than that; you would see how great things grow from small beginnings. That spot was once the only American settlement in two-thirds of the United States."

"Yes, Papa."

"Yes, Papa." But it was still a vacant lot, and even Mr. Fortune conceded that it was the worse for time. "I had hoped the stockade would be left."

"It's been this way as long as anyone can remember," Barton said. "People who come to see it are always dis-

[3]

appointed." Then his voice brightened. "There's something around the corner you'll want to see: a grave from early times. People who like history always go for it." Around the corner, his voice brightened still more. "Hello, there's other visitors ahead of us!"

Dehlia saw two young ladies, one in sober brown kneeling on a narrow strip of grass between the sidewalk and a building, and a slender one in a pink dress and white sailor hat, holding a bunch of flowers. The tableau was broken as the girls started at the sound of hoofs and wheels; the one in brown got up hastily from where she had been pulling weeds and hurried down the street, and the one in pink put down the flowers and followed her friend.

"*Hope!*" Young Barton called.

The girl turned her head for a moment, and hurried on.

"*Wait, Hope!*" When the girl did not wait, he muttered impatiently and touched the horses with the whip. Overtaking her, he swerved recklessly out of the street.

"Look where you're going!" Mr. Fortune shouted, and Dehlia reached for her children. The driver reined in suddenly, with the horses' feet clattering on the wooden sidewalk, barring the girl's way.

"Confound you, you might have upset us!" Mr. Fortune said, but the younger man was too engrossed to hear him. The object of his arrogant and ardent pursuit was a girl of eighteen or nineteen, slenderly mature, with an oval face and blue eyes, and light-brown hair under her backward-tilted sailor hat. She was pretty enough to attract anyone, but Dehlia had no respect for a man who could not control himself. The girl did not show any respect for Barton, either. She was only staying because the horses blocked her path, and she parried his questions and compliments expertly. When she tired of it, she said, "Now, let me past, Ed Barton, or I'll never speak to you again!"

"All right, but tell me one thing first." He pointed with

[4]

his thumb toward the grave. "If I was in *his* place, would you put flowers on my grave?"

"With pleasure," she said, "but if you're a good real-estate salesman you'll keep on the right side of the earth!"

"Thanks, Hope, I intend to." Barton sounded both nettled and admiring as he looked after her. "Prettiest girl in Astoria, but she has a mind of her own!" The Fortunes' cool silence reminded him that he had other business on hand. "Just a minute, and I'll back up so we can have a look at this grave."

A few feet from the edge of the sidewalk there was a thin slab of gray stone, neatly inscribed to the memory of D. MCTAVISH, ESQ., AGED 42 YEARS, DROWNED CROSSING THIS RIVER, MAY 9, 1814.

Young John and Thomas looked politely at the slab, but the inscription caught their father's rarely stirred imagination. "Boys, we read about him in Irving's book! Correct me if I am wrong—he was one of Astor's fur traders—"

Dehlia was sure Irving hadn't mentioned a fur-trading McTavish at Astoria, but young Barton agreed, "That's right. Another trader named Henry was drowned with him, but he didn't get a stone. Both of them courted Jane Barnes, who came out in the *Tonquin*—"

"A woman in the *Tonquin?*"

"That's right. She was a barmaid, out to see the world."

John Fortune was disappointed in history, which had taken an improper turn. "Washington Irving never mentioned a woman in the party!"

"He must have been too polite. This Jane Barnes was the first white woman out here, and that gave her notions. She didn't find the men good enough, so she left to look over the field in China—and these two men were drowned together. You might say they were in the same boat to the last."

John Fortune looked at his inattentive sons. "Well, boys, there is a footnote to history. In time, you will appreciate it more. You might expect this to be an old story to the young ladies who were here, but it means enough for them to pull the weeds, and put flowers on a fur trader's grave."

The brothers said dutifully, "Yes, Papa," but it was clear that they were not stirred by vacant lots, or gravestones, or ancient affairs of the heart. They had other interests. On the way back to the hotel they coaxed for permission to visit the river front for a closer look at the great sailing ships anchored in the stream. Mr. Fortune forbade their going by themselves, but he was in a holiday mood; when they took his refusal in good part, he decided to accompany them.

Dehlia and Marjore went alone to the hotel and the deferential greetings of Mr. Megler, the proprietor, and Frank Gunn, the popular young day clerk, and to the friendly recognition of guests. From the doorway to the dining room, "Old Ben," the Negro steward, made a stately bow to Mrs. Fortune and smiled at Marjorie. Ben was lord of the dining room and master of deviled crabs, fried razor clams and Chinook salmon Occidental that brought epicures from Seattle and San Francisco. Ben was a reserved man, conscious of his worth, and he seldom unbent to flatter guests who had traveled so far in honor of his dishes. His recognition was a crowning honor, and Mrs. Fortune and Marjorie went on from that triumph to their suite which President Hayes had occupied on his Western trip. There were fresh flowers in their parlor; Mr. Megler was conscious of the fact that Astoria was not San Francisco, and he wanted the new official and his family to be so comfortable that they would hardly miss the luxurious city they had left.

The manager would never guess that Dehlia walked tensely through these days, with excitement that she suppressed even from herself. Here it was assumed that the Fortunes had been born to a suite at the Occidental, or a mansion on the hill. People envied the family their good luck—without knowing that there is no such thing as luck, only the iron will to do what must be done. Without discipline the Fortunes would be—she winced to think where, and in what condition.

Here, when Dehlia mentioned having grown up in San Francisco, other women said, "That must have been a happy time—girlhood in California!" Dehlia would smile and say it was, but actually she did not remember much girlhood or much happiness.

Her father had been called from a poor church in Iowa to a poorer one at the far end of Clay Street in San Francisco, and life in the parsonage was often uneasy and always meagre. Her sharpest recollections were of smells: noisy dinnertimes with the smell of baked fish, which was cheap, and of cabbage, which was still cheaper at two cents a head—sometimes at one, if you bargained with the Italian vegetable man. There was also the smell of carbolic acid, which her father used after visiting some of his poorer parishioners. He spent a good deal of time among them, and he was almost as poor as they because he gave away most of his small salary. But he did not approve of their way of life. Sometimes he would say to Dehlia, "Fourteen children in rags, and the father out in the sand lot with the older boys, flying a kite! God should never send the improvident that many mouths to feed." Her father had never had the opportunity to set an example of the proper size of a family; his wife had died in childbirth with the seventh, and he did not marry again.

The provident as well as the improvident came to the church, and it was there, at a social, that she met John Fortune. John was a dark, serious young man, who showed a preference for her company, though at first he was too shy to say much when they were together. Dehlia was then an old maid of twenty, and she had never had a serious urge to marry —perhaps because of family responsibilities, and because of all the wretched and teeming marriages of her father's parish:

[7]

marriages that would have populated a city except for waves
of diphtheria and summer complaint.

Dehlia admired John Fortune because he did not propose
marriage as the answer to all unhappiness. Like her, he had
family responsibilities: a mother and five brothers and sisters
who survived out of an original ten. His father had found the
answer to the unhappiness of too many children in the daughter of a fish peddler, and he had gone away with her to produce more children. John had then left school to become the
main support of the family, and he had found the rest of his
education in books, and later in night school. When Dehlia
met him he was on the way to being a self-made man, working in a hardware store and taking a business course at night.
He had been calling at the parsonage at respectful intervals
for two months before he got up his courage to put a question
to her. His hesitancy made her fear that after all he was like
other poor young men, who hoped to solve their problems by
piling misery on misery. But she had misjudged him. English
was his most difficult subject, he explained, and she was good
at language. Would she help him by telling him when he
said things wrong?

Dehlia helped him unselfishly toward his goal. As he felt
more at ease with language he had more to say, and he expressed well-thought-out ideas, sometimes neatly worded.
The first she remembered was, "Most people learn by their
own mistakes, but it is a shortcut to learn by the mistakes of
others." Dehlia always remembered that; and John made it
one of the rules of his life.

Six months after Dehlia began coaching him, John Fortune
became a clerk in the San Francisco Custom House, and a
year later he discussed marriage with her. By that time their
lives were already intertwined. He could have proposed in
some secluded place and half unwillingly she would have let
him take her in his arms, knowing that this was the beginning
of marriage, which smelled of boiling cabbage and carbolic

acid. But John chose to discuss marriage in the full light and noise of Vittori's Restaurant, which was his only extravagance when they were together. They had finished their six-course dinner, except for the bottle of wine, which they never touched, and he had put down a half dollar in payment. They might have gone out then to the fog and the streetcar and the long ride home; but John had not talked himself out; he had just decided to begin.

He rested his forearm and solid hands on the red-checked cloth and looked at her gravely. "Dehlia," he said, "I have been making a study of marriage."

"Indeed." She waited.

"I hope you don't think it frivolous," he said; "it's a subject which concerns everybody, because everybody is married or unmarried. At odd moments I jotted down on a sheet of foolscap the names of all the married people I know, and after them I wrote what I know about their married life. It's surprising how much I learned by doing that."

"What did you learn?"

He said, "I didn't expect to find many happy marriages, but it was surprising how few I found; really surprising." He sighed. "Most married people are miserable, whether they know it or not."

"I know," she said faintly; "but why?"

"Wrong attitudes; poverty; too many children. Or none at all; that's almost as bad; it's worse after a while."

More faintly she said, "There always seems to be something."

"There generally is. But that's only half the study. On another sheet of foolscap, I jotted down the names of the unmarried people I know—old maids and bachelors—and after them I put down what I knew about whether they were happy or not. It was surprising what I learned by doing that."

"What did you learn?" she asked, a little less faintly.

"I found that unmarried people are more miserable than

married ones. At first they are like couples who don't have any children: they seem to have more fun and get along better; but it begins to wear on them, and after a while they get kind of desperate, even if they're quiet about it. The old maids get desperate first, but the bachelors get that way, too; and they're just as lonely."

It made her feel terribly alone, sitting across the little table from him in the light and noise of the restaurant, and her voice sounded wistful as she said, "It doesn't look as if anyone has a very good chance."

He said, "I guess living isn't easy, when so many people try and so few make a success of it. That's where people should start—knowing it isn't easy."

"What should they do after that, John?"

"A person should be able to figure that out from the facts," he said. "When you have to choose, you take the lesser of two evils." Then, as if he had been too hopeful, he clenched his hands on the checked tablecloth and scowled the way he did when he felt strongly about anything. "Oh, I know, Dehlia, marriage sounds like a desperate step! But it's the only chance: marriage and children." After a while, he said, "It isn't chance; you don't have a chance unless you decide what you want and stick to it! You have to control your life!"

Dehlia said firmly, "I believe that, John. I have seen so many people who didn't control their lives—"

Still scowling, John said, "Marriage, yes. Children, yes; but how many?"

"Not too many," she offered timidly.

He laid his clenched fist on the table, silently, but with a passionate certainty. "The right number of children," he said; "no more, no less!"

A few months before, Dehlia had thought of herself as guiding a timid and hesitant young man, giving him strength. Now he was stronger than she and more certain of himself. She asked, like a disciple, "What is the right number?"

"The number their parents can provide for properly," he answered. "Not just food and clothes; there must be play— in its right place—and education in one of the professions."

"That wouldn't allow most couples many children."

"For people like ourselves, with my prospects, it might allow three or four."

"I think we could manage four," Dehlia decided.

He said, "Four at the outside. Two of them would be likely to be girls; you know what they need better than I do. But no son of mine would be a beginning clerk at twenty-five!"

"I think you are doing wonderfully well," she said.

"I haven't a profession, Dehlia; it's too late for that now." Then he said, "If we have two sons, we would make a doctor out of one and a lawyer out of the other."

"There isn't anything better," she agreed; "a doctor and a lawyer."

John thought it over, then said, "If we have a third son, we'll make a minister of him."

Dehlia had just decided that they would never disagree on anything, but the word brought up a vision of the thread-bare parsonage, with its smell of cabbage and carbolic. "Not a minister!" she said.

John's face was forbidding, but his voice was kind. "I know what you mean, Dehlia, but there are ministers and ministers. Your father just picked it up; he hasn't much of a church, and most of what he gets he gives to the poor. Our son will be an Episcopal minister."

Her mind cleared. "I think that would do: a doctor and a lawyer and a minister."

Dehlia never regretted their mariage, and if she ever disagreed with John it was because she had not fully understood. She had suspected that he was stronger than she, and before long she knew it. He became her prophet, and she the disciple of the controlled life that makes the difference between human animals and men made in the image of God and enjoying the good things created for them.

They had planned to have four children at most, and after the birth of Marjorie, who was the third, John decided that they should consolidate their gains. A fourth might also be a girl, who would do little but add to their expenses.

Mrs. McArthur, in the downstairs flat, laughed at the decision. "It's your bootstraps you'll be lifting yourselves by. Come spring, and you'll both forget it! If you don't, he'll be finding another woman."

Mrs. McArthur was wrong. That was the end of one phase of their life, and it did not alienate them because it was the beginning of another phase.

They started with the theory that children cannot distinguish between right and wrong. Young John disturbed the theory by recognizing wrong at every turn and insisting on doing it, and he took a great deal of disciplining. Thomas was a quieter child who made little trouble during his first few years. He seemed to be trying to decide about good and evil for himself, but it turned out that he was making up his mind whether to side with his parents or with his outnumbered brother. When he was about four he cast his lot with young John, and after that the two boys broke windows and lied and ran away and were whipped together. Marjorie knew good from evil by the time she was able to walk and talk, but she made indifferent use of her discernment.

Her father sometimes said, "The child knows the difference between right and wrong, but she hasn't the moral courage to see wrong punished." That was her greatest weakness: she would foresee trouble and try to keep the boys from mischief; but afterward she would try to shield them and when they were being whipped for it she would cry louder than they. When they were older she continued to cry for them long after the mother was unable to wring a sound from either of the boys.

In the parsonage there had been no whipping, and without guidance Dehlia might never have begun it with her own children, but having started, she never questioned the rightness of it. Only a few days ago, on the steamer, a newly made friend hinted that the Fortunes disciplined their children too severely—and they ceased to be friends. From the beginning, Dehlia had been her husband's faithful follower—and she had never been disappointed in where the path led. Today it was the Occidental, and tomorrow their own big house on the hill, with wide grounds under trees, and a new Knabe piano for Marjorie to practice on. The woman on the steamer had criticized the generalship that made such things possible—without understanding its meaning, and not knowing that the parents disciplined themselves as sternly as they did their children.

The Fortunes' suite was on the north side of the hotel, and the windows overlooked the river that began a few housetops away; the wide river, crossed by masts and yards of anchored grain ships, amber-touched with sunset; the wide challenging river. . . .

In San Francisco there had been hills between the downstairs flat and the bay. To the boys, the water front had been a faraway dream beyond the hills. Here all streets gravitated to the docks, and every house was in sight of the river that mastered everything—as it had mastered the story of two fur traders fighting for a barmaid's hand; the river had taken the hussy away, and drowned both men impersonally. The river was death—and it was the only thing that lived and moved on through the centuries. That afternoon, John had tried to interest his sons in history, and when he failed the boys coaxed him away to the river front, aware of what he hadn't noticed: that history grows old and dies beside the timeless river.

It was dusk in the room, but Dehlia waited a while longer

to turn on the light. Off there to the east, the Columbia bulged to a width of ten miles, like a great bay among the sunset hills. To the west, she had learned to identify rugged Cape Disappointment at the river mouth. But when she looked now, the cape was blotted out by a thick fog bank, ragged-edged against the sky's clear afterglow, and the fishing boats that had been out toward the bar were sailing home.

Marjorie came in and sat at the window opposite Dehlia, too sensitive to her mother's mood or too timid to put on a light without permission. When she had looked out for a while, she asked, "Mamma, why don't the ships sail?"

"They'll sail when they are ready."

"The same ones have been out there ever since we came."

"Your father says they are waiting for sailors."

"Oh." And then, "Where do sailors come from?"

"Some of them from here in Astoria, and some from Portland, I believe." The mother was still intent on the disturbing river, answering questions half-absently. Harmless questions, but in San Francisco Marjorie had never thought about such things.

"Mamma, if the sailors are here, why does it take so long?"

"Your father says it happens every summer. This is the fishing season, and there is work in the logging camps and sawmills, and the wheat harvest, somewhere up the river; many men would rather do those things than go to sea."

"Will the ships have to wait all summer?"

"No, Majorie. Your father says the owners have agreed to pay more money for sailors, and they expect crews any day now."

"It's nice of them to pay the sailors more money."

Dehlia did not answer.

"Look at the boats, Mamma! They're having a race, aren't they?"

Dehlia had observed earlier that the fishing fleet was

coming in from the bar, and now the river to the west was covered with low, slender boats, some dark-hulled and some white, each with a mast near the bow, spreading two sails like great kites. The boats were far apart in the water, but in the air the corners of their sails were tip to tip. It was something like a race but it was more like a rout with all the boats straining in the same direction, wave after wave of them, and hundreds of sea gulls circling excitedly overhead. The last straggling boats were silhouetted against the bank of fog that towered behind them, ragged-edged, like a great pursuing breaker. "Look, Marjorie, they are racing the fog."

"It'll never catch them, Mamma! Hurry, little boats!"

The boats were hurrying under such a spread of sail that it looked as if they would all outrun the fog, but while the two watched, the farthest boats went dim, like shadows, and did not seem to matter any more. They went more dim and were gone, and the creeping grayness overtook the next rank of boats, and the next.

"The fog is catching them!" Marjorie said. "If they don't hurry, it'll catch them all! Hurry, little boats! Faster, *faster!*"

The child's intensity jarred on her mother's nerves. "Control yourself, Marjorie! The fog won't hurt the boats. The same wind is blowing both, and the fog travels faster because it is lighter. Look over that way." The far shore was gone except for the tops of rounded hills that swam above the gray-purple tide of fog. "It's covering the whole river."

"Look at the boats now," Marjorie said. "The fog is catching more of them, but they'll be all right!"

On the near side of the river only one rank of boats was left, spreading wide sails, flying in dramatic rout before the wall of fog that rose above their masts, and above the ragged crest of the fog the sky boiled with the excited flying of gulls. So it came up the river, the pageant of flight and pursuit; spreading sails and darkening breaker of fog and the

[15]

turmoil of sea gulls, building up into the sky in one great wave. The boats went dim, still racing earnestly, with dimming white waves at their bows. They went more dim and were gone, softly, and the fog ghosted on alone. . . . Now the fog was flying over housetops, flitting along streets by the river, where a few lights had begun to shine.

"It's like summer in San Francisco," Marjorie said.

Something like that. But in San Francisco the disturbing water front had been far away beyond the sandy hills. . . . Now the fog had reached one of the grain ships in the stream. The great, complicated fabric of masts and yards and rigging dimmed to a ghost ship, still distinct, but frail as gossamer. Then it was gone, and the next ship became a wraith.

The anchored ships were swallowed quickly by the fog, but they were still there. As the last one dissolved, there came over the invisible water the rapid ringing of a bell. It went on for a minute, ceased, and was answered by the deeper voice of another bell, and another and another, each with a different tone; bells confident, and mournful, and defiant and menacing as ship after ship spoke out of the fog.

"The ships are calling to the sailors in town," Marjorie said, "telling them that they have stayed away from the sea too long."

"No, they are ringing the bells so other vessels won't run into them in the fog." Dehlia hoped that Marjorie wouldn't start asking about the sailors again. She had observed that it was nice that they would get more money, but it was quite otherwise. The boardinghouse masters had won their demand for $150 for each sailor delivered on board ship, and the "blood money" came out of the sailor's pay. That made the sea less attractive than ever, but it was expected to make the boardinghouse masters bolder and more enterprising in securing crews.

[16]

2

At six that morning the Willamette Valley erupted with the volcanic smoke of straw fires under boilers; by seven the dew had dried from the sheaves, and threshing machines thundered and poured out wheat for the grain ships that loaded at Portland, where the Willamette delivered its waters and its wealth to the Columbia.

Soon after eight, on a farm beside the tributary Yamhill River, the harvest panorama was minutely marred by the vanishing of the Hedges' threshing engine. The only warning was a hissed appeal for mechanical aid, and the engine disappeared in a bright cloud of steam.

Pa Hedges, who was better at meeting emergencies than averting them, dived into the cloud and closed the throttle. Dust and chaff and steam and curses drifted away through the tall green-black oaks beside the threshing yard. The engine reappeared, but its owner was not entirely pleased with its condition. In accents which he had brought from Kentucky, he said, "It's that ole stuffing box. Well, we had fun hoping she would take us through the season!" Working cautiously on hot metal, he reported, "Busted wide open! Looks like a trip to Portland for you, Al. Know what to ask for?"

Albert was a big young man who had been feeding straw to the boiler, and accumulated smoke and dust made him look like a minstrel performer. "Sure, Pa; stuffing box for a thirty-horsepower Case, Series A, Model 1879. But they won't have it in stock."

"That's the truth," his father said. "It's a machine-shop

job." He glanced up at the time. "Sun's just over the barn; you'll be in time for the mid-morning train. Get into your store clothes while we tear her to pieces. George, you saddle the horses; put the sidesaddle on Columbine; Nancy can go to the ferry and fetch the horses home."

In the back yard, Albert stopped at the wooden pump ornamented with carved sprays of flowers and took off his sweat-soaked hickory shirt. He pumped with one hand and with the other he scooped water over his face and big shoulders and chest. His sister Nancy came out from the kitchen with a cake of soap, which she handed to him silently, with imperious pity, and a towel which she hung in the convenient mock-orange bush. While Nancy pumped for him, she asked. "What are you aiming to do, Al—go to San Francisco and fight Gentleman Jim?"

"He's not big enough," Albert said modestly, and put his head under the spout to let the water run through his thick red-gold curls. Coming out from under the water, he explained, "I'm going to Portland to get a new part for the old threshing engine; she's all wore out."

Nancy remembered, "You said last season the engine needed overhauling."

"Pa doesn't believe in crossing bridges until he comes to them."

"Pa doesn't believe in *building* a bridge until he needs to cross!"

"Speaking of crossing rivers," he said, "you're going with me to Wheatland and fetch the horses home."

She handed him the towel. "I don't mind; but you're the lucky one—going to Portland!"

"It's nicer here," he said. There were apple and walnut trees around the big southern-style house and they made an island of green in the burnished sea of wheat and fields of stubble like yellow sands. "Portland'll be hotter'n hell in this weather—all those brick buildings soaking up the heat

in the daytime and giving it out at night. I'd rather be here."
While he was drying himself he returned to his sister's
criticism of their father. "Pa's slack about some things, but
year in and year out he gets the wheat raised and harvested;
we're doing all right."

"I want us to do better!" Nancy was a tall, handsome girl
with gold-brown hair and the blue eyes of her brother, but
she had a thinner, more determined face and an aristocratic
scorn of imperfections. "If I had the managing of things—"

Albert interrupted her good-naturedly: "If you had the
managing of things, you'd throw the world away the first
time it got dusty!"

He dressed at the door of his room, which was open to the
second-story veranda. Above the airy top of the English
walnut tree he saw the smokes of distant threshing machines
and columns of brown dust plodding the valley roads beside
columns of wagons heavy with wheat. He saw the Willamette
River winding past golden shores until wheat fields and river
and sky were all one blue in the distance. To the west and
north he saw the Yamhill River going to the Willamette; the
covered bridge over the Yamhill, and on the other side, white
New England houses among their groves. It pleased him to
think of the puzzlement of a stranger set down on the high
veranda. He would know that he was in America, but he
would not know in what part—seeing in one look a gentler
New England and a richer South.

He was in front of the mirror, trying to plaster down his
curls with Bandoline, when he heard the springy thud of
hoofs in the yard. With a second sight born of experience,
Nancy called, "Come on, Al; you'll never get your curls to
stay down!"

"Coming!" he called and put on his hat. The east window
blinds were drawn against the morning sun, but there was a
hole in one of them and dust motes boiled in a ray of light
that pierced the good dim room. The light struck the Rand

McNally map of the world and made a bright splash on hump-backed Australia. The summer sun of Oregon had no business teasing that faraway place that slept in a winter's night on the other side of the world.

Albert would seldom have gone to the city by choice, but he knew how to make use of his time when he was there. While he waited for the stuffing box, he strolled along the river front in the hot sunshine, alertly and with a certain proprietary pride. He felt comfortable about the great black sailing vessels anchored out in the river and loading at the elevators. Ships in themselves did not interest him, but the grain that he helped raise had launched this international fleet, and it deserved his attention.

At a grain dock he stopped beside a ship with the odd name of *Christmas Morning* and watched her loading: slingloads of sacked wheat lowered to the deck beside the hatch; longshoremen heaving the fat sacks into a sloping polished trough; and the sacks coasting out of sight to be stowed in some far corner of the hold. Once when the sling was in mid-air, wheat from a ripped sack poured down in a stream of gold—wasted, but pretty for its moment in the sunshine.

One of the ship's officers came up and stood on the dock to watch the loading: a spry-looking old man with sharp eyes and a pointed gray beard. The captain, Albert decided, and he engaged him in conversation, as he did everyone who had time to talk.

"How much wheat will she take, Cap'n?"

The captain gave him an impatient look before he decided to answer. "About seventy thousand bushels."

"That's the wheat from two thousand acres," Albert calculated; "a tol'able amount of acreage to get in one ship."

"Yes, if you look at it that way."

"Where you bound for?"

"Cork, for orders."

"Then you don't know where you're taking the wheat?"

"Probably somewhere in the United Kingdom."

"Will you come back here for another cargo?"

"Here, or maybe San Francisco. I might touch on the East coast first; that would give me a chance to get home."

"Where is your home?"

"Searsport, Maine."

"I expect you don't get there often."

"It's two years since I saw my wife, and it may be two more."

"That's a mighty long time to be away!"

"H'm." The old captain didn't seem interested in the young man's conclusions, then he asked sharply, "Are you thinking of shipping out?"

"No, thank you, Captain!" Albert remembered that it wasn't a healthy season for lingering around docks when harvesting and shipping boomed at the same time and competed for labor. He also remembered it was time to eat and headed south for a more trustworthy part of town.

At Burnside Street he felt secure enough for a minor expedition. He pushed boldly through the easternmost swinging door of Erickson's Saloon, threw his nickel on the bar, put his foot on the brass rail, and accepted the mug of steam beer that was shoved at him. It was against orders, and he was not fond of beer, but it was worth a nickel to see Erickson's bar. He planted himself at one end, where he could squint down its shining mahogany length, past the jutting headlands of elbows. Near him, big longshoremen and sailors and laborers were drinking big mugs of beer at a wide bar; in the middle distance, medium-sized men were drinking from medium mugs at a medium bar; farther away, tiny men were drinking from tiny mugs at a bar narrowed to the width of a ribbon; and in the far distance, drinkers and bar and mugs tapered away to a pointed blur. Men who had drunk there, and told about it a few times, swore that Erickson's bar was a mile long. Sober men who had measured it with a steel tape found it to be 674 feet. That was better than a mile because it was something people could believe.

From Erickson's, Albert crossed over to the safe side of town and the New Market Theatre. Its massive red brick was already dark with unhealthy smoke and dust, but inside it would always be a place of glamour. Its hundred gas lights had shone on idols of the different members of the Hedges family; Pa and George and Albert had gone there to see the great John L. Sullivan; in a wave of religious fervor, Ma had taken the children there to hear Henry Ward Beecher; Nancy yearned after the great actors and actresses who had played at the New Market: Keene and Sothern and Fannie Davenport. When anyone great was appearing, Nancy went through a spell of declaring that she would go, or die. But with the demands of farm life and the complications of travel, she rarely saw one of her idols—nor had she died.

One look at the billboard was enough to tell him that this time there was nothing likely to provoke any yearning or dying—a foreign woman putting on a children's play. But Nancy would demand particulars; he took out a folded sheet of paper he had brought for noting expenses and jotted down: *Helena Modjeska—A Doll's House, August 11–16.*

He had dinner in the expensive heart of the city, at a good restaurant on Yamhill Street near Sixth, and afterward he went across the street and chewed his toothpick at the entrance to the Hotel Portland's dining room. While he stood there, fed and at ease, he studied the passing crowds. On the farm, when he thought of the city, it seemed to him that he could tell almost everything about people by studying their faces. But when he tried, it was never that easy. About all he could decide was that some people have proud faces, others humble ones. He couldn't figure out the significance of that—so he shifted his attention from faces to posteriors and observed that bustles had disappeared from city women. A few months ago only the daring would have gone without them; now only a few defiant old women wore them. He could tell Nancy definitely that the fashion note in the *Willamette Farmer* had not exaggerated.

Albert left the crowds to make what they could of themselves, and strolled into the hotel to smoke a cigar. Relaxed in red plush and flicking ashes into shining brass, he felt in tune with the soft, expensive storm of echoes in the lobby. He never came to town without trying on the splendor of the Hotel Portland, which gave him a feeling of confidence and success. He had already decided that he would bring his bride there on their honeymoon, and later, on shopping and theatre expeditions from the farm, he and his family would make it their headquarters.

The hotel was a reliable part of Albert's future, but he couldn't enjoy it alone for long. If he had his choice of places in which to do nothing on a summer afternoon, it would be under a tree beside the Yamhill River, or more likely in the river. The thought made the lobby seem dead and artificial and he got up and strolled out to the street, which was hot and noisy, but alive.

He drifted east into a quieter and more sedate part of town, and at Third Street he turned south for a closer look at a span of milk-white horses set off by polished black harness. They were hitched to a gleaming Victoria standing in front of a mansion, and there was a coachman in the driver's seat. Albert could not take his eyes off the horses; they were geldings, beautiful and beautifully matched, and as clean as white pigeons. He took the handkerchief from his breast pocket and rubbed it over the shoulder of the off horse, and it came away as white as it had been before.

"You'll find no dust on them!"

The boy had been too admiring of the team to notice

humans, but now he looked up at the driver's thin, masklike face. "They're certainly beauties!"

"Aye," the coachman said, "a fine pair."

Albert touched a harness buckle that shone like gold. "How do you keep such a shine on brass?"

"It's gold-plated."

Albert whistled. "Someone has lots of goose feathers!"

The mask-face smiled. "Madame is comfortably off."

The young man considered the horses again. "What breed are they?"

"English hackneys; white ones are rare."

While they talked, Albert was aware of the swish of silk and the light sigh of springs—ladies were getting into the carriage.

"These two are high-steppers," the coachman told him; "their action's perfect."

"Is it true they're trained in deep straw, so they have to pick up their feet?"

"Aye, that's how it's done."

"We breed Kentucky saddle horses," Albert told the coachman. "If you're ever at the State Fair—"

"Jackson!" a girl's voice called impatiently. "It's hot sitting here in the sun!"

Albert stepped back in confusion and took off his hat. "I'm sorry, ma'am!" He found himself looking at four intoxicatingly beautiful young ladies who had seated themselves in the carriage in a foam of lace and a sheen of delicate-colored silks and a bewildering sweetness of perfume. The two seats of the carriage faced each other, but the girls were all turned to look at him from beneath tilted silk parasols—beautiful young faces and bold, laughing eyes that made him suddenly conscious of being a gawking country boy.

The carriage was already in motion, but one of the girls cried, "Stop, Jackson!" It stopped with the four beauties just opposite Albert, and the one who had spoken looked at him with challenging blue eyes and held out a white card. "Pay us a call some evening—and have another look at the horses! Drive on, Jackson!"

Albert heard one of the girls ask, "Did you say 'whores' or 'horses'?" Then the carriage rolled away, with their laughter ringing out like mocking bells, and he was left standing in his tracks, hot with humiliation.

He glared at the Taylor Street Methodist Church across the way, then down at the scented card in his hand; on it was engraved the name of Miss Prudence Snow and the address of the mansion in front of which he was standing. He dropped the cool white card on the hot pavement and turned back along Third. It was just like him, making a fool of himself over circus horses prettied up to advertise a bagnio! "Pay us a call some evening and have another look at the horses!" The girls' laughter still burned in his ears.

He was back near the river now, in the wholesale district; there were drays and express wagons, drawn by honest work horses and driven by swearing, tobacco-chewing teamsters who didn't look as if they had ever heard of livery and silk hats; and there wasn't a woman in sight. This part of town was a man's world, where everyone looked as if he had work to do—or was drunk on honest work already done. Only Albert was the sober loafer—and he was on his way to the machine shop to see how they were coming along with the new stuffing box.

He was on First Avenue, a block from the river, when he noticed the old gentleman in the rusty Prince Albert and the squarish derby, standing in the middle of the sidewalk, with his weight all on one leg and his hand on the other leg. Even stooped that way he was a tall man, and he looked as if he had been a powerful one in his prime.

As Albert came up he heard the old man sigh. "Anything wrong, Colonel?" he asked.

"My leg," the man said. "It's all right for weeks and then,

bang! I can't step on it. I'm figuring how to get back to my office."

Albert considered. "Is it far?"

"That's what makes me so mad—it's just around the corner!"

"I'll get you there in a minute; just put your arm on my shoulders and hop along, or however."

"I'm obliged to you, young man." He put his long arm over Albert's shoulders. "It ain't many city people will stop to help a stranger."

"I don't live here," Albert said; "I'm from a wheat farm up the valley."

Hobbling beside him, his companion said, "I wouldn't have known it. My name's Ed Prince; my son and I have a little shipping business; I guess he's waiting for me now, wondering if my leg's caught me somewheres."

Albert introduced himself and asked sympathetically, "Do you have rheumatism?"

"A bullet," Prince told him. "I got it through the leg at Gettysburg, and it's never been right since."

"Gettysburg!"

"Yessiree; that was a battle! Abe Lincoln came there afterward and made a speech, but I was in the hospital, like to lose my leg."

"It must have been hell!"

"It was worse than hell! But I could joke about it then; when the surgeon asked me how I felt, I says to him, 'I regret that I have but one leg to lose for my country!' He says, 'But you got two!' I says, 'Hell, I'm keeping *one* for myself!'"

Albert was still laughing when his companion said, "Here's the office." He pushed open the door and hobbled in, leaning on Albert's strong young shoulders.

After the hot sun outside, the office was dim in the light that came through dusty panes, and it was bare enough;

Albert didn't see much but some packing cases and two chairs in front of a desk, and a man's feet propped up on the desk. The man got up quickly. "Is it your leg again, Pop?"

"That's what," the old man said as Albert helped him into a chair. "Went out on me around the block. I'd be there yet if it wasn't for this young man. Bert, meet Al Hedges."

Bert responded with a muscular handshake. "Much obliged," he said; "have a chair." Indicating his father, he said, "I don't know what to do with this old war horse; sometimes I think I'll have to tie him." Bert was a shabby, middle-aged man with a smooth-shaven face that looked sulky in repose, but it was clear that he valued his father.

"You try tying me!" the old man said. "Anyhow, I got the shipment fixed up for Astoria." Massaging his leg, he added, "And I got back, with the help of this young man."

"I was glad to do it," Albert said, preparing to go. "I hope your leg's better."

The older Prince winked at him and rubbed his leg ostentatiously. "Bert, do we still have a little of that good whiskey? It always makes my leg feel better."

Bert pretended reluctance. "You don't deserve it." Then he relented and rubbed one of his own legs. "My leg feels queer, too!" He opened a drawer in the desk and rattled glassware.

The older man chuckled. "How's your leg, Al?"

Albert laughed. "It might take a little."

"Make it three, Bert." The old man winked at Albert again. "Sometime I'll give Bert an extra snort and see if it'll stir him to wash the windows. When you can see it, we have a view of the new Union Depot."

The office didn't seem a place for a view, but through the smoke- and dust-dimmed window Albert made out the low, level roof of the unfinished depot, and the narrow tower rearing up sudden and high and ending with an overhanging

[27]

cap of roof. Near the top of the tower, under the roof, there were big round holes, like eyes, where clocks would be.

"Here you are, Al." Old Prince handed him the little glass of whiskey and raised his own. "Here's luck!"

"Here's luck!" Albert saluted a rough and honest man's world where there were no mincing whores to laugh at him.

"Here's luck!" Bert said from behind his desk.

They drank, and it seemed to Albert that the glow of whiskey really went down to his legs. "That's certainly good!"

In the dusty dimness of the room, old Prince's sallow face and great gray moustache nodded approvingly.

Beyond the old man, through the smoky window, something was happening to the depot tower; it reared up higher and twisted, looking at Albert viciously with its sightless eyeholes; and the overhanging cap of roof flattened like the hood of a cobra he had once seen in a picture. Maybe an earthquake. . . There was a vast roaring and he was in the center of it. He and Nancy were racing their horses down the road to the ferry, under the willow trees; sunlight and shadow, and the blue Willamette ahead, and the thunder of racing hoofs. The thunder grew louder and boomed in his ears. Boy and girl and racing horses and willow trees disappeared, and only the thunder went on.

3

AT SEVENTEEN, Emily Pearson already had moments of pessimism in which she did not see how all the evils of the world could be done away with before another fifty years. That would be close to 1940, when she was an old woman—a sobering thought now, but with it the assurance of a serene old age.

The slow progress of reform in the world could not be blamed on Emily's lack of diligence; she had been a member of the Band of Hope for five years. And there were now forty-two saloons in Astoria—six more than there had been at the beginning of her temperance work. Probably there were more bagnios, too, but grownups didn't discuss such things with young ladies. For three years she had been a member of the Bethel Society, and she couldn't point to any definite result—

Emily looked sternly at the poster she was lettering, and asked what definite result she could expect. The poster revealed nothing except what was already there:

BON VOYAGE SERVICE
For The Rev. St. John Williams

What results, indeed? Emily was only one alto voice in the Bethel choir; one small neat figure with an earnest, alert face, thick brown hair that curled when there was fog, and steady brown eyes. The choir sang hymns on board while the sailors waited at respectful attention, with their thoughts as fathomless as the sea; Mr. McMillan prayed and preached, and the choir sang the Doxology; then they went ashore and scattered to their homes.

In a few days, or hours, the ship towed down the Columbia and across the bar, bound for Falmouth or Antwerp, Queenstown or Londonderry or Havre, laden with the golden wheat of the Willamette Valley. In their long months at sea, what did the sailors remember? What did they remember in hot tropical days? On nights off Cape Horn, aloft in gales of sleet and snow? Did they hear something beyond the howl of the antarctic wind—the voices of Astoria Bethel girls singing like angels? Not likely. And if they did—she hadn't noticed any change in the sailors' state of grace. When they left their ships at Astoria, they got drunk in "Swilltown," spent their money and shipped out again, or were shanghaied.

Almost certainly evil had another fifty years to go, but meanwhile the world had its undeniable charm. Looking up from the second "S" in missionary, with her face already at the proper angle, Emily saw the great river in the afternoon sun, with its moving waters quivering between blue and green; ships and barks at anchor, with their proud bowspirits pointing upstream; and far away the shore of Washington—rough, blue-green hills touched with the sun's gold.

Through the open window there came the distant clatter of capstan pawls, then a chanteyman's voice in solo:

Oh, Shanydar, I long to hear you,

and the chorus of sailors' voices:

Hoo-ray, you rolling river!

Emily had heard it many times but it always gave her a calm thrill of pride; they were singing of her river; the Columbia had found words for its great song as it went marching to the Pacific. "Hoo-ray, you rolling river!" She had expected the *Challenger* to sail that afternoon, but she knew from the chantey that it was a British ship; Americans would have sung "Shenandoah" instead of "Shanydar."

She went to the window and looked out over the few housetops between her and the river. Seven big grain vessels were anchored off the upper town; five British iron barks and the down-East ships *Patrician* and *Challenger*, with a more buoyant look to their wooden hulls. The capstan chantey was coming from the great four-masted *Falls of Clyde*, and the tug *Columbia* was putting the pilot on board. At that distance she couldn't identify the figure going up the Jacob's ladder; she only knew it wasn't her Uncle Roger, who boarded ships from the moving tug by jumping into their mizzen channels from the top of the pilothouse.

The whirring clang of the door bell recalled Emily to the present. She had been excused from other work to do posters; it wasn't right to spend the time daydreaming. She heard footsteps downstairs, the front door opening; voices expressing pleasant surprise, answered by a voice of reluctance or apology. Through the polite sounds the parlor clock boomed solemnly, *Bong, Bong, Bong, Bong.* Four o'clock on the afternoon of August 12th, with callers arriving punctually on the hour. And out on the river, against water quivering from green to blue, the anchor of the *Falls of Clyde* climbed through the air toward the cathead as the tug began swinging the black ship toward the sea.

Louise came upstairs and along the hall and burst into the room; Louise, tall for a ten-year-old, with long fair hair and dark eyes, her face flushed with excitement. "Mamma wants you to come downstairs," she panted. "The Fortunes are here! Mamma said I could have tea if I'm good, so don't you say I can't."

"Very well," Emily said, "but don't snatch cake when it isn't being passed. And wash your face and put on a clean pinafore."

"Mamma has already told me those things!"

Emily put her drawing materials away deliberately. Even to herself she didn't want to appear too much in haste, but it was an occasion. The Fortunes had just arrived from San Francisco and taken over the big Prosser house. Mr. Fortune was a man of importance. The Pearsons had no corresponding grandeur—a widow and her children living in a jerry-built house near the water front. But Mrs. Pearson was a respected voice in the town; she was also mindful of her social obligations and she had paid the first call on Mrs. Fortune, a call in which Emily had not been able to share because of Bethel services on board the *Highland Lassie*.

People look natural in their right places, but once in a while they get out of place and then they look odd. One of those times is when they go to the photographer's gallery for a family portrait. Another time is when they are strangers in a new town, sitting in a strange parlor trying to make new friends, as Mrs. Fortune and her children were doing now.

Mrs. Fortune was a tall, thin woman, very straight in the straight-backed chair. It looked as if she had been put there because of her immediate resemblance to the severe piece of furniture. Next to her chair, on the slippery horsehair couch, her two sons sat like daring young castaways who had found momentary safety on a floating log. They looked about thirteen and fourteen, wearing identical Norfolk suits and holding identical bowler hats. They had thick straight black hair and dark eyes, olive complexions, and features that were softly but clearly defined. They had the look of self-contained boys, innately neat—the type often described as "little gentlemen" or "manly little fellows." The older boy was introduced as John and the younger as Thomas, and they acknowledged the introduction in low, buttered voices. At the far side of the couch the sister fidgeted in a straight-backed chair, with her feet not quite touching the floor. She was about ten, with dark, velvety, frightened eyes and long, dark hair in glossy curls. She was Marjorie, and she said "How do you do," in a husky doll's voice.

Opposite the lined-up visitors Emily's Irish mother sat with her crocheting: Mother, warm-hearted and quick-moving and small. Emily could remember her father hefting her mother by the elbows, shaking his head and saying fondly, "Witch's weight!" Her father had been dead nine years and her mother was still "witch's weight." She was no bigger than her second daughter, April, who was thirteen; but she was big enough to run the house and keep her children happy, and to keep an eye on the affairs of the town. Barry sat next to her, like a boy on Judgment Day; he was barefoot, in jeans and hickory shirt, with his lock of brown hair hanging over his forehead; it had got that way from hours of bending over the knothole in the sidewalk. While he eyed the new boys across the room, he toyed solemnly with a fish line wound on a piece of shingle with notched ends. Judging by sounds from the kitchen, April was making a fire for tea.

Mother was giving her caller useful information. "We trade at Gearhart's and find them most reliable. I don't know, of course, how our prices compare with San Francisco."

"Meat prices here seem only a little higher," Mrs. Fortune said, "though some cuts are exorbitant. Soup meat at four cents a pound is reasonable, but tenderloin steak at fifteen is ridiculous! And thirteen cents a pound for loin lamb chops! And as for fresh fruits and vegetables—"

Mother said, "I don't doubt they are higher."

"Higher—and such a limited selection!"

"That's because most of our supply comes from California."

"But surely, Mrs. Pearson, it is warm enough in Oregon for some things to grow!"

"Our Willamette Valley is one of the garden spots of the world, Mrs. Fortune; but the farmers up there are too busy raising wheat for Europe to consider the home market."

Emily put in, "Some of them are planting large orchards."

"That is true," Mother said, "but not enough; and it takes

time for orchards to come into bearing. We still have to depend on California for too many things." To Mrs. Fortune she said, "If you are ever in the store, or on your way there, and you hear a cannon fired, it will pay you to postpone your shopping till the next day."

"A cannon, Mrs. Pearson?"

"Yes. When old Captain Hustler sights the ocean steamer coming in over the bar he fires the cannon on the dock. It can be heard all over town and it is a welcome sound because it means a good supply of fresh fruits and vegetables."

"A cannon! What a primitive custom!"

"It is also civilizing. When two housewives are eyeing a last wilted bunch of asparagus in the store and they hear the boom of the cannon, it is remarkable how generous they become!"

They were in the midst of discussing Chinese house boys versus the new phenomenon of Finnish maids when Mother paused to smile at the boys, suffering in the arid world of parlor talk. "Barry, wouldn't you like to show John and Thomas around?"

Barry gave the brothers a still, inquiring look and they rose from the sofa, hats in hand.

Mrs. Fortune prompted them. "What do you say?"

"Thank you."

"We'd like to."

"There's not much to see," Barry said, "but we can look around."

Mrs. Fortune said, "John, Thomas, don't go away from the house."

"Oh, Mamma—"

"Don't go away from the house!"

"All right, Mamma."

"We won't, Mamma."

When the door closed, Mother said, "Such manly little fellows!"

Mrs. Fortune said, "John and I want them to be."

"And so obedient!"

"We expect obedience."

Mother smiled at Marjorie, fidgeting forlornly in the high, straight chair. "Marjorie, wouldn't you like to go upstairs and see what Louise is doing? Maybe she'll show you her dolls."

"I thank you," the child said in her husky doll's voice. "May I, Mamma?"

"Yes, run along." But the child did not run; she crossed the room like a small shadow and went doubtfully up the stairs. Looking after her, the mother said, "Marjorie has always been an obedient child. Boys are more trouble, but they mean more."

Mother looked as if she might question both statements, but she did not, and Mrs. Fortune asked, "You have another son, haven't you, Mrs. Pearson?"

"Willard, our oldest, is eighteen. He's been visiting in Portland, but we expect him on the night boat."

The visitor warmed to another mother of sons. "We're going to make a doctor out of John and a lawyer out of Thomas. What are you going to make out of your boys?"

Mother said with deceptive mildness, "I have never felt wise enough to decide what my children are going to be."

"If you don't, who will?"

"I expect them to."

Mrs. Fortune raised her eyebrows. "Personally, I feel more comfortable knowing that one of my sons is to be a doctor and the other a lawyer. If Marjorie had been a boy, we would have made a minister of her."

Emily saw the lightning twinkle in the gray eyes and she was afraid Mother was going to ask if it had been fair to Marjorie, making her choose between being a minister and being a girl; but Mother only said, "They are all good professions."

Mrs. Fortune asked carefully, "What are your sons going to make of themselves?"

Mother said, "At the moment, I believe Barry wants to be a steamboat captain; he'll probably have many other ideas before he finally decides."

"And your oldest?"

"Willard will begin his second year at the University this fall; he has decided in earnest on a legal career." Which was just what Mrs. Fortune planned for one of her manly little sons.

Later, over cake and tea, the duel of mothers broke out again. With her egg-shell cup firmly poised, Mrs. Fortune asked, "Where can we find hazel bushes, Mrs. Pearson?"

"They grow at the edge of town, but I'm not sure when the nuts will be ripe. We'll have to consult Barry about that."

"I was thinking of them for switches," Mrs. Fortune explained. "There's nothing like hazel; everything else is too soft, or it breaks."

"Oh!"

The visitor felt the disappointing silence which followed. "John and I don't believe in sparing the rod and spoiling the child."

"What have your children done?" Mother asked gently.

"Done?"

"Yes; what have they done that calls for a whipping?"

"They haven't done anything recently; but I can't wait until they have, and then go to the woods looking for switches!"

Mother was smiling reminiscently. "That once happened to Mr. Pearson when Willard was a little boy; he had done something he shouldn't and Mr. Pearson went to the vacant lot to cut a willow switch. It must have been spring; he came back blowing a whistle he had made!"

Mrs. Fortune asked, "Did that teach the boy not to do what he shouldn't?"

"I think it worked as well as anything," Mother said. "Naughtiness is something children get over after a while.

[36]

Probably it doesn't make much difference whether you pass the time whipping them or making whistles for them."

Mrs. Fortune was visibly shocked by the levity of her hostess. "John and I believe that children must be controlled until they are old enough to control themselves. Take young John and Thomas out there; they are mad about boats and the water; do you suppose anything but the threat of a whipping would keep them from running away to the river while we're talking?"

Mother did not see it that way. "My Barry practically lives for the river, but he won't leave the yard because he knows your boys aren't allowed to."

"But wouldn't you whip him if he did?"

"Certainly not! And he knows it; but just the same, he won't leave the yard."

"He is your son"—Mrs. Fortune shrugged one shoulder— "but it sounds like a dangerous way to bring up a boy."

Barry hated parlors, but he was all right when he got outside in the world of sunshine and the smell of the river. Feeling the rough, weathered hide of the wooden sidewalk with one big toe, he looked questioningly at the new boys. "What would you fellows like to do?"

The brothers looked at each other and Jack tipped his bowler hat on one side of his head. "Why don't we just look around and see what mischief Satan finds for our idle hands?"

Barry suggested hastily, "How about fishing?"

"I'd like that better than anything!" Then Tom's dark eyes clouded. "But we promised not to go away from the house."

"That's right," Jack said.

"We can stay here and fish."

"Here?" Jack squinted around from the planked street to the river, which was three blocks away, and back to Barry. "I don't catch on."

[37]

Barry disengaged the hook of his fish line from the soft cedar into which it had bitten and squeezed the fragment of bacon back over the point. "We can fish there." He pointed to an enlarged knothole near the edge of the sidewalk.

Jack looked disappointed. "I meant real."

Tom went over and glanced down the knothole. "There's water down there!" He was kneeling, then lying flat on the wooden street, with one eye inserted in the knothole. "Fish!" he shouted. "Big ones!"

There usually were fish, but never anything big.

Jack looked for himself and his eyes were jaunty with apology. "How do you do it?"

"Do what?"

"Get the water under there."

"It's the river; everything as far back as Commercial Street is on piling; there's deep water under our house; when you go to the backhouse you'll see what I mean."

"Do you save one hole for fishing?"

"We're not allowed. But the Johnsons have a three-holer and their children fish there all the time."

Jack found the idea amusing. "If we had a boat we could have torchlight tours under Astoria: *See Astoria from a new angle; the underside of the houses and the backsides of the people, and children fishing from the sky!*"

Barry smiled out of politeness, but the idea was more dangerous than Jack knew. "I wouldn't go under the town at night for anything!"

"Why not?"

"Crimps. Some of the saloons have trap doors in the back room. After they give sailors knockout drops, they let them down through a trap door. The runners wait underneath with a boat and take the men out to a ship. I wouldn't want them to catch me fooling around under the docks."

"There's a big one!" Tom reported from the knothole. "Golly, he's going away!"

"Here's the line," Barry said, and Tom sat up to receive

it. "Let the hook down in the water about a foot and jerk when you feel a nibble."

Tom's eyes were eager, but he asked, "You want to try first, Jack?"

"You go ahead." Then he asked Barry, "Is that right about the kidnappers?"

"Crimps," Barry corrected him. "It's a business; that's the way they supply the ships with crews."

"*I got one, I got one!*" Tom shouted, horsing in the line.

"Take it easy or you'll lose him—" There was a fluttering thump against wood and Tom held up the empty hook, his face chagrined. "He got away!"

"You pulled in too fast. Take the next one slower and ease him through the knothole."

"You lost the bait, too," Jack said.

"I got plenty more." Barry unpacked his pocket, sorting out a dirty handkerchief, marbles and a knife and a wad of string, and then a little package of butcher's paper stained with grease. Unwrapping the bacon and cutting off a morsel against the sidewalk, he said, "They're not particular; they bite on anything."

Tom landed the next fish and the brothers examined it excitedly as it flapped on the worn planking—a slender, silver-gray fish with a white belly.

"It's a beauty!" Jack said. "I wouldn't have believed you could catch a trout through a knothole in the middle of town!"

Tom said proudly, "It's a foot long!"

The fish was only about eight inches long, and it wasn't a trout, but the brothers' excitement gave it an extra shine.

"It's a tom cod," Barry said. "They're about the only thing you catch here, except in the spring."

"What do you get then?"

"Baby salmon—sometimes."

The younger boy landed half a dozen more tom cod. Jack then took the line for a few minutes and caught three. After he was able to do it well he gave the line back to Tom and didn't seem interested in that kind of fishing any more. Sitting on the edge of the sidewalk, with his hat over one eye, he asked, "Did you ever see the crimps taking sailors through a trap door?"

"No. They do it at night."

"Don't you ever go around the docks at night?"

"I'm not allowed unless someone is drowned, or something special like that."

"I guess people don't drown very often."

"I was at the boat dock all night the time Dan Egan drowned. I was with my brother Willard and we helped grapple for Dan."

"Who was Dan?"

"He was a dwarf. I guess he was about twenty years old, but he wasn't as big as I am. He smoked cigars and hung around the steamboats. That night he was going ashore with some of the crew of the *Potter* and he stepped off the edge of the float in the dark and never came up. One of the others went for help and pretty soon there were about a hundred men there, with boats and grappling hooks and lanterns—"

Tom said, "I guess it would be hard to find a little dwarf in a big river."

"Most of the men went home after a while, but Willard and a few others wouldn't give up. Mother and Emily brought hot coffee, and we went on grappling. We didn't find him until morning."

Jack whistled with surprise. "It's a wonder you found him at all!"

"We didn't find him the way we expected. It was high water when he went in, and by morning the tide had fallen about eight feet. I was on the float with Willard when it was getting daylight. We were going to try another grapple from there when I heard a kind of chuckle; I looked up and saw Dan."

"You mean he wasn't drowned?" Tom asked.

"Where the hell was he?" Jack was as puzzled as his brother.

"He was as close as I am to you, with his arms and legs around a pile and a funny look on his face. I thought he was playing a joke, and then a fish jumped out of his mouth—"

"I bet that gave you a scare!"

"It was scary when I knew that he was dead and not playing a trick on us."

Jack said, "You'd think he would have climbed up the pile until he was out of water!"

"You'd think so, but he just hung on till the tide uncovered him."

Tom said, "I don't see how the fish got into his mouth."

"He was full of water and his mouth was open. Fish always get into you when you're drowned."

Barry and the new boys had started with misgivings about each other, but his opinion of them had risen, and now they listened to him respectfully. He wanted to tell them about more picturesque drownings, but he hadn't been present at any of the others and he had to fill in with general information. "The fishermen are the ones who really get drowned, but most of them are lost on the bar—about a hundred every year."

Jack said, "That's a lot of fishermen!"

"Last summer my uncle saw eighteen fishermen drown in five minutes."

"Who's your uncle?"

"Captain Collins; he's the best pilot on the bar."

The brothers' attention became livelier and still more respectful. "We'd like to know your uncle," Jack said.

"Sometime we'll go up to his house; it's full of things from shipwrecks."

"You tell us when we're allowed!"

The younger boy said, "I like this town!"

"What about the eighteen fishermen—how did they get drowned?"

"They were gill-netters," Barry said; "they're always getting drowned."

Jack asked, "What do you mean, gill-netters?"

"When a gill net is out, it's like a long fence in the water; the salmon try to swim through, but their bodies are too big for the mesh, and when they try to back out they get caught behind the gills. In the river the gill-netters keep hold of one end of the net, but when they're fishing on the bar they turn their nets adrift inside Peacock Spit—"

"Wait a minute," Jack said; he dug in his pocket and found a stub of chalk. "Can you show us?"

"I'm not much on drawing, but I'll try. This is Middle Sands in the mouth of the river, with a channel on each side; and this is Peacock Spit coming out from Cape Disappointment on the north. The gill-netters let their nets go about here, on the river side of the Spit, and the tide drifts them through the shallow water where it isn't safe for a boat. The fishermen sail this way through North Channel and around the Spit, and they pick up their nets in the ocean. When everything works right, they come back loaded with salmon. But if they wait until the tide is running too strong, the bar begins to break and that's the end of them."

Jack said, "You wouldn't think they'd wait that long."

"They didn't the time I'm telling about. It was near the beginning of the ebb and it looked safe; but there's currents there that nobody understands, and one of them started the bar breaking. Uncle Roger said it was smooth one minute, and the next it was all steep breakers. There were nine boats with two men in each one, and the breakers folded them under one after the other. In five minutes the last boat was gone."

"I'll be damned!" Jack said.

Tom asked, "Couldn't your uncle save any of them?"

"He's saved lots of men, but he couldn't do anything that time. He was piloting a ship that was towing into the river. Captain Smith, on the tug, couldn't do anything either. He'd have had to cut loose from the ship, and she'd have gone on Peacock Spit."

Jack said, "I suppose they never found any of the fishermen."

"Not alive; but the Life Saving crew found fifteen of them in Dead Man's Hollow; they found most of the boats there, too—what was left of them."

Jack took off his bowler hat and considered it thoughtfully. "How did they know where to look?"

"Nearly everyone drowned in the river or on the bar fetches up in Dead Man's Hollow. The current sets that way, and there's an eddy that pulls them into the Hollow."

"Nice name—Dead Man's Hollow! What's it like?"

"It's a cove here on the south side of Cape Disappointment. There's a little sand beach with cliffs around it, and caves in the cliffs. Some of them are supposed to go all the way under the Cape, but I guess nobody really knows."

Tom wasn't even pretending to fish any more. He and his brother were looking at each other and seeing a snug beach strewn with wreckage and dead men, and cliffs with pirate caves that echoed the roar of the ocean.

"Can you get to Dead Man's Hollow with a boat?" Jack asked.

"Not alive."

Jack looked disappointed. "No use going the other way."

"You can land here in Baker Bay and take a trail to the Hollow."

"That's better," Jack said. "I'm glad we got to know you, Barry."

Tom looked at his brother. "Shall we ask Barry about the island?" It had a mysterious sound.

"What island?" Barry asked.

Jack hesitated. "It's something we don't savvy."

"What's it like?"

"Well, the first morning we were here we looked out of our window and saw an island in the river—an island with houses and men driving horses; looked like ploughing. When we were up getting cleaned for dinner, the island was gone—"

"That's right," Tom said. "Everything gone—houses and men and horses."

Jack said, "We decided it was a mirage and forgot about it; but next morning the island was back there, with the houses and the men driving horses—"

"And the next time we looked it was gone again, honest!"

"That's happened three times now," Jack said; "we can't both be crazy." He became conscious of Barry's knowing smile. "Do you ever see things like that?"

"Sure," Barry said; "that's part of Desdemona Sands; it's an island at low water. What you saw was the men seining on the morning tide."

"What about the houses?"

"And the horses?"

"They use the horses to pull in the seines, and the houses are on scows. When they're through fishing for the day they drive the horses up the gangplank and tow the whole business away."

Jack covered one eye with his hat. "We're pretty green, but anyway we're not crazy!"

Tom asked, "Were you ever out there when they're seining?"

"Sure, lots of times."

"What's it like?"

"It's wet work—but it's exciting when they draw the seine —full of big fish!"

Jack asked, "The fishermen don't mind your being there?"

"They don't mind; sometimes they even let you help, only you have to be careful not to go too near the horses; they get cranky living on scows and working in salt water. Sometimes they're almost swimming when they start to pull in a net, and it's hard work with a few tons of fish in it—"

"What kind of fish?" Jack asked.

"Mostly Chinook salmon and English sole; there's always

sharks and sturgeons in the haul. The fishermen club them and leave them on the sands."

Jack asked, "How big are the sharks?"

"Twelve feet long, maybe. Some of the sturgeons are almost that big, too. Uncle Roger has a sturgeon smoked every year and it's the best fish there is; but most people won't touch them because they look different, so the fishermen just club them and leave them."

"Are the sharks dangerous?"

"No, but the wolf fish is; golly, you have to look out for him!"

"What's a wolf fish like?"

"It has a body like a ratty-looking eel, and it would slip through the net only it has a big round head with a face like a man's."

Jack was sceptical. "Not really like a man?"

Barry nodded gravely. "Like an old saloon prize fighter, all battered, with an ugly turned-down mouth. Uncle Roger says a wolf fish looks like a criminal from the slums of the ocean. Lots of times I have bad dreams after I've looked at one. And they're mean!"

"What do they do?" Tom asked.

"They have big teeth, sharp as knives; if you get your hand near one of them, it'll take your fingers off."

"They are mean!"

"If you get one in a boat with other fish, it'll slip out of the pile and start working toward you as if it wasn't going anywhere in particular. When it gets close enough it'll make a rush and sink its teeth into you—and it won't let go until you've cut it to pieces."

"I'd like to kill a wolf fish!" Tom said.

Jack was less interested than his brother in picking a quarrel with fish he had never seen. "Wolf fish or no wolf fish, that disappearing island is one of the first places we visit!" Thinking it over, he said, "When we get a boat we'll have a lot of exploring to do!"

Barry asked, "When are you getting a boat?"

"We don't know if we are. We're trying to talk the old man into it, but so far it's no go."

"Nearly everybody in town has a boat; it's the only way to get anywhere."

"I wish you would tell that to the old man!"

Tom asked, "Have you got a boat?"

"We have a cutter."

"A cutter! Golly!"

"What's a cutter?" When Jack didn't know a thing, he went about learning it without pretending.

"It's an open boat with four oars; it has a mast and sails, too."

"Can you go out in it?"

"Sure, when Willard or the girls are along; it's too big to manage alone."

Jack asked thoughtfully, "Where is your cutter?"

"At the boat dock, this side of Hustler's."

"That's not far, is it?"

Barry admitted it wasn't.

"Can we see it?" Tom was winding the fish line back on the piece of shingle.

"You're not supposed to go away from the house."

Jack sounded as if he had never heard of such a thing. "Who said so?"

"Your mother."

"Oh!" The brothers looked at each other, then Jack said, "She's forgotten by now. Anyway, we'll be back before she misses us."

Barry still hesitated. "I don't want to get you into trouble."

"What about you?" Jack asked. "Do you have to stay around the house?"

"I can go where I like, so long as I'm home for supper."

"That settles it!" Jack chalked three words on the planking and got up, dusting his hands. "Come on!" He had the air of a leader of men. On the way to the dock he told Barry,

"We'll get a boat out of the old man somehow. Will you teach us to sail?"

"Sure! Any time you're allowed and we can get hold of a boat."

Tom said, "We could start this afternoon."

"Not this afternoon," Jack said piously. "We're only going to have a look."

When Mrs. Fortune was ready to leave, her sons and Mrs. Pearson's son were nowhere in sight.

Beside the fishing hole the women found a string of tom cod which must have taken some time to catch; on the planking there was a chalk-drawn map which might or might not have been a clue as to where the fishermen had gone; and underneath the map was the bold legend: *Down went McGinty*.

The hostess was distressed. "Barry knew that your boys weren't to leave the yard; it isn't like him to go away with them!"

"I dare say John and Thomas are as much at fault as he," Mrs. Fortune said. "All three of them need to be controlled."

Mrs. Pearson smiled politely. "The boys can't be far away."

"They're sailing in our boat," Louise announced. "Marjorie and I saw them out on the river."

"It isn't like Barry!" Mrs. Pearson said again.

The caller seemed to think it was just what one could expect from a boy with Barry's upbringing, but she only said, "When the boys do come back, please tell John and Thomas that they are wanted at home." Her voice was almost mild, but the little girl began to whimper. "Stop sniveling, Marjorie." Then she said, "Thank you for the tea, Mrs. Pearson."

"It was a pleasure to have you."

Both mothers showed great restraint for women who felt the injustice of having to suffer for each other's sins.

4

THE *Thompson* was on the night run and she left Portland at 11:20 for Astoria and way points on the Columbia.

At 11:02 by the watch which had been his father's, Willard
Pearson set his carpetbag down in his stateroom. On his way
to the dock, keeping to the best-lighted streets, he had felt
comfortable enough, but in the close little room sweat welled
to the surface of his skin. He stayed only long enough to
tidy up, but while he was combing his damp brown hair
before the little mirror sweat was again coming out on his
freshly washed face and he had to dry it a second time. It
was a thin, serious face that looked older than its eighteen
and a half years, and Willard found these things acceptable—
particularly that it was a serious face, which seemed the
right kind to wear in a serious world.

Outside it was almost cool after the close stateroom, and
he felt light, no longer carrying his carpetbag. The port
side of the deck was almost deserted; Willard walked its
length without seeing more than half a dozen people, and
no one he recognized. The afterdeck was deserted, except
for a young couple sitting on the thwartship bench at the foot
of the great drum of the paddle-wheel guard.

On the starboard side overlooking the gangway to the
cargo deck a half-noticed figure called him by name. He
turned and stopped. "George!"

Willard had caught up with George Black in the eighth
grade, and they were graduated from high school together.
George had been twenty then, with the look of a solid citizen,

but he had found studies difficult and he hadn't shown much aptitude for the series of jobs that drifted him out of sight.

George had always looked up to Willard, and that made a barrier between them as well as a tie. The big young man was looking up to his friend now. "You were starting to college the last time I saw you. That must be wonderful— going to college and having brains enough to learn!"

Willard smiled. "I try to learn."

"College life must be pretty wonderful!"

"It isn't as exciting as you think," Willard told him. "They're very strict at Willamette. President Mather was a New England minister, and he lays down the rules. A man's not allowed to walk on the campus with a girl, or even speak to one without special permission."

"Holy Moses!"

"Not that it bothers me. Willamette has a good law department, and law's what I want. I room in town where I can study all night, and I limit myself on college activities. A literary society and a debating society are all I have time for. But what have you been doing?"

George said, "My last job was at Carter's Livery Stable in Portland, but it didn't pan out. Right now I can do better at home, in the cannery."

"It takes time to settle into a job," Willard said.

His friend's big face was wistful. "I'm not like you, Willard. You always wanted to be a lawyer. I jump around from horses to salmon, and I don't know what next."

Willard leaned at the rail and watched the thin trickle of passengers coming on board the night boat. "Give yourself time, George; when you find the right business you'll make a million!"

George said, "You learn a lot around a livery stable, but I guess it don't do you any good—the swearing, and the things you hear—"

"It's not the job for you, George."

"You wouldn't believe how many whores rent livery rigs."

"Really."

"Some of them are pretty."

"They don't stay that way."

"The first two I saw looked so pretty and talked so nice I thought they were rich people's daughters. I wouldn't have caught on, only the horse switched his tail and caught it on a girl's hat. Swear? I cuss, but I never say the things she said!"

Willard said with conviction, "You're better away from there!"

"It don't sound nice," George said, "but there's something about a livery stable—the old smell of horses and the smell of fresh hay, and the talk, and all kinds of people coming for rigs."

"You're better off at the cannery, George."

"One man said he was going to make me his partner."

"Partner!" Willard started. "What business?"

"I don't know; he never came back."

"He was probably drunk and feeling good."

"He was drunk. He said I had one face in a thousand—an honest face."

Willard looked at his friend and realized that a drunken customer had seen more at a glance than he had in a dozen years. George's big face looked as if it had been hewn out of wood for a trademark of honesty—and it had taken a stranger to point it out!

George said, "Look what's coming."

The trickle of passengers had almost stopped, and now it swelled to a flood that bore along a flotsam of baggy mattresses. There might have been twenty men. Four who carried nothing were in charge; two of them stopped on opposite sides of the gangway while two drove the others on board like sheep carrying their own wool in bags. There were bowed heads and raised ones; glimpses of faces, old and middle-aged and a few young; faces wholesome and corrupt, defiant and blank and sullen; big tanned forearms steadying mattresses, and hairy pale old arms with blue tattooing.

From the rail above Willard counted the men as they disappeared through the cargo door: "Twelve, thirteen, fourteen—" Fifteen was a robust young man, bare-headed, with curly reddish-brown hair and a healthy look. Within a step of the gangway he suddenly pushed the mattress from his shoulder into the face of the guard, lowered his curly head and lunged to the right to get away. It was a quick move, but the tall, stooping rear guard took one step with his long legs and swung with an amazingly long arm. His fist struck low down with a solid thud. For a moment it seemed to support the young man, then the gangway guard disentangled himself from the mattress and got one hand on his collar. It was over in a few seconds; under blows from front and back the young man reeled and allowed himself to be pushed into line. On the gangway he stopped, caught the rail, and began vomiting into the river. He clung there a few seconds, then he was pushed on board after the others.

On the deck above the two friends looked at each other. "The God-damned crimps!" George said.

"The Dirks," Willard said. "I've seen them before, taking crews to Astoria; but never anything like this!"

"Did you see old Dirk slug that fellow?"

"I heard it, too!" Willard boiled for a minute, then he said, "Let's go below and have a few words with them!"

Across his friend's broad face Willard could see the march of simple thoughts: the chance of getting his best suit damaged and the unpleasantness that might result from a public fight. But George was only adding up the inconveniences he had accepted. "I'll back you up. They'll fight, won't they?"

"I wish they would, but they're cowards; they keep things quiet."

[51]

"I'll back you up, anyway."

The men had been rounded up on the freight deck near the shallow well of the boiler room. Most of them were sitting on their straw mattresses beside the seagoing outfits provided by the crimps: a cotton quilt and a tin plate and a tinned knife and fork and spoon. A hairy old man was already asleep on his mattress, and number fifteen was half sitting up, vomiting into a bucket. The younger Dirk and the two lieutenants stood near a pile of cordwood, watching over their flock. Old Dirk was not in sight, but he appeared almost immediately, jingling a handful of keys. He was tall and slightly stooped, with pale gray eyes and a sallow face, smooth shaven except for his drooping gray moustache— so big it was like some morbid growth which had drained the strength from its surroundings. Willard hated the old crimp's unhealthy face and his squarish derby hat and rusty Prince Albert with its stooped shoulders. His hatred was mixed with a desire to do physical damage, but violence was out of his field. At the right moment he got in the crimp's way, with George's square bulk aiding him. "Well, Mr. Dirk!"

Dirk grunted, "Hi, boys," and started to pass.

Willard blocked his way and asked in a voice louder than was necessary, "Where are you taking the convicts, Mr. Dirk?"

"They ain't convicts; they're sailors, going to their ship."

"Why can't they find the ship themselves? Or are you and your son going to ship out, too?"

The suggestion brought a snicker from the flock, and old Dirk growled, "That's our business."

"It's a dirty business!"

"Yes," George put in; "shanghaiing men!"

Willard had meant to work up to that more gradually, but maybe it didn't matter. "I'll tell you why you're here. When you get these men on board a hell wagon you'll sell them for

$150 a head, and you want to be there to collect your blood money!"

"Mind your own business!" Dirk said. "I paid their bills and gave them outfits and transportation; I'm out money on them. If it wasn't for me, they'd be in the Portland gutters!"

"You lie!" a voice said deliberately. The hairy old sailor was sitting up on his straw mattress. "You lie, Dirk!" He might have said more, but one of the lieutenants moved over and stood with one heavy foot touching him. A few passengers had been drawn by the raised voices and were standing around, hoping for a fight.

The old man was silenced, but a fisherman from Astoria took up his theme. "Yah, everybody knows Dirk is a liar; he never gives sailors anything but knockout drops!"

Willard met the appealing blue eyes of the young man beside the bucket. "They kidnapped me!" the young man said. "I'm a farmer—" He began retching again.

"You boys clear out of here!" old Dirk growled and tried to get past.

George blocked his way. "Not so fast, you old bastard!"

Willard said, "First you're going to tell us about that kidnapped boy. Why is he sick?"

"He's drunk," Dirk said; "that's what!"

"You liar!" Willard shouted. "He was all right until you hit him in the stomach."

Dirk was sweating and his huge moustache trembled. "I never hit nobody. Now let me pass or I'll have you put off the boat."

"I saw you slug him," George said, "and one of your bums hit him in the back!"

"He didn't!"

Willard raised his voice. "Look at that one now, ready to kick the old man if he opens his mouth!" He looked contemptuously at young Dirk's red, sullen face and the cold, indifferent faces of the lieutenants. "Father and son, you aren't men enough to do your own shanghaiing; you have to hire thugs!"

Dirk made a show of dignity. "Those gentlemen are United States marshals, and you have insulted them!"

"Marshals, my eye!" George said. "They're Portland bums!"

Willard said, "If they're marshals, let's see their papers!" There was no response. "You're too cheap even to buy them tin badges!"

More passengers had gathered, and Willard directed his oratory toward them. "Gentlemen, this is a bare-faced kidnapping of seventeen Americans by a crimp who isn't even a citizen; by this corrupt old man and his half-wit son and two armed thugs!"

A drunken voice shouted fervently, "God love you, boy!" and the Norwegian said, "I wowed a wow that next time Dirk comes to Astoria I'll throw him in the Columbia!"

Willard continued with added confidence, "In the dark ages, Negro slaves were treated this way—and our fathers fought and died to make them free. Is this the freedom they died for: seventeen white citizens snatched away from their families, kidnapped and beaten and sold like cattle?"

"God love you, boy!" the drunk shouted, with tears running down his red face. "We won't let them; we'll throw the crimps in the river and let the sailors all go free!"

It was the logical response, but Willard was not prepared to lead a mob. He realized with chagrin that he had assumed leadership without having thought of a destination.

"For God's sake, what's all the noise?" The *Thompson's* first mate pushed confidently through the crowd, the gold braid of his cap gleaming officially above his full face. "What's going on here?" He stopped, with his eyes resting on Willard. "What is it, Willard? Not fighting, are you?"

"The boy's crazy!" old Dirk said. "He insulted me!"

Willard indicated the sailors. "The crimps are shanghaiing these men!"

The mate spoke soothingly. "This is no court of law. Their fares are paid and we have to carry them. And we can't allow any hot words on board; the old man's madder than hops!"

Willard decided to settle for what he could. He pointed to the curly-haired young man doubled up on his mattress. "That boy's been kidnapped and beaten—"

Old Dirk was indignant. "Nobody touched him!"

Willard raised his voice. "I saw this old crimp slug him!"

"I saw him, too," George said.

The mate became belligerent. "If there's any slugging on board, I'll do it! If there's any slugging, By God—" It was a brave threat, and while he was making it old Dirk got to the other side of the mattress islands, where he was giving papers and keys to his son. "There'll be no slugging on board," the mate said again, "and no hot words!" His statement was emphasized by the final blast of the whistle and he turned away hastily. "Tom, Rance!"

The deckhands appeared from the thinning crowd and manned the gangway. Old Dirk took long steps to the cargo door and hurried over the gangway as the stand-by gong clanged; then the shrill bo'sun's whistle, and the gangway came in with a rush. The gong clanged again, and there was a hiss of steam and the deep sigh of the engines, answered by the awakening thunder of the paddle wheel, and the *Thompson* trembled to life.

Old Dirk was safely ashore, and the jingle bell ringing "all clear" came like a great echo of the jingling keys which the crimp had turned over to his son.

The moment had passed when Willard might have accomplished anything. The most he could do now was to cover his retreat. He moved nearer young Dirk, looking intently at his red, sullen face. "Aren't you ashamed of yourself?"

[55]

Dirk shifted his weight from one foot to the other. "You clear out of here!"

Willard said, "You're so hungry for money that you take stiffs from the flop houses and sell them for live sailors with too many knockout drops. You steal honest men from their families, and you rob the gutter and the morgue. You can't even say you're a tool of the shipowners, because you cheat them with corpses. You're jackals, slinking around flop houses and back alleys and morgues!"

"You shut up!"

"You ought to ship yourself out in a hell wagon and have some sense beaten into you!"

George said, "If you had a rope around your neck, you wouldn't have enough sense to untie it!"

"Oh, shut up!" Dirk turned to his indifferent lieutenants. "Get them moving; we're taking them upstairs."

Dirk's phrase was echoed by an English voice. " 'Upstairs,' my word! I wonder if the man's competent in nautical matters!"

"He can't tell the difference between a stiff and a sailor!" Willard said.

The clash ended in sniping and name calling, with Dirk and his "United States marshals" herding their flock toward the after companionway. Congratulations were then offered by some of the passengers: Hanson, the fisherman; Sam Frye, who clerked in the drug store; a logger from a way port on the Columbia; the drunkard who had invoked God's blessing; and last of all Joe Wells, the English remittance man. "Well done!" he said. "You didn't half give that press gang a going over! Your diction was excellent and so was your invective." Then, as if Willard might think he was presuming, he explained, "I was a great admirer of your father. My name is Joseph Wells; I saw you often when you were a boy."

Willard said, "We never mention Seaside without speaking of you. Do you still live there?"

The remittance man quoted in Greek—which Willard understood imperfectly—something about the shore of the wine-dark sea. "I am a fixture. This is the first time I have been inland since the Queen's birthday—selecting a little gift for Sinj'n Williams; he's going as a missionary to some beastly islands."

For the past week at home Willard had heard about little else but the impending departure of Mr. St. John Williams. "My sister Emily is going to sing on board his ship with the Bethel choir; they're giving him quite a send-off."

"It's good of them to make Sinj'n's departure as jolly as possible—but look here, this chap's waiting to speak to you."

"This chap" was the drunkard who had already thanked Willard for his speech, but once was not enough and he again struck his hand into Willard's. "God love you, boy!" His moist eyes gazed more and more fervently out of his red bumpy face. "God *love* you!" When his eyes and voice could not express his emotion, he drew a flask of whiskey from his coat pocket and urged it on Willard. The flask had a cougar stalking across its label and it bore the virile name of *Panther Piss*. "Let's drink to the unhappy sailors!"

Willard escaped the drink of the brave by retreating with George up the main companionway and through the saloon with its suave glow of lights on polished mahogany and plush, chords struck on the piano, and comfortable voices that suddenly changed. The young man was aware of the stir and flutter as he passed and went out on deck with his companion. He was a hero for a moment, but the adventure had a bad aftertaste: a prospective lawyer doing a vocal exercise in public while seventeen poor devils thought it meant something and put their faith in him.

The *Thompson* was already on the Columbia, passing Sauvie Island. As they walked forward, adding their speed to hers, the low shore seemed to race by in the darkness, rotating past one distant farmhouse light. It was cool now, with the smoke of the city gone and stars beginning to shine above the great river.

They paused at the rail and stood looking down at the low foredeck that tapered to nothing at the bow, with a naked flagstaff rigid against the still-undisturbed river. A passenger from the starboard side passed with a regular step, then turned back and stopped beside Willard. "You certainly gave that crimp a scare," he said.

"I started to, anyway."

"You gave him all he could stand; I'm betting we don't see him before Astoria."

Willard was immensely relieved. "Where is Dirk? We've been looking for him."

"He locked the sailors in three staterooms and himself in another, and put out the light. His helpers are in the smoking room, playing poker with some gamblers."

"Thank you for telling me."

"Thank you for speaking out. Good night."

"Nice fellow," Willard said when the stranger was gone.

George said, "I was scared Dirk and his bums would be waiting for us; and they're more scared than we are."

"We have public opinion on our side—and they know it!"

"Your speech was wonderful," George said. "Some of the men were crying!"

Willard had noticed only one, and he wasn't sure whether that one had been moved by his eloquence or by *Panther Piss* whiskey. He was dissatisfied with himself, and just now he didn't want any more praise from strangers or friends. He said, "I wish we'd been able to help the fellow who got slugged. Maybe we can do something in Astoria. Let's get some sleep."

He was almost surprised to see his red-and-white carpetbag in his stateroom; years and multitudinous events seemed to have gone by since he left it there. He undressed slowly and turned out the light; but he was not quite ready for sleep. He drew back the curtain and stood at the window—a young man in his nightshirt looking out at the strip of dimly lighted deck, the dark river and the darker shore, and a strip of spangled universe above the black treetops. Stars on their courses, and the *Thompson* on her course, flying down the dark river, cradling good and evil in the same sure arms.

At the edge of sleep Willard remembered Joe Wells. The remittance man had introduced himself almost as if he were a stranger, though for years he had been their summer neighbor in the lost world of Seaside.

While Willard's father had lived, Seaside had been a recurring summer reality: eighteen miles by horse and carriage over the Clatsop Plains, within sound and smell of the Pacific, and through big spruce woods; then the roll of wheels and thunder of hoofs on the wooden bridge over the slow Necanicum; the board cottage among coarse warm-colored pines; huckleberry and salal in the sandy dooryard; everyone tracking in sand; little red ants finding their way into the food safe, and great distant ships edging up over the hill of the world as they stood in toward the mouth of the Columbia.

Their nearest neighbor had been Joe Wells, who raised vegetable marrows in his garden and fished delicately for trout in the Necanicum while waiting for his monthly draft from England. Willard's mother still had silverware that Joe had given her—plain sterling spoons with a crest: a crown surmounted with an acorn between two oak leaves. Joe gave Mother the spoons because he did not want the saloonkeeper to have them.

One morning in summer Father lugged home a ship's figurehead which had washed up on the beach: the wooden torso of a woman with generous breasts and an enchanting smile. Father was smiling, too, as proud of his salvage as a boy. He would have carried the wooden lady over the door-sill, but Mother said there was no room for her in the cottage and she had to be content with the shelter of the porch.

The following summer she was gone. During the winter, when Joe needed extra cheer, he had borrowed the lady and pawned her at the saloon. Before her ransom arrived from England, the saloon had embarrassed Joe by burning down. Joe was quite unmercenary; he never suggested making restitution. Neither had he accepted anything in return for his ancestral silver.

Nearly everyone in Astoria went to the beach in those days, the wealthy to the Seaside House, the others to the old Grimes Hotel, to cottages, or tents.

Willard remembered the Oregon Trail wanderers arriving in big farm wagons, and on horseback, with blanket rolls behind their saddles and rifles slung in front. There were families of old and young, and parties of young men who slept under wagons, half living off the land, hunting in the hills, fishing and spearing salmon in the river, and digging razor clams on the beach. In the evenings their campfires lit up the pine grove, silhouetting horses tied to wagon wheels and deer hanging from the lower branches of trees. Fiddling, and the sound of an accordion, and lively songs which Willard never heard anywhere else:

Oh, don't you remember sweet Betsy from Pike,
Who crossed the big mountains with her lover Ike,
With two yoke of cattle, a large yellow dog,
A tall Shanghai rooster and one spotted hog—

The wanderers were heroes to the town-bred children, who told each other that these were Oregon Trail pioneers still searching for the perfect place to settle down.

When Willard asked about it at home his father told him that the strangers were pioneer farmers and their families, who took to their wagons when the wheat harvest was over and roved again as they or their parents had done on the Oregon Trail, living close to the earth and camping under the stars. "That is one of the four great loves," Father said: "The love between a man and woman; the love between parents and their children; the love of one's fellow men; and the love of people for the earth. The human race would perish if men lost those simple things from their hearts."

Willard's father was a man of faith and it appeared that his faith had made the cottage at Seaside a reality. When the family returned to the beach the summer after his death, all trace of their cottage was gone. Joe Wells, their nearest neighbor, could not recollect seeing it disappear, but he recalled a loose board, which explained everything. A winter inhabitant was within his rights in taking a loose board for the repair of his own cottage; and others were at liberty to help themselves from a partly dismantled structure, and the more dismantled it became, the less need there was for delicacy.

The Pearsons never replaced the Seaside cottage. It was not so much that they had less money, but they had less expectation of getting more. In his lifetime, the father had observed that a family needed money. He considered the problem seriously and decided that the best thing to do about money was to make a large amount at one time and not have to bother about it any more. His attempts gave life the many-colored glow of rainbow dreams that added nothing to the family's wealth.

The last dream was of making a fortune by shipping salmon to distant markets; it took Father to California, and shortly before Christmas it produced a telegram which read: SAILING TUESDAY ON GUILDENSTERN. CHRISTMAS JOY. BRINGING GOOD NEWS.

A few mornings later it was blowing hard and the air was full of driven rain and peppered with flying leaves and twigs. When the recess bell rang at school everyone went to the basement to play. But instead of the usual games on the boys' side, some of the big eighth-graders were sharpening crayons, marking strange symbols on the basement walls, and arguing, while younger boys listened worshipfully.

Ed Barton, the gambler's son, chalked his name on the wall and pointed to it. "That's sacred," he said. "If I find salvage on the beach and put that name on it, it don't matter who finds it afterward; it'll be there when I come back with a boat or a wagon. That's the code!"

"This is better!" Chris Anderson drew a large X with a wavy line under it. "That keeps it safe, you bet!"

Ed told him scornfully, "That's for fishermen who can't read!"

Chris was a fisherman's son and he was as big as a man; he looked at the gambler's boy ominously. "Fishermen get the most salvage. What's the good of your name when somebody can't read?"

"What's the good of a mark that anybody could draw?"

"What's the good of anything if people aren't honest?"

Willard thought it was a lot of excitement over nothing. "Why don't they wait until there's a shipwreck?"

The boy next to him looked surprised. "There's a ship on Peacock Spit right now!"

"Who said so?"

"Paul Grimes."

"A grain ship?"

"Nope, steamer; the *Guildenstern*."

Willard's heart turned to a lump of ice and he didn't say any more. It seemed to him that if he did he would lessen his father's chances on board the little steamer. He listened to the heartless salvage talk, with his mind working swiftly; he had to get to Peacock Spit.

The bell rang for the end of recess and Willard marched upstairs with the others, then ducked into the cloakroom and waited. A moment after the halls had quieted, he was flitting downstairs, dressed in his oilskins and sou'wester.

He waited outside the door until four big boys came out, quickly and quietly. Chris Anderson, in the lead, started at the sight of a waylaying figure, then hurried by.

Willard followed close on their heels and no one said anything until they were out of the school yard, hurrying along the rain-lashed street. Then Chris said over his shoulder, "Go back to school, kid."

"Please," Willard begged, "I want to go with you!"

"Run along; we're not going anywhere."

"You're going to the wreck; I have to go with you!"

Ed Barton turned on him menacingly. "You get out of here!"

Willard ignored him. "Please, Chris, it's important! I have—" Before he could say "reasons," he was sprawling on his skinned elbows and Ed, who had tripped him, was hurrying on with the others. Willard scrambled to his feet and caught up with them. "Please, Chris—"

Ed tried to trip him again, but Willard side-stepped and tagged along beside the fisherman's big son. "Please, I've got to—" Then Ed was holding his neck with one hand and twisting his arm with the other. "Ow!"

"You let him alone!" Chris said.

"I'm trying to get rid of him."

"You don't have to hurt him." Chris then turned on Willard. "Go back to school, kid. You're too small. Anyway, we don't know if we're going. If my old man has our boat, we're out of luck."

"You can take our cutter," Willard said; "I have the key."

"It's a good boat," Paul said.

"What'd your old man say if you got drowned?" Chris asked.

Willard played his final card, which he hadn't wanted to reveal. "My father's on the *Guildenstern;* you have to take me!"

It was mid-afternoon when they reached the Cape, battered and exhausted and half seasick. They climbed the steep trail through the roaring spruce woods and came to the open space and the lighthouse on North Head, in the full rush of the gale and the furious drumming of seas in Dead Man's Hollow at the foot of the cliff.

There were people around the lighthouse, but the boy was aware of them only as shadows and dim faces all looking in the same direction. He had expected a steamer on the beach, but all he saw were two tall black crosses a mile or so away, standing out of the white boiling of the surf—crosses with green plumes at their tops. Then he realized that he was looking at the masts and crosstrees of a vessel. The figures of a few men stood on the crosstrees, huddled close to the masts.

Willard told himself that maybe the others had been taken off the steamer, though he couldn't see how when there was no real water out there—only the unending breakers, like the rolling snows of doom. He pulled at the sleeve of the man next to him and asked if anyone had been saved.

The man looked at him in sad surprise. "How, in God's name?"

Chris Anderson came back from somewhere with exciting news. "Your old man's alive!" he told Willard. "We just saw him!"

Willard could hear the thunder of ice falling from his heart. "Father! Where is he? Where is he?"

Chris pointed toward the black spars rising out of the breakers. "He's on the foremast. See the three men up there? He's the middle one! You can see him plain through the telescope!"

They waited their turn while others looked through the telescope on the stand: a sea captain and two fishermen and a man from the Life Saving Service. One after another they looked in silence, or said, "Poor devils!" The Life Saver said approvingly, "Those are good masts. If she doesn't break up, they'll stand till Judgment Day!"

When it was Willard's turn, he adjusted the telescope feverishly until the blurred shapes leaped toward him, as large and clear as life: above the white hell of breakers the masts of a steamer, and men lashed in the upper rigging with their feet on the crosstrees—two men on one mast and three on the other. Above each huddle of survivors there was a little, storm-blown fir tree lashed to the truck of the mast, after the custom of ships during the Christmas season.

On the nearest mast Willard saw his father, between two sailors. His face was turned away, but the boy recognized the shape of his bare head and the bald spot on top, and his long black overcoat crossed by a rope under his arms. The powerful glass brought him so close that when he turned the boy could see every feature. All expression seemed to have gone from his cold, haggard face and gathered in his eyes as he looked toward the land.

"Father!"

He seemed almost close enough to touch, but when the boy stumbled from the telescope his father was suddenly a faraway figure on one of the black crosses above the boiling surf on Peacock Spit.

A little later Willard's uncle found him and took him home on the tug *Columbia*. Uncle Roger was his mother's brother and a bar pilot, and he was very comforting. He was certain that the wrought-iron steamer would hold together until the shipwrecked men could be rescued. "They have only to endure," he said. "You have to endure, too, and your mother needs you at home."

Uncle Roger had great hopes that the gale would blow itself out by morning. But the gale lasted three days, and it was two more days before a boat could get to the wreck.

The boy was not allowed to go back to the lighthouse, but other watchers looked on helplessly as one after another the

[65]

five wilted and died at the foot of the green Christmas trees. They were all dead when rescuers cut them down.

At college and at home Willard heard himself spoken of as a "serious young man," and the reference always pleased him. It seemed a good beginning for a world where rainbow dreams had led his father to crucifixion between two sailors.

Willard slept, half waking when the steamer whistled for a way port, the bellow of a bull with golden lungs; deep bells in the engine room; the engines stopping; silence after the deep breathing and the thunder, with voices coming out of the silence; bells, and the engines taking a few more deep breaths, with the stern wheel thundering briefly in reverse; the creak of mooring lines taking hold; the outward rush of the gangway, bantering voices, and the rumble of freight being wrested ashore. Then the gangway coming in with a rush, the blurred rumble of mooring lines crawling back on board, and a clear cry, *"All clear, sir!"* Deep bells in the depths of the steamer, and the deep breathing and the everlasting thunder. . . .

5

Sinj'n Williams had not received much attention while he lived and labored in Astoria, but when he was leaving the town did him honor.

When Willard and Barry and Emily reached the boat dock, the Bethel cutter was on its way out to the *Cape Fear*, loaded to the gunwales, and Willard could not take half of the crowd that was left: members of the Bethel Choir and the Band of Hope, a deputation from the W.C.T.U., and non-churchgoing women who were making the occasion an excuse for an outing. There were also a few men, and small boys on errands devoid of religious significance.

Willard packed a dozen people into the boat, and Barry and Emily found themselves sitting in the bottom; on the stern sheets, Willard and Miss Susie Nye sat on opposite sides of the tiller; and on the after thwart, Emily's special friend, Hope Morris, sat between old Judge Boardman and pale, plump Mrs. Cross, the doctor's wife.

The boat had been loaded in no special order, but the female passengers who happened to be nearest the halliards raised the sails and one of them tended the jib sheet. They were all good Astorians and they did the right things in a boat as naturally as women of other parts of the country would have hitched a horse to a buggy.

Nautically, the trip out to the bark was short and pleasant, but socially it was difficult. Emily wanted to talk to Hope, but while her brother handled the tiller and mainsheet, he engaged Judge Boardman in a lively dispute over the merits of a Supreme Court decision and the judge's ornate bass voice drowned out Hope's soft soprano. Hope would have preferred to talk to Willard, but that was out of the question. Hope had light brown hair and a pale oval face under the white sailor hat which she wore like a halo; when she sang, she made her mouth oval, too, and with her blue eyes turned upward she looked like a singing angel. Emily wasn't even sure that Hope was a good Christian, but you don't inquire into the religious convictions of angels. Just now, as she sat between the doctor's plump wife and the booming judge, her look of laughing dismay was almost as companionable as words.

Out of politeness, Emily turned her head to speak a few words to Miss Susie Nye, who thereupon fixed her with an Ancient Mariner gaze and began a monologue so urgent in tone that there was no escaping it. Miss Nye took almost personal credit for the display of shipping on the river, and she implied that, except for her family, the girl would be alone in a howling wilderness. The lady's parents had been members of the "Peoria Party," the first American settlers in Oregon; in her mind that made her a member of the royal family, and she explained at endless length the significance of arriving by horseback in 1839 rather than with the vulgar wagon-train stampede of 1843.

Emily's neck was spared a permanent crick by her brother luffing the boat alongside the deep-laden *Cape Fear*. The passengers began scrambling up the Jacob's ladder. As befitted modesty, the men went first. Willard and Barry, who were the crew, remained with downcast eyes; they did not even look up by impulse when Hope Morris turned imprudently to ask a question while halfway up the ladder.

Emily was the last to leave and as she was about to go up Willard told her mysteriously, "Don't mind if I'm not on board for the services; I'm going to have a look at the *Challenger*."

[68]

She partly understood. Before docking, the *Thompson* had gone alongside the down-East "hell wagon" with the shanghaied crew—all of them except one man. "What do you suppose could have happened to your young farmer?"

"That's what I'm going to find out," Willard told her. "He can't have disappeared into thin air. I'm working on a theory—"

"Don't get yourself shanghaied in the process!" Emily warned him—and climbed the unstable ladder with the assurance of a Bethel choir girl used to visiting ships. At the top, Judge Boardman reached up a hand to help her, raising his silk hat with the other. "May I have this dance, Miss Pearson?"

"With pleasure!" she said, jumping down to the holystoned deck.

It looked like a party with so many people visiting in the bright sunshine. Emily saw friends everywhere, but Hope Morris was nearest and she took Emily's hand and drew her to the bulwark. She asked laughingly, "Now do you know all about the Peoria Party?"

"Do you know all about the Supreme Court?"

Hope made a face of dainty dismay. "I expect that of a judge, but why do I like Willard when he only talks about things like the Supreme Court?" Then she said, "Oh, my heart! Isn't he handsome?"

In the boat below them, Barry had just hoisted the jib; Willard pulled in on the mainsheet smoothly and swiftly, put up the helm, and the boat heeled as she filled away for the dock. Hope sighed. "Doesn't he look romantic?"

Emily was proud of her brother and she considered him good looking, but she did not think he was romantic. He was young and serious, and though he liked Hope, he was more interested in planning a career. Emily thought it a pity that Hope was ready to be romantic when he was not, but she didn't know how serious her friend was. Hope had the gift of being able to say almost anything without giving offense. She could even say improper things so daintily and with such an angel's face that you did not think of her as saying them; it was more as if the thoughts had come out of your own mind to dance, naked and unashamed.

Today Hope was romantic. "It feels so good to be on board ship again that I won't want to go ashore! We really haven't anything to go back for. We could sail forever, visiting new places and seeing what other people think is right and wrong, and what they wear or don't wear, and what they dry their eyes on in this vale of tears. We might even find a place where people don't think the world is a vale of tears. We would stay for a long time and if Sinj'n started to tell about sadness and sin, we'd feed him to the cannibals."

Emily overlooked the disrespectful reference to Sinj'n. "A voyage like that would be nice as long as it was summer and we were young—"

"It would always be summer, and we would always be young! Don't you feel that way?"

"I do," Emily admitted, "but—"

"That's two of us—so there must be something in it!"

"Other people have felt that way—" Emily began.

"And they were young as long as they felt that way," Hope told her. "If unpleasant things happened to them, it was because they lost faith."

They were still standing at the bulwarks when the Bethel cutter came back on its second trip. The cutter was loaded with passengers, but the girls did not find any of them interesting except Emily's Aunt Rita and the Fortune brothers, Jack and Tom. The boys were sitting in the bow, among the W.C.T.U. deputation, as good as gold, with the river breeze ruffling their thick black hair, and their clear young faces and piratical eyes alive to every visible detail of the bark.

Watching the brothers, Hope said, "We'll take them on

our voyage; you've only to look at their eyes to know how close adventure is!"

Emily had only to look at the boys' bare heads and hickory shirts and jeans to know how close they were to trouble. Mrs. Fortune would never have sent them to a religious gathering in such attire; anyway, she had forbidden their leaving the yard for a week. "You can see they're dressed to work around home," Emily pointed out. "I hope they have a good time, because they'll certainly go home to a whipping!"

But Hope's attention had already shifted to Rita. "We'll take your Aunt Rita along, too. She's even dressed for an expedition to the Spanish Main in that coral dress with the flowing black sleeves and that black sailor hat! We'll find a dagger for her wide belt—not that she would ever use it; she could slay anyone with her beauty!"

"She's a good cook, too."

"There are many good cooks, Emily, but only one Rita; she has the secret for staying young and beautiful."

Emily had to admit that so far her aunt had done very well; she was all of twenty-seven and there was still a suddenness about her beauty that was apt to give a man a moment of forgetfulness and a look of foolish joy, like one who has come to the end of a quest. Almost immediately, of course, he learned that Rita was the wife of Captain Roger Collins. . . .

For Emily, Rita's beauty was an old story; she knew that her aunt was no wiser than other people and no less subject to the misfortunes that befall human beings, and probably no happier. Emily had seen her look wistfully after a young squaw with a papoose on a carrying board at her back.

The cutter was alongside now, with its sails fluttering in the wind and passengers reaching for the boat ropes. Mr. McMillan called, "Down jib!" and the jib came down with a rush that nearly tore it from the hanks. Looking from above, the startled girls saw the Fortune brothers pounce on the sail and smother it, like two earnest terriers annihilating a pigeon. Either of the girls could have downed the jib with one hand, and the boys' concerted vehemence was too much for them and they gave way to unladylike laughter. It was funny, and it was also something to think about: this was the brothers' second experience afloat and they already showed the dash, if not the judgment, of men-of-warsmen.

While the passengers were still coming up over the side, the girls saw Willard and Barry sailing back alone; they waved and passed under the stern of the *Cape Fear*, and Hope lost interest in standing at the rail. "We ought to pay our respects to Sinj'n Williams," she said. "He is the reason for this gathering."

The young missionary was surrounded by well-wishers and because he was shorter than most of the women Emily got only a glimpse of his fair head and spectacles. Hope stretched on her tiptoes and reported, "I can see his lamb-chop whiskers!"

"You mean mutton-chop whiskers!"

"No," Hope whispered; "they're too young and tender for that, and he looks like a lamb going to the slaughter!"

"You shouldn't make fun of him," Emily said. "Sinj'n is going on a serious and dangerous mission."

Hope embraced her. "If I didn't make fun of him, I might cry!"

They were still waiting their chance to speak to him when Mr. McMillan appeared at the break of the poop deck, rangy and tall and a little shabby, beside the stubby, sharp-faced master of the *Cape Fear*. The Bethel minister clapped his hands for attention and called, "Brothers and sisters, Captain Dixon has been kind enough to allow this gathering of Brother Williams' friends, and we do not want to delay his sailing. We shall hold our service at once, and whatever time is left can be spent in sociability." He turned to the captain. "Perhaps you have a word to say, Captain Dixon."

The captain looked down a trifle cockily and said: "Ladies and gentlemen, I'm more used to talking to sailors than to beautiful ladies and distinguished gentlemen, so I hope you'll excuse me if my language is a little rough. As your minister told you, you're welcome here; but we have time and tide to think about, and we don't want to be late arriving in Australia. (Laughter.) The pilot will come on board at eight bells; until then, make yourselves at home." They applauded, and Joe Wells cried *"Hear, hear!"* so fervently that everyone looked at him, and saw that he was drunk. The captain then bellowed to the mate, "Mister, send the hands aft!" After that he nodded to Mr. McMillan, "It's your watch, sir."

They gathered on the raised poop deck, with the choir in a double thwartship row forward of the binnacle and wheel, and the visitors along the starboard and port rails, making three sides of a hollow square. Some of the children sat on deck, with their elders standing behind them, like people posing for a group photograph; then Aunt Rita sat down and a few of the younger women followed her example. They were still settling themselves when they heard the tramp of feet on deck, and then the crew began coming up the port ladder, uncovering their heads respectfully as they reached the poop. They lined up in a double row, facing the choir, and the captain and the mates stood a little apart from them.

As usual, Mr. McMillan opened the service with a prayer for "those who go down to the sea in ships." Emily stole a look at the bowed heads of the men who were about to go down to the sea: bald heads and graying heads, and dark, shaggy ones, and opposite her a head of curly red-gold hair that made a brighter spot in the bright afternoon.

Emily felt that she could be as religious with her eyes open as with them closed, but she could not justify using the time of prayer to admire a sailor's curls; she looked up and away to the spars and white furled sails and dark intricate rigging: a forest, romantic and geometric, where nothing stirred.

[73]

. . . Now something was stirring—two small figures in blue cautiously ascending the ratlines of the main shrouds. For a moment she thought they were sailors diminished by distance, then she recognized them as the Fortune boys, exploring while people who would have forbidden them were at prayer. It was dangerous and probably wrong, but there was something worshipful about their careful, unfaltering ascent, like two boys climbing up for a reverent peek at heaven. In their own way they were as brave as Christian martyrs; if they didn't break their necks, they would go home to a beating. But no stripes, however numberless, would take away their pride in having been aloft, or dim the vision they had had in high places.

The prayer ended and Mr. McMillan turned to the choir and announced the hymn: *Shall We Gather at the River?*

Hope whispered, "We're doing it, aren't we?"

Emily's impulse to giggle was just saved by the hymn.

> *Shall we gather at the river,*
> *Where bright angel feet have trod—*

As she sang, with conquered laughter dying away in her eyes, she found herself meeting the steady gaze of one of the sailors, and she looked away in confusion. He was the young man with the bright curly hair whom she had noticed during prayer, and he didn't look at all like a sailor: he wasn't more than twenty—big and straight and good-looking.

After the hymn, Mr. McMillan spoke. "Brothers and sisters, my text this afternoon is, 'Go ye into all lands and preach His word.' One of us is doing that today. We have with us a missionary who is leaving the comforts and ease of civilization to plunge into the jungle; to travel among dangerous islands in distant seas, and among barbaric peoples, to preach His word. . . ."

When Saint John Williams acknowledged the introduction, Emily felt as much as saw the look of disappointed incredulity on the faces of the crew. It was as if a lion had been described to them and they had been shown a mouse. Sinj'n was a slight young man, not over five feet tall, and his spectacles and fair sandy hair and pinkish "lamb-chop" whiskers gave him a frail, unworldly look. He stepped forward and said in a weak, earnest voice, "I am doing only what I feel the Lord has called upon me to do and I pray that He will give me strength to perform His work." He stepped back among fervent "Amens," and Mr. McMillan began his sermon.

It was a dry sermon, but for Emily it was made tense by the sight of the Fortune boys against the sky near the head of the mainmast, apparently debating whether they should go through the lubber's hole of the top or do the seamanly thing and take the futtock shrouds. Hope saw them, too, and whispered, "Do you think they're all right?"

"I hope they are!" Emily hoped they would decide not to go any higher. As she watched, they decided on the futtock shrouds which slanted outward and upward to the top, and the first boy began the perilous climb, hanging by hands and feet, back downward, a hundred feet above the deck. By then all the choir were looking upward tensely, and some of the congregation were turning their eyes in the same direction. The boy paused, his head level with the top; he reached up one arm, then the other; his legs dangled against the empty sky; and as he pulled himself over the rim, the smaller boy began the upward and outward climb.

By that time the inattention had spread to the minister himself; he faltered in the middle of a sentence, looking upward anxiously. The *Cape Fear* became as silent as a derelict. Then the captain growled, "Mister, get those boys down out of there! Don't scare them enough to make them fall!"

The mate hurried away and the sermon was resumed, but it was doubly a voice crying in the wilderness, with all eyes watching the mate surge up the ratlines. On the futtock shrouds, hanging back down, the smaller boy had paused as if uncertain whether to go on or retreat. He decided to go on, and his brother helped him over the rim as the mate came storming up. For a few moments the boys stood in the top, enjoying their bird's-eye view of the ship; then the mate was upon them; through the faltering words of the sermon you could hear the growl of his voice.

The mate had orders to bring them down, but while he growled and pointed through the lubber's hole to the lower shrouds, the boys pointed in all directions. Emily was puzzled until she realized that they were making use of the mate, trying to turn their ejection from the top into a lesson in ship's rigging. The mate's voice became loud and profane, and presently he swung through the lubber's hole to the main shrouds and began to descend slowly, keeping an eye on the boys, who followed him.

By the time the boys reached the safety of the deck the sermon had limped to a close and Mr. McMillan called for the Doxology.

As Emily sang with a will she found her eyes again meeting those of the curly-haired sailor. She felt less self-conscious when she was singing, and he seemed less a stranger; he was almost handsome and quite refined, not at all like the other members of the crew. Among the rough and the hairy and the tattooed and the dissipated and the drunken, he looked young and fresh. She turned her eyes away because she felt her heart suddenly beating faster.

The blessings of the day blended into one warm glow of praise: the glory of feeling that it would always be summer and they would always be young; the sound of Hope's sweet soprano voice and the touch of her hand; the safe return of Jack and Tom Fortune from the high places; the red-gold curls and fresh, tanned face and blue eyes of the young sailor, who would always come back to her in memory when she recalled that afternoon on the great river—the color and light and warmth and excitement and the singing voices, and the flash of sunshine on the white breast of a flying gull.

Praise Father, Son, and Holy Ghost. Amen.

The sailors had been served their ration of religion, and now the mate growled at them to "lay for'ard," while Mr. McMillan apologized to the captain for the misbehavior of the Fortune boys. Their antics aloft had distracted the service and made everyone forget the missionary who was being honored; but now everyone thought of him again and crowded around, eager to make it up to him.

Emily and Hope held hands and kept close together as they worked their way through the physical turmoil and babble of voices from people milling on the poop deck. In the thick of the crowd, Emily felt a touch on her arm and a man's voice said, "Miss." She looked up into the troubled, deep-blue eyes of the young sailor. He was even taller than she had thought—her head came just to his shoulder. He was anxious and secret, whispering like someone bringing her a message in a dream. "Miss, can I talk to you?"

"Yes."

"I've been shanghaied; I don't want to go to sea! I want to get off this ship! Will you help me?"

"I'll try," she promised.

"My name is Albert Hedges; can you remember that?"

"Yes; Albert Hedges."

"We have a farm near Lafayette. The threshing engine broke down and I went to Portland for a new part. I was drugged and robbed and brought down here—"

The story matched a pattern that was already in Emily's mind. "Were you on the *Thompson* last night?"

He nodded. "The crimps had twenty of us, and a young man tried to help us."

"That was my brother! He's around the *Challenger* now, looking for you."

"You're good people," he whispered earnestly. "What's your name?"

"Pearson, Emily Pearson. My brother's name is Willard."

"Emily Pearson; I'll remember that."

Standing close beside him in the crowd, whispering, she felt all the excitement of a conspirator and a rescuer; it was also pleasant to be near him, though she couldn't account for his being on the *Cape Fear*. "You disappeared from the steamer—"

"Yes, Miss Emily. Your brother kept saying that I was kidnapped and they were afraid of trouble. When the *Thompson* stopped at Rainier, they put me on this ship. I don't want to go to Australia—"

"I'll do everything I can," Emily promised. She felt his hand close over hers.

"Thank you, Miss Emily! They need me at home in the harvest; the wheat is beginning to shell out. Pa is waiting for me to bring back the part for the threshing machine; my folks don't know what went with me—"

Both of them started as a voice blasted from close by: "*Sailor, get the hell off the quarter-deck! Who d'ye think you are?*" Emily saw one of the mates ploughing through the crowd, his eyes glaring cold and gray in his big red face. She told her companion, "I'm going to see Mr. McMillan; we'll try to get you off this ship."

"Thank you, Miss Emily!" His hand tightened over hers. "You're mighty sweet!"

"You'd better go!" she said. Then the mate was upon them, with his mouth opening for another roar. Emily stepped between him and the sailor. "I'll thank you not to swear in the presence of ladies."

Her aggressiveness surprised herself as much as it did the mate, but the rebuked man closed his mouth; then he opened it again, more civilly.

[78]

"Excuse me, Miss, but that sailor—was he bothering you?"

"Indeed not! He's a friend of mine!" Her face flamed under the curious glances of friends and acquaintances, but the delay gave Albert Hedges time to escape the mate's immediate anger.

When both of them were gone, Emily pushed her way through the crowd until she found Mr. McMillan, and his warm tired smile made her feel less desperate.

"Well, Emily, we couldn't have had a more beautiful day for Sinj'n's departure." Then he noticed her troubled look. "What's the matter?"

They stood at the rail, watching the sea gulls and the anchored ships, while Emily told him about the shanghaied sailor.

"I noticed him as soon as the crew appeared," Mr. McMillan told her. "I thought then, 'There's someone who isn't used to earning his bread and butter on the sea.'"

"He's never been on a ship before," she said; "his people are wheat farmers and they need him in the harvest. You must get him off this ship so he can go home!"

Mr. McMillan sighed. "I've preached sermons about it, trying to show people that no one's rights are safe as long as any group is denied its rights. When you deny a sailor human rights, the crimps have only to kidnap a farmer or a grocer and call him a sailor—and his rights are gone."

Emily listened, watching Willard and Barry in their boat that was drifting alongside the *Challenger*, with the sails down and the boys fixing something—or pretending to. When it became apparent that the minister was restating a problem rather than offering a solution, Emily asked, "What are we going to do? The ship will be on her way to Australia in less than an hour. We have to get him off!"

The minister looked thoughtful. "I haven't any special powers," he said. "All I could do is talk to the captain, and

[79]

that isn't likely to do any good. He's paid blood money for the boy; he won't want to lose it and delay his sailing. And I wouldn't want to be in the boy's shoes if the captain knows that he's stirred up trouble."

"There is a law against kidnapping," Emily told him.

"That's out of my field; but Judge Boardman is here; I'll find him."

He came back in a little while with the judge.

"I'm surprised at you, Emily," the judge said, "bothering your pretty head about things that go on in a man's world!"

"It's a woman's world, too, Judge Boardman; I can't stand by quietly while someone is being kidnapped!"

"You have only his word for it, Emily. Probably every sailor who gets drunk and accepts an advance fancies himself kidnapped."

"He wasn't drunk," she protested hotly; "he was drugged!"

"That happens, too," the judge admitted. "The young man may very well have a case, but it isn't against the captain, who paid the blood money in good faith. If the crimp procured the young man under duress, he is criminally liable —if it can be proved. You would have to know the name of the crimp and the county in which the alleged kidnapping occurred—"

"It was the Dirks, and they kidnapped him in Portland."

Judge Boardman looked interested. "The Dirks are an unsavory pair. With the right case, it might be possible to get a conviction against them in the Multnomah courts. When the young man returns—"

"*Returns!*" Emily cried. "He doesn't want to go! We must get him off before the ship sails!"

"That is what we were hoping for," Mr. McMillan put in.

"That's impossible," the judge told them. "It would mean securing a writ enjoining the ship from sailing and requiring the captain to produce this young man in court, and getting the sheriff to serve the writ"— he consulted his watch—"all in half an hour. It's physically impossible."

"We could try!" Emily said.

He shook his head. "I'm liberal-minded, Emily, but when I was a judge I would have thought a long time before I delayed the sailing of a vessel and gave the town a bad name with shipmasters and shipping interests. No, Emily, the town depends on shipping, and we can't be quixotic."

Emily said bitterly, "So you think it's right for the town to be a party to shanghaiing men!"

The judge smiled and chucked her under the chin. "Look at it this way, Emily: your young man is a wheat farmer; if it weren't for vessels with shanghaied crews, his wheat would be rotting in Portland warehouses. Tell yourself that this time he's helping to deliver his own crop. Is that so unfair?"

She scorned to answer the question. "Then you won't do anything for him!"

"On the contrary," he said, "I'll be glad to give him legal assistance when he comes back." His eyes twinkled encouragement. "It should be less than a year, Emily, and you're rather young to be serious about a sweetheart."

"He's not my sweetheart!" she told him indignantly.

The judge made a gesture of quizzical dismay. "Then why are you making such a fuss over him?"

In her headlong rush to save the young man, she had not considered her motives, and now that the question had been asked, she found herself blushing. It was all very well to tell herself that it was only right to help a human being in distress, but would she have taken up his cause so passionately or gone to so much trouble if he had been distasteful to look at, or an old man?

She did not cry until after the judge and the minister had left her—Mr. McMillan to round up his first load of passengers to take ashore. Then she cried only out of vexation because they had failed her. If Willard had been there, she

[81]

thought, he would have accomplished something; but he and Barry were still loitering around the other anchored ships—every place except the right place.

Willard did not come back to the *Cape Fear* until the Bethel cutter had started ashore with its second load of passengers, and while he took off the last stragglers, the tug *Clatsop* was lying a little way off, waiting to put the pilot on board. Emily could hear the fateful clatter of the capstan pawls as the anchor chain was hove in.

Joe Wells was the last to come down. When he had stumbled into the boat, Barry hoisted the jib and the boat's head fell away from the scarred black side of the *Cape Fear*. Emily looked back eagerly, hoping for a last glimpse of the young sailor. She did not see him anywhere, but she recognized a lonely, bespectacled little figure in black at the break of the poop, looking after the departing boat, and she felt ashamed. The gathering had been in honor of Sinj'n Williams, and she had not even wished the departing missionary Godspeed! He was waving now, and she waved back and called, "Good-bye and good luck!" The others in the boat waved, too—Hope and Aunt Rita and the Fortune boys; and Joe Wells leaned out over the water, shouting hoarsely, "Good-bye, old man! Good-bye, old thing! Good old Sinj'n, God bless you! God bless you! Good-bye, old man!" He choked with emotion at last and collapsed in the bottom of the boat.

Now the tug was coming up from astern of the *Cape Fear*, with a familiar, graceful figure poised on top of the wheelhouse. The tug almost brushed the quarter of the bark, and then the tall pilot disappeared. Then the passing smokestack revealed him in the mizzen channels of the bark, where he had jumped from the top of the wheelhouse.

"There goes Uncle Roger!" Barry said, and Emily saw her aunt smile in acknowledgment of the pride in the boy's voice.

When she looked back again, the tug was hovering near

the bow of the bark, sending the hawser on board. Now it was going ahead, with the hawser unflaking and sliding out over the stern. You could see the black cable chain straight up and down, and hear the clatter of pawls change to a slow clanking as the capstan took the weight of the anchor. Then the clear tenor voice of the chanteyman came over the water:

Oh, Shenandoah, I long to hear you

and the deep, stirring chorus:

Hoo-ray, you rolling river!

Then again the clear solo, made mournful by distance:

Oh, Shenandoah, I love your daughter.

For the first time Emily felt the sadness of the chantey that had been raised on board departing ships for a hundred years in a thousand thousand farewells.

Hoo-ray, you rolling river!

For the first time she felt that the river was rolling over her heart. That's the way it is. It was her river and the song she loved . . . and you can't love anything deeply and for long without its becoming intertwined with sadness.

When the other passengers had gone, Emily and Hope lingered behind while Willard stowed things in the locker at the boat dock.

"I didn't have any luck with the *Challenger*," he said. "I managed to talk to one sailor, but he had signed on here."

Emily said a little sadly, "I didn't have any luck, either, but I talked to him."

Her brother looked blank. "Talked to whom?"

"The man you were looking for; he was on the *Cape Fear*."

"Great Scott! That's one chance I never thought of!" His

[83]

look of dismay was almost comical, and then he began firing questions at Emily. "What's his name?"

"Albert Hedges."

"Where does he live?"

"Near Lafayette."

"Did he say he had been shanghaied?"

"Yes. He said he was drugged and robbed."

"How did he get on board the *Cape Fear?*"

"The crimps were afraid you would make trouble for them. They put him on board the bark when the *Thompson* stopped at Rainier."

When Willard had finished his cross-examination, he embraced Emily and kissed her. "We've got something at last! Now our shanghaied sailor has a name and an address! And if he wants to sue the Dirks when he gets back, he has witnesses! You did it, Emily!"

Hope was dancing around them like an excited butterfly. "What about me?" she asked. "Don't I get congratulated, too?"

"What did you do?"

"I flirted with the mate so Emily and her sailor would have time to talk. It was hard work, too, because he wasn't as nice as you, Willard!"

"Oh, all right." Willard embraced her with the look of a man interrupting himself in important work to close a window. Hope clung to him for a moment with a delicate shiver and kissed him on the mouth.

When Willard let her go he looked startled and confused. But he was himself again almost at once. He announced, "We're going to the telegraph office and wire Albert Hedges' parents right away!" He put his hands in his pockets and produced a very faint jingle. "Well, as soon as I go home for some money. This evening we'll write and explain things in detail."

When they looked after the *Cape Fear,* she was far down

[84]

the river, with half her sails set and drawing. Willard was making their day's adventure sound like a triumph, but Emily watched the departing bark with a feeling of loneliness and defeat. She had gone on board to help save souls, and stayed to save a handsome young man from being shanghaied. She had failed in both endeavors.

6

THE HOUSE was still called the "old Prosser house"; but the Fortunes were growing into it and touching it with their family personality. Dating from the seventies, it lacked some modern conveniences, but it was well built and positive. It was a two-story building with an attic under the mansard roof, but its high ceilings and narrow windows gave the impression of a taller structure. Like other well-to-do houses of the period, it drew itself up loftily, as if disclaiming any relationship with the common earth.

The immediate surroundings consisted of a quarter of an acre of land sharply defined by a white picket fence. From the front gate the path went to the narrow porch, between the dark, shaggy pyramids of two cedars. For those who shied away from the severe frontal approach, the flagstone path turned the corner and went past the side of the house, under the shade of large cherry trees. At the back was the woodshed and vegetable garden, and a wide expanse of grass under apple trees.

When the Fortunes had bought the place, the grounds were overgrown, and along one side of the wood shed patent medicine bottles were piled up like rick wood. According to the neighbors, Mrs. Prosser had been a strict temperance woman, and her husband relied on *Golden Balm* for his alcohol. However, the medicine was guaranteed to cure consumption and syphilis and other fearful ailments, which fact had inspired Mrs. Fortune to give the house an extra cleaning.

Now the bottles were gone, flowers and shrubs were rescued from oblivion, and the tall grass was mowed. John and Thomas were raking the last bits of trash and rusted hardware from around the wood shed and the interstices of the fence. Following their father's instructions, they had made two neat piles of the rubbish, one of materials that would burn, and one of materials that would not burn. Even when they disliked a task, the boys united in tackling it, and there was never any quarreling or shirking. There was something almost mysterious in the balance they kept, each doing what was best suited to his size and strength, with the resulting accomplishment greater than the sum of what each did.

In the guise of a northwest breeze the tide of summer flowed sweetly over the clean grounds and through the leaves of the fruit trees about the tall house, and it stirred the black hair of the boys who were working along the fence; it entered the open windows of the parlor where Marjorie was practicing "Three Blind Mice" on the new Knabe piano; and it flowed pleasantly through the long, high-ceilinged kitchen where Mrs. Fortune was icing a novelty cake. When it was served at tea that afternoon, there would be cries of admiration over the different-colored layers that had been concealed inside the white icing.

Anna, the Finnish girl, should have been there but her husband had been drowned on the bar, and Mrs. Fortune was left without help; but a hundred extra duties could not crowd out the perfection of the morning. It flowed in over the great river, over the town and the square stone Customs House where her husband was a man of respected authority; through the trees of the clean grounds where her fine sons worked, and in through the open window of the parlor where Marjorie was practicing. "Three Blind Mice—"

Three blind mice, and ever so many blind people. At tea, openly or in private, the women would envy Dehlia's good luck: her well-appointed home and her husband's position. Rita Collins, the childless pilot's wife, would envy her the three handsome children; Rita Collins with her startling beauty that would come to nothing, like wealth with no inheritors. She would envy plain Dehlia, with children handsomer than herself. Mrs. Baldwin—who had borne thirteen and raised nine of them, poorly, and was an old woman at thirty-six—she would envy Dehlia her well-cared-for children from another angle. Even the opinionated Widow Pearson would feel the harmony of the Fortunes' life and wish that she had things easier. She was raising five and giving them some opportunities, but she could not hide all the nakedness of the ramshackle house above the river. Three blind mice— In different degrees all the women would envy what they called "luck." Young John and Thomas, working out there in the wide sunlit grounds, with the breeze ruffling their hair—even they didn't understand that in a life without a master plan they would be waifs in a slum. They had had countless examples of their parents providing the right thing at the right time—and still they tried to dash ahead and do things on their own account.

Since they had moved to Astoria, the boys' dream was a boat; they had already been whipped for disobeying and going out on the river with Barry Pearson; they had made themselves ridiculous scurrying about the water front and bringing word of dubious old boats that could be had at a bargain; they had wanted passionately to spend their savings on the wreck of a boat that had been smashed by the Portland steamer; and they had come home sighing like young lovers about a craft Ben Jacobs was building for a man up the river: a boat of Port Orford cedar copper-riveted to frames of white oak, with oak transom and stern sheets.

Young John and Thomas never remembered for more than half a day that life has to be controlled and planned. Their father had told them that they would have a boat when he thought it advisable and when he had a safe and suitable one for them, yet they never once suspected that the "man up the river" might be a fiction; they had no faith in anything but their own instinct for pitfalls.

"Three Blind Mice" ended again, without false notes and in good time. Marjorie called, "Mamma, I think I have it right!"

"That's better, Marjorie; it should be livelier, though."

"My arms are tired."

"You may stop now, but remember your practice tomorrow!"

"I will. Thank you, Mamma!"

Marjorie was not supposed to linger in the parlor after she had finished practicing, but there was the sound of her moving tentatively, as if she were looking for something. Dehlia was about to speak to her when she heard the door slide shut, and the child's footsteps in the hall.

Marjorie stopped in the kitchen doorway. "Oh, Mamma, you have it iced! It's a most beautiful cake!"

Dehlia agreed. "It did turn out well."

Marjorie came in for a better look and stopped beside the table, looking wistfully at the frosting bowl.

"Well?" Dehlia said amiably.

"If I put on an apron, could I scrape the bowl, please?"

"If you wash it afterward, and then give me some help. Anna couldn't have chosen a worse time to be away."

Sitting on a stool and covered by her apron, Marjorie scraped and ate frosting neatly while she visited. "It's the most beautiful day," she said. "Not too warm and not too cool, and everything just right."

Dehlia had already observed its harmony. "It is a fine morning," she agreed.

"Ever since I woke up everything's seemed just right." She licked the spoon, and added. "This is such a nice house to wake up in."

"That's the way we want it to be," Dehlia said.

"Jack and Tom are making the yard so nice." She licked

the back of the spoon and said with mature judgment, "They're good workers."

That was Marjorie, seeing the best in everything and calling attention to it. It wasn't as much that she had a happy disposition as that she wanted other people to be happy. For a child, she thought very little about herself and she had too much anxiety about others.

"The boys have worked very well this morning," Dehlia said. "I don't believe they've stopped once." She looked out to verify the impression and saw them leaning on the fence, talking to a young man and a boy: Willard and Barry Pearson. Well, she hadn't expected them to work every minute, and the Pearson boys were better than most, even if she didn't like their mother.

When Marjorie was washing the bowl, she asked, "Mamma, when we lived in San Francisco did we keep a black box of tools in the parlor?"

Dehlia paused in her sandwich making. "What gave you that idea?"

"Sometimes I dream about them."

"Tools in the parlor! What kind of tools?"

"Measuring things, in a black box—a square and a ruler and things. They're on a table with wooden eggs on a stick around the top. The table has twisty legs that spread out, and a shelf near the floor, bigger than the top."

"That's a library table," Dehlia told her. "We had one like that—it belonged to the parsonage—but you wouldn't remember it. When we were married we borrowed some furniture from Father's parsonage, but we took it back when we were able to buy our own. That was when you were very young; you wouldn't remember."

"Were we really poor?"

"Poor enough, although it isn't the kind of thing you talk about."

"We're rich now, aren't we, Mamma?"

Dehlia said, "We aren't rich, but we have enough of this world's goods so we can hold up our heads."

"And be very happy," Marjorie said.

"That's what we've worked for."

She looked out again; the two pairs of boys were still talking from opposite sides of the fence; but after a few seconds Willard put one hand on the top of a rounded picket and vaulted cleanly over the fence. Barry climbed over after him. Then all four boys started walking toward the house.

Dehlia met them at the back door. Willard Pearson was quite a gentleman, standing on the porch, hat in hand, praising what the Fortunes had accomplished.

"You have done wonders," he said. "This place used to be an eyesore, and now it's a pleasure to pass this way." But he hadn't come just to praise Caesar, and after a minute he went on: "I know you're busy, Mrs. Fortune; I wouldn't have stopped if I hadn't thought maybe we could be of some help. You won't want Jack and Tom underfoot at your tea and I'd like to look out for them for the afternoon."

"Please, Mamma!" Thomas said.

"That's thoughtful of you, Willard," Dehlia said, "but I'm afraid you'd find it too much trouble."

"It won't be any trouble at all," Willard assured her. "There's a fine breeze today and I'm taking the boat out. It'll be a help to have two extra hands, and your boys will get a lesson in sailing."

John said, "Please, Mamma; you can trust Willard to get us back when you say."

Dehlia hesitated for the sake of form. "That's kind of you, Willard, but Mr. Fortune set the boys a task—"

"We're almost through," John interrupted. "We'll be done before noon and you can inspect the job!"

Dehlia was in too generous a mood to be suspicious. "Your father expected it to take you all day."

Thomas' eyes were burning with eagerness. "It was a

day's work, Mamma, but we hurried and worked hard to get done in time."

In time for what? Dehlia saw John's look of disappointment with his brother, who had said too much. The picture changed: the Pearson boys' visit and her sons' industrious morning fitted into a pattern that might have been weaving for days. As likely as not, it was Mrs. Pearson's idea.

Even then Dehlia was in a mood to let them go. She would let them go if they could be made to understand that the control had not been taken away from her. First they would have to be tested out, refused, or almost refused; if they controlled themselves and took it in good spirit, she would remember some altering circumstance. "It was very thoughtful of you," she told Willard; "I hope you ask the boys again, a few days in advance, if possible. Today I have other plans for them."

"Please!" Thomas begged.

John said impatiently, "Oh, Mamma, you and your plans!"

"John!" she said, giving him the first warning.

"You and your plans!" he said again. "You plan things so we never can do anything! Never——"

"*John!*" It was settled now, beyond recall from either side. When one of the children overstepped the bounds, and she spoke in that tone, only one thing could follow. The cold silence was broken by Marjorie slipping away indoors, and Dehlia said, "Thank you for the invitation, Willard, but the boys cannot go this time. Thomas, you may go on with your work. John, I wish to speak to you."

When they were indoors, she turned on him. "Why did you speak to me that way?"

"I'm sorry, Mamma." He always was when it was too late.

"Why did you say that, and in the presence of others?"

He answered evenly, "Because I was mad. Tom and I had

worked so hard so we could go sailing, and you wouldn't let us."

"What do you think your father would have done if he had heard you insult me that way, in the presence of other people?"

He didn't answer.

As they stood there in silence, facing each other, the door opened and Thomas came in swiftly, then stopped as if he hadn't expected to find anyone in the kitchen.

"Thomas, go back to your work," Dehlia said.

He stood his ground, with his face dogged and pale. "You're not going to whip him, Mamma!"

"Thomas, go back to your work!"

"Go on, Tom," his brother said, "don't get into trouble."

The younger boy gulped and looked at his mother. "If you whip him, you can whip me, too!"

Dehlia said, "You controlled yourself. If your brother had done as well, everything would have turned out differently." Then she added, "For the last time, go back to your work!"

Thomas hesitated.

"*You go!*" John said.

Thomas looked at his mother's unyielding face, and about the room. For a moment his eyes rested on the rack of knives above the sink. Then he went out quietly.

Upstairs everything was routine. Dehlia said, "Take off your clothes!" Jack began undressing, deliberately. When she had unlocked the chest by the window and taken out the hazel switches, he was just pulling the shirt off over his head.

"Don't be so slow about it," she told him; "I have other things to do!"

His head emerged from the shirt, with his black hair tousled, but his face calm. "If you haven't time, I'm willing to call it off."

"Don't be insolent!"

"I was only trying to help you," he said. "If you're in a hurry, you can whip me with my jeans on."

"You take everything off!" She did not look at him again until he had stripped himself. He stood in the middle of the room, straight and well-knit and smooth-skinned, his face sullen with shame and anticipated pain, but defiant.

Dehlia had selected the toughest switch, and laid the others, separate and parallel, on top of the chest, where one could be snatched up without disturbing the others. Advancing on him with the hard, limber hazel in her hand, she said, "You know that this hurts me more than it does you!"

Unsympathetically, he said, "It was your idea."

"Don't be insolent!" She struck at him tentatively and he side-stepped, warding off the blow with one hand. "Keep your hands out of the way!"

"You could be doing something more useful with your own."

When the worst had happened, his mind was always cold and sharp and he said things he wouldn't have dared to say in anger. His insolence put an end to her hesitation and she began lashing his legs and buttocks and back with the too-limber switch. There was a frustration in beating him; it was like beating a statue, and the more she lashed him the more certain she became that his feelings were too deep in his flesh for a whip to reach.

Dehlia's anger ebbed with diminishing blows, and she did not want to beat him any more. She put down the switch, panting. "I hope this teaches you to control yourself!"

He did not answer; when she looked at him she was not even sure that he had heard. His face was twisted with pain, but it was calm, as if he were thinking of something more important than his hurts. Standing in the middle of his parents' bedroom he looked like a boy alone in a hayfield, with the shadows of tall grass weaving a pattern of red stripes on his white body. In spite of her warning to keep his hands out of the way, the switch had cut the inside of one of his fingers, and blood was dripping from it."

"You may put on your clothes," she said, "and put some arnica on that finger and tie it up."

"All right, Mamma." He was reasonable now. It was a pity that he hadn't been in control of himself earlier, when she had so much to do.

As she hurried downstairs, the clock was striking eleven through the still house. Thomas would be back at his task, and Marjorie somewhere outdoors, as far away as possible. Dehlia had heard her scurry from some hiding place in the parlor and rush out of the house, away from the sound of blows. In her haste she had left the parlor door partly open. From the stairs Dehlia had a glimpse of the room: Brussels carpet and delicate West Paris chairs with carved seashell backs, and the dark mahogany gleam of the Knabe piano.

The perfect order held until she was in the hall, where she saw a trail of scattered crumbs from the kitchen. Hungry Thomas! The moment her back was turned— But she had never known him to be so clumsy, or to eat anything while his brother was being whipped. In the kitchen she was bewildered by the sight of a plateful of fragments and crumbs that spilled onto the table and the floor. It was several seconds before she recognized the shapeless heap as her novelty cake. Beside it on the table lay the butcher knife with which it had been hacked to pieces.

She didn't have to search for Thomas; he was near the back fence with a hoe, quietly pulling small rubbish from between the pickets. He looked up at her, pale and determined and only a little frightened. He stood his ground until the last moment; apparently he had not meant to run at all, and when his courage fled it was too late for him to follow. There was just time for one useless attempt, then Dehlia had him by the wrist and was leading him to the house.

She was speechless, but as she hurried Thomas along, he said, "I told you not to whip Jack," as if he were a small oracle reproaching her for not listening to him.

They were within a few steps of the porch when Marjorie appeared around the corner of the house, drying her eyes. She had assumed that the whipping was over, and she was coming back, composing herself to help compose others and make some second-best thing out of the wreck of the morning. When she saw her mother dragging Thomas to the house she stopped, with a despairing wail, "Mamma, Mamma! Why can't we love one another?"

They met John coming downstairs. With his clothes on he showed no marks of his beating except for a bandage on one finger and the pallor of his face. He had combed his hair, and he looked gentlemanly and grown-up. Instead of stepping aside to let them pass, he blocked the stairway and looked sternly at his mother. "You're not going to whip Tom!" he said. "It was my fault; he didn't do anything."

Dehlia said bitterly, "He didn't do anything except hack my novelty cake to pieces!"

John looked at his brother sadly. "You shouldn't have done that, Tom." Then he said to his mother, "It was my fault in the first place, and I'll pay for it. If there isn't time to bake another cake, I'll buy one out of my money. But you're not going to whip him!"

"You'll buy one!" Dehlia was already under torture from the thought of what her neighbors would say when she served a cake from Cleveland's Bakery. "What kind of a cake can you buy?"

John said, "I'll get the best they have. You're not going to whip Tom!"

"I'm going to whip him within an inch of his life!" she told him. "You stand aside!"

His dark eyes blazed up and he continued to block her way. "You'd better not!"

For a few seconds she thought he was going to use force, but when she stepped forward and up, dragging Thomas after her, he moved aside reluctantly and she was in control again. "When you have finished in the yard," she said, "you can cut some wood since you feel so energetic!"

With Thomas there was no need of exchanging taunts before she could strike; she began the moment his underwear was off. Through her panting and the sound of blows she could hear John sawing wood—the sound of fierce sawing and the hard, clanging thud of wood falling. All the doors must be open for sounds to carry so clearly from the woodshed. She stopped to listen, and at the unexpected pause, braced against pain, Thomas began to sob. Surprisingly, she had managed to hurt him at the very beginning. It was also surprising the way sounds carried from the woodshed; they seemed close enough to be in the house. Suddenly she was rushing downstairs.

John was working in the parlor, and she burst in on a scene of mutilation. One corner of the new piano gaped hideously; a shining mahogany leg lay among sawdust on the Brussels carpet, and John was sawing furiously at the other leg.

Dehlia screamed and threw herself on him, but even while she was striking him she knew that something had changed in the house: it was the last time she would ever dare to whip the boys. She had done her best and now it was her husband's turn.

7

THE TUG *Clatsop* steamed down the river against the last of the flood. Joe Ball, the oldest bar pilot, slept in the port corner of the wheelhouse settee, with his regular, moaning snore ticking the time away like a rusty clock. Captain Smith sat next to him, full-faced and thick-moustached, with his placid eyes aware of the wheelhouse clock and the small dingy back of Cummins, the mate, at the wheel. In the starboard corner of the settee the young bar pilot, Roger Collins, was cutting letters in a piece of blackened teakwood with the small blade of his claspknife. Through the pilothouse window the men had a distant glimpse of coal smoke from the tug *Columbia*, followed at a respectful distance by the three masts and clewed-up sails of a large ship.

The crew of the tug and the two bar pilots were in a situation that was commonplace to their professions: their day's work might have been over hours ago, when the *Clatsop* took Pilot Ball from the outward-bound *City of Topeka* and towed the English bark *Peter Iredale* in from sea. They had been reasonably sure of it, with the *Columbia* lying below Sand Island in sight of the pilot grounds. But now the *Columbia* was in the North Channel, bringing a ship in past Middle Sands. Where there had been one ship, there might be another. Captain Smith had bet his usual dollar that a grain ship would be waiting with the last of the flood tide, and Pilot Collins had taken his bet. While they waited for it to be settled, Captain Smith took his ease between the snoring old pilot and the young one whose sensitive, smooth-shaven face and quick blue eyes were intent on his busy work. So far he had carved: S.S. *GREAT REPUBLIC*, WRECKED APRIL—. While he added to it, old Joe Ball's moaning became more sonorous as he sank deeper into sleep.

The captain turned his big round face toward the snoring pilot in cheerful exasperation. Then he shook the old man by the shoulder. "Stop snoring, Joe!"

Joe blinked and sat up. "What ship?"

"I said stop snoring; you make me nervous."

From the other end of the settee, Roger Collins said, "Every time you snore, we think it's a steamer blowing for a pilot."

Captain Smith looked blank for a moment as the aptness of the simile went home. Then he slapped his thigh, and his laugh filled the wheelhouse. "That's good, Roger! 'Every time he snores—'" He laughed again.

"God damn," the old man grumbled, and settled himself to sleep again.

Smith rocked comfortably on the settee, chuckling an echo to his belly laugh. "Did you hear that, Mr. Cummins? 'Every time he snores—'"

"Yes, sir." The mate gave the wheel a smooth spoke and glanced over his shoulder with polite appreciation. "We can count on Captain Collins."

Roger Collins was the best-liked pilot on the bar, and people in town had got into the habit of saying that he was also the best pilot. That was horse manure. Nine times out of ten a pilot was put on board a ship only to get the papers signed and to drink coffee and take credit for what someone else did. The man who did the job was the unnoticed tugboat captain. It was his responsibility to estimate conditions on the bar and decide whether or not they could make it. Having decided they could, he supplied the brains and the tug supplied the power—and the sailing ship followed at the end of a thousand-foot towline. Any helmsman who could follow a tug could do the rest and keep in the channel—and the pilot drank coffee and yarned with the captain and got credit for being a clever fellow.

That was nine times out of ten. On the tenth time a pilot might need as much brains as a tugboat captain. That was when he took a steamer across in a hard chance, or got stuck with a sailing vessel when a tug wasn't available. The odd times were the reason why not every man could be a pilot, not even every man with a master's papers; the crooked off-chance required a certain instinct, even if it was used only once in six months. That was why the bastards had to be pampered; each one was good in his own way, and it was horse manure to speak of Roger as the best pilot on the bar. You had to admit, though, that he had a touch of genius. If there was any difference you could put your finger on, it was this: other pilots put in the day afloat and then hurried to their homes ashore. Roger put in his nights ashore—and hurried back to the river and the ocean. And that was puzzling because one glimpse of Mrs. Collins could make a young seafaring man dream of staying ashore forever; she even had that effect on a solid tugboat captain, near middle age and putting on weight these ten years.

The *Clatsop* was past Desdemona Sands, lifting to the increasing swells. If there was going to be a tow for her, it should be in sight by now.

"There's our ship," Cummins reported from the wheel. Roger Collins put aside his carving and went to a forward window, a handsome figure of a man, five-feet-ten maybe, with square shoulders and a proud, likable head. He stood there a few seconds, swaying easily with the uneasy tug, then he reached into his side pocket and turned with a flicker of laughing light in his blue eyes. "Catch!"

The captain's thick hand snapped the silver dollar out of the air. Pocketing it, he asked, "What have we got?"

"Grain ship," Roger said. "A four-masted lime-juicer, about eighteen hundred tons."

From the gyrating settee Smith had a glimpse of close-set towers of canvas beyond the bar, and he went to a window for a better view. "Looks like the *Kinkora*," he said. "What's-his-name is master—the fellow who looks like the Prince of Wales."

"Captain Lawrence," Roger supplied. "But that's not the *Kinkora;* her masts don't rake that much and the cut of her spanker is different. Looks more like the *Mistley Hall*."

"It don't look big enough for her."

"The *Kinkora* is bigger."

"The hell she is!"

"1799 tons for the *Kinkora* against 1772 for the *Mistley Hall*."

What can you do against figures unless you know they are wrong? Smith said, "I still think it's the *Kinkora*."

"Want to bet on it?"

"Not with you." Smith had never won a bet with Roger on the identity of a ship. Neither had anyone else. He asked, "Is there a ship afloat you don't know something about—her tonnage, the cut of her jibs, and all that?"

Roger was lighting his pipe, steadying himself with one elbow against the side of the reeling pilothouse. "Thousands of them." Then he said, "Probably I know something about every ship that has come into the river in my time. If you're dealing with ships, it's a good thing to know them."

The captain said, "I know more about ships than most men, but the way you know them is indecent. If you heard that the *Scottish Lassie* was getting a new doctor, you could cable him where to reach for the pepper and salt!"

Roger laughed. "The *Scottish Lassie* doesn't stock pepper, only salt."

"I'll catch you on something yet," Smith said. They were running past the end of Sand Island, past the wreck of the

Great Republic. Earlier in the day, when the tug was lying below the island, Roger had rowed to the wreck of the old China liner and sawed out a chunk of teak. It had been smooth then, but now it was breezing up from the southwest, and the rising swells burst dirty-white and sullen through skeleton paddle wheels—all that remained of the largest ship that had ever entered the river. The captain inclined his head toward the wreck. "I won't ask you about her. You were there when she was wrecked!"

"Not quite; but I got there while they were taking the passengers off."

"You took some off, yourself."

"A boatload or two." The pilot didn't seem to favor the subject. Drop it, Smith; a man doesn't always want to talk about his romance. For the sake of form, tapering off, he said, "She was built in New York, wasn't she?"

"Rockaway Beach."

"Never heard of the place."

"It's on Long Island," Roger said. "I don't know how they happened to build a big ship there; it's a summer resort."

Smith was on the point of saying that you would expect a gay ship to be built in a gay place, but the pilot might take it as a reflection on the beautiful wife who had come to him from the wreck, and by now the *Great Republic* was anything but gay. Drop it, Smith.

Standing at the wheelhouse window, the young pilot was not conscious of discouraging Smith. For ordinary conversation the two men had exhausted the subject of the *Great Republic* long ago. Just now Roger was feeling rather than thinking, absorbing the interwoven relationship of the river and the wind and sea. There was an hour and a half left of the flood, and the rising southwester worked with it smoothly. Together they had mastered the current of the river, and the Pacific rolled in over the bar in great, even swells that had not begun to break, and the *Clatsop*, alive with power, surged over their almost smooth tan-green hills. There were limits, though, that you could feel; the free, fathomless ocean swells striking the shoaling sand and rebounding in higher swells—sullen power close to bursting into fury.

Conditions would hold like that or a little worse until the ebb joined the great push of the river against the swells being driven in by the rising southwester. Then the river would go mad and froth at the mouth, with breakers five miles long roaring and cracking all the way across from Clatsop Spit to Peacock Spit; a bar that was all breakers, heavy with churned sand, with no water between. That was how the day would end on the Columbia bar; it would be no place for vessels or men, and even the salmon would not try to enter. But before things got unreasonable they would snatch the tall grain ship into the safety of the river, and they would all go home to one thing or another: Roger to a good dinner cooked by his wife, Rita, and a new copy of *The Guide*, with shipping news that spun a web around the world.

Pilot Ball stumbled to the port window which, at the moment, was looking up at the gray scud flying overhead. "It's coming up dirty," he said.

The vista of dirty sky changed to a slope of rough green water as the tug swooped downhill. Smith said cheerfully, "It'll keep until we get in."

Ball grunted as if to say maybe it would and maybe it wouldn't and, as they climbed the next slope of water, he turned his sour old face to the captain and asked, "Which one are we going to take first?"

Which one? Roger saw nothing up toward Peacock Spit; to seaward there was only the big iron ship, close hauled and ranging ahead slowly, and out toward Clatsop Spit there was nothing—or had he glimpsed something out of the corner of his eye? From the top of the next hill of water he saw the other vessel, hanging up to windward, well south of the jetty, as if she were bashful about showing herself on the pilot grounds.

"What do you make of her?" Smith asked.

"A little bark," the old pilot said. "She's in ballast; probably American."

Smith said, "We can't take both, and it'll be too late to come back. Want to take the bark, Joe?"

The old plumage of Joe's whiskers looked ruffled. "Under sail?"

"Sure. We got two pilots and one tug, and I have to hook onto the ship that pays most."

"God damned if I want to; my sailing days are over if I can help it."

The captain was embarrassed, looking ahead at the next big swell and the smoother water beyond the bar. "Well, Roger?"

Roger had already thought it over: an hour of the flood after he got on board and a fair wind that would hold all the way to Astoria. In addition to that, it wasn't every day that he had the chance to handle a wind-wagon under sail. "I'll take her," he said, "and with luck I'll beat you to anchorage."

When the *Clatsop* stormed past the end of the jetty the bark was backing her main yard two miles away to the south. She was a wooden three-master under a thousand tons, neat and positive-looking and showing a great deal of freeboard even for a vessel in ballast. She was definitely not American, and at the moment between falling off and coming into the wind again the Tricolor stood out, as flat as a board, below her spanker gaff.

"French," Ball said. "I thought she was American."

Smith relieved the mate at the wheel and looked at the younger pilot. "I suppose you even know where they keep the cognac!"

"Never set eyes on her before." Roger was studying her through narrowed eyes. "I doubt that she's French, though."

"You can see the flag," Ball said grumpily.

"I mean she wasn't built in France; the Mediterranean, maybe, but not even Marseilles. There's something different—"

Smith looked at him with a feeling of pride. The stumped expert appears most expert of all, groping delicately beyond the edges of knowledge.

Roger gave it up for the moment and began pulling on his oilskins. On deck the crew had cleared the boat and were standing by, with scupper water boiling about their feet as the tug rolled down toward the disputed bark. They were close enough now to see the heads of the crew above the high bulwark in the waist; square-cut black beards and black tarred hats, and among them the flash of a red-pomponed beret from the French Navy. Putting the souvenir of the *Great Republic* in his oilskin pocket, Roger said, "I wish they'd kept her sailing until now."

Smith said, "You have plenty of offing to clear the jetty."

"Enough," Ball said.

The captain reached for the bell pull. "Tell Mr. Cummins to get you away as fast as he can make it." He rang for half speed. "I'm going to come up close, and I don't want to drift down on her."

"You'll never catch her," Roger said. "She's going to loo'ard like a crab." He paused with his hand on the doorknob. "If you don't see me at the anchorage, will you stop by and tell Rita I'll be late for dinner?"

"If you're not in sight," Smith said, "I'll come back for you; my old lady can wait as well as yours."

He stopped a risky fifty yards to windward of the Frenchman, turned broadside to the weather to provide a lee. The pilot and two deckhands were already in the small boat, poised at the boom, with Cummins and the other hand standing by the falls. Two seas passed under them, then the boat lowered away swiftly and disappeared, then shot up with a sea, almost level with the wheelhouse window, clear of the tackles, with one deckhand already rowing and the other getting out his oars. In the sternsheets, Roger was adjusting his chunk of teak in the pocket of his slicker. The pilot was getting on in his thirties, and he would probably never grow up.

In the small boat, close to the foreign ship, Roger still couldn't find a birthplace for her in the cyclopedia of his mind. She was built of oak, as he expected, probably in a Catholic country; her worn figurehead was an angel or a saint with hands together, palm to palm, praying night and day for the sailors in the foc'sle at her back—a full-time job for any saint. He also noted a wooden anchor stock, bound with metal, and a cathead that was true to its name, with a cat's face on the end of the timber as fine as a carving in an old cathedral. The bark's name was *Jocelyn,* which didn't prove anything except that she was French-owned.

The boatmen were old Columbia River fishermen, wise as sea serpents. They fetched up smoothly abreast of the Jacob's ladder, then hung off because the *Jocelyn* was too much up in the wind to provide a proper lee. Roger bellowed up, "Starboard your helm and give us a lee!"

The captain, with a pointed beard, leaned over the poop rail. "She will roll, Pilot!"

"To hell with the roll! Give us a lee!"

The captain gestured with both arms and disappeared, and the bark began falling off, with the boatmen edging away warily so she didn't drift down on them. The Frenchman had said his ship would roll, and she rolled like the wheels of hell while the small boat ranged up and down beside her, one second looking up at the copper sheathing under the turn of her bilge, and the next level with the square beards above the bulwark, and through the murderous arc of her roll the ship's massive oak guard struck up at the boat from underneath, and down from above.

Roger watched her through two furious seas, then grinned at the nearer boatman. "Back in, and watch yourselves!"

"Yes, sir, and watch yourself!"

They backed in cautiously and poised just clear of destruction, the pilot crouching in the stern, with his feet free of his oilskins. The boatmen rejected an inferior sea, then the boat ranged up on the next sea, level with the scuppers of the bark in the last moment of her loo'ard roll. A smooth push sternward, and the Jacob's ladder looked Roger in the face, like a sweetheart. He went to it lightly, then hung on like iron through the weather roll. Over his shoulder he saw the boat, ten fathoms away, pulling smoothly back to the tug.

Going over the rail, he sang out, "Fall off on the port tack! Brace your yards up sharp!" His shout was re-echoed in French, and while the watch was hauling the yards around, he exchanged greetings with Captain Raoul Lannes of the *Jocelyn,* 142 days out of Le Havre and bound for Portland to load wheat. It wasn't a bad passage for a little bark in ballast, and the captain looked like a sensible man. He was also a civilized one, and after a minute a cabin boy came up the companionway with cups and a silver pot.

When he had tasted the brew, Roger said, "Only the French know how to make French coffee!"

Lannes bowed, accepting the compliment to France, then looked doubtful. "But perhaps only the French know how to enjoy it."

Cup in hand, the pilot was squinting across the binnacle, taking a bearing on Clatsop Spit. "I've cared enough to learn how it is done."

"But yes?"

The pilot straightened up. "First you burn the coffee beans to a crisp; then you shellac them; then you throw them away and use chicory. Am I right?"

Captain Lannes considered. "That is the broad principle, but one does not throw the coffee beans away; one grinds them to mix with the chicory." After a moment he said, "Perhaps the pilot would have cognac?"

"Later, Captain, with pleasure. But first shall we show the main t'gallant and the mizzen topmast staysails?"

"But certainly, if it is desirable."

"It's essential!" Roger had taken it for granted that the little bark was losing ground while she was hove to, but he was scandalized by the amount of leeway she had made.

When the last kites were sheeted home, with the *Jocelyn* heeling far over as she thrashed to windward, the pilot accepted a tumbler of cognac and relaxed to enjoy his visit on board. "I admire your bark, Captain; she also puzzles me; I can't decide where she was built."

The captain's eyes were appreciative. "You notice, then?"

"She's not French built, and not Italian, and not quite Spanish, but she's from somewhere to the south—"

"You are a scholar," Lannes said. "She is Austrian, built at Trieste."

"I'd forgotten that they built ships there."

"But yes! Some think the best in the world. My *Jocelyn* is all Adriatic oak, seasoned for years, and fastened with bolts of red Italian copper. She was made to last forever."

"When was she launched?"

"That is uncertain. Perhaps fifty years. She was not young when my owners bought her, and she is not old now."

"She was renamed when she was sold French?"

"But yes. Before that she was the *Saint Therese.*"

"The figurehead and catheads are the originals?"

"Certainly; also the picture of the Virgin Mary; you can see her from the deck." They looked into the cuddy above the companionway at the mild face of the aging painting under glass.

"Your crew travels in the best of company," Roger said.

Lannes said, "They contemplate her daily, and when they go ashore at a quay, Saint Therese looks after them and prays."

"And when they are around the corner?"

"Then she prays harder than ever. Therese is no fool."

Two miles or so to starboard, the big *Mistley Hall* was walking over the sea in the wake of the *Clatsop*, with her sails being clewed up swiftly: jigger and mizzen, and now the main, as her tall masts made their first bow to the big swell running on the bar. And Roger had offered to race her into Astoria! He took another bearing on Clatsop Spit, and swallowed the rest of his cognac. He looked at the Frenchman. "Are you satisfied with the way she sails?"

"She does magnificently!"

"To windward?"

Lannes hoisted his shoulders. "She is in ballast."

"I was wondering if she had any ballast. Is this the best she can do?"

"Under the condition she could do no better."

"What does she draw?"

"Fully loaded?"

"Empty, as she is now."

"Under four meters."

Maybe twelve feet, and Roger had been wondering why she wouldn't go to windward! He took another bearing on the end of Clatsop Spit, which was closer to loo'ard and more abeam than it had been at the beginning of their futile thresh to windward; almost close enough to hear the breakers on the beach, and close enough to make out the seas spouting along the jetty beyond. He had been in a trap from the moment he boarded the *Jocelyn*, and he had half known it all along.

Even Captain Raoul Lannes suspected something of the sort. After all, he was enough of a seaman to bring his ship this far from Le Havre. "There must be some current here," he suggested.

The pilot said, "There is a hell of a current that sets us in toward the Spit."

"We are in danger?" the Frenchman asked.

"Not yet, and we don't want to be." The pilot looked thoughtfully to windward at the cloud masses pushing up and up on the horizon toward Asia. There wasn't any comfort from that direction: a full gale by evening, and it might last three days. There was an hour left of the flood. They might keep off the beach that long, and the ebb would carry them clear of the jetty, with luck. But then there would be no hope of getting into the river. And they could never hope to get enough offing to weather the southwest gale. The *Jocelyn* wouldn't go to windward, and to loo'ard there were only the beach and the jetty. . . .

Lannes saw his smile. "You have thought of something, Pilot?"

"I think we can make it," Roger told him. "Square away; get her off before it and let's see what she can do!"

"The course?" Lannes asked.

"North by west will do for now."

The Frenchman was sailor enough to be startled. Then he said, "We are in your hands." He looked as if he would rather be anywhere else.

Roger said, "Clew up the courses so we can see where we're going—I'll want to take a bearing on the Cape— Leave the headsails as they are."

Lannes had boasted that the *Jocelyn* sailed magnificently, and she did. With the skirts of her main and fore tucked up, she ran off to loo'ard like a deaconess pursued by lecherous men; too fast for comfort and too fast for thought. Maybe just as well. . . . There's McKenzie Head in line with your fading high notch on North Head, like the sights of a rifle from the muzzle end. *Port a little, port a little. Steady so.* North by west, a quarter point north. If your bearing's wrong, you'll lie forever uncorrected. . . . There go Mc-Kenzie Head and the heights of North Head, obscured by clouds and driven rain. North by west, a quarter point north. *Starboard a little. Steady, steady. Ease your wheel. Steady so.* . . . The French are a voluble people; talk all the time, especially when they're excited. That is odd because twenty-some Frenchmen are gathered about, and there isn't a sound on board but your own voice as *Jocelyn* comes storming down on the jetty with its brutal stones almost concealed by a curtain of spouting seas; a white curtain rising and blowing away to loo'ard, and rising again, thinning in one spot. *Port a little! Steady! Ease your wheel! Steady so!* No sound on board except your own shouting that fades to a gnat's voice in the mounting roar of breakers trampling over walls of stone. No slips now, or out of this lonely dream France will be sprinkled with widows from Dunkirk to Le Havre. *Starboard a little! Steady, steady so!* If the chance comes, take a good look and a quick look, and don't get drunk on the excitement of learning what the sea and dead men know. . . . *Starboard a little, starboard a little! Starboard! Starboard! STARBOARD! You fool! You fool!*

8

WHEN VISITORS LOOKED around the Collins home, Rita's dark eyes and red lips would flash their half-Spanish smile and she would say, "Yes, we live among wreckage!" The wreckage was interesting to the eye and enlightening to the mind that fitted its clues together. One piece appealed to the ear as well: the bell pull beside the white front door worked a ship's bell inside; Roger had stayed the clapper with a spring so that an ordinary pull produced a deep golden whisper from a bell with power enough to waken the dead. The deep whispering resonance reminded different people of different things. Rita would have preferred something more ordinary; she felt that the bell should be under the rolling bar of the Columbia with the *Vandalia's* crew.

The bell prepared the caller for the wreckage inside—the flotsam and jetsam mixed with comforts that had never known shipwreck. The front-door stop was a round of cedar from the stockade of Fort Astoria. In the hall, above the wainscoting, a copper sheath held a rust-pitted fire ax from the *Desdemona*—the ship that had died to give her name to Desdemona Sands; and the brass hanging lamp had once swung above the cabin table of the *Morning Star*.

There were more trophies in the parlor: a camphorwood chest from the *Nimbus*, wrecked on Middle Sands; a revolving table built on the wheel of the *Ariel*, lost in the breakers off Clatsop Spit, and a corner cabinet made of wood from the *Shark* house. Among lesser relics in the glass case were a Chinese compass from a junk that had drifted across the

Pacific; a brown lump of beeswax stamped with an obscure hieroglyph; and beside it a piece of teak from the Acapulco galleon that sometimes raised her enduring frames from the Nehalem sands.

In her own parlor Rita could close her eyes and feel centuries of time and the Pacific rolling over her. She didn't enjoy the feeling, and she didn't understand her husband's liking for mementos of shipwrecks. It was his business to see that such things didn't happen; in eleven years of piloting he had not lost a vessel. She liked to think of that on an evening like this, when he was late getting home and the west windows were wet with rain; that meant southwest weather and bad conditions on the bar—a poor time to wait dinner among mementos of lost ships. Oh, well, she was a memento of a lost ship, herself.

It was Rita's own story, but she never knew just where to pick it up. The story of her life was a knot with no loose ends.

Like her inquisitive neighbor, Mrs. Fortune, Rita had grown up in San Francisco. But unlike Mrs. Fortune, Rita had not had a happy girlhood in the parsonage of a well-to-do clergyman. Her parents were not the enduring kind, and she had been brought up by her Aunt Dolores, who drank a little, and beat her a little, and put the fear of God into her about men, young and old. Her aunt also allowed her to go to high school, and in her mellower moods she let Rita spend holidays, or even vacations, with Mary O'Malley, her classmate. The O'Malleys lived on Telegraph Hill in their own rickety big house, full of good cooking smells and the arguing voices of children. The O'Malleys were Catholics and good people, and toward the end they were the only ones Dolores trusted; that was when Rita emerged from adolescence and Aunt Dolores grumbled over the trick that had been played on her: a girl born and raised poor coming into such an inheritance of beauty.

[113]

Except when she stayed with the O'Malleys, Rita had to be in the house every evening at nine o'clock, but that did not keep her from having admirers: boys from the boys' high school and boys from the neighborhood. There were others more mature, but too earnestly bent on marriage or sin. And there was Charlie Hollis, who was such a man of the world that he neither begged her to marry him nor tried to make love to her the moment they were alone.

Charlie worked at the El Dorado Ice Cream Parlor across the street from the high school; a man of twenty with a bright voice, a friendly smile, and long, wavy hair. He dressed stylishly and talked with great assurance. Charlie was the girl's window to the garden of the world; he spoke of people who lived in New York—Belmonts, Astors, Vanderbilts—and sometimes he talked about the Latin Quarter in Paris, or mentioned what the King of Spain was doing.

Not that one had to go to Europe for a good time, Charlie told her. A cable-car's ride away was the heart of the gayest and most golden city in the world, but the real San Francisco was as far away as Paris when she had to be in the house at nine o'clock.

The bright and worldly clerk was alert to other possibilities of life. One afternoon, mixing an orange phosphate, he told Rita he would not be in the store the following week; he was taking a sea voyage. He mentioned it casually, but the news overwhelmed Rita, who had never gone farther than the Alameda ferry. "A real sea voyage, Charlie?"

He put the phosphate in front of her and said, "I am sailing on the *Great Republic* day after tomorrow. From the Golden Gate we go north to the Columbia River and up the river to Astoria and to Portland. Next week we make the return trip."

Rita was too awed to touch her phosphate. "It's nice to have money," she said.

[114]

Charlie tossed back his wavy mane of hair. "That was a mere trifle. My trouble was getting time off. I only managed it because business will be slow next week with school closed for Easter vacation."

"You must be rich!" she said.

"You could go, yourself, if you didn't have to be home by nine."

Rita didn't believe it. "How much does it cost, Charlie?"

"Four dollars!"

She had expected him to say twenty, or some other unattainable amount—but four dollars! "For what?" she asked sceptically.

"Everything: round trip, stateroom, wonderful meals, and dancing to the music of the ship's orchestra!"

Rita couldn't believe it. "All that for four dollars! How can they do it?"

"They can't," he said, polishing glasses. "The company's losing money hand over fist!"

"Then why do they do it?"

"Rate war. The Oregon Steamship and the Independent Line are fighting for the monopoly and losing thousands every trip. One will go bust, then the other will jump prices. While it lasts, it's the chance of a lifetime!"

"It really is, Charlie!"

"An ocean voyage, with moonlight and music and dancing! Oh, Rita, if you could only go with me!"

"Maybe I could."

He looked incredulous. "What about your aunt?"

Rita had already made her plan. "I'll tell her I'm going to visit Mary O'Malley. She lets me stay with Mary as long as I'm invited for."

Charlie was enraptured. "You darling! I'll dash out this afternoon and buy our tickets!"

She hoped he hadn't misunderstood. "I'm paying my own way."

"Sure, but I'd better get the tickets; we're not the only ones taking advantage of the price war."

Charlie had been daring when he promised moonlight and dancing in April; but they had both, and except for the cold their first night was like a young dream of an ocean voyage. Charlie had also guessed right that others would jump at the chance of a lifetime; the *Great Republic* carried a thousand passengers, hundreds of them young people like themselves, enjoying a week's voyage for less than it would cost to live at home.

Because of the great press in the saloon, Charlie and she and a hundred other couples took their moonlight and dancing together on the upper deck with the music of the ship's band coming to them up the main companionway. Rita, who always had to be in by nine o'clock, danced until midnight; with flying feet she hopped through polkas, Charlie's hands on her slender waist and her hands firm on his broadcloth shoulders while she looked up into his face: Charlie, who had the imagination to know where you could buy a new, exciting world for a song. They hopped through schottisches with hands clasped warm in the cold night air and his warm arm around her waist, while the deck throbbed to the hopping of reckless feet and the muted blare of the band pulsed up from the heart of the great, warm ship. Around them dimmed and shone the faces of others like themselves: gay blades; pale young bookkeepers from out their dusty cubicles, with the pallor still on their faces and their eyes reckless with life; thin young clerks prancing through a night that was all profit, with no buying or selling; girls with bold, undenying faces; girls with the faces of waifs; and girls with inexperienced faces, timid at their moment of awakening to the reckless dance of life.

At either side of the throbbing deck the round guards of the paddle wheels towered up like giant bass drums, rolling out soft thunder; overhead the black walking beam of the engine pumped up and down against the sky, and the smoke-stack flaunted its inky banner through yards and furled sails that waited for the creaking engines to give out. In faraway, lonely distances and on nearby waves, the moonlight was liquid gold on the roughening Pacific, and it was pale gold on the faces of the dancers; reckless young faces lit from within by buried dreams and desires which had risen at last in the moonlight; faces that had come into a heritage of youth—accidentally and for a moment by virtue of companies battling for a monopoly.

That was how Rita remembered it afterward. At the time she was part of the reckless dance of youth. Older men watched from the rail each time she came around, with a look of recognition; Rita saw them and forgot them and saw them again, their eyes reflecting a little of her youth as she passed before them.

There were women, too: disapproving women who saw sin broken loose and hopping all over the ship in the heathen moonlight; and here and there one who watched with a smile that was like a sigh. And there was one older woman who watched with neither disapproval nor envy; a tall woman dressed in dark velvet. She watched all the girls intently, but her eyes followed Rita longest, with growing approval, and the girl wove her into her moonlit dream: a great lady who would come to her afterward and say, "My dear, you remind me so much of a daughter I had, and lost. Her room in the mansion is empty, her saddle horse is in the stable, and the garden is waiting; I want you to come and take her place and share my wealth."

It was a light dream that went away, and after a while the woman was gone, but the *Great Republic's* band played on, with its music pulsing up from the heart of the warm ship; the deck throbbed on under prancing feet; thin, flushed young faces dimmed and shone in the moonlight; the towering paddle wheels rolled out their soft bass thunder; the

[117]

black walking beam teetered up and down; and the great smokestack unfurled its inky banner against the sky forever; and Charlie's warm arm held her forever. . . .

At last the band played "Good Night, Ladies," and youth sang with it.

> *Merrily we roll along, roll along, roll along;*
> *Merrily we roll along, over the deep blue sea.*

They sang it boisterously, with the feeling of having come into their heritage. They had taken over the ship for a night; they had taken over some of life, which they would not give up again.

The music and the singing ended, but the glow went on. Charlie's arm was warm around her waist as they went to the rail and looked away across the moonlight on the roughening Pacific. Charlie was no longer the poised man of the world; he was as young as she, and as glowing, and as happily overwhelmed by what they had bought for four dollars.

"Gee, Rita," he said, "we'll do this every time we can; I didn't know it would be so wonderful!"

She hadn't known, either, and she didn't want to think or talk about it ending, even to begin again.

"And only four bucks!" he said. "Did you ever have such a dinner? And the crowd on board, the nicest lot of young men I ever met, and the nicest girls!" He held her closer. "You're the prettiest of them all, Rita!"

"You're the nicest young man," Rita said.

The moonlight was like melted gold on the waves, but it was not the way she expected; it was too cold and there were too many leagues of lonely sea. They turned their faces to the reassuring vessel and walked around the deck, arm in arm.

"She rolls a lot, doesn't she?" Charlie said.

Rita had hardly noticed. "I like it. Don't you? It makes the ship feel all alive."

[118]

Charlie said, "It's a stroke of luck that we're both good sailors!"

Most of the young people had disappeared, but they passed a few couples, arm in arm like themselves, or embracing in dim corners. From darkened staterooms there were giggles, and now and then a girl's voice raised in sudden protest. Ahead of them, down the dim long deck, they saw young couples disappearing into staterooms. For a minute Rita wondered that there were so many married people; when the truth came to her, it made strangely little difference. This was a reckless new world, full blown on the night of its creation, and tonight was more real than seventeen years of yesterdays.

One side of the ship was moonlit, and the other dim. On the shadowy side Charlie put his arm around her with sudden awkwardness. She didn't think he noticed how his hand was resting against her breast. He was fumbling in his side pocket for a key, and when they had walked a little farther he stopped at his stateroom and unlocked the door.

Even then she didn't want to leave her hero, who had discovered a new world for her; but there was still tomorrow and the day after. "Good night, Charlie," she said; "I'll see you in the morning. It's been the most wonderful night I ever had!"

"Oh, Rita!" His face was pale and hungry in the dimness, and his thin arm was closer about her. "*Rita!*" The door opened and shut again, and they were inside, in the close air with its smell of mildew and paint. With one arm holding her, he locked the door, not so much to imprison her, she thought, as to shut out the world. Then he was holding her with both arms, kissing her mouth hungrily.

She broke away at last when he was trying to undress her, as much frightened by herself as by him. All of her had surrendered except her voice, which argued with him.

"Charlie, you mustn't! You're here to protect me! I trusted you—"

"Rita," he kept saying, "*Rita!* You're so beautiful, beautiful!" As if that gave her no choice but ruin.

"I could never go home!" she told him. "Auntie would beat me to death when she found out! I couldn't go back, and I don't know what would become of me!"

He kept saying, "Rita, you're so beautiful! There won't ever be another night like this!" When she most wanted to be secure in the thought that there would be nights and days without number.

"What about tomorrow?" she asked. "What about when we get back?"

While she argued and he cried out about her beauty and the night, the ship rolled on, shaking up the close air of the little stateroom with its smells of mildew and paint and stale furnishings; the kerosene lamp rocked in its gimbals, and on the wall Charlie's jaunty coat swung back and forth, advancing and retreating as if it still heard the music of a schottische.

"What about when we get back to San Francisco, Charlie? What'll we do then? What'll I do?"

Charlie's face was pale. "You're so beautiful, Rita! Beautiful—"

"We have to think what we're going to do."

Unexpectedly, he took his arms from around her with a sickly smile. "I guess you're right," he said; "we'll talk about it tomorrow."

"I think we should." She was immensely relieved—and disappointed.

"Maybe you'd better go now." He unlocked the door, almost hastily. "Guess I was carried away."

"I know how you feel, Charlie; I was carried away, too."

"I know." He gulped. "Hurry!"

As Rita went out, she heard the first great upheaval of his vomiting.

The sea was rougher next morning, and Charlie was sick all that day, and all the next.

Rita went to his stateroom twice to find out if she could do anything to make him more comfortable, but he could only groan and say there wasn't. By the second time she guessed that her look of health and cheerfulness only made him feel more wretched.

Rita was not touched by the malady that struck down hundreds of the untried passengers, but she hated the unfeeling sea which had gone gray and cold, and she thought about what her aunt would do if she learned of the voyage. And her clothes weren't warm enough for her to be comfortable on deck for long. She had a bleak, uneasy day, with a few warming spots, exchanging gossip with girls temporarily widowed by the sea, and talking with young men until they seemed in danger of forgetting their seasick girls. She was disappointed in Charlie, whose weakened stomach had overtaken his weakened morals, but she felt a certain responsibility for him and she was lonely partly out of loyalty.

The third afternoon, when she was on deck, one of the mates stopped beside her and leaned his arms on the rail while he talked about the ship and the voyage and the green mountainous shore in the distance. It was the Oregon coast, he said, and about midnight they would reach the mouth of the Columbia River and take on a pilot. Not that they would cross the bar immediately. "Ships always wait for daylight," he said. "It's a tricky sort of bar, and we'll lie to outside until morning." The mate's face was honest and friendly, and they might have talked for a long time if he hadn't offered to conduct her to the 'tween deck to see the horses. There were twenty-seven of them, he told her, and they belonged to some of the steerage passengers—immigrants who were coming to try their fortunes in Oregon.

If Rita would like to have a look at the seagoing horses—

Rita was dubious about the presence of horses on a passenger ship, and from childhood she had been warned about going anywhere with a strange man. She said, "No, thank you," so hastily that the mate knew what she was thinking. He was half angry and half amused because she didn't trust him, and she left in embarrassment.

She was trying to find an obscure corner in the saloon when a ball of crochet yarn rolled in front of her, unwinding as it went. She picked it up and looked for its owner; she was the queenly woman who had watched the dancers with such interest. The woman looked older than she had in the moonlight, but she was beautifully dressed and very kind.

"Thank you, my dear," she said; "that was sweet of you."

Rita smiled. "You are welcome, ma'am."

"Won't you sit down for a minute and talk?" She introduced herself as Mrs. DeVore of Portland, and after the girl had taken a chair beside her, she explained, "I find it lonely traveling by myself."

"I know how you feel," Rita said; "I'm alone, too, in a way."

Mrs. DeVore answered with her firm little smile as she crocheted. "I expect your parents are seasick."

"I haven't any parents," Rita said. "At least—" She stopped, embarrassed, not knowing whether she had or not.

"Excuse me for asking!" She looked compassionate, then puzzled. "But you're not traveling alone?"

"No," Rita said. "I have a friend on board, but he's seasick."

Mrs. DeVore wasn't sure whether that was better or worse. "I would expect your relatives would make better arrangements for your traveling, particularly in these times when so many people aren't any better than they should be."

"I have only my Aunt Dolores," Rita said, "and she—"

"She thought it proper for you to make this trip?" Mrs. DeVore looked surprised.

"She doesn't know about it."

"That was wrong of you, Rita!"

"Yes, ma'am, it was." It was comforting to be told that she had done wrong, particularly by someone who wasn't going to beat her for it, who didn't seem to think any less of her.

"You might have lost your honor."

"I know." Rita knew it very well and she blushed to think how near she had come to it.

Mrs. DeVore looked at her evenly. "Rita, you didn't—"

"Oh, no, ma'am!"

"How lucky for you!" After a while she asked, "Why were you so reckless?"

"I'd never been anywhere," Rita said; "and I never have much fun—"

The woman sighed over her crocheting. "At your age I was poorer than you, Rita, and now I have a business that brings me in a pretty penny; but it doesn't give me as much pleasure as a new dress would have done when I was seventeen. You're at the age when you should be enjoying yourself— and someone should be looking after you."

"Aunt Dolores does her best," Rita said.

"I don't doubt it, Child; but is her best enough for a beautiful, high-spirited girl?"

Rita wondered if Mrs. DeVore wasn't going to offer herself for the task, but the woman spread her crocheting on her knee with the air of dismissing the subject. Rita got up, feeling there was nothing more to say; and the woman, seeing that she was hesitating, said, "Don't let me keep you from the other girls; we'll have another talk before you go ashore. If only you were staying longer in Portland—"

There was moonlight that night, but there was no dancing, and Rita went to bed early in her little stateroom. She felt chastened and reborn and more real. And strangely there was some substance in her most fantastic dream of all: the moonlight dance of youth was over, but the tall watcher had become her friend, and perhaps her guiding star.

She was half awakened by distant pounding; then someone was hammering at her stateroom door. "What is it?" she asked, sitting up, wide awake.

"Get your clothes on, and get out on deck, ready to go ashore!"

It was morning outside the curtained window; the ship was steady as a house, and the engines had stopped; but there was a great deal of bustle on deck. Dressing, Rita thought, "We must be at Astoria already." She knew that the ship stopped there soon after crossing the bar.

She went on deck with her carpetbag, but there wasn't any city, only distant wooded shores and a near island of barren sand. But the ship was like a city, foreign and confused with strange customs. Young men and girls milled up and down the deck, arguing and laughing, and a few of the girls crying; groups of older men talked and smoked like men standing on street corners; women gossiped and knitted, or clung to men's arms, or straightened each other's hats; and a small man hurried by urgently, with a carpetbag in each hand and a wide hem of nightshirt showing underneath his coat. Clean sailors and grimy men with blackened faces were uncovering lifeboats and swinging them out; and at one boat a passenger and a sailor were playing a game, the passenger tossing his carpetbag into the lifeboat and the sailor tossing it back again. They did that several times, then the sailor suddenly looked disgusted and threw the carpetbag into the sea.

Passengers hurried up and asked Rita what had happened, before she could ask the same question, then hurried away. It was some time before she learned that the *Great Republic* was in the Columbia River, aground on Sand Island. When she got to the rail, waves were crashing against the side, but the ship lay firm and still without noticing them.

Charlie's pale face and wavy mane of hair appeared out of the welter of strange and half-familiar faces, and she stopped him as he was hurrying by, carpetbag in hand. "Rita!" He shook hands excitedly. "I was looking for you!"

"Are we all right, Charlie?"

"How much money have you, Rita?"

"About two dollars."

He looked disappointed. "If I'm not back on time, I may lose my job." He hurried away while the girl was still wondering.

The ship and the passengers were real, but things were disjointed. A tug was stopped a little way off, and there were lifeboats out in the water, full of people, though Rita hadn't seen any boats lowered, and none of the boats seemed to be missing. But when she went to the side toward the sandy island, the last boat there was poised in its davits, full of women and children. They were waving and calling messages to men on deck, and then they were lowered out of sight in a flutter of handkerchiefs.

Farther forward Rita heard her name called, and she saw Mrs. DeVore standing like a pillar of strength among a group of girls. The sight of her friend was like reaching safety; the woman seemed to have that effect on others as well, and the girls around her looked prettier and more confident than any of the hundreds that were wandering around the deck.

Mrs. DeVore put a reassuring arm around her. "I have been looking for you, Rita. You're not frightened, are you?"

"No, ma'am, not now." Then she asked, "What are you supposed to do?"

Her friend said, "We have to wait a while; the other side is too exposed to launch boats full of passengers; they're going to bring the boats around empty, so we can board from this side." She was the first person Rita had talked to who was calm and sensible.

"Where will the boats take us?"

"To Astoria; it's only a few miles, and there are steamers from there to Portland. Ah, but you're going back to San Francisco; there's a train daily, or you can get a steamer in a few days."

A train fare—or a few days' wait for a steamer! And she had only two dollars! She asked hopefully, "Won't the company do something? I have a round-trip ticket."

"I spoke to the purser about it; he is sure they will do something, but this is their only ship and it'll take time."

The girl said, "I hadn't planned to stay—"

Mrs. DeVore looked down at her unhappy face. "Are you worried about money?"

"I haven't much."

The comforting arm was around her again. "Don't think about it, child. I want you to be my guest."

The girl blinked, trying to make her eyes swallow their tears of relief. "I'll pay you back!" She hugged the woman who had seemed so distant the day before. For a moment she was completely happy and at ease. Then she saw one last dark cloud in her sky. "Aunt Dolores will go crazy when she finds out that I didn't go to the O'Malleys. I'll have to send her a telegram."

"Of course, Rita; I'll send it myself."

Rita felt better, but not altogether at peace in her mind. "Then she'll know what I did. Do you think she'll take me back?"

Mrs. DeVore's face looked serious. "We can only try." Then she asked, "Have you so much to go back for?"

When Rita thought of it that way, there was very little. "If I could make a living—"

Her friend gave her arm a pat and smiled hearteningly.

"If that's all that's worrying you, child, forget about it! Portland is the city of opportunity, and I'm well acquainted there. But just now you ought to be watching the shipwreck; it's something that doesn't happen to one every day."

When Rita's mind was happy and at ease she was almost able to enjoy physical disaster. A little later she realized that others could enjoy it, too.

At her first glimpse of the boat coming up from around the stern, she thought it was one of the lifeboats for which they were waiting; then she realized it was a lighter and slenderer boat, strikingly graceful and buoyant, with a professional look. Four men were rowing so like a smooth machine that there seemed to be some trick about it, but Rita couldn't give them any attention because of the fifth man. He was standing in the stern, tall and easy, swaying with the motion of the boat and holding the steering oar casually. His uniform cap was pushed back on his head, giving a glimpse of brown curls, and his laughing young face was turned up toward the stranded ship, taking everything in and enjoying all he saw. Opposite the pilot house he recognized the mate and called in a big voice, easy and amused, "Henry is that the best you could do!"

Henry was leaning over the rail of the bridge, and he called down, "Don't tell me about it, Roger! Talk to your God-damned pilot! I told him he was too close to Sand Island!" The mate's voice was like a strained croaking, and it made you realize what a voice the young man had to fill the space between the sea and sky without effort. Even his name was grand: Roger.

Roger was laughing at the mate's bluster about the pilot. "We're only human," he called. "We have to miss once in a while!" He hadn't had any share in the disaster, but he was taking some of the blame, as if making mistakes was as much a part of life as doing the right thing.

Rita wasn't the only one who was admiring Roger; the

other girls of the little flock were crowded at the rail wondering who he was and saying, "Isn't he handsome!" And one girl, with big dark eyes and a pale waif's face, said, "I think he's beautiful!"

Rita thought it was a silly thing to say. Then she was jealous because she hadn't thought of it herself. Roger was beautiful, standing there in the restless, swaying boat, as easily as a bareback rider at a circus, laughing up at the grumpy mate and raising his big, easy voice in conversation —loafing there, beautifully at ease, doing nothing. As far as Rita could see in either direction the rail was crowded with admiring faces, and their side of the ship was growing quieter. Roger was doing far more than nothing; he was showing people that the sea was nothing to be afraid of, telling them they were safe and that there was plenty of time. Gropingly, out of her inexperience, Rita recognized the touch of genius.

While the girls admired Roger, Mrs. DeVore was forgotten. Then she spoke, and became more important than ever. "That's Captain Collins," she said; "he's always like that."

"Do you know him?" they asked. And the girl with the big eyes and the pale waif's face asked, "Is he married?"

Mrs. DeVore said, "Captain Collins is the youngest pilot on the Columbia Bar, and the best. If he had been on board, this would never have happened."

Next to Rita, a plump and shapely girl sighed, "If he were on board, I wouldn't care what happened!"

"My dear!" Mrs. DeVore said reprovingly.

Another girl asked, "Do you really know him?"

As if it were no great matter, the woman said, "Of course. When Captain Collins is in Portland he always stops at my hotel."

The plump girl sighed again. "I hope he stops at nothing else!"

Mrs. DeVore was shocked by the rowdy she had taken under her wing. "Marie!"

"Is he there often?" the waif asked, as if she meant to stay until he appeared.

"Fairly often." By the crisp sound of her voice it was clear that she felt the girls were giving the pilot too much attention. Rita decided that the woman didn't like Roger.

Swaying easily with the restless boat, the young pilot raised his voice again. "She looks safe as a church, Henry! I'm coming on board. Will you drop me a ladder?"

Henry answered. "Damned if I will! We've had one pilot too many!" But he disappeared from the bridge and presently a rope ladder was dropped over the side, breathlessly near the group at the rail.

The boat eased in toward the side of the ship, and the young pilot stowed his oar. A moment later the bow of the boat swung out, the stern flashed from under his feet, and he was coming up the ladder with triumphal grace.

"Showing off!" Mrs. DeVore said. Rita thought, "Why shouldn't he?" She only hoped that after shaking the tree he would look around to see how many hearts had fallen.

He came on board with a gesture of dismay at seeing so many people; everyone was pressing toward him, but he slipped through the crowd quickly, laughing and handing out assurances and compliments as he went. He disappeared too soon, but he was on board, and his being there made the ship feel safer.

They were safer almost immediately; the first empty lifeboat appeared around the stern and drew in out of sight behind the great paddle guard, and another boat followed. Mrs. DeVore took up her carpetbag. "Come, girls; it will soon be our turn."

But the girls lingered beside the pilot's ladder.

"Girls, we're moving aft, nearer the boats."

They continued to linger, and one of them said, "There's

lots of time, yet." And the waif said, "I want to see him again!"

"And maybe lose your life, child?"

The waif answered, "I can't think of any nicer way of losing it."

"It would be nicer for him to get here first!"

Rita was afraid that if the plump girl said anything more their stately guide mightn't take her to Portland, and she put in hastily, "The sailors are telling people not to crowd. Maybe it would be better to wait."

"It would be much better," they all said.

Mrs. DeVore put down her bag and looked at them tolerantly. "Girls weren't so forward in my day, but I live and learn."

The plump girl said, "That's why we like you, ma'am; you're a lady, and you know how girls feel."

The redhead said, "—and you help us in times of trouble, like the Bible says."

They were still complimenting her when the young pilot loomed up suddenly, hurrying back toward his boat. In the thinned crowd they were almost face to face with him; they could see him plain, and he couldn't help seeing them. He stopped, with his hands in his pockets and his feet apart, and looked down at the girls with a big, admiring smile. "I'll be damned," he said softly, "if this isn't the most *ornamental* shipwreck I ever saw!"

The plump girl said, "You're ornamental, too, sir."

Mrs. DeVore said, *"Marie!"*

Roger laughed. "I'm certainly not useful!" He was still laughing, looking from one girl to another, when he met Rita's eyes. She was used to having men stop and turn to look at her, but she hadn't expected to have that effect on the lordly young pilot. He had stopped laughing and his eyes had a look of hurt glory. Then he asked, almost roughly, "What are you doing here?"

[130]

"Captain Collins," Mrs. DeVore said, "these girls are shipwrecked, like everyone else; they're not here to be stared at!"

"I am!" the plump girl said.

"*Marie!*"

Roger was laughing again, and Mrs. DeVore said, "Girls, meet Captain Collins." She introduced him to each by name, which Rita thought remarkable, since she had gathered them at random in the confusion of the shipwreck.

Roger had asked Rita a question which she hadn't answered, and when they were introduced, she said, "I was making the round trip, but when we got wrecked Mrs. DeVore invited me to stay at her hotel."

Mrs. DeVore seemed to think that Rita was talking too much. "It was nice to see you again, Captain," she said. "Girls, if we expect to get into a lifeboat, we had better go."

Roger asked innocently, "Are you going ashore?"

"I believe everyone hopes to."

"I have an excellent boat down there—it won't cost you anything."

Mrs. DeVore smiled. "Thank you, Captain, but I wouldn't think of inconveniencing you; we'll wait for a lifeboat."

"I'm going with the captain!" the plump girl said.

The red-headed girl said, "So am I!"

"I am, too," the waif said.

The pilot questioned Rita with his eyes.

"I am going with you," she said.

Another girl said, "So am I!"

Mrs. DeVore laughed. "And so am I!"

Roger went to the rail and called in his big, easy voice, "Boat ahoy! Bring her up to the ladder; we have some passengers." He sent the baggage down by tossing their bundles and light carpetbags to one of the men in the boat; it took only a few seconds, but before he had dropped the last one other passengers were pressing their bags upon him. "Sorry," he said, "I have a full passenger list. Step aft and the lifeboats will take care of you." Starting down, he paused and addressed the little flock: "Only one on the ladder at a time, and hang on all the way; it isn't as easy as it looks! Mrs. DeVore, see to it that we don't get any stowaways; when you come down, that will complete our load."

Rita was the last girl to descend; she had the experience of watching others clinging to rough, swaying rope and feeling for narrow wooden steps with unaccustomed feet; she was glad of that much experience, and glad when she felt the pilot's steadying hand as he helped her into the tossing boat.

"Sit down, Rita!" He handled her name as surely as her arm.

She sat in the bottom of the boat and looked up involuntarily, among the expensive undergarments of Mrs. DeVore, who was beginning to descend the ladder. She looked away and met the eyes of the plump girl, who was about to make a rowdy comment, but instead suddenly covered her rosy face with her hand. "Mercy!" she said; "and I haven't any—"

The pilot had already shipped the steering oar, and he spoke quietly to the oarsmen: "That's all; bear away!" The boat slid out from the black side of the *Great Republic*, and when Rita looked back she saw the tall woman descending the rope ladder that led to the Columbia River. She heard the other girls exclaiming, and she saw the blank look on her neighbor's face. "Why did he do that?" the plump girl whispered. Rita came out of her stupor of surprise and said, "Captain, you forgot Mrs. DeVore!"

The pilot didn't seem to hear.

"You forgot Mrs. DeVore!" she said again, looking up at him.

Chuckling, he said, "As if I could forget her!"

"She'll climb right into the river!" the waif said.

Roger didn't seem to think it any great matter, but he

spoke to his crew. "Avast rowing!" Then he called, "Mrs. DeVore, watch where you're going!"

The woman looked down, and stopped. Then she turned as far as she could while holding on with both hands, and her voice came to them, hard and thin: "Captain Collins, come back for me! Do you hear me? Come back!"

"Wait for a lifeboat! I'll leave your bag at the Occidental!" He was enjoying his cruel prank.

"Please go back for Mrs. DeVore," Rita begged, "she's been very kind to us!"

Roger said, "Listen to her!"

They heard her voice in rising anger. "Captain Collins, come back here! God damn you! Come back here, you low Irish bastard! You rotten, lousy longshore—"

"Bear away!" the pilot said. As the boat surged forward, he smiled at the girls. "That is the voice of the meanest bagnio keeper north of the Barbary Coast!"

They were still for a few seconds, then one of them began to cry, and the redhead said in awed tones, "You saved us from something worse than death!"

Roger's face was almost solemn. "At least I'm giving you the chance to make up your minds. I don't usually interfere with other people's business, but she has no principles."

"She told us about her nice hotel," the waif said; "she was going to find me a job—and she runs one of those places!"

"That's the way they work," the young pilot said. "But she shouldn't have taken advantage of a shipwreck; any girl could have been caught off guard."

It made Rita feel like a miserable fool. She wanted more than ever to thank him. She didn't know just what to say. He was steering with one arm on the oar and his free hand hanging by his side near her, and suddenly she caught his hand and touched it with her lips.

The pilot said, "Don't!" as if she had hurt him. Even then she wasn't sorry, but she didn't want to meet the eyes of the other girls. She looked away and saw the black bulk of the *Great Republic* looming high out of the receding water, with white lifeboats clustering beside her. Passengers still crowded the deck where young men and girls had danced in the moonlight, but they had a departing look; and above them the great black walking beam of the engine was still against the gray sky, one end down and the other up, with an unsatisfied look; and the black banner from the smokestack dwindled to a ghostly wisp as life went out of the ship.

An hour later a tug brought the rescued girls to the oldest American settlement in the West.

Rita's first impression of Astoria was of houses standing above the river on piling that was covered with green moss, and of a dock with nets spread on it and hung over racks, and old boats pulled up. The dock and the old boats were covered with moss that was soft green under rain that had begun to fall. The April rain was falling over everything, and pitting the gray river that went sliding by the town, and ashore church bells were ringing. She was gently surprised that here, too, they had days of the week and that she had arrived on a Sunday morning.

That was the wreck of the *Great Republic*, which had begun and ended quietly for Rita and for most of the others who had been on board. All the passengers and crew were taken off and all the boats came ashore safely, except the last one, which was swept under the stern of the ship and capsized, drowning ten of the crew.

It had been a quiet shipwreck, but it was also a tenacious one, that went on affecting the lives of people and their children. The round trip cost four dollars when the *Great Republic* steamed out of San Francisco; but when she lay mortally injured on Sand Island the rate war was over and the fare jumped to twenty dollars one way. Many of the young adventurers were a long time getting back to San Francisco; others never got back. A few of the young men found work in Astoria, and more in Portland. Some of the girls found work or husbands, and others found their way to the bagnios of the river towns.

The wreck of the *Great Republic* affected the lives of people who had never seen the ship, or who were there only as spectators. Like the young pilot, Roger Collins, who fell in love with Rita's beauty. In the ten years of their married life he had taken hundreds of steamers and grain ships and lumber schooners across the bar without loss, but a few of the other pilots were less skillful, or less fortunate; occasionally a pilotless vessel found the bar in a smiling mood—and died by its treachery; or one was driven by necessity. Roger visited other shipwrecks, but never one like the *Great Republic*, which was the shipwreck of his life.

9

FOR THE THIRD TIME that evening Rita went to the kitchen and made up the fire and comforted the dinner that was wasting its youth on the back of the range. In the dining room the table was perfect from repeated inspections and adjustments, and in the parlor everything was ready: Roger's carpet slippers beside the Morris chair, the papers neatly arranged on the revolving table—the *Astorian*, the Portland *Oregonian*, and the San Francisco *Guide*, solid with shipping news—and a fresh supply of matches beside his pipes and tobacco jar. There was nothing to do but put another piece of wood in the fireplace—stoking the fires of passing time.

Worrying, she knew, was only being too much aware of what always is: the surrounding uncertainties which you accept more easily for yourself than for someone you love. And a pilot's homecoming could never be more than an approximation. Once when she had been waiting dinner, Captain Smith stopped by with word that Roger was on his way to San Francisco in the steamship *George W. Elder*, the sea having been too rough for them to take him off outside. Another time he boarded the *Amphitrite* when the bar was breaking too heavily to risk a crossing, and was missing four days, having worked the big grain ship offshore to ride out a southwest gale.

It was nothing that Roger had estimated that with luck he might be in by six, and was not there by seven. And she had never proved anything about premonitions; sometimes it turned out that he had been in danger, and other times, when her premonitions had been strongest, he had been enjoying himself in safety—unless there had been some danger that he never saw.

At ten minutes after seven there came the deep whisper of the *Vandalia's* bell. She got up so hastily from her sewing that she spared the thread she was about to cut and the scissors clanged on the floor. But halfway across the room she knew it wasn't Roger, who would come in immediately after announcing himself. It would be a neighbor calling, or one of the tugboat captains with word that Roger was on some ship outside the bar, waiting for daylight and better weather. It could be almost anyone, so long as Rita didn't find a sea gull at the door. Roger would never have told her the superstition about the souls of dead sailors turning into sea gulls if he had known how it would affect her in troubled moments.

When she opened the door the light from the hanging lamp shone on the smooth faces and dark, lustrous eyes of the Fortune boys. They were standing in their school-going oilskins against the background of the dark and the windy rain. "Come in, boys!" She opened the door wide, smiling a welcome. "It's a wet night."

"Hello, Mrs. Collins," Jack said. "Is Captain Collins home?"

"Not yet, but he should be here any minute. Come in."

"Thank you." They stepped in and looked apologetically at the water dripping from their oilskins. "We're kind of wet," Tom said.

"The floor is used to it," she told them. "Take off your slickers and come in where there's a fire."

"We mustn't stay," Jack said. He took a dry book from under his oilskins and put it carefully on the hall stand. "We were returning a book the captain lent us."

"Thank you, Jack; I'll tell him—if you don't get to see him."

Hanging up his oilskin coat, Tom said, "Captain Collins said there was another book we could have when we brought this back."

Rita picked up the book. "If you know which one it is, you're welcome to take it." She and Roger were fond of the boys; in spite of their reputation and the apocryphal stories told about them, they were better mannered than most boys, and better company.

When they went into the parlor, Rita invited them to make themselves at home rather than to sit down. They responded by roving about the room like well-behaved young panthers, soft-footed and light of touch and soft-voiced, alive to things that other people missed; more appreciative and more civilized than most boys, but always with a touch of something untamed; always saying "we" instead of "I," banded together against the world.

She left them exploring, and when she came back from the pantry with oatmeal cookies and cider, Jack had come to rest in front of the glass case, where he was contemplating the lump of wax from the Nehalem treasure ship, and Tom was kneeling at the bookcase, considering volumes: *Coast Pilots, Lloyd's Registers, Vancouver's Voyages* and the *Wilkes Expedition,* miscellaneous volumes on naval architecture, oceanography and navigation, and the seven gray ledgers in which Roger kept his records of ships.

The boys responded to food willingly, but after a minute Jack went back to the case with his glass and a handful of cookies. "There's something about that old wax—"

Rita laughed. "Anyone would think you were Roger's son!" She wished he were—he and Tom—Roger's sons and hers; why didn't the two who loved the boys have them? Why didn't the two who had them love them? She got up and went over to the case and stood beside him, looking at the cracked brown lump of ancient wax. On the impulse, she said, "If you're very careful, you can bring it over to the table where the light's better and look at it while you eat."

His eyes were lustrous with excitement. "I'll be careful, Mrs. Collins!" As she unlocked the glass door, he asked, "Is it broken?"

"I believe it's one solid piece," she said. "You can probably tell when you lift it."

He lifted it accurately off the shelf, without touching the smaller objects on each side. "Must weigh twenty pounds!" Then he said, "Treasure coming!"

"Treasure coming!" Tom stepped well out of the way. Rita smiled and knew the treasure was in safe hands. There were stories about the boys hacking valuable things to pieces in revenge for punishment, but they seemed the least likely ones to damage a thing because of clumsiness.

The older boy put the big chunk of wax gently on the center of the table built on the *Ariel's* wheel, and the three of them looked at it while Jack revolved the table by turning the spokes. "Wouldn't you think the table was made for something like this?" he asked.

The value of the treasure was mostly in its age and associations: a cracked, dull-brown mass that seemed very dry for wax. It wasn't much to look at in itself, but the boys couldn't take their eyes off it, and Rita had to bring Jack's forgotten cider and cookies from the top of the glass case. He was so seriously keen, and so much a boy; as he handed the spokes, he pretended that he was a pilot giving instructions to a helmsman: "Port a little, port a little, port a little! Steady! Ease your wheel! Steady so!" He stopped rotating the table and looked at the date on the big lump of beeswax: 1657.

"That was a long time ago," Tom said.

Rita told them, "Roger has never made up his mind

about that date. It seems right, but he thinks it may have
been added after the wax was found. It looks as if it had been
carved, and the other mark was stamped or branded with an
iron."

Jack said, "It came from an Acapulco galleon, anyway."

"It seems most likely," she agreed. "When Roger first
got interested, he spent weeks looking up things in history.
He finally found an account written by a Spanish governor
of the Philippines in the sixteen hundreds. The governor
mentioned some of the things they were sending to New
Spain—gold, and cakes of white and yellow wax."

"This must have been the yellow," Tom said.

Jack turned the table smoothly. "Starboard a little, starboard a little, starboard—" In the fierce earnestness of play,
handing the polished spokes, his eyes had the glow of a well-
mannered young demon's storming down some Spanish Main
of the imagination. *"Starboard a little, starboard a little.
Starboard. Starboard! STARBOARD!"*

"Don't!" Rita cried.

He stopped the table smoothly. "Here we are," studying
the hieroglyph branded into the wax, an "N" with an added
ellipse on a vertical line up from the diagonal of the letter.
"It looks like an 'N' with a lantern on a pole."

"Or someone's head on a pole," Tom said.

"It's probably a trademark, or an ecclesiastical mark,"
Rita said. "There were candles in the cargo, too. When we
were at Nehalem we dug a piece of one out of the sand. They
and the wax seem to have been intended for churches in
Mexico. Roger can show you how the North Pacific drift
could have brought the ship to the Oregon coast."

"And this kind of southwest weather could have put her
ashore," Jack said. They listened instinctively and heard a
gust of it stumble against the house.

"We still have some of the candle." Rita went to the case
and came back with it. "This is much the way it looked when

we got it out of the sand. The wick was gone, but you could see where it had been."

"There's a wick in it," Jack said.

"I put that in. We burn it for a few minutes every Christmas Eve; it has to last a long time."

Tom put his nose close to the ancient, heavy candle stub and inhaled audibly. "How does it smell when it's burning?"

"If you didn't know," she said, "I suppose it would seem like any beeswax candle. But it seems more than that when you know that in a way you're smelling a candle that burned in a Mexican church more than three hundred years ago."

The older boy bent his thick-thatched black head over the table and inhaled the smell of ancient wax. "If we may, Mrs. Collins, we'd like to come over on Christmas Eve when you're going to light it."

Rita said, "You're both invited for as many Christmas Eves as you like!" She hugged Tom, who was nearest, and he responded timidly, like a wild thing unaccustomed to human caresses.

"You're so nice!" he said, like a sigh.

Without looking at her, Jack said, "You and the captain are the best friends we have."

A little wildly, on the impulse, she said, "Would you like to light it now, for a minute?"

"Would you?" Tom asked.

"If you would!" his brother said.

She took a match from the cup, struck it at the fireplace and carried it to the table and touched the blackened curled wick with the flame. The wick was unresponsive at first, then it answered with its soft pure blade of flame that should have burned for worshippers who had been dust three hundred years. The flame was warm on the young hands held up to it, outlining them with light transparent red, and it made a warm light on the boys' faces, dangerously close to the candle.

Jack reported, "I can smell it now!"

Tom said, "It's like a field in summer."

"Don't burn your noses!" Rita said. In her mind the faint perfume brought up the picture of worshippers in a church, but there was the field beyond. She said, "You're smelling the flowers of tropical islands when the world was young!" Then she thrilled to the clanging whisper of the bell. "That must be Roger now!"

But the door remained closed, and when she opened it, there stood Mr. Fortune, closing his big black umbrella. From his black mutton-chop whiskers to his dark topcoat he looked severe, but his voice was friendly. "Sorry to disturb you, Mrs. Collins, but are my sons here?"

"They are," she said. "Come in, Mr. Fortune. The boys stopped for a minute to return a book and I delayed them, talking."

Coming in, he said, "I didn't know the boys went around borrowing books, with their school books waiting for them at home."

The boys had heard their father's voice and they came out of the parlor, genteel and a little guilty, but not quite meek.

"Boys, do you know what time it is?" their father asked.

"No, sir," Jack said; "I forgot to look." It was the first time that evening he had said "I" and not "we."

"You promised to be back in half an hour, and you were gone an hour when I left home."

"You'll have to blame me for that," Rita said. "Jack and Tom told me they couldn't stay, and I forgot and delayed them with refreshments, and then I got them interested in the captain's museum——"

Mr. Fortune interrupted. "Mrs. Collins, you are a charming hostess and I wouldn't have you any different. But the boys can control themselves and remember their obligations. I won't hear of your blaming yourself."

"I do blame myself!" she said.

[142]

While the boys were putting on their oilskins their father told them, "I might have overlooked this if you had your school work prepared for tomorrow; but lessons don't study themselves." Then, as if he were afraid that Rita might think harshly of him, he explained, "Before I was John's age, I had to leave school to help support the family. I wouldn't wish that experience on anyone else. I only ask that my boys learn from the experience of others, and hew to the line."

When she had closed the door after the Fortunes, Rita remembered the precious candle she had left burning, and raced into the parlor. She stopped with a smile of relief and gratitude. The candle had been blown out, and it and the treasure wax were back in the glass case, and the cookie plates and glasses were stacked on the table. Before going to meet their displeased father, the boys had thought of her and stowed everything neatly, even to eating the last cookie.

She was in the kitchen making up the fire again when she heard the whispering clang of the *Vandalia's* bell. The sound of blowing rain came to her clearly through the open door, and when she reached the hall Roger was there, taking off his dripping black oilskins. "Hello, dear; I'm late." He looked tired, but triumphant and amused.

"Roger," she said, clinging to him as if to make sure that he was real. "Roger!"

He looked down at her with a little of the old hurt glory in his eyes. "Rita, you weren't worried about me, were you?"

"Yes."

"You shouldn't have been."

"Anyway, you're here; it's all right now."

"We're here," he said, kissing her.

When he ended the kiss she said, "That must have been good brandy!"

"Cognac *and* Napoleon brandy."

"You don't get a French ship every day!"

[143]

"Not very often." Releasing her, he said, "I brought a little of the brandy with me; it was the captain's last bottle." He fumbled in the pocket of his oilskin coat, dripping on the hall stand, and pulled out a chunk of dark wood. Laughing, he said, "I can still tell the difference between a bottle of brandy and a piece of teak!" He handed it to her while he looked for the other pocket.

"What ship is this from, Roger?"

"Souvenir of the *Great Republic!*"

Rita was disappointed. "Roger, you went back to the old wreck?"

"That was a long time ago today."

She, too, was a souvenir of the wreck, and she didn't see why he wanted others. "I thought you had enough of her already."

"It brought me luck," he said.

"The *Great Republic?*"

"This piece of her paddle wheel."

She was disappointed again but he did not notice, holding up the half-empty bottle of ancient brandy. "It was the last one Captain Lannes had."

"It must have been quite a day! What happened, Roger?" Then she said, "Don't tell me now. You must be starving."

Roger wanted to tell about his adventure as much as she wanted to hear, and at dinner he began while he was carving the overdone roast.

"It was a quiet sort of day with a sting in its tail. All morning we lay below Sand Island, in company with the *Columbia,* waiting for something to show up over the hill. While we were there, I took the work boat to the wreck of the *Great Republic—*"

Rita didn't want to hear about that part of it. Long ago Roger had visited the wreck, magnificent and laughing, at the steering oar of the *Halcyon's* whaleboat. He had visited the wreck at the right time, and no time afterward could be the same. "What about the French ship?"

"I was coming to that," he said cheerfully. "In the afternoon we brought the *Peter Iredale* in and went for another look at the pilot grounds. It was late by then and getting dirty. We were ready to call it a day, but the *Mistley Hall* was there, standing close in, and there was a little bark floundering a couple miles south of the jetty. The bark needed to get in, too, so they put me on board to bring her under sail while Smith went after the *Mistley*—"

"So that was your French vessel?"

He nodded, smiling. "The *Jocelyn*, ex *Saint Therese*, French-owned, but Austrian-built. She's been knocking about the seas for fifty-odd years, but she'd never been out here before."

"Was she very bad?"

"She was wonderful! Built of Adriatic oak with hand-wrought copper fastenings, and copper-sheathed; tight as a bottle; a sturdy, honest design; nice old-fashioned touches about her, too: a praying saint for a figurehead, and hand-carved catheads, and a painting of the Virgin Mary in the cuddy."

Rita knew that he hadn't told her everything. "She sounds nice; what was wrong?"

He said regretfully, "She was in ballast, riding so light she wouldn't go to windward, and her captain had her on a lee shore, pocketed by the jetty."

"That was bad."

"Bad enough."

"Didn't the tug tow you out of danger?" she asked.

"That's what we should have done," he said, "but Smith was in a hurry to get the *Mistley Hall*, and I was over-confident. I was sure I could manage; it hadn't occurred to me that maybe she wouldn't go to windward—but that's the way it was. By the time I knew I was in a trap, the tug

[145]

had the *Mistley* in tow, with her sails clewed up; she'd have gone on Peacock Spit if they'd let her go."

"What did you do?"

She looked so troubled that he laughed and patted her hand. "I always think of something. I thought, 'We're losing ground even when we're trying to get to windward; that means we have to go to loo'ard. What's down that way? There was Clatsop Spit'; I could hear the breakers on the beach, and I ruled it out. That left only the jetty. So I asked myself, 'Is there any particular place on the jetty you would like to take this little bark?' When I thought of it that way, there was."

Rita was horrified. "That's just a wall of stones!"

"But some stones are softer than others, and as soon as I thought of it that way, I knew the spot I wanted to try for. I remembered that the last gale had knocked a hole in the jetty; not a very big one, but wide enough for the *Jocelyn* if we could get them together, and I remembered that it bore sou'east by south from a high point on North Head—"

"How could you know that much about a little break in the jetty?"

"I must have taken a cross bearing on it from the channel at some time, though I don't remember doing it."

"Expecting to take a ship through?"

"Heaven forbid!"

"Then why would you have done that?"

He was smiling at her again. "Rita dear, this afternoon Smith was joking about the way I know ships; he said that if they were getting a new cook for the *Highland Lassie*, I could cable him where to reach for the salt and pepper. That's the way I try to know the bar and the ten miles of the river; I'm a pilot and it's my business to know where things are."

"I know why you're the best pilot on the bar!"

His face was serious again. "No one is the best pilot, Rita.

All of us are terrible sometimes; I made one of my mistakes this afternoon."

"You got the ship in," she said. "Or did you?"

"She's anchored at quarantine; but I shouldn't have taken her, under sail on a lee shore."

She brought him back to his story. "So you ran for the break in the jetty."

"Yes. It was getting dusk, with the sou'wester coming up fast. I don't think I'd have found it except for that bearing. I wasn't sure even then, because it was something that just popped up in my mind; I couldn't remember having taken it. All I could do was hope, and keep a little weather gauge; if we fetched up to loo'ard, there wouldn't be any getting back. With that strong northerly set to the current we had to hit it fast.

"We came storming down on the jetty, and even when we were almost on top of it I couldn't see the gap; the seas were spouting against the stones and blowing away to loo'ard, so there was a white curtain hanging over everything. I was wondering if we hadn't missed when I noticed that the curtain was thin in one spot, dead ahead, where it should have been. Then I made out the gap in the jetty underneath, but it was so narrow it didn't seem possible that anything could get through."

"How wide was it?"

"Maybe thirty yards. It didn't look any wider than a gate someone had forgotten to close, but it was a welcome sight!"

"How did you know the water was deep enough?"

"We drew only about twelve feet," he said, "and I'd seen the gap at a minus-two tide with no rock showing; and we were near the flood of a plus-twelve. We were as good as in the river when the gap showed up—or we should have been."

"Why 'should,' Roger?"

[147]

"The helmsman," Roger said. "At the last minute he took it into his head that I was going to kill us all on the jetty; he shouted something in French and started to bring her up into the wind; if he had, we'd have gone to kindling wood in a minute! I tried to take the wheel, but he was frozen to it in a panic—"

"What a time to have to fight with a madman!"

"He was sane enough; he thought I was crazy. It was a misunderstanding, and a few more seconds of it would have piled us up on the jetty. But the *Great Republic* saved the day."

"The *Great Republic*, Roger?"

He explained, "While we were struggling, I felt that chunk of her in my pocket; I tapped him over the head with it and took the wheel."

"So you had to knock him out!"

"It wasn't the democratic thing to do, but there was no time for debate. It all took only a few seconds, and then the rocks were flashing by on each side of us as we stormed through. I pulled in my elbows and Captain Lannes put his hands over his eyes. When we were out of the noise of the breakers, he told me he hadn't known the entrance to the Columbia River was so narrow!" Roger laughed in retrospect. "We didn't miss the weather rocks by twenty feet, and the loo'ard ones were almost as close."

Rita felt as exhausted as if she had just lived his adventure. "And you were safe after that!"

"There was only the bar, and the slog up the river, with the flood slacking off. We might have had to anchor if Smith hadn't come back looking for us. We towed the rest of the way in."

Roger looked tired, and Rita didn't want to hear any more about the sea or anything connected with it. "At least you won't have to be up early in the morning," she told him.

"No; we'll be bar-bound tomorrow; we got those two in just in time." Then he said, "Listen to it!"

They were still for a minute, listening to the drunken gusts stumbling against the house and going away muttering. "I like the sound of it now," she said. "It'll be nice to lie in bed and listen to it, knowing that we don't have to get up in the morning until we feel like it."

"I was thinking of that on the way up the river. We'll go to bed early, the way we used to, and listen to the wind and rain."

She said, "It isn't early now."

"I'll just have a look at the papers before we turn in."

She made up the fire while he changed to his slippers and reached for the *Astorian* on the revolving table. He gave a minute to the front page, with its shy headlines and casually told news packed in a dunnage of advertisements: Lots in the Warrentown swamps at $140 each, and certain to double their value in a year; Golden Balm at five dollars a bottle; Hood's Sarsaparilla, Elixers and Discoveries, all guaranteed to cure syphilis and cancer and consumption, trumpeting hope to the desperate and the dying. For cases where the remedy failed, with the money cheerfully refunded or the fifty-dollar reward paid, there were undertakers' advertisements with inviting pictures of new-style caskets.

From the front page Roger turned familiarly to the shipping news, his glance running down the columns of "Departures" and "Arrivals" and "Ships Due." He paused at one name questioningly, like a music master sensing a false note, put the *Astorian* aside and laid open the heart of the *Oregonian* with a swift motion. When he found what he was looking for, he took up the *Astorian* again and penciled a correction. He paused at another name and reached into the bookcase for *Lloyd's Register*. That usually meant an unfamiliar vessel.

"What ship is it?" Rita asked.

"The *Glenalvon*, new in the grain fleet. I believe she's a big one." He found her in the *Register*. Big enough: 2072 tons; Clyde-built iron ship, two years old. They're sending out some fine ships." He finished with the listings of vessels, ran through "Marine News and Notes," and began on the shipping news in the *Oregonian*.

At half past ten Rita put more wood on the fire, and at eleven she sat on the arm of his chair, shoulder to shoulder with him, looking at the close-packed columns of *The Guide*. "It's eleven o'clock, Roger."

He looked up with a boyish, apologetic smile. "I didn't know it was that late!" Then he said, "The *Down East Maid* is posted as overdue at Falmouth—168 days. Hargrave's average with her is about 120, and he's never taken more than 135."

"You think she's lost?"

"There's no telling. Hargrave was racing Slade in the *Christmas Morning*; he'd have been off the Plate River at the time of the great pampero."

Rita asked, "What about the *Christmas Morning*?"

"She was past Santos when it struck; she made it to Cork in 110 days."

There was a gale blowing outside now, and Roger had saved a French bark from it, as he had saved other ships. And he had once saved her. He was the one who needed saving now, and if he would only come to bed she would make him forget about ships and past gales on distant seas. "Roger, we were going to bed early and listen to the storm, remember?"

"I'm almost through, dear. You go along and I'll be there in a few minutes."

She wavered. "You won't forget?"

"As if I could!" he said.

"All right; I'll have the bed warm for you."

"I'll be there in a few minutes."

After she had gone he could still feel her living sweet presence beside him. She had thought he was taking a long time over the shipping news; actually he had skimmed through it. She didn't know how longingly he had thought of her on the cold, wet slog up the river—as soon as he dared to think at all. He had seen her clearly then, waiting for him in the warm, bright house, with all the comforts ready to welcome him, and her own affectionate welcome; everything about the house and herself as perfect as things can be in this life. He had thought beyond his homecoming and dinner, to bed, with the gale and rain turned to a luxury by windows and roof and walls; he had thought of her swift loveliness and her tender fire, and love-making in which there were no frustrations and no after feeling of grossness, or anything but timeless well-being.

He had seen her clearly, coming back to this pleasant earth from a vision of death on the jetty, with wreckage and the bodies of Frenchmen who have never liked the sea. He had seen her clearly then, and he saw her as clearly now, and loved and desired her as much; but when he had come back to earth there were a few chores which he had forgotten about.

When he had skimmed through *The Guide*, he thought of the *Jocelyn* again. All these years she must have been in *Lloyd's Register*, waiting to come to life; a hundred times he must have skimmed by her, missing her sometimes by the thickness of a page and sometimes only by the distance of a line of type. He reached for the *Register* and turned to the "J's"; *Jocasta*, *Jocelyn*—she had been there all the time. *Jocelyn*, ex *Saint Therese*, French bark, 827 tons, 147 feet length, 38 feet beam; depth of hold, 16 feet; construction, wood; fastenings, copper; built Trieste, Austria, 1839. Sold French 1864, renamed *Joselyn*. Rated A 1, after all these years!

What did the encyclopedia have to say about shipbuilding

at Trieste? He sat on his heels at the bookcase, in front of the dark volumes. "T—" He brought the volume to his chair, opened it, and stormed down on "Tr," with the turning pages making a tiny roll of thunder. "Trieste." He read through the article, getting the history and feel of the place, but he didn't find what he was looking for until near the end, and there wasn't much of it: there was some shipbuilding, making use of native oak. Captain Lannes had said that the Jocelyn was built of Adriatic oak; but what kind—live oak or white oak or some special variety? Whatever it was, it must be good to be rated A 1 in the latest *Lloyd's Register*. Try "Adriatic."

There was a map showing the Adriatic Sea, rich in the history of ships and sailors. Trieste was across the way from Venice, home of Venetian galleys. Columbus had visited that sheltered northern bight of the Adriatic, and there Elizabethan shipmasters had listened to Juan de Fuca's story of his explorations in the Oregon country—too fantastic to believe, and fitting the geography of the country too well to be rejected. Trieste and Venice were only eyebrows' distance apart on the blue Adriatic, and the *Jocelyn* would have been built of the same stuff as the Venetian galleys. Try "Italy" and see what kind of oak grew in the northern provinces. Her copper was from there; Lannes had said red Italian copper. See if there is any special merit in that kind. Smith had said that his knowledge of ships was indecent; it was intimate, anyway, and gained out of a passion to learn the last secrets of their being.

When he had tracked it down, there were several kinds of oak on the Adriatic; but the white would have been used in shipbuilding, and part of its enduring quality would have come from years of seasoning in a climate which was now familiar to him. When he saw the *Jocelyn* again he would know more than where they kept the cognac. He would know what kind of winds had blown through the trees from which her timbers and planking had been formed, and he would have a memory of the mines that had produced her copper.

Jocelyn was only a name superimposed on the positive and unchanging personality of Saint Therese. Who was Therese? When and where had she lived and what had she done? Was she a patron saint of sailors?

While the mystic Carmelite nun was coming to life out of the encyclopedia, the lamp dimmed a little, and when he turned it up the wick answered with protesting sparks. Out of oil, when he was within a few minutes of being through! Once in a while Rita was negligent like that—forgetting to fill the lamp so it burned out by midnight! And he was so near to being through that it wasn't worth blundering through the house looking for another lamp; he could make up the fire a little and finish by its light. But the fire had burned down very quickly; there wasn't an ember left to revive. And now that he thought of it, the house was cold, with the gale having sucked the last warmth out of it. It really was time to turn in. If only there had been a few more drops of oil in the lamp! Its dying light gleamed faintly on the glass case and reminded him of the candle. He opened the door and found the heavy stub dug up in the Nehalem sands. It was supposed to be lit only once a year, for a few minutes; but it had already burned for ten Christmas Eves and it wouldn't make any difference if he lit it for a minute now.

The candle was a luxury at first, with its perfume and light coming out of past centuries; then it was only light on the pages he consulted and he forgot about it until the light began to waver. When he looked, there was nothing left but a wick hove down in a pool of wax on the table; and the clock was striking four in the cold house.

He couldn't believe it, and he felt guilty and sad, remembering that Rita had been waiting for him all these hours. She would be asleep by now, her disappointment healed over by sleep that would still leave scar tissues on her mind. Tomorrow she would say that he had sent her to bed only to get rid of her; that she was only a souvenir of the wreck of the *Great Republic*, gathering dust among the souvenirs of wrecks while he went on to new adventures. She would say and think unfair things, without knowing how he had come home to her with love and desire, without knowing how he loved and desired her now. Rita hadn't been at fault in any way, and his intentions had been as good as hers.

10

IT WAS THE NIGHT they had prepared for, but they did not know this was it until they saw its moonless face and heard the west wind in the apple tree outside their window. The breeze was fresh and steady, blowing up the river, and the flood began a few minutes after eleven; they would have both wind and tide to help them against the current.

It wouldn't be accurate to say they were running away that night; they had been leaving piecemeal for two weeks— smuggling things out of the house and down to the boat dock. Now they didn't have much but themselves to get out of the house.

They lay in bed, with the covers up to their chins, over their clothes, wondering whether their mother was asleep. They could hear their father snoring, and Marjorie had gone to bed hours before. The best way to find out about their mother was to stir around a little. If she was awake, she would ask from the other side of the hall what was the matter. They would tell her that it was blowing outside and they were looking to see if Marjorie had enough covers.

"I'll try now," Jack whispered. He got up, without making any special effort to be quiet, and went out. The hall was dark except for a dim line of light under Marjorie's door. He opened it and went in. She was sleeping sound and warm, as he had expected, with the night light burning in a glass on the stand. She was afraid of the dark, and because less was expected of her than of the boys, she was allowed the night light. Her face was calm and sad and her hair looked very black, and her stuffed monkey doll was beside her, with its head on the pillow. "Good-bye, Marjie," he thought. "I hope you have a good time when we're not here to fight with the old man and the old lady." As he was turning away, she moved in her sleep and said distinctly, "Don't let them touch the window." Whatever that meant.

When she was quiet again, he went out. His mother hadn't stirred across the hall, and he could still hear his father snoring. The house was asleep; there was nothing to keep them from going. Back in their own room, he whispered to Tom, "The coast is clear. I'll go first and pick up some grub. Give me about ten minutes."

"All right."

Jack lit the bull's-eye lantern, with his cap over the lens. "If mother hears me, tell her I went to put out the cat." He went out. The hall floor creaked and the stairway landing creaked louder, with a sleeper stirring in response. He stood still until everything was quiet again. Then he got astride the banister and rode down smoothly, almost without a sound.

In the pantry he uncovered the lens of the lantern and swept food into the flour sack he had brought: a slab of bacon, two fresh-baked loaves of bread, as many eggs as he could pack in a covered can, a print of butter, and four oranges, brought by the ocean steamer, a cake of chocolate and a sack of raisins. He was adding useful odds and ends when Tom came in, his shoes in his hand. He hadn't had to tell his mother that Jack was putting out the cat; he was as quiet as a cat himself, and his brother hadn't known he was there until the door opened.

Jack closed the neck of the bag and muffled the light with his cap. "Let's go," he whispered. In the entry they took their oilskin coats from the wall and Jack blew out the lantern. No one was in sight on the street. They put on their shoes, sitting on the bottom step, and went away across the lawn, avoiding the gravel path until they reached the gate.

From the far side of Seventh, the place looked nice: the high white house in the wide grounds, guarded by big leafy trees under the dark night sky. It looked like a place where a family would spend happy days and sleep soundly at night; but all the boys wanted of it they already had in a flour sack, and they hurried by like strangers.

It was a good time for going through town; late enough so few people were out, but not so late that anyone would ask questions about their being there. They went along Seventh toward the river. Crossing Commercial Street, they came within sound of gongs and drums and flutes from Chinatown, and then they heard the banging of pianos and a swelling uproar from the saloons and bagnios and gambling houses of Swilltown. Three big ships had come in that day, and the *Telephone* had brought an army of loggers from closed camps up the river. From blocks away they could hear the loggers and sailors parting with their money, and if there were any objections they were drowned out in the roar of the mill that took it from them.

They passed beside the Pearsons' darkened windows; the widow's house, sleeping in dim white innocence in the tide of drunken sounds that beat around it, with the night-black river flowing underneath. . . . Now the hollow planks of Bond Street were underfoot.

Tom said, "Someone's up late at the Pearsons'."

Jack had been so sure the family was asleep that he hadn't noticed the front of the house. Now, when he glanced over his shoulder, he saw the lighted upstairs window and a figure silhouetted by the light. Emily's room, and that was Emily. He didn't look back again, but his mind carried the image of the still, intently waiting figure—waiting for what, he didn't know. "This way," he told his brother, wanting to be out of sight as quickly as possible.

They turned the corner, and almost ran into a familiar young figure. "Hi, fellows!"

"Hi, Barry." The meeting had been too sudden to give them any choice. "You're out late," Jack said.

Barry nodded gravely in the gaslit dusk. "I've been on board the *Cape Fear*."

The brothers had been too occupied with plans to notice what ships were in, but the name had a familiar sound, and it was connected with a whipping. Jack said, "We had a look at her last summer, when that missionary was leaving for the islands."

Tom asked, "Wasn't it kind of dangerous going on board at night?"

"I don't know." Barry had a way of going through dangers dreamily, without noticing. "Emily had a friend in the crew; she'd had a letter from him, and she was kind of expecting him. You know how girls are."

Jack didn't know much about it, but that explained the still waiting figure at the window back there. "Did you find him?"

"No. The crew had cleared out hours before. The mate said the fellow I was looking for was in a hurry to get home. He must have taken the steamer to Portland. Emily'll be disappointed." Barry was looking gravely at the brothers, loaded with oilskins and plunder. "Are you fellows going somewhere?"

"Just around," Tom said.

Jack said, significantly, "If anyone asks, will you say you didn't see us?"

"Sure," Barry said. "I'd better be getting home." He went away through the roistering gaslit dusk like a thoughtful young deer walking alone in the woods.

The boys reached Front Street without seeing anyone else they knew, and walked beside the reassuring river. They were less likely to meet neighbors there, and they were at least on equal terms with the few people they did meet: a group of drunken sailors and a painted lady, also drunk, who tagged along with them for most of a block, trying to take Jack's arm. After they had shaken her they did not see anyone but a Swede logger, sitting on a stringpiece, holding up a round tin of snuff and singing to it as if it were his sweetheart.

"Must've been drinking something pretty strong," Tom said.

"Blue Ruin whiskey, I'll bet." It would have to be something like that for the logger to sing so blissfully through the blood of a nose that was broken flat on his face.

At the boat dock they looked things over before going down the steps. On the float, among others, was the *Flying Dragon*, the four-oared boat which their father had had built for them—and which he had let them have, months afterward, when Jack earned enough to pay the cabinetmaker for putting new legs on the piano. The boat was padlocked to the float, and their father had the key; but it had been easy enough to have a duplicate made and to resist using it until now. Along one side of the float was the long shed, with lockers where boat owners kept their gear. The oars and mast and sail and the supplies were in one of them, the supplies tagged with Barry Pearson's name on the chance that their father might inspect the locker. He was forever emphasizing to his sons the need for methodical planning, and he should be pleased at the way they had learned the lesson.

Looking things over from the wooden street, Jack reasoned, "She's our boat, and we can take her out when we want to; but we don't want to have to argue about it with anybody. Let's sneak the stuff from the locker into the boat and shove off."

"We could take everything to the end of the float, where it's in the shadow," Tom suggested, "and load from there." It sounded more complicated, but it meant that they wouldn't be making trips back and forth across the float in the light from the gas lamp on the street above.

"That might be safer," Jack agreed. "Let's try."

On the float everything was quiet and friendly, more peaceful than in the daytime. They were able to keep out of the light while they emptied the locker and carried their gear to the shadowed end. The incoming tide had almost mastered the current of the river, and the west wind was blowing steadily upstream. It was like a train, passing forever; when they were ready they had only to jump on board. Everything was the way they wanted it to be, except that the river looked very wide and untamed in the dark.

When their equipment was ready to load, Jack singled out the key to the padlock. "We'll shove off now," he said. The open gaslit float was as peaceful as the shadows under the shed. He undid the padlock, and he and Tom grunted together as they wrestled the *Dragon* into motion and slid her, buoyant and white and dry, into the troubled night water.

"Someone's watching!" Tom said.

"Don't notice," Jack told him, leading the boat along the side of the float.

He had almost reached the corner when a bullying voice roared down from the street: "Where do you think you're going with that boat?"

"It's our boat!" Jack's voice sounded very small, even to himself. "We're moving it!" In a still smaller voice he said to Tom, "Start putting things in as soon as we're alongside." It was the night patrolman who had challenged them. Jack could have identified himself and Tom, but he didn't want to. The patrolman was only suspicious now, but if he knew it was "those Fortune boys," he would be certain they were up to no good.

By now the boat was alongside the face of the float and Tom was raining in equipment and supplies. He might have been more cautious if he had been using his own judgment, but he was following Jack's orders with passionate energy.

The sound of things thudding and rattling into the boat made up the policeman's mind. "Keep your hands off that loot!" he bellowed. "Stay where you are or I'll shoot you full of holes!" They heard his heavy feet galloping on the hollow planking.

"What'll we do?" Tom asked, still dumping in supplies.

"Get in! We'll take what we have!"

As Tom scrambled on top of the gear on the forward thwart, they heard the policeman's feet clattering on the rungs of the ladder. Jack took a final look to see what he could salvage in the last moment. But Tom had done a good job; the edge of the float was swept clean except for a can of paint and the twenty-two rifle. Jack snatched them on board as the patrolman came thundering across the float. As he shoved off, he saw a big foot reach out to catch the stern. He started to strike at it with the butt of the rifle, but the momentum of the boat carried them safely past the float, with the locker shed screening them from the law.

"Close shave!" Tom whispered.

His brother didn't say anything immediately. They were free, with everything on board, but nothing in its right place; food and clothing and gear were all tangled together. They couldn't sail; they couldn't even row until they unearthed the oars and oarlocks; and they could hear the patrolman rattling in a locker, getting out oars to give chase.

"Try to find the oarlocks."

"That's what I'm doing." Tom was groping underneath their gear. "They're in the bottom, somewhere."

Jack had dragged two oars from under the mast and sail, and was feeling for oarlocks in his end of the boat—and finding almost everything else.

"Tide's going to carry us under the dock," Tom said.

The piling of Ben Holladay's dock was looming up ahead

[161]

and above them. Jack saw it was already too late to miss it, but he tried steering around it with one of the oars. Then he changed his mind and decided to go under; he paddled with the oar to get there faster. "Maybe we can lose him in there." They heard the rumble and splash of a boat being launched as they glided into the shadowy world under the dock, like sailing between avenues of trees in a flooded forest at night.

Sometimes the pilings were so close-set that they propelled the boat by pushing against the slimy columns with their hands, and sometimes they paddled with the oars; there was never room to row. At times they had to work along a wall of close-set piling until they found a gap wide enough to let them through. When they paused to listen, there was no sound of pursuit; presently they heard horses' hoofs and the rattle of wheels overhead. They were a long way beyond Holladay's dock, under one of the streets of town.

"He'll never find us here," Jack said. "I'll light the lantern and we'll get straightened out, then head for the open."

"I just dumped things in; I'm sorry about the oarlocks."

Jack told him, "You did fine. I expected to lose half our stuff and we didn't leave a thing." He lit the lantern, which showed them in a world of slimy pilings and black water; Tom made the painter fast to one of the piles and with the aid of the light they found the oarlocks and the other pair of oars. They stowed their supplies in the bottom of the boat and covered them with the tarpaulin. On second thought, Jack took out the rifle and leaned it againt the stern sheets, and broke out a box of cartridges, which he put in his pocket. "Just in case," he said.

Tom nodded wisely.

Jack shipped the rudder, and flashed the bull's-eye lantern on the high planking overhead. "There's room to step the mast," he decided. "We want to be ready to sail when we hit open water." Together they stepped the mast and Tom set up the forestay while his brother rove the mainsheet. When they were through they had a well-stowed boat, with oars and sail where they could use them.

They cast off from the piling and in the dark began working their way toward the open river. They heard sounds of fiddling and dancing feet over their heads, and in one place there was a sudden milling hum of voices and one loud voice shouting, "This is on the house, boys!"

As they went on, pushing their way past black slippery piling, Jack remembered, "We used to say we were going to have a look at the underside of town at night."

"Yep. Like Jean Valjean in the sewers of Paris."

That reminded Jack of another danger. "Maybe we ought to put on our sou'westers, Tom; you can't tell what minute somebody's going to crap on our heads!"

They passed under more dance halls and saloons, and sounds of human activity which they did not identify, and once they stopped for a sound like the creaking of hinges; there was a churning crash in the water ahead of them, then a dull "bang" like the closing of a heavy door.

"What was that?" Tom asked.

"Something dropped."

A little farther on they came to a pale blur in the water. As it went by, Jack leaned over for a closer look, and decided not to turn his lantern on it.

"What was it?" There was a quaver in Tom's voice.

"Piece of paper." It might have been that, but it looked more like the face of a man, with his throat cut.

That was the underside of town, which people were never supposed to see; particularly not nice boys who should be asleep in their comfortable beds in the tall white house, with their God-fearing parents snoring across the hall, and their troubled little sister asleep in her high bed, with her doll's sad monkey face on the pillow beside her. The boys were asleep there and this was a dream. Let us rise up in our sleep and go to the underside of the town, under the saloons and whorehouses, where, under the water— Never mind; it was a piece of paper in a dream. . . .

"*Jack, there's a boat coming!*"

They stopped, holding to slimy piling in the dark, and heard nothing. Then they heard the dip of oars. A hundred yards away a bull's-eye lantern was flashed under the piling from a boat. They were already too close to chance a dash for the open. "We'll go back, underneath, until they're past."

"N-not—where we were?"

Jack didn't want to go there any more than Tom did. "No, off that way."

They turned the *Dragon* through a gap and angled away through the flooded dead forest of piling, pushing past somber columns, sometimes with the oars and sometimes with their hands. When they paused for a moment, they heard the swift puffing of a steam launch, racing downstream. There was no telling if it had anything to do with the search for them, and its noise drowned out any sound of pursuing oars. They were startled into motion again by the sound of a fish jumping near their boat, and they passed under the muffled thunder of a saloon. Ahead of them a pelting shower began and ceased suddenly; as they went through its area, they heard the clink of floating bottles against the side of the boat. After that the wake of the steam launch swept among the piling with heavy flapping sounds, like a flock of big birds caught under the docks and trying to find their way out. The *Dragon* stirred and lifted easily to the chop; then something went wrong and three jarring shocks ran through the boat.

"We're hitting!" Tom said.

They were, but not with the keel.

Jack shone the lantern upward and they saw the truck of the mast bump against the planking. He had forgotten about the rising tide. A little more of that would break the mast— or would hold the boat down while it filled. "We've got to get that mast down!"

Tom was already standing by the forestay, and as the chop went flapping away among the piling, Jack lifted the mast from its step; it lifted halfway, then bumped against the overhead again. He had a moment of trapped panic, then he recalled a pointer Captain Collins had given him: *You can sail a boat with a thirty-foot mast under a twenty-foot bridge if you have her heeled over far enough.* "We've got to heel her," he said; "get over to port!" He shifted his own weight in that direction until the black water almost lapped the gunwale.

"Look out!" Tom cautioned.

"She's all right." The mast bumped the overhead again, but its heel was clear of the thwart. "That was close!" he said, laying it down. "Better cover the light."

Tom started to obey, but the lantern was already under the tarpaulin in the stern. The light was coming from a square that had opened in the black planking overhead a few yards away. Suddenly a voice asked, *"What are you waiting for?"* impatiently and almost close enough to be in the boat with them.

"Somebody was after us," Jack muttered.

"The hell!" The voice was quieter and the square of light dimmed. "Did you give him the slip?"

"Sure!" he sounded almost boastful.

There followed a brief consultation, then the sharp order: "Get under, and make it quick! We can't keep him here!"

"Let's get out of here," Tom whispered.

"We can't go back!" Jack could hear the other boat behind them. They pushed ahead and stopped under the dim square. "Hold her there!" he muttered. That would keep Tom facing away; he wasn't looking up, and he didn't want Tom to look, either.

Overhead they were dragging something limp and heavy and presently the light dimmed still more. Jack glanced up to see a man's feet and legs dangling through the trap-door square.

He didn't look again until the voice cal ed, "Heads up!" The feet were almost level with his shoulders now. He opened his claspknife, reasoning there would be a rope to cut. The experience wasn't real any more. This dream under the city at night. . . . "Take his feet!" he ordered. He had a glimpse of Tom's pale face as he took the dangling feet and guided them under the forward thwart. He was scared, all right, but he was game.

The rest of the body settled quickly into the boat—into Jack's arms. It was warm, at least, and the rope was under the arms, not around the neck. He sawed through the hemp with his knife, and called, "Haul away!" To Tom he whispered, "Shove off!" As they clawed past the slippery piling the voice growled after them, "You didn't have to cut the rope!" Then the lighted square was gone.

"Let's get out of here," Tom begged; "I'm scared!" His teeth were chattering.

"You don't want to get out of here any more than I do!" Jack remembered that they had been heading away from the river; they still were. "The next gap to the left," he said; "when we see a straight track to open water, that's where we're going!"

They went on until they opened a dim avenue to the river, and turned, gratefully. They were as good as safe, none the worse for their wandering in the underworld, and the terror of the lighted trap door was gone. Jack gasped, suddenly, and Tom asked, "*What?*"

"Nothing." He had put down his hand on the head of their passenger, who was so quiet that he had forgotten him. "Listen!" he said suddenly, though he wasn't sure he had heard anything. Just then a lantern flashed abreast of them, not fifty feet away, shining upward on the planking. The light disappeared and they could hear the sound of oars against piling, pushing the boat forward. "We'll wait until they're past," he whispered.

But the boat did not go past; it stopped almost immediately and the lantern was shone upward again. In its light Jack saw an oar reach up and he heard it knock three times against the planking—at about the place where their mast had bumped as they tossed in the swell from the steam launch. "Shove off! We're getting out of here!"

They fled down the dim avenue, pursued by fear, and carrying fear with them in the form of a body lying under the thwarts of their boat. Halfway to open water they heard an uproar of curses in the dark forest behind them, and they rushed on, sacrificing caution to speed, thrusting the slimy black pilings away from them with stabbing oars.

The wide river had been there all the time, and it was strangely indifferent to the miracle of their getting back on it. The river went on about its business, and the night wind went on about its business, as the boys stepped the mast with desperate haste. The river had not noticed when they had gone away, or that they had come back to the comfort of its wide, impartial flood.

"What's your hurry, boys?"

Jack looked up, violently, and saw the bearded face and the shoulders of a man, twenty feet away, leaning from the window of a house at the edge of the dock. A little farther away he heard the thrust of oars against piling; he forgot the man in the window as suddenly as he had become aware of him, because there was no time to answer.

He hoisted the sail and stumbled aft, stepping on their passenger in his haste, put up the helm and let the sail draw. The *Dragon* came to life and gathered speed, but not enough. He let out more sheet, bringing the wind on the quarter, and headed diagonally out into the wide darkness of the river.

"Should I row?" Tom asked from his thwart.

"Not yet; they might hear us." They were sailing almost

silently, and they might lose their pursuers out there in the dark.

"Where we heading?" Tom wanted to know.

"Up the river." That was where they had planned to go, and there was even more need for going there now. "We have the police and crimps on our trail, besides the old man."

"Guess they're after the man we got."

"Sure; that's why I was in a hurry to get out of there!"

"Guess they're pretty mad!"

"You bet; they'll lose a hundred and fifty dollars blood money."

"If they don't catch us," Tom said.

"They're not going to catch us!"

Like an echo, a voice came to them over the water: "*What's your hurry, boys?*" The idiot was still calling after them! No, he was calling to a boat that had just appeared from under the dock.

"They're coming!" Tom whispered.

"Not yet." The boat was lying to—a dark-painted boat with two men at the oars, and a third standing in the stern; maybe talking to the man at the window. Never mind. Come on, *Dragon*, faster. . . .

After a minute Tom said, "They're coming now!"

Jack could hear the creak of oarlocks and the pull of oars in the water. The boat was heading out toward them, a little upstream, as if it planned to head them off; and it was moving fast. "Start rowing!"

Tom's oars leaped into the locks and he began to row desperately.

"Don't wear yourself out," Jack warned.

"I won't!" He continued to row prodigiously and the *Dragon* flew over the dark water, under urge of sail and oars. It seemed to Jack that nothing could keep up with them, but when he looked back the other boat was foaming after, close enough now for him to see its bow wave as it burst through the chop.

"They're gaining!" Tom panted.

"They can't keep it up, and we can sail all night." But Tom couldn't row all night, and even with his efforts they were being overhauled. "You take the tiller—I'll row awhile."

"No, Jack. You sail her better'n I do."

Jack tried to justify the compliment by getting more speed out of the boat: shifting his weight, shifting the tiller a little, and trimming in the sheet. She seemed to sail a shade faster with the wind more on the beam, but that spoiled it for rowing, and Tom caught a crab and almost lost an oar.

As he squared away again, a voice bellowed from the pursuing boat, "*Ahoy, there! We want to talk to you!*"

"Don't answer," Jack said.

"*Ahoy, there! Lay to!*"

The only answer was a groan from their passenger, who stirred under the thwarts, and was quiet again.

"*Lay to or we'll shoot!*" The boat was foaming after them, less than fifty yards away in the half-dark of the river. Probably the rowers were getting winded by the furious pace and they wanted to have it over with. It was their first admission of weakness. But Tom was weakening, too, judging by his sobbing breath. "Ship your oars," Jack ordered.

Tom shipped them obediently, but his voice protested. "We're not stopping—"

"You sail her. I'll row; I'm fresh."

Tom saw the sense of it and they changed places quickly.

"Keep the wind a little on the quarter, so you won't jibe." As the older boy took up the oars, there was a flash of light astern; something whined past, well off to port, and an instant later a pistol banged.

"They couldn't hit a barn door!"

There was another flash, and a bullet whizzed close overhead and popped through the taut sail—so close that they ducked, too late for usefulness, as the pistol banged.

"Almost hit me!" Tom said.

"Get down in the boat!" his brother ordered. "You can reach the tiller." The bastards! he thought, the God-damned bastards! They almost killed Tom! If I could get at them! If I could get into their boat with a knife, I'd cut them to pieces, and keep on cutting, even if I was shot full of holes! He took out some of his rage in furious rowing, and this time he ducked as the pistol flashed. The bullet whined past, high and to starboard. He ducked for the second flash and heard the bullet skipping over the water, low and still to starboard. Two shots each time—they were using a derringer, not much of a weapon, but they had almost killed Tom, and the next chance bullet might do it. The God-damned crimps! The bastards, the bastards!

As he rowed, furiously, with clenched teeth, his eyes fell on the twenty-two, sticking up from the side of the stern sheets, black against the gray-black water; he remembered, ages ago, an inexperienced boy putting a box of cartridges in his pocket, "just in case." He shipped the oars, found the box, tore it open and dumped the cartridges loose in his pocket. As he scrambled down beside his brother and reached for the rifle, there was another flash astern and the bullet whanged by and through the sail, close overhead. He had been up there a few seconds ago! And they had almost killed Tom. The bastards! The bastards!

He rested one arm on the stern sheets, aimed at the pursuing hull, above the foaming bow wave, and pressed the trigger. "Crack!" The feeble report of the rifle understated his rage, but he felt some satisfaction at the sound of the small bullet plunking into wood, and the whiff of powder smoke inspired him. He began shooting as fast as he could load and pull the trigger. The bastards! The bastards! It took time to reload between shots, but he thought of himself as pouring a hail of lead into the pursuing boat. Through the sound of firing he heard a shout of rage and then the other boat was falling astern. The crimps had stopped rowing, but the one with the derringer was standing up to shoot again. He ducked at the flash of Jack's rifle, and answered with two shots that skipped into oblivion before they reached the boat.

"Out of range!" Jack reported. "We've fought them off!" As he reloaded, he noticed that the barrel of the rifle was almost hot to the touch of his hand. The warmth went through him and brought a glow of satisfaction. "We've done it!" he said. "We fought them off! They're turning back! They couldn't stand up to that hail of lead! Feel how hot the barrel is!"

Tom put his hand on the rifle. "Sure is hot! The smoke was thick down here! That's how I kept the wind on the quarter—watching the smoke. I was scared to death I was going to jibe, but the smoke showed the way the wind was blowing."

During the battle they had been huddled together in the stern, but they had been facing in opposite directions and had different stories to tell.

While they were talking, Jack thought of their passenger, who was the cause of their adventure. "We ought to have a look at him."

"Guess so," Tom said, "but I wish it was daylight. I hope he's alive."

Jack uncovered the lantern and shone it under the thwart, on the curly head and relaxed face of a young man in sailor's clothes. He was sleeping heavily and he didn't show any signs of injury.

"Will he wake up?" Tom whispered, though he hoped that wouldn't happen until daylight.

"Sure, he'll wake up."

"What's the matter?"

"Knockout drops. He'll be all right when he sleeps it off."

"Put a blanket over him."

"Sure; we don't want him catching pneumonia. Better put one over yourself, too; you're shivering."

When they had tucked their passenger in, Tom wasn't afraid of him any more. "He's nice-looking; hope he'll be all right in the morning." He got a blanket for himself and curled up in the bottom of the boat, beside his brother at the tiller. "I'm not sleepy," he said, "but it's good to be under cover. I'll rest awhile, then take my trick at the helm." He was asleep in a minute, with his head against his brother's knee.

Jack was wide awake, glowing with the excitement of having fought a naval engagement and steadied by the responsibility of sailing the town out of sight around Tongue Point before daylight and the end of the flood. He drove the *Flying Dragon* on through the wide darkness of the river, watching over the sleeping and the drugged.

11

ALBERT HEDGES decided that they must be off Cape Horn: the foc'sle was miserably wet and cold, waves tossed the ship as if it were a little boat, and all hands had been called a minute after he fell into his bunk. If he didn't get into his sea boots and oilskins pretty quick, the mate would drag him out. He had seen Tommy Wentworth in the spare bunk in the carpenter's shop, dying of a beating Martin had given him. Mustn't let anything like that happen. He told himself that, but did nothing about it, unable to make headway against overwhelming sleep. He had thought Cape Horn was past; after that the tropics, then cooler weather. And hadn't they towed into the Columbia River and anchored off Astoria? He remembered thinking about a girl named Emily Pearson, who had tried to save him long ago. He was looking at houses along the river front and white houses on the darkening hill, wondering which one she lived in. That must have been a dream. . . .

He half woke again, with cold water striking his face.

That wasn't a dream about Astoria. They had towed opposite the town at sunset, with a flock of four-oared boats racing to be first alongside, fighting to be first at the ladder. Before the anchor was let go, the runners were climbing on board— sportily dressed men with hard derby hats and hard faces and flashing jewelry. They greeted the crew with handshakes and backslapping and cries of "God love you, boy!" and even embraces. They opened whiskey bottles and thrust cigars and boarding-house cards into the sailors' hands, and exhibited French post cards.

Albert fled the welcome and took refuge in his bunk, but almost immediately the foc'sle was filled with his shipmates and with runners who helped rope their sea chests. To those who still hesitated they promised lodgings and food fit for captains, women of marvelous skill, and a bulldog fight in the back room of the Fallen Angel Saloon. Albert closed his mind to all inducements and his hands to all bribes. "I'm not a sailor," he told the runners. "I was shanghaied once, and I don't aim to let it happen again!"

They gave him up and the foc'sle was empty except for Albert and the poor litter of belongings left by his shipmates. He stayed where he was until he heard the bump of the last sea chest being lowered over the side. After that he hid three dollars in his shoes and he did not venture out of the foc'sle for some time.

He was frightened by what had happened to him, and what might happen. A year ago he had stepped out of the safe, comfortable world, and since then he had had glimpses of it but had never been able to get back. His watch mate, Roth, had told him about the time he made three voyages out of the Columbia, with three hours of liberty in between. Each time he had gone ashore for some fun—and woke up in an outward-bound ship. If Albert wasn't careful, that could happen to him.

He had been careful, but now he was in the foc'sle of a ship off Cape Horn. How did it happen?

After the boardinghouse runners had gone, the lawyer came on board and called Albert by name and asked him if he wasn't the young man who had been shanghaied. Albert told him he was, and the lawyer said, "Thank God, I got here in time! You're not safe alone, and you know how much help you could expect from aft!"

Albert knew, never having got anything but abuse from that quarter of the ship.

The lawyer told him, "I shouldn't be surprised if they

came back to take you by force, but we're going to give them a surprise!" He touched the leather portfolio under his arm. "With the evidence I have now, and with what you can tell me, we're going to put certain crimps behind the bars!"

When they were in the boat, going ashore, the lawyer asked Albert if he had a revolver. Albert didn't. "It's only a chance that we might meet the runners," the lawyer said. "If they try to bother us, I have an old derringer that will make them regret it!"

He was disappointed at first by the lawyer's office. It was on the water front, and by the sound of it, next door to a saloon; but he decided that a lawyer who looked out for the welfare of sailors couldn't afford expensive quarters.

They sat on opposite sides of a table, and the lawyer made notes while asking endless questions. When Albert's throat got dry, the lawyer poured each of them a glass of ginger beer. Albert finished his without thinking about it, then he noticed that his friend hadn't started. The lawyer reached for his glass, and asked, "Are you sure you could identify Dirk in court?"

Albert said drowsily, "Yes, sir; he has a big white moustache, like this——" The table and the lawyer opposite him and the shabby room were like a reflection in calm water with something happening to it, distorting reflections. . . .

Now he was in a ship off Cape Horn; all hands had been called, and he wasn't able to stir from his bunk because of overwhelming sleep. He opened his eyes, with cold water dashing in his face. It was dark, but he had the feeling of being outdoors, and the water was fresh and sweet.

A voice near him said, "Don't let her jibe!"

He managed to raise his head, then he tried to sit up.

"Keep down! Do you want your head knocked off?" The voice was emphasized by an appalling crash of thunder.

Albert did not want his head knocked off; he lay still, with

[175]

his mind clearing a little. He was not in the foc'sle of a ship, but in a small boat running in a rough sea, with rain dashing down on him. He had been shanghaied, but he was still in the crimp's boat being taken out to a ship, and they were in a heavy squall. When he had raised his head he got the impression of being close to land, and now he could hear waves dashing against the shore. If he could wake up enough to jump overboard— There was another crash of thunder, and lightning blasted through the watery clouds. He raised his head a little and saw the loom of forested land against the sky, almost overhead.

The boat must have been driven off its course by the squall; it was close in, running parallel with the shore. Any time now he could throw himself overboard. But when he tried, his arms and legs were like rubber. He lay still, trying to gather strength.

His captors were talking in youthful voices. One of them said, "It's taking a chance, but we can't let him get pneumonia. Where is the light?"

"It looked about two hundred yards ahead, but I don't see it now."

"Think it was a house?"

"Maybe. It was like a doorway, only it closed down from the top and one side, and the light was gone."

"You're not thinking of the trap door, are you?"

"No."

"How is our passenger?"

One of them leaned over Albert. "Asleep again."

"I thought he was dead when they lowered him down."

"So did I. What would we have done with him?"

"Dumped him into the river. We couldn't afford to go back and get caught."

With his eyes closed, Albert decided to steer a middle course between having his head knocked off and appearing too lifeless.

There was a rolling crash of thunder, and through his eyelids Albert saw a glare of lightning.

"There's a house!"

"I didn't see it this time."

"It was dark, but it's shelter."

"Think we can make it?"

"We'll try. I'll steer in close; there must be a landing."

The sound of waves on the shore grew louder. One of the voices shouted above it, "I don't see anything yet!"

"We have to take a chance! Be ready to jump."

"There's a boat on shore!"

"Good! We've found the landing!"

Their own boat grounded with a sliding rush that Albert felt through thin planking. He heard the splashes of the crew going overboard; a sea knocked the boat broadside, then it was pulled farther up the shore.

"That's the best we can do until we get the passenger out!"

A hand pulled at Albert's collar. "Rise and shine; you can't stay here and get pneumonia!"

The wet blanket was pulled from over and around him and he sat up unsteadily in a black deluge of rain.

"Can you walk?"

"I can walk." Albert stumbled to his feet and stood wavering, supported from each side.

"All right, step out!" With their help he stepped over the gunwale into water halfway to his knees, and then he was led ashore and left there.

Albert was at the crimps' rendezvous, wherever that might be. He didn't see anything but the black land in the rain, and blacker shapes around him, like enormous birds that had crept up out of the troubled river—birds as big as boats, with stubby tails and long raised necks with little heads. Beyond them in the darkness there was something with fire in it: a few dim cracks of light and, above, a long strip of half-luminous smoke rising evilly.

His captors were grunting as they pulled at the boat. This was his chance to escape! But he only stood there on his unsteady legs, with his teeth chattering loudly. He didn't want to escape into the wet brush to shiver to death, and he was afraid of the evil, smoking place ahead of him.

"Looks like the banked fires of hell." His captors had come up from the river and were standing one on each side of him. "Come on, we have to get you warm."

As they took him by the arms, thunder crashed around them and there was a wild gush of lightning. The smoking place leaped into sight before them as plain as day: A low weathered building as long as a barn, windowless, with smoke boiling up the whole length of its ridge pole.

"There's a door!"

Albert was led to where there was a slash of smoky light. One of his captors banged on the wall and started back at the appalling uproar that answered him—like the sound of a thousand dogs all going mad at once.

On his first sight of the building, Albert wondered if it was a place where he was going to be burned to death; now it appeared that he might be fed to savage animals.

At first there was only the dogs' uproar; then there were shrill and guttural voices scolding them. They quieted a little; a curtain was drawn aside and an Indian face looked out. *"Klahowya!"*

"Klahowya!" one of the captors answered. "We got caught in the storm. This man is nearly drowned."

"Come in." The Indian drew the curtain farther aside. *"Hyas piah. Hyas muckamuck.* We fix him."

They stepped out of the cold driven rain into warmth thick enough to swim in: suffocating smoke packed with the smells of fish, animals, human beings and earth. It vibrated with the fierce barking of dogs and the shouting of Indians;

it flickered with shadows and the hot murky light of fires that made Albert think the whole place was about to burst into flames.

The fires burned in a trench down the center of the narrow, endless room. There was a double deck of bunks on each side, and through smoke the firelight touched on disturbed sleepers sitting up in the bunks—naked and half-naked men and children and women, and furiously barking dogs with glaring eyes. The place looked like the foc'sle of a burning ship on some mad voyage, and outside there was thunder and rain and the dash of waves. It seemed to Albert that the wild, firelit voyagers were rising and falling and reeling with the motion of a ship. Indians were crowding around him, and he felt ill with only smoke to breathe and no rain dashing in his face to keep him awake. He caught the edge of a bunk to steady himself.

"He's had knockout drops," one of his captors explained. "Better put him to bed."

Albert resisted feebly as the Indians unlaced his shoes and unbuttoned his wet clothes, but they paid no attention. *"Hyak!"* they ordered him. *"Marsh nika shoes."* He heard the clink of his last hidden dollars as his shoes were "marched" away.

"Marsh nika yuteskut!" A squatty Indian with a lined face stripped off Albert's coat, and it was whisked away.

"Marsh nika shut!" As his shirt was being pulled off over his resisting head the air shook with a crash of thunder. Albert started violently.

"Hiyu Sahilee skookum wawa!"

The shirt came off over his head, and he saw dim Indian faces laughing at him through the smoke and murky firelight as "heaven's strong talk" died away.

"Marsh nika sakulex!" His trousers were stripped off and carried away; he shivered in his wet red underwear, steadying himself against the edge of a bunk, with pictures reeling

[179]

around him through the smoke: broad Indian faces smiling at him; his young captors, heartlessly happy, visiting with Indian boys beside a fire; firelight flickering on half-naked wild voyagers looking out from their bunks, restraining furious dogs; a hand holding an evil-looking glass of liquor in front of him.

"*Muckamuck lum.* This fix you up!"

The glass was being held to Albert's lips; he knocked it away violently and heard it rolling on the earth floor. The Indian who had taken his coat looked at him sternly. "*Anah, nawitka mika halo shem?*"

Albert was not ashamed of himself for guarding against knockout drops, and the undressing went on.

"*Marsh nika keekwilly sakulex!*" His drawers were hauled off.

"*Marsh nika keekwilly shut!*" His undershirt was hauled off over his head, and a stout woman with a withered face began rubbing him down with a sack. He climbed into the bunk with unsteady haste and pulled an old blanket over himself. The woman brought another blanket and spread it over him, then went away. He stopped shivering and was drowsily warm.

From the bunk Albert looked up at rows of black bottle-shaped things hanging from poles near the ceiling; salmon, probably, curing in the smoke. Practical, living in the smoke house and being warmed by its fires, but how did they keep from being cured like a fish? He closed his smoke-stung eyes, and half-opened them in the shadow of one of his captors.

"How are you feeling now?"

"Sleepy," Albert murmured. He was going to appear drowsier than he was until he could work out some plan of escape.

"Have a good sleep; you'll be all right in the morning."

The place was quieting down and the sound of thunder was going away in the distance. When everyone was asleep, he might be able to slip away and steal a boat—if he could find his clothes. He raised his head with great effort, but the firelight and smoke balanced each other; he couldn't see anything but a dog's eyes glaring watchfully from the bunk opposite him, and his captors sitting beside a fire, examining fishing tackle with two Indian boys. His captors looked like boys themselves. When he got back to civilization—if he ever did—he would have to make them a little older than they appeared. Not much more than boys, and they had talked brazenly about knockout drops and dumping him into the river, and one of them had told him to "have a good sleep." That was what they wanted him to do; he had to stay alert and plan his escape.

He woke with fleas biting him violently. The long windowless hall was still in a twilight of smoke, but he saw daylight and a glimpse of blue sky through the open ridge of the building. He had slept all night, but he was awake and alert now, and the building no longer seemed ominous. The dogs had disappeared and most of the bunks were empty. At the far end of the room the smoky sunlight touched on a group of old Indian men and squaws sitting peacefully around the fire, and a squatty woman in red calico was working at the fire opposite him.

When the woman saw him sitting up, she waddled over to him, with her wrinkled broad face smiling. "*Klahowya!* You had *hiyu moosum. Spose* you *muckamuck?*"

He made the motion of dressing. "I want my clothes."

"*Nawitka,*" she agreed, and went away.

There was no sign of his captors; inside the building everything was safe and peaceful except for the smoke and overpowering smells, and the biting of fleas. He was fighting them when the old woman came back with his clothes. She handed him his underwear, which was warm and dry and pungent with smoke. "*Hiyu dly.*" His socks and shirt were also *hiyu dly* from the same smoky fire, but his trousers and

[181]

coat were *tenas pahtl chuck*. The shoes were also a little wet, and the silver dollars were gone, as he knew they would be.

When he had dressed, and combed his tangled curls with his fingers, he glanced casually toward the door curtain. There was no one to stop him, and he strolled in that direction.

"*Muckamuck* now!" the old woman called from beside the fire; her voice was friendly and persuasive, and he was hungry. As he was hesitating, he put his hands in his pockets and felt his missing dollars.

The discovery decided him; he went back to the fire where he sat on a mat of woven rushes and ate from half a broiled salmon on a slanting rack of twigs. He tried another dish, which proved to be huckleberries floating in fish oil, and he ate more of the salmon to take away the awful taste. When that did not do it, he accepted *kaupee*, which the woman poured from a black pot into an old-fashioned willow-ware cup. The cup, she made him understand, had been a wedding present to the daughter of Comcomly, who was a *hyas tyee*.

Albert felt that he was being treated well for a shanghaied sailor, and when he could not *muckamuck* any more, he got up and strolled to the unguarded door.

Outside, the world changed to clean air and sunshine on the little clearing and on the broad Columbia. The only ominous thing in sight was a three-masted ship being towed by in the distance. On his side of the river there was no sign of the crimps' boat; only a graceful dugout canoe with a high, forward-slanting stem that ended in a carved figurehead. Last night, in the dark, he had seen more canoes, and to his drugged mind they had looked like sea monsters that had crept up out of the storm. But there was nothing sinister about the beautiful remaining canoe. It had been bailed out since the storm and, like a miracle, there were paddles in it.

[182]

If he could get it into the water, the Indians in the long house would have no way of pursuing him.

The canoe was pulled up on a grassy shelf of land, still wet from the thunderstorm, and the shelf was separated from the river by only a few yards of muddy beach. The ticklish step would be getting the canoe down from the shelf of land without splitting some cross-grained part. Better shove it along until it was almost balanced, then go round to the stern and ease it down.

No one was in sight. Here's your chance for freedom, Albert! He shoved at the black bow and the canoe started smoothly toward the river. It had a beautiful light hollow feeling; it must be almost on the balance now—

"*Kopet!*" a voice shouted close behind him. "I help you!"

Albert stopped, and the Indian came up to him: a short bowlegged man in dirty jeans and hickory shirt and black felt hat. "It break," he said mildly, indicating the canoe.

"I know." Albert felt ashamed of trying to steal a canoe from anyone so reasonable. He hadn't been stealing a canoe —he was trying to escape from a nightmare of captivity on sea and land.

"You *klatawa* now?" the Indian asked.

"Yes." Then Albert asked, "Where can I go?"

"*Spose* you take steamboat?"

Albert remembered his voyage on the *Thompson*; but a steamboat was the only way back to civilization. "Where?"

The man indicated the wooded point to the north. "Steamboat landing. *Potter* come soon."

"All right," Albert said.

Together they carried the canoe down to the river and launched it, and together they paddled north.

Albert's relationship with the Indians was still undefined, but so far they had treated him well. He felt quite comfortable, wielding the bow paddle and talking to the Indian behind him. "What tribe?" he asked.

"Chinook," the Indian told him, "not enough to fill *oleman house*. The others—Clatsop, Calipooia, Cowlitz, Multnomah—*ahnkutty* people; all come here in *waum illihee* for salmon." Then, as if Albert might think him uncivilized, he explained, "My papa and mamma had white-man house at Chinook. White *tyees* at Fort Vancouver send Captain Grant to mama and papa when he has snakes: too much *lum*. You *kumtux* Captain Grant?"

Albert didn't know Captain Grant.

"No *kumtux*?" The Indian was surprised.

"Bye-m-bye he *hyas tyee* in Washington."

Albert only half heard him, thinking about his white captors of the night before, and wondering if they would be at the steamboat landing with other runners and other shanghaied men. Casually he asked, "Where did the white men go, the ones who brought me?"

"Those boys? *Klonass*. They go after *hiyu wind* before *sun chahco*."

They rounded the point and came to a salmon cannery, where they stopped beside a float. When Albert got out he was still ashamed because he had tried to steal the canoe that was waiting to take him to civilization. He gave the Indian one of his dollars. "You were mighty kind to me."

The Indian smiled at him. "Remember *oleman house*: Chinook, Clatsop, Calipooia, Cowlitz, Multnomah; long time *skookum* tribes—enemies. Now"—he made the gesture of holding them all in one cupped hand—"brothers."

When Albert had climbed to the dock, he saw the Indian paddling away without looking back; in the distance a white side-wheel steamer was churning up the sunlit river, standing in toward the cannery with flags flying.

The passengers waiting on the dock looked reassuring: women with children, one old man, and a pair of sweethearts holding hands. He didn't see anything of his captors of the night before, or anyone who looked like a crimp. Last night he was shanghaied, and today he was a free man! Some miracle had happened and he was back in civilization!

He looked after the Indian, paddling away around the point, with a confused tickle in his mind. White men had drugged and robbed him and sold him into slavery, where he was starved and kicked. The Indians had given him shelter and warmth and food; they had dried his clothes and returned his money and brought him back to civilization. Or had they? His fleas began biting again, and he forgot it. Then he forgot the fleas as he was swept by the full realization of his freedom.

12

THERE WAS A BREEZE blowing up the river; they had sailed all night, but it was not night now. The land was still dark and asleep, but the sky was beginning to waken in the east and the river was growing light in answer to the sky. There were no islands in the river ahead, and this time when the boys stopped they would have to lie up in sight of traffic on the river. It seemed as safe as hiding on islands, and maybe safer, because if They had any sense they would look in places like islands, but they couldn't examine every yard of bank on each side of the river, which was still a mile wide.

The brothers had been on the river ten days, and the vague pursuing They weren't very real any more. There hadn't been anything to suggest that a search was going on, and their surprise passenger wouldn't be any help in one. The boys had gone on as soon as the storm went down, and left him with the Indians, sleeping off his knockout drops. But Jack thought it likely that their father would be looking for them, or have other people doing it. There was danger in the fact that there didn't seem to be any danger. Yesterday they hadn't been as cautious as the day before, and today they would be tempted to take more chances than they had yesterday. Too much of that could lead them into a trap.

Tom was asleep in his blanket in the bottom of the boat, while Jack sailed. He was sailing close to shore because there was least current there and he could keep on longer that way; when it grew too light for safety, it wouldn't take more than a few minutes to find a camping place in a cove or where they could pull the boat up under the overhanging branches of a tree.

Even when he passed up a possible hiding place, Jack kept it in mind until he saw another. There was always the chance of coming in sight of a steamboat landing and having to drop back downriver. The boys had reaoned that every steamboat running between Astoria and Portland had eyes that were looking out for their boat. By the same token, settlements around steamboat landings were also their enemies; they never passed one except in the dark of night.

There was a passable hideout a hundred yards astern and, by the looks of it, a cove just ahead. Jack was sailing the *Dragon* delicately in the chill of early dawn, getting all he could out of her until the last minute when he settled on the stopping place for the day. Probably he would pass the cove, too, and push on in hope of finding the perfect arrangement of shore waiting for them: one where they could build a fire far enough away so it wouldn't call attention to their boat, and a good place to fish and swim, and to lie in the sun afterward.

They had learned things on the river that they hadn't had to talk about to each other and they couldn't have communicated to anyone else: the river had received them when they trusted themselves to it; it had accepted them as something to work on, and had started immediately to educate and change them—fitting them for the life they had chosen, changing them quietly, inside and out.

At first they had to be careful when they went swimming because their bodies showed up clearly against every kind of background—they had been the wrong color for everything. Now they were the color of half-breeds, and by the end of another week they might do still better. Anyone seeing them from a distance would mistake them for Indians—maybe from closer up, too—with their straight black hair. Only yesterday Tom had tried combing his hair down over his forehead, like the boys at the fishing camp, and by making a solemn face and speaking a few words of Chinook jargon he looked and sounded like an Indian boy whom anyone would want to take home and adopt.

That was the outside. There was the inside, too. The river changed you all the way through, to the center of your thinking and to the way you thought about the river. The river wasn't just flowing water: it was that, and the great pulse of sea tides which they could still feel, sailing far inland; and it was the shores, and the sun and weather, and the stars that came out at night and stood still above the moving river or wheeled slowly over the black forest against the sky. The river was those things and many more, and altogether it was still more; it was a wise and living world, changing and shaping you so you would be fit to live in that world.

There were no books or newspapers or speeches or sermons, but the river was talking to you all the time, in the steady or changing pressure and direction of a breeze, in the sound of flowing water, in the warmth or coolness of the air. When there was a change in one of these, it was like the tone of a voice changing to tell you to get ready for something else. If you failed to understand the quiet warning, the weather might lose its temper and fly at you in a squall, or bellow at you in a voice of thunder. Maybe you got a wetting or a beating, but when you had lived through your punishment the river was kind again. The wind and waves went down, the sun came out to dry your clothes, and maybe you found that you had taken shelter in the mouth of a creek where you caught wonderful harvest trout. Or it might be a slough leading into a great island in the river: a slough that branched, and then branched again, until you were safe beyond all chance of pursuit in the heart of the island. There you might shoot a grouse, and roast him over a fire; or find little trees loaded with service berries; you could wander through beds of wild peppermint with white and purple flowers; or sleep in the warm sun—and wake to see the top-gallant masts and yards of a grain ship passing between the treetops and the sky. . . .

The cove ahead widened, disappointingly, into a marshy bight. Jack was sailing on to pass it when he opened a channel leading inland: a channel that went through the marsh, and then among alders and spruce, to disappear around an unknown bend. Gently he shifted the tiller and turned out of the river channel. The breeze followed him in, with the sail delicately full as the boat rippled past tule beds growing out of the water and beds of *wapatos* with arrow-shaped leaves. Then he was sailing past alder trees, with the ends of their branches pointed and yellow-white where they had been chiseled off by the beavers, and past dark spruce trees with some of the night still in their branches. Tom would be surprised when he woke, expecting to be on the broad river and finding the boat sailing through woods. He wished Tom were awake to help him wonder what they would find around the unexplored bend ahead.

The stillness of the woods was unbroken except for the light whisper of the bow wave, the careful splash of a muskrat taking to the water, and the crying of a swamp bird back in the darkness. As the boat neared the bend, there was something else—a throbbing which he felt rather than heard. Suddenly the sound was all around him, filling the slough. He put the tiller over and, as the *Dragon* came up into the breeze and glided toward shore, he stepped around his sleeping brother and let go the halliard.

Tom was suddenly awake and on his feet, helping stow the sail, and he was ready to unstep the mast as Jack let go the forestay. "Where are we?"

"In a slough," Jack told him, "east of Puget Island. There's a boat coming."

"Sounds like a tug," Tom said.

It sounded like one, but what would a tug be doing at

dawn in a lonely slough that wasn't much more than a hundred feet wide? He got out an oar and found the mud bottom and pushed the boat in toward the bank. Tom, standing in the bow, caught the overhanging branch of a spruce tree and pulled the boat in until it grounded softly. The puffing of the steamboat was everywhere now, throbbing against them and their boat and the junglelike shore behind them.

"Are we all right here?" Tom asked.

There hadn't been any choice, but Jack thought they were all right. Since they had put green paint over their white boat, it no longer stood out like a newly bandaged thumb, and the drooping branch of the spruce tree almost covered them. There was still the white sail, roughly furled in the boat. He was putting Tom's blanket over it when the straight black stem of a tug pushed into sight around the wooded point, twenty yards away. The tug came on with slow confidence: the black-painted bow and then the steady mast; the buff-colored pilothouse with a bearded face at the open window; the sooty, tall stack trailing coal smoke through the clean woods; a fireman standing on deck near the open engine-room door, big and rounded in blue dungarees and close-fitting black cap; abaft of him the low, black freeboard of the tug, and the huge towing bitts, stretching a hawser. That was why she was moving at such a stately pace. "She's towing; probably logs."

"*Look!*" Tom pointed with cautious excitement up and behind the tug. Higher than the tug's mast, a flying jibboom pushed around the wooded corner after her, then jibboom and bowsprit, with furled jibs, black clipper bow and foc's'le, and a schooner's foremast as high as the treetops. The boys looked almost straight up, with their mouths open, as the schooner revealed herself, towering up to the treetops and seeming to fill the slough.

Tom said, "Golly!"

"Golly!" Jack said. There didn't seem to be anything more to say.

The black hull of the schooner was low in the water, with a chained deck load of yellow lumber piled higher than her foc'sle head, higher than the rail of her poop deck, where the helmsman steered with shrewd smoothness, like a helmsman taking a ship along a road through the woods. A river pilot or captain was standing near him, conning the wheel: *"Port a little, port a little. Steady. Ease your wheel. Steady so!"* The schooner was almost broadside to the channel, with her bowsprit driving toward the alder and spruce trees on the other side, about to run her nose into the woods. Jack didn't see how it could be avoided, and Tom gripped his arm excitedly.

"Starboard smartly! Hard a-starboard!" The pilot did not raise his voice, but it came to the boys as clearly as the voice of someone passing in the street, and they heard the creak of tiller ropes as the wheel spun. The end of the flying jibboom grazed the branches on the other side as the schooner swung. *"Steady! Ease your wheel. Steady so!"*

The schooner was passing them now, following a mid-channel course in the straight reach leading to the river. She seemed almost close enough to touch, and there was a smell of fresh coffee from her galley. Looking after her, the boys read the name carved on her transom: *Forest Maid;* a good name for a schooner wandering through the woods with a bouquet of alder leaves caught in the end of her flying jibboom.

Jack said, "It just shows you—you're likely to meet shipping anywhere." But he still couldn't quite believe it: a schooner that almost filled the slough, with the trucks of her masts up among the treetops.

"Where do you suppose she came from?" Tom's face was full of excited surmise about smugglers' lairs and secret harbors deep in the forest.

His brother considered the deck load of lumber. "Must be a sawmill up the slough."

"Of course," Tom said. "It can't be far from here; they wouldn't have tried to get through in the dark."

That sounded reasonable, and it was hardly daylight now.

"Maybe we can find it on the chart." Jack got out the battered chart and unfolded it. "I think we're somewhere east of this island." Sailing at night in a small boat, there wasn't much chance to consult charts. Their usual method was to catch up on their navigation the next day, trying to figure out where they were and where they had sailed the night before.

The channel in question didn't open a slough for a long distance, and the other one, behind Wallace Island, did not have depth enough for anything but a small boat.

"How about this one?" Tom put his finger on a slough much farther west: a snaky, many-branched slough that looked like a plumed serpent on the chart.

"It's the only one deep enough for the schooner," Jack admitted. "Twenty-eight feet, twenty-five, twenty-seven—" Around the bend, and three-quarters of a mile inland, there was a circle with a dot in it, and the legend *STACK*. "There's your sawmill!" he said. "We're on West Slough." Beyond the sawmill, for a dozen miles, the slough traveled east in big, snaky bends plumed with branch sloughs, without an indication of settlement, and then it rejoined the river behind a group of islands. Probably some of the branch sloughs hadn't been visited since they were first charted—

Tom had the same thought. "If we were only past the sawmill!"

Maybe they could. It was just daylight now, and mills didn't start work until six. Anyway, they couldn't stay where they were, jammed against the bank of a narrow slough where there was traffic. "We'll have a look," Jack said.

"Will we try to sail?"

"That would attract too much attention. We'll row till we get to safe waters."

The schooner was out of sight now and it was safe to go on, but it was odd how clearly the puffing of the tug came to them. They pushed away from the bank and the puffing was suddenly quick and clear, coming from the wrong direction—

"It's another tug!" Tom said.

"Under cover again!"

They backed in and shipped their oars, and Tom stood up and caught the branch of the spruce tree as Jack poled the boat against the bank.

Standing beside his brother and looking through the branches, Jack said, "You'd think we were on a main ship channel!"

A kingfisher gave its shrill, unoiled cry, and flashed across the slough as the white bow of a steam launch pushed into sight around the wooded point: a straight-stemmed white bow, and the solid, intent figure of a man standing on deck in front of the pilothouse, and then the long, glass cabin with the buff smokestack coming up through it. The launch was almost as familiar to them as the man on deck.

"It's Father!" Tom whispered.

"And Peterson's steam launch!"

"What'll we do if he sees us?"

There wasn't much doubt that he would see them, from the intent way he was studying the shore. "We'll grab some food and the rifle, and take to the woods! If they all come after us, we'll circle back and steal the launch!"

"We can run it!" Tom agreed.

The launch was opposite them now, no more than twenty yards away, and their father was looking directly at them, his fiercely intent eyes meeting theirs as they peered through the cover of spruce branches.

"Get ready to run!" Jack whispered.

Then their father turned his head away to study the other shore. Through the windows of the pilothouse they saw Gundar Peterson going by, sitting on a stool at the wheel; they had a glimpse of oak woodwork and red plush cushions and the launch was past, puffing down the slough, going away through the woods. Her wake came rolling in to them, rocking their boat and chuckling against the bank.

"He looked right at us," Tom said, "and he didn't see us!"

"I thought he had us, all right!" It seemed to Jack that he hadn't breathed for several minutes, and he was panting now. "That was a close call!"

"Where do you suppose he was coming from?"

"Looking for us on the slough. Probably tied up for the night at the sawmill."

"Maybe I wasn't scared when he looked right at me! What are we going to do now?"

They couldn't stay where they were, or go back on the river where it was broad daylight, with their father looking for them.

"We have to go on," Jack decided.

"Father will have told about us at the mill."

Jack nodded. "Maybe there's a reward for our capture, but we have to chance it." He put his oars in the locks, and they listened for a minute before shoving off. There were no more sounds except for the chirring of a squirrel in the spruce tree over their heads.

"Shut up!" Tom called.

The squirrel shut up, and everything was still.

"All right." They rowed out into the slough and around the bend.

They hadn't planned any strategy for passing the enemy sawmill, but when they came in sight of the tall stack and the wharf and the smoke of buildings in a clearing, Tom had an idea. "I'll lie in the bottom of the boat; if they're on the lookout for two boys, they mightn't pay any attention to you alone. I'm not trying to get out of rowing," he explained; "but you look more like a man than I do."

Jack decided that it was worth trying. If They were watching for two runaways boys in a white boat, one figure in a green one wouldn't arouse immediate suspicion. If anything happened when he was abreast of the settlement, it wasn't far to the next bend and the network of sloughs beyond.

Tom shipped his oars and dug himself in among the equipment. "If anyone starts chasing us, tell me, and I'll help row."

"I'll tell you, all right!" Jack rowed alone, trying to cover distance without appearing to hurry. "When we get around the bend, I'm going to sleep on the groceries and let you row all day!"

"I don't mind," Tom said. His brother knew that he didn't.

The sawmill was silent and asleep, except for a dreaming breath of smoke from the stack against the sunrise sky. Keeping to the far side of the slough, Jack passed the still log pond and the deserted wharf where the *Forest Maid* would have lain the night before—probably the steam launch, too. Then he was passing a floating bunkhouse, and what seemed to be a cook shack on the land, with blue smoke coming up briskly from its stovepipe. Farther back there was a big house, hayfields, and an orchard. Something about the farm at sunrise made him think it would be a nice idea to come back when he was a rich man and buy it.

As he rowed, he edged across the slough to get the shelter of the point. There was no sign of pursuit. At the edge of the shore he passed a frail white-and-red ox that looked as if he had strayed from a bull team where he found the work too heavy for his years. Maybe the last of his strength had gone into his horns, which had a spread of five or six feet and were tipped with balls of brass. The ox stood unmoving, looking after the boat, with the morning sun flashing on his brass-tipped horns.

"All right," Jack said, "the coast is clear."

Tom sat up; there was nothing in sight but the green slough going through the woods.

The breeze still followed them; they stepped the mast again, hoisted the sail, and ghosted on contentedly.

"There was a nice farm on the hill," Jack said; "fields and an orchard and stables, and a big green house with porches. Maybe we'll come back sometime and see it." He didn't say any more. Without having seen the place, Tom wouldn't understand how he felt. And it would probably be a long time before they settled down on a farm.

Tom was steering, and a mile or so after they had passed the sawmill, he said, "There's a fork in the channel ahead. Which side shall we take?"

Jack looked at the chart and saw that it didn't matter. "They both go round an island and meet again."

Tom took the channel to the north, and before it met the one coming around from the south, it forked again. "Now which one?"

"Try the one to the left. Maybe we'll find a camping place."

The branch slough was no wider than a creek, and the breeze followed them more and more faintly until their boat stood still. It didn't matter. They were off the main channel of the slough where nobody was likely to find them, and they could stop when they felt like it.

They lowered the sail and mast, and rowed on up the creek through the woods, exploring. A few hundred yards farther on the creek forked again, and there was a narrow beach of flat pebbles, with high ground above it, and an open space under cedar trees. The morning sun was slanting down into the open space, and the flat foliage of the cedars had a rich, tropical shine, like palm trees. As the boys rested on their oars, they heard the firm splash of a fish that had jumped.

"Harvest trout!" Jack said. It was a sign that they had come to their camping place.

As soon as the boat was beached, Tom began carrying things ashore. Jack stood for a minute, looking over their kingdom for the day, trying to remember something that troubled him—something he had seen recently. Then it came to him: his father standing on the deck of the steam launch, and the fierce, anxious, hunting look on his face. He would never find them here, and from now on they would be more careful. The old man would never find them; but he felt sure that he would never stop looking for them through the creeks and sloughs and channels and islands of the great river. . . .

"When you make that face, you look like Father!" Tom was standing beside him on the narrow beach.

Jack roused himself and smiled at his brother. "We're a stubborn family," he said.

13

THE BROTHERS spent four days on the plumed serpentine channel that went east in great looping bends between the river and the steep forests of the hills. They caught harvest trout, which they fried with the delicious, moldy last of their bacon; they found huckleberry bushes so loaded with fruit that their branches were like heavy blue and purple clubs; they looked into the surprised little eyes and berry-stained mouth of a black bear that had been picking from the same bush with them; and they shot as many grouse as they needed. They also stumbled on a mystery.

Exploring deep in the big timber, they stood on a rise of ground among close-set fir trees that were six and eight feet through and a hundred feet to their first branches. The trees were like the columns of a great cathedral, with light sifting down among them slantwise, making gold light and deep shadows on the carpet of moss and on sword ferns. Trees like the ones around them were supposed to have been big enough for timber when Columbus discovered America, and by the still untouched loveliness of the place the boys might have been the first people to stand there. They were on a rise of ground at the edge of a clear little stream, and suddenly Tom pointed and said, "There's a cabin down there!"

"No," Jack said. There couldn't be a cabin; there wasn't room for one beside the stream that they could have stepped across, and it wasn't more than a dozen yards away to where it wound out of sight past a big tree. "There couldn't be a cabin!" Even before he finished speaking he saw the new cabin. It was standing at a bend of the stream: a settler's cabin with an outside chimney at one end and a window catching a gleam of light.

Suddenly Jack felt mixed up about the size of things. He and Tom were no bigger than chipmunks to the giant trees, and to him the cabin twenty feet away didn't seem any bigger than a doll's house—unless the stream was really a river and he was looking into the distance at a cabin a mile away. He stumbled along the bank, not sure whether he was trying to take two feet or a hundred yards at a step.

He and Tom reached the settler's cabin and stood over it like giants. Tom knelt in front of it, with one side of his face on the damp ground and his behind sticking out over the river. Squinting through the window, he reported, "There's nobody home!"

Jack picked up the cabin and they examined it inside and out. It was newly made of packing-case wood, with a wooden chimney and fireplace, and a small square of glass set in a hole for a window. "A doll's house!"

They looked around them, then at each other, and their puzzled eyes asked, "Where are the dolls? Where are the children who play with them?" A few minutes before they had assured each other that they were where no white man had ever walked, and maybe no Indian either. But here was a doll's house that children must have been playing with a few days ago—or maybe only a few hours. There was no trace of rust on the heads of the nails that held the boards together.

With the little house in his hands, Jack said, "You wouldn't expect children to go away and leave a new thing like this!"

"Not unless they're coming back," Tom said. "Maybe they heard us, and hid somewhere."

"They could, at that." An army could be in hiding in the woods around them, and they wouldn't see anything. The children might now be watching them from the underbrush, wondering what they were going to do with their new plaything.

Jack put the cabin back where they had found it. "We might as well move on," he said.

They went back downstream, following its bends carefully. If they lost it in such deep woods, they might never find it or anything else again. Tom was in the lead, and after they had gone a few hundred yards, he stopped in his tracks. "We're lost," he said. "We've been walking in a circle!"

"No. We came upstream and now we're going downstream."

"That's what I thought, but there's the doll's house again!" Jack was sure that it wasn't the same bend, but he was almost as sure that it was the same cabin. Two things couldn't be so much alike unless they had been turned out by a factory. "This is getting queer!" he said.

"I wouldn't touch it if I were you!"

Jack felt the same way about it, but he had to make sure they weren't traveling in a circle. After a minute of survey, he reported, "It's not the same place. We tramped all around the other one, and there are no footprints here!"

"That's good," Tom said. "Let's go on."

Jack felt a strong urge to go on, but he had to assure himself about the little house. It looked so like the other one that he had the improbable thought that someone might have carried it swiftly, roundabout, and set it there to confound them.

"Come on, Jack," Tom urged.

There was one way he could tell. The first cabin had part of a word stamped on the back: "RI—." He picked up the one before him, with an odd feeling of distaste, and looked at the back wall. It was blank, but on the end opposite the outside chimney were the letters "DL" and part of an "E." The little houses had been made from the same pattern and maybe the same packing case, but there was a difference. He put it back where he had found it. "They have different marks!"

"That's good," Tom said. "Come on!"

A hundred feet farther along they saw the little cabin again—this time on the other side of the stream. Probably it had different markings, too, but it looked uncomfortably like the others, and they didn't examine it.

They didn't feel quite comfortable until the stream led them to the branch slough where they found their boat, undisturbed.

Tom said, "If children played there, we'd have found tracks, wouldn't we?"

"You'd think so, unless it had rained since then." Even then there would have been some signs—unless the little people who played with the cabins, or lived in them, were so light and small that they left no footprints. Jack didn't believe that real children played there. In four days on the sloughs, the dolls' houses were the only sign that human beings had been there before them.

That was their last day on the lonely backwater. They didn't discuss moving on, but they remembered how good it was to be on the broad and honest river, where the trees didn't hide the sun, and where lumber and grain ships and steamboats passed in the distance.

That evening they rowed the last few miles to where the slough entered the Columbia behind the cluster of islands. It was as black as the inside of a boot when they reached the mouth of the slough, with Jack rowing and his brother on lookout. Then they were on wider waters, and ahead of them they saw the channel between the end of the big island and the little island to the east—and the starlight on the broad Columbia.

"There's our river!" Tom said.

It was like coming home, only now there was a touch of fall in the night breeze. Resting from rowing, they put on their coats and hoisted the sail. The boat heeled a little to the breeze as it pressed forward, and the bow wave took up its rippling song.

"We'll make Crims Island by midnight," Jack estimated, "and try for that deep cove on the north side."

"That's good," Tom said. "I want to camp in the middle of the river for a change!"

"You might as well get some sleep," Jack said.

Tom asked from the bottom of the boat, "Is anything flapping?" Then he was sitting up. *"Listen!"*

His brother was already listening to the sudden swift puffing of an engine—trying to remember where there was shallow water that would put a pursuing boat aground.

"There she is!" Tom said.

The lights and the shadowy hull of a steam launch slid out from behind the little island close to the east and parallel with them. Then it turned to cut across their bow. They were caught in the open, in deep water, and the launch could do three knots to their one.

"We can't make it!" Jack said, but he kept on trying until the launch was laid alongside, pressing their boat up into the wind. Then he lowered the flapping sail, and he and Tom unstepped the mast, stowing everything neatly.

"That's right," Peterson's voice said, "do a good yob!" The hearty, familiar voice eased the sting of being caught. "Now yump on board; I have the painter."

Their father was there, but he didn't say anything until he had followed them below, with the launch on its way downriver. The cabin was pleasantly warm from the boiler, and the oak woodwork and red plush cushions looked good. Jack thought how nice it would be to stretch out on one of the seats and go to sleep in the nice warm steamboat smell, but his father was paying for the boat and his father didn't seem pleased. He was looking them over from head to foot as if he were seeing if they were in condition for a thrashing. "Are you boys all right?"

They told him that they were.

His eyes were even and cold as he studied their unrepentant faces. "I suppose you know that you put me to a lot of trouble and expense."

"You didn't have to come after us," Tom said. "We were all right."

It was the kind of reply that usually led to trouble, and Jack altered the course of the conversation. "You caught us neatly," he said. "How did you know we were going to be here?"

"I suppose culprits always want to know why they weren't smart enough. You made the mistake of entering West Slough in daylight. From then on I had both ends of it watched." When that had sunk in, he said, "I could have caught you the day you were reported, but I had to decide what I was going to do with you. If you hadn't come out, I would have gone in tomorrow and brought you out." He sounded disagreeably sure of himself.

"We had a good time, anyway," Tom said boldly.

The father looked at him and at Jack. "You could pass for Siwashes! Look at your fingernails, and your hair, and your clothes!"

They hadn't seen a barber or a tailor or a laundry while they were on the river, but there had been compensations.

"You, John," the father said, "you're the older. Have you any excuse for this behavior?"

"It was something we wanted to do, and we did it."

"You did what you felt like at the moment, without trying to control yourselves, or thinking of the future?"

Their escape to the river had taken a good deal of control and planning, but it might be just as well not to remind their father of that. "It was what we wanted to do—and we didn't like the kind of future you were planning for us."

"You favor a roving life, then?"

Jack didn't like his father's tone, and his words had a stuffy, indoor sound. "We wanted to see the river."

"If you wanted to try a roving life, why didn't you consult me?"

Why not, indeed?

"You wouldn't have let us go," Tom said.

"On the contrary," his father said, "I am going to give you your fill of the roving life! It may be an expensive lesson, but it is one you will remember for the rest of your lives!"

Jack had expected an immediate thrashing, but now it appeared that his father wasn't stopping for anything so trivial. As casually as he could, he asked, "Where are we going?"

"Cape Horn, for one place. You're making a voyage in the *Christmas Morning* with my old friend, Captain Slade."

"In that hell wagon?" Tom sounded as if he didn't believe it.

Jack thought bitterly, "My old friend, Captain Slade!" From his few visits over the years, he had nothing but hatred for the harsh old man who made even the sea sound like a dry tedious place.

Tom asked, "How do you know Captain Slade will take us?"

"I made arrangements with him," the father said. "He's in Portland now, loading wheat for Liverpool; you boys will be at sea before this time next week."

It had a final sound, and the brothers looked at each other with their eyes agreeing, "Now we're in for it!" There wasn't anything to say in words, with their father standing over them.

"I'm being generous with you," he said. "Captain Slade will sign you on at eight dollars a month, and you may spend your earnings as you please; it will give you an idea of the profits of a roving life."

The launch stopped and the cabin door was opened noisily, and Captain Peterson looked in, with his face breaking into a smile when he saw everything going peacefully. "We're by the mouth of West Slough," he reported. "You want me to signal the others?"

"Two shots," Mr. Fortune said. "Listen for the answer."

Peterson went away; a gun banged twice, answered by the sound of a distant gun, and the launch started on.

When their father was through lecturing them, the boys stretched on the red plush cushions in the warmth from the boiler and the pleasant steamboat smells. It was what Jack had wanted to do when they first came on board, but now it was partly spoiled; he and Tom could never store up enough warmth and comfort to last them around Cape Horn. They had planned to go some day, of course, but they had expected it to be on their own terms, with someone like Captain Collins. He hadn't expected it to be now, when he felt so young and unprepared, and with Captain Slade, whom he had always thought of as an ogre.

When he thought of him now, starting fresh, there seemed no good reason why he should hate the old captain. Suddenly a piece of the past came back to him, with its sights and sounds and pain still alive. . . .

It was their house in San Francisco, and it must have been Sunday because his father was at home. His mother was cooking a dinner that filled the house with wonderful smells. It was an occasion because his father was now important enough for a sea captain to visit him. Jack and Tom already had dreams about ships, and they waited in happy awe for "My friend, Captain Slade." When he arrived he was just an old man in stuffy Sunday clothes, with a bald head and sharp eyes with sharp lines coming out of the corners of them, and gray chin whiskers. The children were introduced to him, then they were shooed out of the house into the yard.

It was a small house and a small yard, with one tree growing in it. It was an apple tree, and it must have been spring, because the little tree was in bloom. Their father had fussed a great deal, getting the tree to grow, and the children weren't allowed near it because they might shake off its first blossoms. Now when they had been pushed out of the house where their father was entertaining a sea captain, Jack scowled at the forbidden little tree and saw a chance for revenge. He took out his new pocketknife and hacked off one of the flowering branches. Tom looked surprised, and Marjorie began to cry. She was only a little girl, but she recognized trouble. "Hide it, hide it!" she begged.

The tree looked funny without the branch, but Jack didn't care. He felt better when he had had his revenge, and forgot that he had done anything wrong. He decided it would be interesting if the captain were to look out of the window and see apple blossoms outside. He got under the parlor window and waved the branch, with Marjorie begging him to come away and whimpering softly so the people in the house wouldn't hear her. Nothing came of the branch-waving; maybe the captain thought it was a real treetop.

He became bolder and waved the branch closer and closer to the windowpane, while Marjorie clung to his arm and sobbed over and over again, "Don't let it touch the glass, don't let it touch the glass!" He hadn't thought of doing that, but it seemed worth trying. He brushed the petals against the windowpane; a twig squeaked on glass; from inside there was the sound of someone getting up, and Marjorie gave a despairing little cry, *"Now you've done it! Run! Run!"*

He didn't start running until his father rushed out of the house, and then it was too late. Before he had made one circle of the yard, his father had him by the collar, and was shoving him toward the parlor window where he had dropped the branch. Captain Slade appeared in the yard, and he seized Tom, who was hanging onto one of the remaining branches of the tree; Jack wasn't sure whether he was trying to climb up, or break off the branch. Holding the kicking boy under one arm, Captain Slade observed, "The little devils! If I had them on board my ship, I'd trice them up by the thumbs and take a rope's end to them!"

Jack got a whipping with the butt end of the branch he had cut off, and he thought the whipping was extra hard because of the sea captain's advice. After that one of his legs swelled and he was sick, and there was a doctor, and Marjorie crept in and begged him not to die. Sometimes in his fever a face came out of the dark and looked at him: a bald-headed face with sharp eyes and sharp lines at the corners, and a goat's beard and a wide thin mouth that said, *"The little devils! If I had them on board my ship, I'd trice them up by the thumbs and take a rope's end to them!"*

Jack hadn't thought of the experience for years, and probably everyone else had forgotten it; but Captain Slade was going to have "the little devils" on board his ship at last.

14

WHEN RITA began to be conscious of life again, she reached out her arm for Roger; she couldn't remember his coming to bed, and he wasn't there now. She opened her eyes and found that it was still half dark in the room, but a pale winter daybreak was coming in over the river beyond the square gray mass of the Custom House and the sleeping bulks of houses and stores. At the edge of things, near Holladay's dock, the windmill on the Parker House stood out against the palid river like a dark sunflower.

Roger's pillow was plump and undisturbed, and she knew that she had been alone all night. Sleeping, she had known nothing, but she woke to a feeling of being cheated. One more night of life gone in aloneness. Not right. Her mind hadn't been aware, but her body had. Once she had dreamed of being cold; then her blind body would have groped for warmth and comfort, without finding it, only knowing that something was missing.

It wasn't right that there should be such waste and loss. You come into life alone and you go out of it alone, to be alone forever, and at best you are by yourself much of the rest of the time. You accept what you must; you pay the costs that eat up most of life, but you hate to see the clear profit wasted.

Roger didn't feel that way; he was a spendthrift with time. He knew, of course, that people grow old and die, or things happen to them, but it never occurred to him that he was included. The way he threw days and nights away, you'd think he was God, with his pockets full of shining centuries. He must think that he will be a gay young blade to the end of time—carrying on a love affair with the sea that is too old and wise for him now, and will be too young and unsatisfied forever after. Roger sitting up all night, writing love letters to the sea in his gray volumes; burning up his life and leaving hers to suffer alone in the cold. It wasn't that Roger didn't love her, but he loved something else more; and she didn't like to play second fiddle, nor did she like to see him slowly destroyed by a passion for something with no more body or soul or heart than water with salt in it. It was absurd that she should have to hate something like that and be jealous of it—absurd and hateful and baffling.

Downstairs, the clock struck seven. Roger had to leave in half an hour. Because she was his wife, she would have to go and see that he got out of the house properly clothed and fed. She would have to hurry and freshen up the leavings of the night, so the sea could have the best of him, and she would have to keep her temper in the wretched scramble. This evening, when there was time to talk calmly, she would try, as she had done a thousand times before, to plan some reasonable hour for his going to bed; try to save him and herself with words!

She jumped out of bed, naked, into the cold room. Her neighbors would never speak to her again if they knew that she didn't wear a ruffled nightgown, but Roger liked her to sleep this way. . . . Rita, you fool! He likes you to go to bed this way and run the risk of pneumonia—while he sits downstairs writing love things about the sea! You make a fool of yourself because you love him, but you can't expect him to love a fool. He asks you to do something, then goes away and forgets, and you go on doing it—like the boy who stood on the burning deck. That was a captain's idea, too. Only you are the girl who stood on the freezing deck. All right, go and ask him if he still wants you to sleep this way. . . .

She threw down the woolen dressing gown she was about to put on and ran downstairs.

Roger had become aware of time at last; she heard the crackling of a new fire in the kitchen range, and when she looked down into the parlor from the stairs, she saw him crouched in front of the fireplace, saving the life of the fire which he had almost let go out. It was like Roger: the fire had been keeping him warm, and he had been so absorbed in what he was doing that he had hardly given it enough attention to keep it alive; now he was trying to make amends.

He didn't hear her bare feet, or turn his head until she was in the doorway. Then he started up and stared at her, haggard and anxious, and admiring. "Rita, for God's sake, you'll freeze!"

"Does it matter?"

"Of course it matters!" There were drawn lines under his eyes, and his face was untidy with a day's growth of reddish stubble. "Get something on before you have a chill. Come over by the fire. I'll get you something." He hurried to the windows facing the street and pulled down the blinds.

She said, "The neighbors not seeing me doesn't keep me warm!"

"I know!" He came back and tried to take her in his arms to give her his belated warmth. He was stale with tobacco smoke and a sleepless night in his clothes, and she pushed him away. He looked at her, nervous and anxious. "Rita, why are you doing this?"

"It was your idea; you asked me to sleep this way!"

He looked ashamed. "I'm sorry, Rita. I meant to go to bed right after you did. Let me find you something to put on."

"If you do," she told him, "I'll throw it in the fire!"

He put more wood on the fire, which had begun to blaze

[209]

up. The room was the usual mess of scattered books and papers and spilled pipe ashes and burnt matches. It looked like a shipwreck—the shipwreck of their life. Trying to make her warm with the fire, he said again, "I do wish you would put some clothes on."

She said, "I'm this way because you asked me to be. If you asked, I suppose I'd stand naked in the yard for a statue, and freeze—and you would forget even to look out of the window at me, while you carried on with someone else—"

"Rita, that's not true!" His eyes were anxious and hurt. "You know I never look at another woman—"

"The sea is a woman, damn her! Ships are women, too! You're unfaithful to me with every ship that anchors here. Let a ship come into the river and you're unfaithful to me with your eyes, even while you're holding me!"

He assumed the usual attitude as he found himself on the familiar battle ground. "I know that I stay up too late when I get interested—but you can't make it into what it isn't. I'm a pilot and it's my business to know ships."

"It isn't your business to sit up all night, burning yourself out writing love letters to a siren and never giving me a thought!"

He tried to take her in his arms again. "Rita, that isn't so! I never think of anyone but you!"

"You never think of anyone, including me! Only the sea. The sea's a thing, and it means more to you than I do; I'm nothing but a cook and housekeeper who doesn't get paid."

Roger was hurt and bewildered again. "If you want anything you have only to ask, or buy it without asking. I don't spend anything on myself, except for a few newspapers and a book now and then—"

She interrupted. "I'm not talking about things you buy! Can I pay you to notice that I am here? Can I pay you to go to bed at night?"

"I told you I'm sorry, Rita! But I can't help being interested in my work; maybe too interested sometimes. But it isn't as if I did this every night. I go to bed oftener than I stay up."

"If you do, it's because you're too gone for sleep to stay up, lusting after ships; it isn't any compliment to me. Even when we're in the same bed, you're sleeping with the sea!"

He smiled a little and looked at her admiringly. "I'm sorry to make you mad, and it isn't that way, but you do look beautiful—like an angry goddess!"

"I'm angry, all right," she told him, "but I'm not a goddess; I'm a woman, and that doesn't interest you!"

"The hell it doesn't!" He engulfed her in a sudden surge of desire, caressing her body with fierce, persuasive skill, hurting her averted face with his harsh stubble, trying to find her mouth with his. If he did, she would be lost, and he would take her then and there in a crude, brief mockery of love that would leave her outraged and resentful all day. She twisted suddenly and wrenched herself out of his arms. "You know what time it is," she said. "For pity's sake, go look at yourself—and shave! I'll get you something to eat."

"I'll eat on board." He was panting, with his nostrils dilated, his eyes bloodshot and his drawn face smudged with its day's growth of beard. He looked like a man who has been on a drunk, and he was disappointed and ashamed. She was ashamed for him, too, and sorry for him while she was angry. She wanted him to be handsome and proud, with his cap a little on one side of his curly head, kissing her good-bye, since he had to go—remembering that they had been happy together. Instead, it had to be this wretched and humiliating scene, with Roger looking like a drunken pilferer, caught trying to steal small change when he could have had all the gold of love. No, he looked like someone fine and capable on his way downhill because of some vice or weakness. That was what came of his nights of love-making with the sea. This was what it did to him, and she would have to

[211]

save him, or die. If she didn't save him, they were both lost, anyway. She said:

"Eat on board, if you won't even give yourself time to have breakfast with me. But first go and clean up and shave and put on a clean shirt. You ought at least to look as if you had a wife!"

"I'm sorry, Rita," he told her, as he had done a thousand times before. "I'll try not to forget again." He looked ruefully around the littered room. "I have made a mess of things." Everywhere there were papers and books, open or out of place, as if he had spent the night in a wild paper chase after some elusive fact. He had been writing in all seven of his ledgers—or consulting them; the gray volumes were propped against his chair or lying flat on the carpet. "I'll put these away." Roger dropped on one knee beside the chair to gather up his ledgers.

The sight of him lifting one of the gray volumes tenderly was more than Rita's patience could bear. He hadn't really heard what she had said; he was still thinking of his trysts with the sea, and not of her. She had been wasting her breath, and nothing was settled. As if anything was ever settled with words! She snatched the book out of his hand.

"You go and shave!"

He was about to answer when he saw her look; he changed his mind and saluted her, half admiringly and half mocking, and went out of the room. She heard him in the kitchen, taking the teakettle off the range. Then he was in the hall, whistling, "A Yankee slaver came down the river. Blow, boys, blow!"

Nothing settled by words. He would be more reasonable for an evening or so—not for her sake but for her rival, whom he was protecting, and then he would go back to these damned books that linked him day and night with the sea. He would drift farther away from her while she scolded oftener and more and increased the drift. Even now, though they were in the same house, the same room, they never saw each other clearly because of the cold, misty thing that reached into their home, into his mind. He was too much under its spell to recognize it, and she fought against it with words because she didn't have the courage to cut off the gray, visible tentacles that were wrapping themselves around him. Didn't she have the courage to fight for him, to cut off even one gray tentacle? Like this?

The closed book resisted the fire stubbornly, too proud to let pain show on its face; then a tan blush began spreading, as if it were getting sunburned from the flames, and it began to burn at the edges. She stood the next book on end, with its pages open to the flames; the next she let straddle a blazing log, and the next she stood half open, like a tent among the flames. When they were all burning, she felt more at ease than she had for years. Something was settled at last, and she had had the courage to do what had to be done. She counted the burning books: seven of them. The sea had reached seven gray arms into the house and fastened them on Roger, and she had cut them off; they were all there, writhing slowly in the fire. Seven of them. Then she remembered that an octopus has eight arms. She had never seen the eighth.

When Roger came downstairs, Rita was still crouching at the fireplace, watching the burning books: the naked, pagan woman destroying knowledge. She got up as she heard his quick, confident steps in the hall, and then he was standing the doorway, shaved and refreshed and dressed to go out. His cap was a little on one side, his face was smiling and his blue eyes alight: that dash of something he could throw over himself to conceal disappointment and fatigue and doubt—the air of the pilot coming on board and making tired seafarers feel that they were in safe hands, off the headlands of a pleasant world.

"I'll see you this evening," Roger said; " 'I'll be here though a thousand mutineers—' " He broke off when he saw her face and came in and put his arms around her. Looking into her eyes, coaxingly, he told her, "Don't give up hope! We're young and able and willing, and we'll settle our problems yet!"

"One of them is settled."

"Good!" But he did not seem certain that it was good, troubled by her quiet. "Which one, Rita?"

She nodded toward the fireplace.

He let her go and went over to the fire and stood there, looking from the twisted blackness and the burning black and white to the vacant spot on the floor beside his chair.

"I burned them," she said.

"For God's sake, Rita!" He looked at her as if realizing that he had never really known her.

"I had to save you, Roger."

He didn't seem to hear her. "Ten years' work!" he said, like someone in a dream. "A complete record of shipping on the lower Columbia—"

"The river will always be there," she told him. "But we have only one life."

He said again, "For God's sake, Rita!" Then he brushed past her. At the doorway, he turned with a look of stunned wonder, as if he had never guessed her depths of folly. "*You fool!*" he said. "*You fool!*"

15

RITA STOOD behind the lace curtains, watching for the young people to come up the hill. They thought she was doing them a favor, entertaining them at dinner; and it was the other way round; they would take the chill off the house for the evening and ease the tension between Roger and herself.

Earlier in the afternoon she had had the relief of penance when she bought seven ledgers at Strauss' and carried the heavy parcel up the hill in the beginning rain. By the time she reached Franklin Street the rain was slanting and hard, and for the last block she carried the parcel under her cloak. In past times, carrying things that way, she pretended she was carrying a child. She didn't pretend any more, but the swelling line of her cloak was still becoming.

She had bought the books because Roger's stunned silence made her desperate and she had to do something. The purchase hadn't been a defeat, she told herself; it was only acknowledging that things are what they are. The next step would be to offer her help. Everything in the destroyed records must still be in Roger's head, and she would work with him writing down things as he recalled them.

She had given up hope of saving him from the labyrinth of ships and the sea; where he went wasn't as important as whether it was alone or with her. *Let me never forget this,* she prayed; *let Roger understand: let all who love understand that it is better for two who love to commit follies together than to do wise things separately.*

It was getting dusk when she saw them coming up the hill:

small, neat Emily and tall, strapping Albert Hedges under a big black umbrella that tilted to the westward to meet the rain. They looked well together, and Rita hoped that Albert's visit with Emily meant something.

Their acquaintance had been drifting along for more than a year—more than two years counting Albert's shanghaied voyage. Rita knew it wasn't Emily's fault that it had been limited mostly to the exchange of letters and a barrel of apples from the Hedges' farm in the fall. It must be Albert —dallying so long, wasting golden time when he and Emily could be happily married.

If young people could take advice, Rita would set Emily and her young man down in the parlor and make them understand that they were throwing away the best of life, and she would tell them how easy it is to attain happiness. She and Roger had come so near, that their failure showed how simple it was. With a few bits of good advice, any young couple could make a success of marriage.

She opened the door, without giving them time to ring the bell; she kissed Emily warmly and shook hands with Albert, and told them that Captain Collins wasn't home but she expected him in a little while. As Albert was helping Emily out of her long Newmarket, Rita asked, "How do you like our weather, Albert?"

He answered, "We have rain at home, too, Mrs. Collins." He hung Emily's coat on the hall stand and started taking off his own. "City people apologize for rain, as if it were their doing. On the farm we figure it's that much better for next year's wheat crop, and we let her come down!"

Rita laughed. "In town people apologize to each other for the weather and say, 'Well, it's good for the farmers.' You've no idea how much rain we put up with for your sake, Albert. I only hope it didn't spoil your afternoon."

"We didn't let it, Ma'am."

"It hardly interfered at all," Emily said. "Before the rain

we climbed to the top of Coxcomb Hill, and since then we've been to the site of the Fort, and McTavish's grave, and we called on Hope."

"You've seen her, then?"

Only two days ago there had been the surprise announcement of Hope Morris' engagement to Ed Barton. Rita still wasn't used to the idea of her marrying the coarse-grained real-estate promoter—pretty and high-spirited Hope, whom Willard could have had for the asking. But Willard had given himself, body and soul, to the study of law, and Hope couldn't be expected to wait for him. "How did you find Hope?"

"Well," Emily said.

"And happy?"

"She was in better spirits than she was earlier this winter, but she can't be happy about someone she never even liked."

"She could change her mind," Rita said.

"Not Hope! I told you that Ed boasted to her that a man can get anything he wants, with money and persistence and a thick hide—" Emily paused, with the sudden dreadful thought that maybe he was right. "It isn't like her to forget a challenge like that; she's so strong-willed. It's just as if she had stopped fighting—and that isn't like Hope, at all!"

Rita smiled at her vehemence. "You make it sound quite doleful, Emily! Albert, you'll have to excuse all this about people you don't know; we're so fond of Hope—"

"It interests me, too, ma'am," he said. "I was there, and I noticed that Miss Hope's Ma never let us out of earsight. If you ask me, she helped make up the girl's mind—and she's not going to let her unmake it!"

Rita looked at him with approval. "You size things up very well, Albert. Shall we go into the parlor?"

Since Rita's last and only glimpse of Albert, he had grown a moustache and gained an air of confidence befitting his size and good looks. He was almost elegant in a new blue cheviot suit and the latest fashion of collar, with a standing band and rolled points, and the knot of his silk cravat neatly filled the notch of his waistcoat. There was the unmistakable air of an occasion about him, and Rita devoutly hoped that it concerned her good and reliable Emily.

There was the air of an occasion about Emily, too, as she showed Albert the mementos of the sea which had been powerless to tempt him. Her old-rose challis dress had been freshened with muslin frills at the throat and wrists, and the rainy weather had given richness to her thick brown hair and color to her cheeks. "This is the table Uncle Roger made from the wheel of the *Ariel*. When you want something on the other side, you have only to turn the wheel and it comes round to you."

"A Lazy Susan," Albert said. "We have one on the dinner table at the farm. Pa brought the idea from Kentucky; they're used a lot there."

"I think all tables should have them," Emily said; "it would save a lot of passing."

"They're right handy," Albert agreed. "If you want the pepper and salt or horseradish or tabasco sauce, you only have to give Lazy Susan a turn." He illustrated, rotating the wheel and checking it as the imaginary condiment came around. "There's others in our neighborhood, too; most of the families around Lafayette came from the South." As they talked, he went on playing with the wheel. Everyone who came to the house played with it. There must be a nice feeling about pretending to steer a ship in the warm lamplit room, where even the wildest helmsmanship would bring no one to grief. Rita left them and went to the kitchen to put more wood in the stove.

"Here's another piece of furniture you must see." Emily led Albert to the corner cabinet. "Uncle Roger made this out of wood from the *Shark* house."

Albert ran his hand over the smooth cedar cabinet and

cocked his ear to the sound of rain against the windows. "Miss Emily, don't tell me it's so wet here that sharks have to live in houses!"

They laughed together, and Emily was very proud of him; he was big and strong, and he could say such amusing things. "The *Shark* was an American sloop-of-war that was wrecked at the mouth of the Columbia in the 1840's," she explained, "when Astoria was only a few cabins in the woods. The sailors built themselves a house and spent the winter here. They carved a record of the shipwreck on a rock and later, when the ship *Industry* was lost, her survivors carved a record of their shipwreck on the same rock. Uncle Roger has looked for it; he thinks it's buried——" She stopped in confusion, meeting Albert's ardent, admiring eyes.

"Miss Emily, you look sweet when you're telling things!" He looked as if he would take her hand with the least encouragement, but Aunt Rita might be back from the kitchen any minute, and if she started holding hands with him she wouldn't want to stop. She hurried on to the glass case. "Here is a piece of beeswax from the Acapulco galleon that was wrecked on the Nehalem sands. Uncle Roger can tell you about it; he'll take it out of the case and show you the trademark branded on it three hundred years ago."

She paused for breath. Albert was still looking at her admiringly while he shook his head. "Your uncle's right fond of shipwreck things!"

Emily smiled. "It only seems that way because they take up more room. What means most to him are those tall gray books in the bookcase."

"The ledgers?"

"Yes, only they aren't used for bookkeeping. Uncle Roger has written in them all about the ships that have come into the river since I don't know when. I read a little in one of them once—about a ship built in Maine: all kinds of dates and specifications and things. The ship was built of oak, and he had written about the white oak trees—the way they grow, the wind and rain, the autumn colors and the late autumn gales and the New England winters—all the things that go into a ship."

She paused for breath and Albert said, "Your uncle surely loves ships!"

"Yes," Emily admitted; "even the wood they're made of. He wrote about the way they tested the oak in the shipyard: one man would hold his watch against the end of a timber and one would put his ear against the other end; if he could hear the ticking of the watch, the timber was sound all the way through."

"Hearing you tell about it, Miss Emily, makes me feel as if I had been there."

"I haven't told it very well," Emily said, "but that's the way I felt when I read it."

"You told it beautifully!" Albert said. "You could almost make me love a ship built of oak like that!"

"I don't want you to love a ship!" It wasn't the way she meant it to sound and she covered her confusion by suggesting: "You can look into one of the books; Uncle Roger won't mind." As he took one of the volumes down from the shelf, the deep resonance of the *Vandalia's* bell sounded through the house. "There he is now!"

Rita heard the bell in the kitchen and ran into the hall, then slowed to a sober walk because the front door remained closed. There was the old fanciful terror of finding nothing but a sea gull outside, and she opened the door half fearfully. The light from the hanging lamp gleamed on a bulk of wet black oilskins and a solid friendly face. "Come in, Captain Smith."

He stayed outside, with his wet cap in his hand, half in courtesy and half in apology. "I know you hate to see me here of an evening, Mrs. Collins; Roger asked me to stop by."

"Is he caught outside the bar again?"

"Yes, ma'am. He's safe, but not what you'd call accessible. I'm afraid you won't see him for a day or two."

She had known it the moment she opened the door, but she couldn't help feeling ill-treated. The sea was spiteful and unforgiving, like other females—more unforgiving than Rita, who had surrendered herself and Roger to the sea; and the sea had snatched him away and shut the door in Rita's face. "What ship is it?"

"The *Huntress*. A good, able ship."

The name was unfamiliar. "Is she new?"

"She's an old clipper, but she's just gone into wheat carrying. Neither of us had ever set eyes on her before, but when we were two miles away your husband recognized her by her elliptical stern."

"Trust Roger to know ships!" she said.

"He offered to bet me that she was the *Huntress*, and she was. He gave me her pedigree: she's the last Mystic clipper."

Rita said jealously, "It must have pleased Roger to get a ship like that."

"Very likely. He said he had always wanted to sail a full clipper."

The sea would tempt him with her best! And Rita was left to ask useless questions. "Was it too rough to bring her in?"

"Too rough, without enough water on the bar. We couldn't chance it."

"Did Roger know that when he went on board?"

"He did. We agreed that the only safe thing was to work her off shore to ride out this blow. He'll bring her in when the weather permits and I'll be on the lookout for him."

She asked, "He didn't have to go on board, did he?"

The tugboat captain was surprised by the question. "It's up to the pilot's discretion, but we usually do it that way, ma'am."

"Of course." Her question had only lacerated herself. Roger had gone where he wanted to go. "Thank you for stopping, Captain Smith."

"No trouble, ma'am." As he was putting on his cap, he said, "You've nothing to worry about; Roger has a fine ship under him. Good night, Mrs. Collins."

"Good night, Captain Smith." He went away into the dark and driving rain, and she went back into the house.

In the parlor, Albert was putting another log on the fire while Emily stood by with the hearth broom, ready to sweep up any litter.

"You won't see Captain Collins this time, children," Rita told them; "he's on a ship outside and it's too rough to bring her across the bar."

"I'm right sorry to hear that!" Albert said. "I counted on meeting the captain."

"Why couldn't the bar behave itself long enough to let him get in? If I were you, Aunt Rita, I'd be jealous of the sea!"

"Sometimes I am, Emily, but little good it does." Then she smiled and said graciously, "I'll bring in the dinner."

"I'll help," Emily said.

"I'll help, too," Albert offered.

"Fine," Rita said; "Emily, you can help serve, and Albert, I'll ask you to sit at the head of the table and carve."

"I'll do my best, ma'am."

Albert decided that Mrs. Collins was the sweetest aunt anyone ever had, in addition to being downright pretty for a woman who must be nearly thirty. It was a shame that her husband had to be outside the bar on a stormy evening.

Judging by all the books in the long case, Captain Collins was a well-educated man; he would have to be just to know where to find so many books about ships and the sea and history and geography. And there were the seven books he wrote in, very clean and fresh-looking. He had been on the point of looking into them when the doorbell rang—

Respectfully he took down the first volume and opened it, turned through blank ruled pages. Empty! Apparently the captain hadn't written in them all. He put it back and took down the last volume; the same blank pages. He tried the middle one, and it, too, was empty. He tried the next to the last then the next to the first, and then the remaining two. Nothing! These couldn't be the books Emily was talking about.

He put the last book back in its place with a queer lonely feeling about Captain Collins. He had been invited to dinner to meet the captain, and he wasn't going to be here; he had been told about the rich records in these books, and there was nothing.

Emily was proud of the way Albert sat at the head of the table and carved, and the way he entertained. With a little encouragement from Aunt Rita, he told about the time he was shanghaied in Astoria, and about his night at the Indian camp and the unsolved mystery of his escape. "At the time, I didn't doubt that the Indians were in cahoots with the runners," he said, "but the more I think about it the more I feel they were my friends and I was free as soon as the runners disappeared; but what went with them, I can't figure out."

"That was one of the things Captain Collins wanted to talk to you about, Albert," Rita told him. "That night there was a gun battle on the river, and later Doctor Ward treated a bullet wound in a runner's shoulder. Roger believes that rival crimps were stealing men from each other and came to blows, and that the ones who got you were frightened away because they had shot someone."

Albert nodded gravely. "I expect it was something like that. The runners were scared. The Indian chief told me they left before *sun chaco*, as soon as the *sahilee skookum wawa* and *hiyu wind* had stopped—Mrs. Collins, may I help you to some more of this delicious roast?"

"No more, I thank you."

"Miss Emily?" Albert looked at her, with the carving knife poised over the roast.

"No, thank you, Albert." Then she said, "That was the night Jack and Tom Fortune ran away; it's lucky they didn't get caught in the gun battle."

Albert looked inquiringly at her. "Did we see the Fortune boys today?"

"No; we met their young sister—Barry was walking home with her. The boys have been at sea for a year. Their father punished them by sending them around the world in a down-Easter!"

"Their own father did that to them, Miss Emily?"

"Mr. Fortune did it for their own good," Rita explained; "and he expected the *Christmas Morning* to return from Liverpool instead of going around the world. Roger and I think it is hurting him more than the boys!"

Their talk had wandered away to people Albert did not know, and when they were having dessert Rita brought it back to his experiences. "It must have been a strange feeling, being free and not knowing it."

Emily asked, "Weren't you frightened at all?"

"Mostly I was too drugged; at first it was like things happening in a dream." He smiled reminiscently. "Only once I woke up enough to be scared—I mean scared!"

"Was that when they talked about dumping you in the river?" Rita asked.

"No, it was a picayune thing; it was when one of the runners knocked at the door and all the Indian dogs started barking. I thought they were figuring to feed me to wild dogs that would eat me bones and all, so no one would ever know what went with me."

"Albert, what a dreadful thought!"

"That must have been the effect of the drug," Rita said.

Albert smiled at her. "No, Mrs. Collins, it was the effect of something that once happened to Pa and Ma."

"What happened to them, Albert?"

"It's a long story, Miss Emily, and I don't know if it would interest you—"

"Albert, you can't put us off that way!"

Rita said, "Please tell us."

He submitted gracefully. "It's about the time when Pa and Ma were first married. That was soon after the War Between the States, when Oregon wasn't as civilized as it is now. Pa was a cattle dealer, going around buying up herds and driving them to market in Portland or to the mines in Jacksonville. Usually he was toting the price of a herd in gold."

"Wasn't he ever robbed?"

"No, Miss Emily. Pa was wary and bold." Albert gave his shy, rueful grin. "I can be wary and bold, too, but I'm nearly always the one when I should be the other."

"I like you as you are," Rita said.

"Thank you, ma'am. But Pa managed better; he always had a loaded revolver, and he toted Ma along. You wouldn't think it, seeing Ma in the kitchen at home, but when she was a girl she crossed the plain on horseback. Ma could ride and Ma could shoot, and she told Pa. 'Wherever you go, I go!'"

"That's the way it should be," Emily said.

"It's the only way," Rita said. "The worst can't happen to people who are together."

"That's the way Ma and Pa saw it. They went on two good Kentucky horses and kept their revolvers handy, and Pa carried the gold in his saddlebags.

"The time I'm telling about, Pa sold his cattle at Jacksonville and he and Ma headed north. On the Umpqua someone told them about a herd of good steers in the mountains near Roseburg. They headed for the place, but when they got to the foot of the mountains it was late in the day; there were a powerful lot of trails and Pa wasn't sure which one to take. He stopped at a cabin to ask, and when he was leaving the settler said, 'If I was you, I wouldn't go up there now.'

"Pa asked, 'Do you know any reason why I shouldn't?'

"The settler said, 'It's getting late, and I have a feeling that you shouldn't.'

"Pa laughed at him and he and Ma rode on into the mountains. It was nice country; grassy mountains that were bare except for trees growing in some of the draws—myrtle and bay and incense cedars; and the air was clean and dry.

"It wasn't quite dusk when they reached the cattle ranch in a mountain valley; there was a big corral and a log stable, and a nice log house. Pa was a little surprised that the corral was empty; and the stable was empty, too. He put the horses in there, and took his saddlebags, and he and Ma went to the house.

"The rancher gave them a nice welcome, and his wife hurried to get dinner for them. She was a large, dark woman in a silk dress, with a cameo brooch fastening a lace collar that was as wide as her shoulders. Ma noticed her because ranchers' wives didn't usually dress like that on a weekday.

"The log house was better than usual, too. It had a room where they cooked and ate, and a big room with a comfortable bed and fireplace and chairs.

"After dinner Pa asked to have a look at the steers; if they were as good as the steak he'd eaten, he and the rancher could do business, and he wanted to make an early start in the morning.

"The rancher said it was too near dark to see anything, but the cowboys would fetch the cattle in the morning and Pa wouldn't lose any time.

"They talked till after dark; then the rancher and his wife left Pa and Ma in the big room and told them to make themselves at home.

"They'd got themselves a fine stopping place for the night, but Pa couldn't enjoy it because he had a toothache from being up in the mountains. He told Ma to go to bed while he reasoned with his tooth. He had a piece of linen that he folded up and kept heating at the fire and putting against his jaw, and that made it feel better.

"Ma had been riding all day, and she went to bed and fell asleep. Pa dozed by the fire, and the next thing he knew something woke him, and he heard Ma calling, asking him to help her.

"The fire had burned down and there was just enough light for him to see that the bed was gone; there was only the frame, like a curb around a well, and he saw Ma's head, and her hands holding on—"

"Mercy!"

"It cured Pa's toothache all right; he pulled Ma out, and made up the fire, and they looked to see what kind of bed they had.

"They made out that the mattress was on a trap door, hinged at the head, and it opened into a black pit. Ma said she'd been lying over to one side of the bed to leave room for Pa, and she remembered half waking and rolling toward the middle, and some kind of trap sprung and she caught the end of the mattress as she was going."

"A good thing your father was sitting up with a toothache," Rita said.

"If he hadn't been, I wouldn't be telling the story, ma'am. While Ma and Pa were looking down into the pit, they heard the most fearful sounds of hogs. They seemed to be outside at first, then they were in the pit, snuffling and grunting and fighting with each other. They were starved crazy, Pa said; lean as shadows with glaring eyes, and teeth that they kept clashing together. If anyone fell down there, there wouldn't be a trace of him in five minutes."

"For Heaven's sake!"

"What a horrible trap!"

"That's what it was," Albert said, "and you can see what I was thinking when the runners took me to a place that sounded as if it was full of starving dogs."

The women could see very well, but Albert's story paled his own adventures, and he had to go on.

"Pa and Ma pulled up the trap door and fastened it, and they sat with their revolvers in their hands the rest of the night. Pa said their only chance was to act as if they didn't suspect anything, and then go out of there shooting.

"When it was daylight, Pa took his saddlebags and went to the stable, and pretty soon Ma went to the kitchen room, where the woman was cooking. She still wore her good dress with the lace collar and cameo, and she was making enough breakfast for a dozen people; but she looked mighty startled when her guest came in. Ma acted as if nothing was wrong; she found out what time breakfast was and said she would tell her husband, who'd gone to the stable to look after the horses."

Emily said, "Not many women would have had the courage to go through with that!"

"She's brave," Albert said; "and she was doing what Pa told her to do. She had her revolver in her blouse, ready to shoot anyone who tried to stop her.

"When she got to the stable, Pa had the horses saddled, and they mounted up and rode hell-for-leather down the trail. Until then they hadn't seen anyone outdoors, but they were hardly in their saddles before a band of horsemen dashed down from the hills, yelling and shooting and trying to cut them off. Pa and Ma exchanged shots with them, and the bandits chased them, but their cayuses couldn't keep up with Kentucky saddle horses.

"When they got down out of the mountains," Albert went on, "they told what had happened. The settlers weren't surprised; they said that other people had gone into the mountains and disappeared.

"Pa and Ma went on, and the next year they settled down on the Yamhill; they never were back that way, and they never heard anything more about the bandits."

After dinner Emily and Albert sat on the couch by the fireplace, with the roar of the gale outside answered by the comfortable roar of the fire. "You entertained most beautifully," Emily told Albert. "I didn't know anyone could tell stories the way you do!"

Albert took her hand and this time she did not draw it away. Aunt Rita was busy in the dining room and Emily was glowing with a quiet, reckless warmth.

"I never had such pretty listeners before," Albert told her. But he was willing to take some of the credit. "Do you notice anything different about me today, Miss Emily?"

She had been noticing it all along, but she despaired of putting it into words. "I don't know how to say it, Albert; you're more yourself—more sure."

"I've had me a birthday, Miss Emily."

"Albert, and you didn't tell me! I congratulate you!" She gave his hand a little squeeze. "You're grown up!"

"That's the way Pa and Ma figured it," he told her. "Pa gave me a hundred and sixty acres for a birthday present."

"Albert! How wonderful! Were you surprised?"

"Not exactly. Pa and Ma had promised it to me if I stayed on the farm and didn't do anything foolish."

"Imagine your doing anything foolish!"

"They meant like getting married before I was old enough to know my own mind. Ma says a man wouldn't look twice at the girls he fancied when he was a boy."

Emily didn't think that was always true, but she only said, "You haven't done anything foolish, and you're a man now."

"I don't aim to do anything foolish, but I still fancy a girl I saw when I was nineteen."

Her heart was beating too fast for her to do anything but hope that Aunt Rita wouldn't come back just then.

"I've looked at her more than twice, Miss Emily, and I'm looking at her now."

She had been half afraid that he might be talking about someone else. Now she met his ardent blue eyes and his look seemed to encompass her like a warm summer sea. "Are you sure?"

He raised her hand to his lips and kissed it with a grace she didn't know he possessed. "Miss Emily, I knew it would be you the first time I saw you—that time on board ship when you were singing in the choir. I was looking at you all the time, and you smiled at me—"

"I didn't smile at you, Albert. I was smiling because Jack and Tom Fortune were climbing up in the maintop, where they weren't supposed to be; they looked so daring and innocent—"

He said, "I suppose you didn't look at me at all!"

"I could hardly help it—we were facing each other."

"And I suppose you didn't try to save me from being shanghaied?"

"I did. I tried so hard!"

He swept a big arm around her and held her close. "Miss Emily, I suppose you didn't think then that you could like me?"

"I thought about it a little, Albert; maybe more than I should."

He sighed, holding her with gentle strength. "No, Miss Emily, there isn't that much thinking!" Then he said, "I'm asking you to think about it now."

[230]

She told him, "I don't have to think about whether or not I like you, because I do."

He sighed again. "That was another time I was wary when I should have been bold. I didn't mean 'like'; I meant 'love.'"

"That's different," she told him; but it wasn't, because she hadn't been thinking "like" either.

"We'll have to start over, Miss Emily. I'm asking you if you could love me; I mean enough to be a farmer's wife."

"Yes, Albert—enough to be a farmer's wife."

"Miss Emily!"

She ended the kiss because she knew that one of them had to exercise some control.

He looked a little disappointed and altogether happy. "Why did you have to stop?"

"Aunt Rita might come in."

"Let's find her now and tell her we're going to be married. When shall we say?"

She thought while the gale-driven rain beat against the window. "The spring would be just right."

"That's a long time to wait!"

She smiled encouragement. "Not when you have things to do—and it takes a long time to make a wedding dress."

"I expect it does. And I have to build us a house," he remembered. "I've picked out a spot, near the Yamhill River. It's not a very big river—maybe you'll miss the Columbia."

"I won't miss it, Albert." The Yamhill flowed into the Willamette, and the Willamette into the Columbia. She wouldn't really be giving up the river, only moving nearer to one of its sources.

He asked, "Where shall we go for our wedding trip?"

"A wedding trip, Albert!" She hadn't thought of having one. "Where would you like to go?"

Albert hesitated. "I always thought it would be nice to go to the Hotel Portland—"

"The Hotel Portland! Why, that's the grandest place in the city!"

"That's why I thought of our going. If you like, we could put up there."

"That would be wonderful, Albert! I'd never imagined staying in such magnificence!"

He said, "It would be nice to have us a few days in the city, with nothing to do. When we get to the farm we'll be there a long time, and there'll be a lot to do. We're not going to stop with a hundred and sixty acres, and we're not going to stop with raising wheat. The valley grows wonderful fruit —we'll have us an orchard—"

While they planned, the rain blasted like shot against the windows, unable to reach the warm security of their love. It only made the indoors seem safer and more comfortable.

"It is our rain," Emily said. "The rain is working now for the crops we will plant in the spring."

In the kitchen, Rita washed dishes slowly. Judging by the silence, the young people were getting along very well, and Rita was determined to make the dish-washing last until they appeared. She felt a pleasure in being forgotten, and her tender smile went away only when she winced at some new sound of violence from the rising gale.

16

IN 180 WEST AND 43 NORTH, the *Christmas Morning* was running her easting down. It was Jack's wheel watch, but he was not allowed to stand his trick.

The day before had been Friday, the thirteenth; they had roared across the 180th meridian at night, and in the morning they were faced with a second and stormier Friday, the thirteenth. The day had missed them with one barrel, but they were keeping their fingers crossed until it fired the other. That was how Jack would tell about it afterward—if he told about it at all. Actually, he hadn't felt unlucky when the mate waved him aside and called for Cyrus Pringle, who was the best helmsman in their watch. A little later the mate called Leif Johnson to bear a hand; and after that he passed a line around Yankee and Norwegian and lashed them both to the jolting wheel.

There were things about the ship in a gale that Jack would have to explain to landsmen at home: the Sunday feeling, and, for the time being, at least, the absence of work. Instead of being horsed about the main deck, pulling unnecessarily on sheets and braces, the watch was gathered on the poop for safety, and in the last hour they had not been called on to touch a rope. The *Christmas Morning* was running under rigid topsails and reefed foresail, and forestaysail and jib sheeted flat, and Captain Slade did not seem to have any new ideas about sails.

The ship was going like a race horse under her reduced canvas—rising and falling as she ran with the long rolling surges that charged down from the westward, breaking white as they came in range of the eye, roaring heavily in sound of the ear, and blasting spray over the poop as they towered up behind the fleeing stern. Each one seemed confident of toppling itself down on the quarterdeck to overwhelm the ship; each time the stern rose lightly and cleverly—and the outwitted sea lunged by, under and on each side, so close you could hear the disappointed bellow of the monster that was being carried past by the impetus of its leap. Triumphantly, the *Christmas Morning* rode the monster's back, rolling downhill toward home, shaking off masses of water that leaped her bulwarks and spilling them out through the wash ports. Then she was in the wild mountain valley of the sea, with the next great roller towering up to overwhelm her, its deepening roar fading the high whistle of wind through naked rigging.

The ship was doing nobly under her few sails, racing faster than the boys had ever seen her go before. It didn't look as if there would be anything to do for the whole watch, unless—

They had learned a multitude of things about a ship and the sea, but something new was always coming up. They looked about for Noah, the foc'sle sage, who had been second mate in half a dozen ships and was now in his more usual position as a seaman.

Noah was standing near the break of the poop, contemplating the row of fire buckets in their rack—little brass-bound wooden tubs, with two opposite staves higher than the others and joined by a square wooden handle with a rounded grip. The buckets were half full, and the water slopped from side to side and forward and aft with the motion of the ship. When she steadied, the wind found its way down into the buckets and chased little waves across the surface of the water. Maybe Noah found the Pacific less convenient to watch than ripples on a two-gallon sea. The brothers stopped beside him and helped him contemplate. "Well, Noah—"

[234]

"Aye, Jack."

"Th' gale don't seem to be going down, does it?"

The whiskered face and steady eyes looked at the boys impartially from under the sou'wester brim. "It's rising."

Jack had suspected that, and he knew that a ship could not run forever before a heavy gale. There was a point at which she had to heave to or risk being overwhelmed by following seas. "Do you think the old man's going to heave to in our watch?" If he were, it would be good to know how to go about things in such a sea and wind.

"He won't heave to now," Noah said, without emphasis, but with meaning.

"But if it gets heavier—"

"We'll still run."

"Oh."

"Are you afraid, boy?"

"No," Jack said, "only—"

"You might be afraid," the shellback told him. "The old man's run too long; it's too late to heave to! Even if it blows a hurricane, it's roll and go—or the deep six for all of us!"

The brothers walked away in silence and left their oracle contemplating his tempest in a tub. Near the foot of the mizzenmast they paused.

"That means we're in for it." Tom's voice was matter-of-fact and there wasn't any sign of fear in the smooth tanned face under his sou'wester.

Jack didn't like the situation of the *Christmas Morning* as it had been represented to them, but he couldn't be squeamish about it when his younger brother didn't show any concern. "It's roll and go," he said. "Now we'll see what the old ship can do!"

At the moment, the old ship was doing very well—twenty-five days out of Shanghai, twenty days from the mouth of the Columbia at her present rate—rising and falling as she ran the easting down, her sails lifting her and the send of the long rolling surges driving her on: the *Christmas Morning* running like a race horse pursued by countless ranks of wolves, trying to outrun them all and each rank overtaking her at last—the gray wolves of the sea with white fangs, slathering white foam, launching themselves at her, leaping up at her flanks—and the *Christmas Morning* shaking herself free at the last moment, trampling on them as they passed under her feet. Come on, *Christmas Morning!*

The ship didn't need any urging, or anything but the steadying hands on her jolting wheel: Pringle on the starboard side, Johnson on the port; the New Englander's face keen and grim, and the Norwegian smiling fiercely, showing his teeth through his red beard. They were good men and good helmsmen, but even they couldn't quite ignore the seas at their backs. By hearing or feel, they recognized the last critical moment when a great roller hung in the air, poised to launch itself down on them and the ship; their faces would harden, and sometimes, when the roller seemed to poise too long, one or the other would glance over his shoulder. When they did, the mate would growl at them, but his words were lost to the watching boys in the sound of the wind and sea and the racing ship.

When you're at the wheel, you're not supposed to look back, uselessly, at a following sea; it could only shake your nerves and endanger the ship. Captain Slade had explained that in the past with loud and profane clarity. Now he left reproofs to the mate. He was standing at the starboard rail, his sharp-bearded face calm and cold, and his senses intent on the ship and the sea. He didn't seem to notice the occasional backward glance of the helmsmen, but after it had happened a few times, he raised his voice in a bellow of impatience: *"Chips!"*

The carpenter, who was standing by with the watch, hurried aft, deferentially, like a willing angel in rustling oilskins. Captain Slade gave him an order, and he rustled off the poop and forward along the main deck, with an overtaking sea following him on both sides, leering at him from the level of the bulwarks as if it had a mind to pounce on him and give him the wetting of his life. Jack disliked Chips unreasonably, because of his anxiety to please the officers. More reasonably, he had to admit that Chips could not remain Chips if he failed to please; but that did not alter his dislike.

In a few minutes Chips was back again, with his oilskin wings rustling vehemently, burdened with lengths of iron pipe and a tarpaulin. While the crew watched and speculated, he secured two heavy pipes in sockets near the taffrail, and jointed them at the top with a horizontal pipe screwed into elbow fittings. The result looked like a larger and lighter version of the gallows frame, a resemblance which Noah was the first to observe.

"There," he said gloomily, "Captain Slade is going to hang the first man who looks over his shoulder!"

But it was only the framework for Captain Slade's masterpiece. When it was further secured with lashings, Chips called for help, and obliging hands muzzled the thundering tarpaulin, and passed lacings through grommets and around pipes. When it was done, Chips looked to the captain for approval, and was rewarded with an impatient nod. Jack thought he deserved more; the masterpiece had been erected with remarkable speed, inspired by Chips' desire to please and his desire not to have a ridge of the Pacific fall on his head.

Chips had succeeded in both desires and there was the masterpiece—a wide and gloomy screen bellying at the helmsmen's backs.

Jack had just understood its meaning, but Tom was still questioning. "To keep off the spray?" Captain Slade had never cared who was wet or dry.

"To keep the helmsmen from looking back."

[237]

"So that's it!" Tom wasn't certain that it was a Christian idea. Maybe it wasn't, but Captain Slade was a practical man. What the helmsmen couldn't see wouldn't hurt them—not until the last moment, when there would be no time to flinch under an avalanche of thundering water.

The helmsmen didn't look back any more. They steered with sure hands and set faces: one shrewd and grim, the other smiling fiercely; the Yankee rejoicing in the clever ship that overran and outwitted all the devils of the sea; the Norwegian glorying in his physical strength, glorying in his day of battle.

The boys had become mere spectators, but they were appreciative ones. Now when it seemed likely that they wouldn't have anything to do during the whole watch, Jack thought they should see as much as possible; it wasn't every day they were in a ship running for her life. The real thing would be to go aloft where they could see the whole show: the fleeing ship and the pursuing rollers, the wild smoking sea and the wild sky from horizon to horizon. The best place for that would be the maintop, in the shelter of the box for overhauling gear—but that was out of the question when they were on watch, and it was no longer satisfactory for two. Somewhere along the way, he and Tom had developed such long arms and legs that they couldn't fit themselves into their early nest with any comfort. The maintop was out of question when they were supposed to be standing by aft; the foretop even more so. There remained only the less satisfactory mizzen top above them—and that was unpromising because it was under the eyes of the captain and the mate. Only yesterday, early in the gale, the brothers had started aloft for their own entertainment, and the mate had called them down profanely. He had also given each one a kick as he reached the deck; they had still to settle with him for that.

Jack gave his brother a look which said, "We ought to be

aloft in a comfortable spot, where we could really enjoy this, but I can't figure out where."

Tom's eyes said, "I've been thinking the same thing."

The older brother continued to cast about in his mind, without finding anything suitable; then Tom asked, "What about that lashing?" He pointed at the spanker overhead. The boom was secured in its gallows frame aft, and the furled sail secured by double lashings around boom and gaff.

The spanker wasn't much of a vantage point, ten feet above the deck, but it was better than anything Jack could think of. The sail was as safe as a church, but the second lashing had put a little slack in the first. "It could stand taking up." He shinnied up the mast until he got his hands on the jaws of the gaff, put one foot on the spider band, and drew himself up astride the spar. Tom followed like a monkey, and together they worked a foot of slack out of the lashing and secured the end again.

The task had been neither necessary nor worth doing in itself, but it had a solemnly plausible look and no one bellowed from aft for them to "lay down out of there." They continued to sit astride the gaff, with their feet stuck comfortably between the lashings and the heavy roll of sail.

The vantage point was better than Jack had expected. Facing aft, they could look over Captain Slade's screen at the big seas as they towered up behind the stern, and the matter of being ten feet above the deck lent a feeling of security. It also gave them more of the exhilarating motion of the ship, the easy roll and the racing rise and fall, and the send of the long seas thundering after her.

The speed and the great rhythmic motion and the sound of the gale were exciting at first, and then it made them feel pleasantly drunk; not afraid any more and not separate from the gale. It couldn't hurt them because they were part of it. *Come on,* CHRISTMAS MORNING, *race on forever with the lift of your iron-hard sails and the send of the sea! Be ready for the next wolf pack springing up, showing their white fangs, slathering white foam, blowing their smoking breath over us; be ready to answer the trumpet of the wind. Now! Shake yourself free! Rise up and trample the wolves under your racing feet! Come on,* CHRISTMAS MORNING!

Astride the spar, at his back, Tom made a game of the pursuing rollers. When it was a large and angry one, he shouted in his brother's ear, *"Here comes Mamma!"* If it was larger and angrier, he shouted, *"Here comes Papa!"* Jack joined in the game, and they elaborated on it until they had five classes of waves: *Mamma, Mamma-with-a-stick, Papa, Papa-with-a-stick,* and *Mamma and Papa*—the last a rarer variety produced by a swift wave overtaking a slower one and merging with it in an oversized tumbling fury.

It was good to shout from the reeling spar, and they shouted unreproved; the gale whipped their voices away and the sound never reached the officers aft. Not every overtaking sea deserved a title, and there was time for other noise. Riding the swaying spar, Jack thought of a song that fitted the rise and fall and roll of the ship and the buoyant send of the sea. He looked over his shoulder and met his brother's eyes, bright and dark and fearless in his smooth young face. "Shake out the topsails," he said; and together they shouted the homeward-bound song:

> *Shake out the topsails, and roll along home;*
> *Roll along home;*
> *Roll along, roll along, roll along home!*

They shook out skysails and moonsails—and paused because no sail higher than a moonsail had ever been set. They consulted with their eyes, and started over with the courses. Now and then they paused when a roller of unusual size lifted out of the welter astern, and one or the other shouted, "Here comes Mamma!" or, "Here comes Papa-with-a-stick!" With the wave classified, they went back to their song.

Below their feet, the sou'westers of their shipmates gleamed somberly, wet with driven spray. Farther aft, the still figure of Captain Slade watched the ship and the sea from near the cabin companionway. He had been on deck all day and he looked ready to go below and leave the mate to the remainder of his watch. Still farther aft, the oblong bulk of the mate stood on the port side of the binnacle. Behind him, at the wheel, Johnson and Pringle steered quietly, no longer glancing back when a threatening sea rumbled astern and rose evilly to look down at them over the fragile screen.

The furled spanker on which the boys were perched extended to the counter of the ship, over the center of the wheel, obscuring the hub and spindle and leaving a segment on each side, one for the Maine man and one for the Norwegian. They handed the spokes smoothly, steadying the *Christmas Morning* as she ran with the great, rolling surges.

> *Shake out the skysails and roll along home;*
> *Roll along home;*
> *Roll along, roll along, roll along home!*

Captain Slade had gone below at last and the mate was standing his watch alone. The brothers had still to get even with him for kicking them yesterday with his hob-nailed shoes; but it would have to be planned carefully, and he had enough to think about today.

> *Shake out the moonsails and roll along home—*

"Here comes Papa-with-a-stick!" Tom shouted.

The big one was rearing up three seas away, gray and white under the racing gray sky; they could hear the rumble of it across the lesser seas.

> *Roll along home;*
> *Roll along, roll along, roll along home!*

When the big one reached them it was nothing. It broke

[241]

clumsily, too soon, with spindrift flying over the poop, then it was toppling by in ruins, with the ship trampling it under her racing feet. Come on, *Christmas Morning!*

They had shaken out the moonsails, and now they had to start over again with their song that had become a part of the gale and the rush of the ship and the send of the sea.

> *Shake out the courses and roll along home;*
> *Roll along home;*
> *Roll along, roll along, roll along home!*

"Here comes Papa *and* Mamma!" Jack shouted.

"Where?" Tom couldn't see it at first because he wasn't looking far enough into the distance. The ship coasted down into the trough and began rising again; and then he saw it, seven seas away, rolling and smoking and building up as it came. "It's Papa and Mamma with *two* sticks!" That was a new classification. Jack conceded that none of the earlier ones fitted this chance roller, but they had already observed that the big ones could be clumsy.

> *Shake out the topsails and roll along home—*

The big one was now four seas away, like a wintry mountain range avalanching snow. Jack wondered if he should tell the mate—to what end he didn't know, unless it would be to worry the two men lashed to the wheel. And unless he was deaf, the mate could hear the thunder of it for himself.

Now it was two seas away, not breaking, but building up and smoking—building up bigger and steeper than he had thought any wave could be.

"I don't like that one!" Tom shouted.

Jack leaned from his perch and yelled down to his shipmates, *"Look out! Big one coming!"*

A wet sou'wester tilted and turned, and Noah's whiskered face looked up at him. "Plenty of big ones, boy!" But others of the crew were already scrambling for the mizzen shrouds.

The big one was astern now, towering above them, fascinating and steep and almost silent. How would the *Christmas Morning* ever rise to such a sea? She hadn't started yet. Come on, *Christmas Morning!*

The stern lifted desperately; then the ship stumbled and the roller toppled forward with an unending roar, and the ship disappeared. Gone! There was nothing but the furled spanker on which he was sitting, extending out over the rolling white torrent, a bridge leading to nowhere. A man's arm reach up out of the rushing white water, and was gone. There was only the torrent, and the bridge to nowhere; the thunder of water and the crash of things breaking up and being carried away. "*Tom!*" He couldn't hear the sound of his own voice, but he looked over his shoulder and Tom was there behind him; Tom's good face, safe and unhurt! *Safe!* No one was safe unless they all were—if there were any others. "Come on, Tom!" He didn't know if his brother heard him, but he would follow, anyway.

He scrambled and slithered along the gaff, past topping lifts and lazy jacks. When he looked back, Tom was close behind him, and when he looked ahead, the broken port taffrail rose at an angle out of the welter of white water. Under it, heeling over, the *Christmas Morning* was fighting for her life; the spar he was on shook with her struggle as she tried to rise. Just underneath him, part of the wheel rose out of the water; the wheel with part of the rim gone. He turned and shouted in his brother's face, "*I'll go first! Follow me if I make it!*"

Holding on to the sail lashings, he let himself down until his feet touched the wheel box. He let go and jumped down abaft the wheel. The water was only up to his hips on the windward side of the wheel. There should be no loo'ard or windward. They had to be running before the gale to live. And they were broaching to. He found two good spokes and began grinding the wheel over. Come on, *Christmas Morn-*

ing! He gained a little, and lost it to a savage kick of the wheel that left his shoulder numb. He tried again, gaining a little and holding it. Tom—where was Tom? Then he saw Tom on the other side, standing on the broken rim, climbing the wheel to give it his last ounce of weight. "Don't!" he shouted. "If it kicks, it'll throw you—to Kingdom Come!" Tom didn't seem to hear; so he put his shoulder under a spoke of the wheel and braced himself. If the wheel kicked now, it would have to crush him before it threw Tom. *Come on,* CHRISTMAS MORNING!

Grinding at the wheel, he gained a little, and got his shoulder under the next spoke. The wheel jolted and lightning seemed to blast through his shoulder, but he stayed braced, and Tom was still on the other side, climbing the wheel. Once more, and once more! He ground at the wheel and gained another spoke, and held it with the furious pain of his shoulder. *Come on, God damn it! Come on,* CHRISTMAS MORNING! *Rise up and run before it! Rise up and trample the seas under your feet! Rise up and answer that high screech of wind in your rigging! If it's Gabriel blowing the last call for us—ram his trumpet down his throat!*

17

In the city of Salem, Winter Street and Summer Street are only a block apart. When Willard rode out to the University in the morning, he might get off the horse car where it turned from Trade Street into Winter; or sometimes, when he was having a political discussion with young Hoover, who drove the car, he would ride as far as State, then continue east along the edge of the campus on foot. Going that way, he crossed the end of Summer Street a block from Winter, but there was no dramatic change in temperature; whatever season it was in one street, it was the same in the other.

Tonight it was winter in both streets, and over all of Salem. Winter expressed itself in black teeming rain that dimmed the few lights on the far side of Front Street and fought for mastery with the sputtering arc light at the north intersection of the block. The rain came down in icy walls that encouraged one's person and thoughts to stay indoors, and it made good studying weather.

In his room above the Valley Harness Shop, Willard studied without his attention straying beyond the walls and roof of sounding rain. At night he was the only occupant of the building, and he made the most of his deliberate loneliness. At the dormitory, lights had to be out by ten o'clock, and here, if he chose, a young Abraham Lincoln could study all night. Rooming in town also revealed another facet of Willard's independence. Dormitory students were required to attend morning chapel in Waller Hall, and Willard, who championed freedom of worship, rebelled sternly against compulsion.

His independence might hardly be noticed now, but it would take on significance in a biography. It would be important to a biographer that Willard Pearson had lived in an attic while attending college, and at present it was important to Willard that the attic was reasonably comfortable. Mr. Boyd, the proprietor, had planned it for himself and had lived there until prosperity and matrimony had taken him to a house on Fairground Road.

A flight of wooden steps led up from the street to a hall with three doors. The first door was to Willard's big room, which occupied the front of the building; the second opened to a modern water closet; and the third, outside of Willard's domain, led to a locked storeroom where rats scrambled among old sleigh bells and over ox yokes that had weathered the Oregon Trail.

In Willard's room everything was snug and efficient. The kitchen table at which he was reading served both as a dining table and a desk, and the heating stove also had a double purpose: from his place at the table, Willard could reach out to put in another chunk of wood or to mind whatever was cooking on its flat top. Against the back wall, near the door, a wooden sink with a big, verdigrised brass tap provided the luxury of running water. The other furnishings of the room fell naturally into place: the food cabinet by the sink; the barrel of apples which the Hedges had sent, in the corner farthest from the stove; the bed against the serene far wall; and the clothes press in the corner made by the partition to the storeroom. As a concession to college life, on the wall over the bed was tacked a pennant with *Willamette* in diminishing letters of cardinal on old gold.

At the moment, Willard was conscious only of Blackstone, and of the rain's curtain of sound and the diminishing heat from the stove. In a minute or two he would put in another chunk of wood. He turned a page, and there was a knock at the door. That surprised him, because he hadn't heard any tramp of feet on the stairs, and it was late for visitors. "Come in!" he called, and went on reading. No one came in, but there was another light, insistent knock. He got up, with one finger between the pages of his book, and went to the door. He opened it, and started at the sight of a very wet young woman with a pale oval face and upward-looking eyes. "Hope Morris!" He couldn't believe that she was there. "Hope!" he said again.

She gave him her hand, which was cold and wet. "It's all of me that the rain couldn't wash away!"

"For Heaven's sake, come in and get warm before you catch pneumonia!"

Hope came in willingly. "You don't know how good it is to see you, Willard!"

He closed the door and hurried to make up the fire. "Take off your wet things and hang them here." He drew up another chair, with its back to the stove.

Her India silk dress was as wet as the cloak she hung over the chair; and when she took off her Climax hat with its rain-wilted lilies-of-the-valley, her light-brown hair was dark and plastered with rain.

"I'll fix you something hot to drink," Willard said. "Would you like tea?"

She was unbuttoning one of her slender, sodden shoes. "I'd like coffee; that's what you take, isn't it?"

Willard had observed on other occasions that many different worlds take turns occupying the same space. A minute ago he had been in a male world of study, with everything in harmony. If some of the boys had dropped in, they would have talked politics or study or college; they would have helped themselves to apples from the barrel, and found chairs for themselves. If one of them made a threatening gesture toward the sink, or started to open the side window, Willard would remind him of the plumbing in the hall. But it would continue to be the same world.

Instead of boys, it was a young woman, who brought another kind of world with her, and the earlier one was knocked helter-skelter. He wouldn't be aware of anything but awkwardness and defects until the two of them were in harmony and things around them settled into a new pattern that was neither the one she had disturbed nor the one she had brought.

While he was filling the coffeepot, he asked, "How did you get here, Hope?"

"On the Shasta Limited from Portland."

"You look as if you might have swum up the river!"

She looked ruefully at her wet clothes, which had begun to steam. "It was easier to find my way from Portland to Salem than from the railroad station to here. I had your address, but I was a long time finding it in the dark."

He was as puzzled as he had been at the beginning. "You came here to see me?"

"I was in Salem already. I'm going to Roseburg to visit Aunt Matilda, but it didn't seem right to go through without seeing you."

She looked so bedraggled and pretty that he could only scold her in a fatherly way. "So you got off the train in the middle of a downpouring night, without an umbrella!"

She said, "When I want to do something, I think more about doing it than what time it is." She got up and stood with her back to the roaring heater. "Aren't you at all glad to see me?"

"Hope," he said, "you know I am!" He was surprised to find how pleasant it was. It was also disturbing. "You aren't getting a chill, are you?"

"I don't think so, but my back was beginning to feel cold."

"You're soaked through!"

"Completely," she told him. "From the top of my head—" She put her hands up to her wet hair. "I can't take that off to dry, anyway." She began taking out hairpins.

"There ought to be a woman here!" Willard lamented.

She looked at him with dainty surprise. "I am a woman!"

He blushed. "To help you, I mean. It's bad to let clothes dry on you."

She shook out her wet hair. "I know; you're supposed to go into a decline. I doubt that."

Willard doubted it, too, but he was aware that things happen when you least expect them. "Shall I get a towel for your hair?"

"Please."

He brought his next to the last clean towel, and when she did not seem to make sufficient progress, he took it from her. "Sit down!" he said masterfully. She obeyed, and he began rubbing strands of wet hair between the folds of the towel. "You need someone to look after you!" Immediately he was afraid that she might interpret it as meaning more than he intended.

But she only said, with light regret, "I know; so much hair and so little sense!"

He rubbed strands of wet, dark hair until they became light brown and fluffy again, and he began to feel a proprietorship in the young woman whom he was restoring. "Tell me if I pull your hair."

"You do now and then—but you're managing beautifully."

He was more careful. "Why didn't you tell me before?"

"If I'm never more hurt than that, I won't complain."

"I don't want to hurt a hair of your head!" he told her gallantly. Her upward-looking eyes disturbed him, and he concentrated on the top of her head. "Your hair's more dry now than wet."

She responded by sneezing.

"God bless you!" Though he didn't believe that colds could be warded off that way.

"Thank you," she responded.

"Are you cold?"

[249]

"In spots."

He felt dissatisfied with the way he had evaded a problem on which a girl's health might depend. "You need to get out of your wet clothes and into something dry!"

She said, "You've stated it very well."

"I haven't anything suitable," he said, "but I could let you have a nightshirt and a dressing gown while your clothes dry."

"They would do nicely, Willard."

"And slippers," he added, going to the clothes press.

"I feel warmer already!"

He brought the clothes and put them on the chair beside her. "Now get into these dry things as fast as you can!" He pulled out his silver watch and opened the case; it was twenty minutes of eleven. "I'll wait in the hall. How long will it take you?"

"Not more than ten minutes," she said; "but I don't feel right about driving you out."

"It was my suggestion. I'll knock in ten minutes; if you're not ready, let me know."

"Thank you." Then she asked, "Would you mind unhooking the back of my dress?"

He unhooked her, impersonally; she thanked him, and he went out. He was more excited when he was alone. What an adventure! Then it occurred to him that it could be an embarrassing one. He hurried down the wooden stairs and locked the door to the street. The door hardly dimmed the feeding sound of the rain. It was raining all the time, but not evenly; it came in waves that increased in intensity, then sank like the trough of a sea, and the next wave swelled to the same intensity—trying to build a solid wall forever between the world and the Valley Harness Shop. What an adventure! And how some coarse-minded young men would have talked about it afterward! Some of them might have tried to take advantage of Hope, who was so pure and candid.

Suppose . . . but no—her ideas of right and wrong couldn't be much different from his own.

He hadn't intended to wait at the foot of the stairs like a bashful boy, but since he had lingered this long, he would stay. It would be awkward to tramp back upstairs—Hope would think the time was up. . . . Oddly, the stairway didn't seem to be a place; it was a time of waiting inside the timeless wall of rain. . . .

He struck a match and looked at his watch; it was six minutes of eleven; the time was already more than gone. He went upstairs with a feeling of excitement that seemed more profound than the circumstances called for.

The smell of coffee welcomed him in the hall, and when he knocked, Hope's voice called, "Come in, Willard!"

She was at the stove in his nightshirt, with her soft drying hair over her shoulders. The clothes she had taken off were draped on chairs around the stove: an imposing drift of chemise and drawers and embroidered petticoats, corset and corset cover, stockings and garters. He turned his eyes from them in embarrassment. In the white nightshirt, Hope looked simple and pure beside the vulgar trappings of modesty. Hope felt it, too. She said, "Men should have beautiful dispositions at night; I never felt so angelic as I do in this!" She looked like an angel in the absurd garment, a sweet and profoundly disturbing angel.

"Wouldn't you be warmer if you put on the dressing gown?" Willard asked.

"It felt so good just to get into something dry. Then the water boiled and I looked for the coffee; I hope I made it strong enough."

He helped her into the dressing gown and felt safer. But she was still disturbingly sweet, and whenever their eyes met he was conscious of the fact that he was a man and she was a woman.

Willard had started to make coffee with the idea of saving

Hope from pneumonia; but it ended by Hope making the coffee, and they had it together with bread toasted at the open door of the stove, and wild blackberry jam from home —a young man and woman at ease in front of their hearth, with the sounding rain shutting them away from the world. The only thing that troubled Willard was the naturalness of it, and the fact that Hope did not seem troubled at all. "Hope, don't you ever think ahead?"

She looked up from the bread she was toasting, with her eyes dreamy and the pink glow of firelight on her delicate oval face. "No, Willard. Should I?"

With fatherly sternness, he told her, "There are times when you should. You might be compromised by coming here."

"Then I should have stayed out in the rain?"

He wondered if she was being willfully perverse. "You should have gone to a hotel, and then got in touch with me."

"It would have been so late by then," she objected.

He had to admit that. "But there was tomorrow."

"You would have been at classes."

"Not all day; I have nothing after three o'clock."

"You make it sound so difficult," she told him. "If I had to stop in Salem until tomorrow afternoon, just to shake your hand—"

"I wouldn't expect that!"

"You mean I shouldn't have stopped at all?" The toast was burning, but she was too troubled to notice.

He put his hand on hers. "You don't know how nice it is to see you; but I'm trying to point out that it's also awkward for you."

She said, "It doesn't seem awkward. I wanted to see you, and you wanted to see me. I'm glad I stopped."

"It's awkward just the same; here you have to hunt a hotel in the middle of the night—"

[252]

"I can't, Willard! My clothes aren't dry, and listen to it rain!"

"You can't at that. I have to hunt a hotel," he amended.

"Willard, you wouldn't leave me alone in this strange place!"

He felt a certain relief, because he had just remembered that he didn't have the price of a hotel room. "You see, it's awkward any way you look at it. You have to sleep, and it's only a question of whether you would feel safer alone or with me here."

"Naturally I would feel safer with someone I know and trust."

It was the sensible way to look at a not too sensible situation. "In that case, you're welcome to my bed."

"Thank you," she said; "but where will you sleep?"

"I can sleep in a chair."

"No one ever slept comfortably in a chair."

"Or I can roll up in a blanket on the floor."

"That doesn't sound comfortable, either."

"I'm used to roughing it," he told her, "and you can see for yourself there's only one bed."

"I can see that, Willard." Then she said, "It's a pity you haven't a sword to put between us, the way the knights and their ladies did at times like this."

He didn't have a sword, and the fact made it safe to discuss the daring subject. He thought, this is the nineteenth century; there wouldn't be any progress in the world if we couldn't talk more daringly than our elders. He asked her, "Would you really trust to something like that?"

"It would depend upon the man."

He asked without looking at her, "Suppose I was the man?"

"Yes, if the sword were sheathed."

He was startled. "But that would defeat its purpose!"

"It would be less dangerous."

[253]

Looking grimly at the stove, he said, "You forget that I am a man."

"No, Willard; I am quite conscious of it."

He admired her for not pretending not to know what he was talking about, and because there was a delicacy about her even when she was being most candid. "You would be exchanging one danger for another."

"Aren't we always choosing between dangers?" she asked.

He pointed out, "You could be safe at home, instead of being in danger here."

"I could be at home, but I mightn't be safe."

He wondered if there was some special reason for her being there—something she hadn't told. "Why mightn't you be safe, Hope?"

"There was a big gale; it had been blowing two days when I left. The house might have blown away; or a tree might have fallen on it."

"Had it done any damage?" he asked.

"Nothing special." Then she recalled, "Your Uncle Roger was caught outside the bar in a ship."

"He knows how to take care of himself, but Aunt Rita will worry until he gets in." Then he said, "Here we didn't get anything but this rain."

"It sounds ever so comforting—in here," she said.

The rain did sound comforting. It was telling Willard that there was nothing beyond its walls of sound—no world; everything that mattered was here: shelter and warmth and the warmhearted young woman beside him. He knew better, but the rain was telling him so persuasively that the real problems didn't seem very real. They would have to wait for morning. There was no use trying to break the spell, or disturb the new world that had been created in the room.

In the morning there would be practical, unpleasant problems, but he would be able to tackle them better after he had slept; and Hope had yawned once. He said, "Don't let me keep you up, Hope. The bed is yours—and the 'House of Parliament' is in the hall."

"Thank you, Willard. I am ready for bed, but we have to decide where you're going to sleep. I can't put you out of your bed and forget you."

She helped him make a bed on the floor with spare clothes and a blanket, with a chair cushion for a pillow. It was not a good bed, and Hope was not satisfied with it. She sat on the floor, with her arms around her knees, shaking her head and stirring the light-brown hair over her shoulders. "I really feel conscience-stricken! You'll be cold, and have bad dreams —all because of me!"

It seemed to him that he wouldn't be in a makeshift bed on the floor; he would be in a pleasantly excited state of mind that would leave no room for awareness of physical discomforts. "I'll have pleasant dreams."

Hope shook her head again. "Not here. Just sitting on this hard floor convinces me that it would be impossible. Maybe some of my clothes are dry enough to make you more comfortable." She started to get up, but he stopped her.

"You'll do nothing of the kind, Hope!" He was touched that she should be so much concerned with his comfort. "You go to bed; I'll make out all right."

"But you won't be comfortable, Willard, and I won't be, either, knowing that you're not!"

"I'll be all right," he told her. "You just forget about me."

"I couldn't do that." Looking down at her arms clasped about her knees, she asked, "Would you be shocked if I told you what I am thinking?"

"Of course not, Hope! We're young moderns!"

Still looking at her arms, she said, "I was thinking that if you were very good, as I know you would be, you could sleep beside me."

[255]

"No!" he cried. "No, Hope; that would be wrong! You go to bed; I'll be all right here."

She went, without saying anything more. He turned out the gaslight, felt his way to his bed on the floor, took off his shoes and coat, and crawled under the blanket. In the dark, shut in by walls of rain, the feeling of profound excitement returned to him. What an adventure! He wondered if anything like this had ever happened to anyone else. A pure and beautiful young woman had offered to let him sleep in the same bed with her; had offered because she didn't want him to spend a wretched night on the floor! He was overwhelmed by her trusting tenderness. And he had cried, "No, no! That would be wrong!" He hadn't said that; it was his elders, living and dead, who had answered her. When he consulted his own mind, the answer was still "no," but in a different tone; not because it was wrong in itself, but because it was dangerous and unwise. It was also brave, and his voice had answered in the condemning tone of his elders. He raised himself on one elbow, feeling the hard floor through his bed. "Hope, are you awake?"

"Yes, Willard." Her voice was clear and gentle in the dark.

"Are you comfortable?"

"The bed is very comfortable, thank you."

"What about you?"

"I was wondering if you were angry with me for saying what I did."

"No. It was kind and sweet of you, only I was taken by surprise."

"I'm glad you're not angry."

"I'm not. I admire you for being frank, and I am very proud that you trust me."

"It wouldn't be much good if there wasn't someone you could trust in every way—if there wasn't someone to whom you could say whatever you happened to think. I wouldn't want to live without anyone really knowing me. That would be too lonely; I would feel like a ghost." Her voice was ghostly in the dark; it was also gentle and appealing: a ghost not wanting to be a ghost; wanting to be human and warm and alive.

He said quietly, "Hope, you can say whatever you feel like saying to me."

"Thank you, Willard. And I expect you to say whatever you think."

The bond of understanding between them was so perfect that he didn't feel any need to make use of it, but after a minute he asked, "What do you think about the way people should act—about what is right and wrong?"

"It doesn't seem complicated to me," she said, "but maybe that's because I don't bother about things unless they are simple enough for me to understand. I think the only real sin or wrong is hurting others; the rest is a matter of taste."

"That's the basis of all laws," he said, "to keep people from hurting one another. You're very wise to put it all in one thought."

"Not wise, only lazy; it's much simpler to think of it that way. Perhaps I should go to sleep before I say something foolish."

He said, "There's something nice about talking in the dark; you can think clearly, and be more honest. But I mustn't keep you awake any longer."

Her quiet voice said, "I could talk all night—or I could sleep now, if you tucked me in and said good night."

He got out of his hard shakedown and made his way across the room. He sat on the edge of the bed and took her hand, almost without excitement, but with affection and respect. "Good night, Hope."

"Good night, Willard."

It was a small and quiet "good night," and he sat a while longer.

With her hand nestled in his, she said, "You look very nice there; shadowy and strong."

In the faint light that came in from the rain-tormented street, he saw the dim oval of her face, and the darkness of her eyes looking up at him, and the soft shadows under her cheeks that told him she was smiling. "You look sweet, Hope." It was pleasant to have her there, but it also seemed improbable and unexplained. "Hope," he asked, "is there any special reason why you are going to Roseburg?"

"Yes. Ed Barton."

Ed was someone Willard had never liked. "What about Ed?"

"I got engaged to him."

Willard let go her hand. "You're an engaged woman and you came here?"

"That's why," she said.

He didn't understand. "But you accepted him."

"I had to, to get some rest. Father and Mother were after me day and night to marry him."

"Your parents must know Ed's reputation."

"They do; but Father insists that wild young men make the best husbands."

"I doubt that," Willard said.

"I do, too. But I was outnumbered."

"So you agreed to marry Ed without intending to?"

"Yes."

He was more troubled. "And now you're running away?"

She said, "At nineteen, a girl doesn't run away; she leaves home."

"What will you do in Roseburg?"

"Find some kind of work. Aunt Matilda can't afford to support me—and if I went home it would be the same thing over again."

He thought unhappily of going home for the holidays and not finding Hope there. In the past, he had seldom sought her company, but he had a feeling of emptiness knowing it would no longer be there for the asking. "Astoria won't be the same without you."

"I won't be the same without Astoria," she told him.

He gave her hand a friendly little shake. "Hope, I admire the natural way you take life. When you came here tonight you were going through a crisis, and on top of that you were wet through—yet you were as calm and pleasant as if nothing was troubling you."

"I was happy to get here, and the rest didn't matter." After a minute, she said, "You take things calmly, yourself."

He told her honestly, "Things disturb me more than you might think; I suppose it's the excitable Irish."

"I would never have known it, Willard; you seem so calm." She disengaged her hand from his and put it over his heart. "Does it always beat so fast?"

"No," he said, "but it always would when your hand was on it."

She put her other hand over her own heart. "Yours is twice as fast as mine." She took his hand and put it inside the borrowed nightshirt. "Can you feel it? I have a quiet heart."

He didn't feel anything but her delicate young beauty answering his awkward hand, and the blood thundering through his own arteries. "Hope," he whispered, *"Hope!"* He started at the dim, smiling oval of her face and the darkness of her eyes. "Hope, I must leave you—and I can't!"

She was caressing his arm, and her voice was calm and sweet. "Willard, I don't want you to leave me; you mustn't go away!"

"I must," he stammered, still caressing her. "This is wrong, Hope! I mustn't take advantage of you!" His lips said the words, but they were inaudible in the thunder of his blood.

Hope drew his head down to hers and kissed him tenderly.

"I don't want you to go away, ever!" she whispered. "Take off these rough clothes and come to bed."

The voices of his elders dwindled in the roar of rain and the drumming of his heart.

That night, he thought, his mind should be most aware and most present, but it kept going away to clear visions of past times, or hovering about the sky and the horizon of the new world. . . . That winter night in the city of Salem. It was there that the miracle happened. That evening, when I climbed the worn, familiar steps to my room, I had no way of knowing that it was going to happen. I didn't know that wooden stairs could turn to gold; that rain-sodden time would catch fire and burn with a precious flame; that moments would become warm jewels, each one too precious to be lost or hurried by. I didn't know that time would suddenly become timeless. Out there in the winter dark and rain over Salem—the groves of Arcadia; instead of the cold, swollen Willamette, with its flood of dead black water going to the Columbia—rivers of Paradise. I didn't know that the dull, slow stammering prose of life would become a song. The beauty I had sensed in a thousand fragments at a thousand different times; the beauty that always escaped like a flying bird, and left me on the ground—I didn't know that it would come to me at last, complete and splendid in my arms; that it would all be there for my hands to caress. . . .

Sometimes only his mind was there, like a mirror, reflecting clear pictures; sometimes there was only darkness and Hope, warm—and cool—and piercingly sweet; and sometimes his mind saw all of her white body in the light of thunderbolts that dazzled through them.

He was never certain that he was quite awake, or conscious of having slept, until he woke in the cold room. The rain had dwindled to a quiet dripping, and in the wet gray light of morning he saw his unused shakedown on the floor, and near it the blank, silver gleam of his watch, which looked as if it had expired there, trying to time timelessness. Over the three chairs he saw the white drift of Hope's clothes, trying to warm themselves around the cold stove. It hadn't been a dream. The fact lit up his mind with an excited light—a feeling of newness touched by fear.

Hope was sleeping quietly beside him, with her soft hair drifted across the pillow and her lips smiling. He had never seen her look as angelic; never as pure as now after she had sinned. There was a mystery in that, and a contradiction in the fact that someone so slender and gentle should have been capable of such passion. He wondered how she would feel, what she would say when she woke. He hoped she wouldn't blame him too much. He should have been stronger-minded, but it had been partly her fault.

While he was watching, Hope's eyelids fluttered and opened, and she smiled at him, dreamily and trusting. Then she took his hand in hers and held it against her cheek.

Conscience-stricken, he whispered, "Hope, I have seduced you!"

She looked at him as if he had said something ridiculous. "Willard! And you are going to be a lawyer!"

He almost thought that she had known what would happen. He took her in his arms and kissed her, without desire, but tenderly and with affection. "Hope," he asked wonderingly, "why did you come here?"

She answered, "To be near you."

"Like this?" holding her closer.

"To be near you," she said, "whatever that included."

He sighed with happy wonder at the fact that she was so one with life. His own mind kept going back to the past, rushing ahead to the future, hovering about the sky and the horizon of the present. "I don't see how we can get married until next week, when I get my check," he told her; "I've used up the last one."

This time it was she who sighed happily. "You want to marry me, Willard?"

He wondered at her question, when nothing else was thinkable. "Hope, of course I do!" He held her closer while he wondered more. "Don't you want to marry me?"

She kissed him sweetly. "More than anything else, except having you love me. But are you sure you can afford it?"

He had already been thinking of that. "I'll find some work; with what I get each semester, we'll manage."

"I'll find work," she said. "You have your studies."

"Never!" he said. "I believe in being modern, but there are limits. Anyway, you can help most by keeping house. That way, even with a job, I'll have as much time as ever for my studies."

"I'll keep house for you most beautifully," Hope promised.

They were still making plans when they heard the clomp of hoofs in the cobblestone street and the roll of iron wheels on iron. The wheels stopped, a bell clanged, and a voice called, *"Halloo, Willard!"*

Willard, who had forgotten time, started at the hail, and reached for his dressing gown. Hope asked, "What is it?"

"The streetcar." He jumped out of bed. "The driver stops for me on the mornings when I have an eight o'clock." He went to the front window, raised the sash, and put out his head. "Herbert," he called, "I overslept. Don't wait for me!"

The driver leaned out of the car, with his shoulders hunched and his square young face looking up disapprovingly. "I *can't* wait for you!" he answered. "I have a schedule to keep!" With his whip poised, he added, "You have a schedule, too. You'll never get ahead that way!" He cracked the whip. The gray horses lurched forward and iron wheels rolled on iron.

Willard decided not to go back to bed. He was fully awake in a chilly and unsentimental world that ran on schedule.

18

FOR THREE DAYS the southwest gale battered Astoria. The wind came rolling over the hill and down into the town, to see what it could overturn or tear loose. Sometimes it was visible waves of rain, and sometimes there was only the roar of its coming. On the land streets even the smallest mud-puddles caught the excitement and little wrinkled waves raced across them. It was the kind of weather Barry liked when he couldn't have summer. There was excitement even in the small things about it, like the fierce tiny waves on the mudpuddles, and in counting umbrellas that were turned inside out. The first day, seeing Marjorie Fortune home from school, Barry and she had counted seven, and the second day they counted only five, which was a little disappointing. It wasn't that they wished people or umbrellas bad luck; it was the gale and not they that did it.

The gale was exciting in larger ways, too. The river was rolling with long waves that went charging by the town; the steamboats coming down from Portland reeled and pitched like old ladies who had forgotten their dignity and their temperance pledges; they had trouble coming in to the famil-iar dock, and on the return trip they went staggering up-stream with unbecoming speed and a great flourishing of their stern-wheel bustles. Out in the stream the bar-bound grain ships rode uneasily to extra anchors, with their running rigging bowed back like sails turned inside out. Sea gulls flocked into the river and took possession of the water front, where they scolded everyone as cheekily as if they were pay-ing for the use of the docks and did not want any loiterers.

Ashore everyone was more alive and excited and at ease with other people. On the way to school Barry stopped at the Fortunes for Marjorie, and in the afternoon he saw her home, and no one took any notice when they held hands. Barry had never thought he would come to holding hands with a girl, and he did it partly to keep Marjorie from blowing away, but mostly because she wanted to and he liked it. There were other things that brought them closer together: his Uncle Roger was somewhere offshore, riding out the gale in the *Huntress*, and Jack and Tom were at sea on their way from Shanghai.

Looking out for Marjorie hadn't been easy at first. When he had walked her to school three mornings without her having said a word, he thought maybe he was being a bother and he asked her if she would rather he didn't stop for her any more.

She said in a husky whisper, "I want you to, Barry; you're the only one who ever stopped for me!" After that she began to tell him things and he forgot that he was looking out for her because her brothers had asked him to.

In the course of a year Barry got to know Marjorie better than anyone else did, but she puzzled him. She worried about her family all the time, which wasn't sensible. He just let things happen in his family and nothing bad had come of it. Marjorie was the youngest, and a girl, and Barry didn't see why she should do any of the worrying. Yesterday at school he had read her most of Jack's letter from Shanghai, stopping with the information that the *Christmas Morning* had a new second mate, but the best part followed:

> . . . *Remember the old one, who kicked us when we were saying good-bye to you? He promised to boot us around the world, but he didn't quite manage. After a squall in the South China Sea an oilskin coat was left on deck and he tried to kick it overboard through a wash*

port. He is stopping in the American Hospital with some broken bones in his foot. . . .

Barry hadn't read that because Marjorie might think her brothers had put the holystone under the coat. Even then she found something to worry about. Jack observed that the sea was a rough life, but he and Tom liked it and they thought of making another voyage. Marjorie begged Barry not to tell her father about that part of the letter. "Father said it was 'kill or cure'; if he thought it wasn't going to cure them—"

"He certainly wouldn't kill them!"

"I don't know."

"Well, I'm not going to tell your father, or anyone else, so you can forget about it."

"Thank you, Barry, but I mustn't forget. I have to see that nothing bad happens."

"They won't do any more than have a row," he argued. "If people want to quarrel, let them."

"Not the way they quarrel!" She held his hand tighter. "I'm afraid."

"You're afraid of too many things."

"I'm only afraid for other people."

"Aren't you afraid of things for yourself, Marjorie?"

"Only one or two."

"What are they?"

"Being dead."

"Who isn't afraid of that? What else?"

"Something silly."

"Like what?"

"It's silly!"

"You don't have to tell me unless you want to."

"Promise you won't laugh?"

"I promise."

"Apple blossoms brushing against glass."

[265]

He looked at her with sober blankness. "Is that all?"

She nodded without looking at him.

"I don't see anything bad about that."

"It's very bad, Barry."

"Why is it?"

"I don't know."

He felt her hand trembling, and he knew that it was what she was most afraid of, but he couldn't see why. "What would happen if they did touch?"

"It would be a sign."

"Of what?"

She said softly, "I don't know."

"I think you like to worry."

"I hate it!" she cried. "I hate it. But I don't know what would happen if I stopped."

Marjorie was a queer girl, all right.

He missed her the third day of the gale. Other mornings she had always been ready; the door opened and she came out the moment he reached the gate. This time it didn't happen, and he stood looking at the yard and some fruit-tree branches that had been broken off by the gale. Then Mrs. Fortune came out on the back porch in her wrapper, and called, "Don't wait, Barry! Marjorie has a cold; she isn't going to school today!"

The gale was letting up in dying gusts; you could tell there was a sun somewhere, though you couldn't see it; and it might be a week before the breakers on the bar went down enough for Uncle Roger to bring the *Huntress* across. Aunt Rita knew that as well as anyone, but so far Barry's mother hadn't been able to persuade her to leave her house for an overnight visit, or even for dinner—as if she meant to stay at home alone until Roger came back. This morning, with the gale clearing, his mother was trying again. Barry was stopping with an invitation for Aunt Rita to come over and have breakfast with his mother. If she didn't appear within an hour, his mother was coming over to visit.

Barry's mother thought Aunt Rita might be sleeping late, but when he turned the corner he saw blue smoke blowing away from the chimney in a gust of wind. Before he had time to ring the *Vandalia's* bell, the door opened and his aunt stepped out on the porch. She had on a woolen dressing gown and slippers, and her black hair was in braids as if she had just got up. She looked very fresh and young and pretty, and she was smiling. She kissed Barry and asked where Marjorie was. When he told her, she said, "It's right for Mrs. Fortune to keep her at home; there's so much influenza going around—or do you call it *la grippe* at your house?"

"We don't have it—but if we did we'd call it influenza; except maybe Emily—she tries on airs sometimes."

Aunt Rita laughed. "I'm glad none of you has it by either name. It's better to avoid influenza than to be fashionably dead with *la grippe*."

Barry told her about the letter from Jack Fortune and she was pleased to hear that the boys were safe and well and on their way home. "We have a letter, too, but I haven't opened it. It's addressed to both of us and I'm waiting to read it with Roger; he means more to the boys than I do." She talked about "the boys" with fond pride, as if they were her own and she would have liked to mean as much to them as Roger did—the way Barry would have liked to mean as much to her as the Fortune boys, who weren't any relation.

"Jack and Tom said you're the nicest woman they ever knew."

Her eyes shone when he told her that. "That's mostly on account of Roger. He loves the sea the way they do; I can only pretend."

When Barry was about to leave he gave her the invitation, which he had almost forgotten. She thanked him. "It'll be ever so nice to see your mother. I'll wait for her to call; I want to stay here until Roger comes home."

"It doesn't look as if anything could get across the bar for a few days yet, Aunt Rita."

"Just the same, I want to be here all the time." She walked with him as far as the gate. Barry was glad for her sake that no one was passing; it would be a scandal if anyone saw her dressed the way she was; but he was ashamed to tell her, and she didn't seem to notice. She walked beside him, with her hands in the pockets of her dressing gown, taking long, slow steps, and talking quietly. "Staying here until Roger comes home is a kind of penance," she told Barry. "When you are old enough to do penance you will find out how much happier you are doing it. There is a difference between being lonely and being alone. I have so much to plan and think about, I have no time to be lonely."

She was saying good-bye to him at the gate when a dim shadow passed over them, and he saw a sea gull light on the eaves of the porch. It was a large, handsome bird, snow-white with soft gray wings, as clean and fresh as if it had been created that morning.

The sea gull appeared to think well of himself, too. As Aunt Rita turned back on the path toward the house, he began scolding her, after the manner of gulls driven in by a storm. He was an uncommonly cheeky one, though, with a bell-like voice that sounded almost as if he were talking. He stretched out his neck and opened his beak as he shouted at Aunt Rita, gull-fashion.

His aunt stopped in the middle of the path; from the back she looked like a girl, standing there in her dressing gown and braided hair, with her head raised, looking up at the handsome sea gull that was shouting abuse at her.

Barry had seen other gulls behave in much the same way, but he had never before heard one that sounded as much as if it were swearing. Aunt Rita, too, was fascinated, or afraid to go in while the gull stood possessively on the house and laid down the law. She hadn't moved an inch from where she had stopped on the path.

"You'd think he owned the place!" Barry called.

His aunt did not answer; she was standing, looking up, as if she had turned into a statue, while the handsome sea gull repeated its bell-like shout.

In another minute or two Barry would be late for school, but he couldn't leave. He lingered at the gate, beginning to feel queer. It didn't seem possible that his aunt could be scared by a gull; he could only think that she saw or heard something he missed.

He left his books on the gatepost and went back along the path and stopped beside his aunt. The gull stood on the eaves looking down at Aunt Rita with eyes that were bright and impatient, but not really unfriendly. It reached out its snowy neck and half opened its beak and gave its sea-gull shout again, short and harsh, then the bell-like sound.

"I never saw one stick to it the way he does," Barry said. "You'd think he was trying to tell you something."

Aunt Rita did not seem to hear; she was trembling, more swiftly than he thought anyone could. "Aunt Rita!" he said. She did not answer. "Aunt Rita!" he repeated, and stepped forward where he could see her. Then he felt his hair bristling and rising, and cold goose-pimples all over him. Between her black braids her face was a strange dead-white, and her dark eyes were fixed and staring upward, with a kind of growing fire in them; he could feel it blazing up and up while she made no sound, or any motion except her trembling.

In the distance the school bell was ringing, but it did not have anything to do with him. He was with Aunt Rita in the presence of something he did not understand. He thought she understood more than he, but all he got from her was fear. He reached out and touched her hand because he was afraid, and because she was more afraid than he. At first her hand was cold and it didn't seem to notice; then it gripped until his fingers hurt.

"Aunt Rita, what is it?"

"Barry, I didn't know you were here!" Her voice sounded as if she were in a dream. Then she whispered, "Can you make out what he is saying?"

"Who?"

"*He; up there!*" She had never taken her eyes off the handsome new gull; he began scolding again.

The boy began to tremble because he had already thought the sea gull's cry sounded like words. It was shouting now: a short, harsh word, then a bell-like one; something reproachful and impolite. . . . He heard his aunt whisper words that had the same sound as the cry of the gull, and he agreed. "It sounds as if he was saying '*You fool!*' "

She repeated it in a burning whisper, "*You fool! You fool!*" Then she reached her arms up toward the sea gull with a terrible cry: "*Roger, Roger!*"

The sea gull stopped his clamor and launched himself into the air. Barry saw him rise above the house and soar away toward the river bar and the ocean beyond.

19

WILLARD'S KITCHEN TABLE served as both dining table and desk, and until recently the two pieces of furniture in one had always been at his command. At this moment he had neither, and his chair was drawn up beside the bed, which served as a desk in such an emergency.

But there were compensations. While he reviewed his notes on Doctor Hawley's lecture, the smells of coffee and frying ham drifted in and out of his consciousness; and sometimes he heard Hope's voice, which Emily had always said was like the voice of an angel. She sang very softly, not to be heard from the street and not to disturb him at his studies: "Flow gently, sweet Afton, among thy green braes—" Her voice was so light that he didn't have to hear it unless he wanted to. The song drifted out of his consciousness and he became wholly absorbed in political science; then Hope's voice said, "Willard, breakfast is ready!"

He left his books where they were and washed his hands at the sink. It was the wooden sink of his bachelor days, but it was scoured to luxurious cleanliness; there were no dishes to interfere with the washing of his hands, and the old brass tap shone like massive gold. (Last evening, with Hope sitting patiently in the dark storeroom, one of Willard's classmates had approached the sink with evil intent—only to be abashed by its elegance or by some divination of a feminine presence, and he had apologized and gone away to the plumbing in the hall.)

Willard dried his hands on the fresh towel that waited

on the rack and took his place at the table; Hope poured his coffee. He had become reliably used to her caring for all his needs, but he still marveled at the completeness with which she managed. For breakfast there were oatmeal, ham and eggs and toast, and applesause made of apples from the Hedges' barrel.

The ham particularly pleased him. "I thought we were out of ham," he said, helping himself.

"We were, but I got more."

"But I didn't have any money left."

"No," she said, "but we did."

He frowned. "Hope, I've told you that you mustn't spend your money on food for me."

"Only half of it's for you," she pointed out.

"Not any of it for me," he told her firmly. "My check should be here any day, but even if it's delayed another week, we have enough simple food to last us. Remember, you're not to spend your money on anything for the house."

"I'll remember," she promised.

"You'd better," he told her masterfully. "You've already done more than your share."

Living in sin had not turned out to be the dark, insidious drug that Willard had once imagined it. His living quarters had no vestige of red velvet curtains and leopard-skin rugs and oppressive perfumes. Instead, the attic room was fresher and cleaner than when it had been a monk's cell; the bare wooden floor was scrubbed and wholesome-looking; the lampblack hue had gone from the pots and pans that hung, shining, on the clean wall; and light and air came in through the clean windows and fresh curtains whose grime he had once accepted as one of the conditions of life.

Living in sin was refreshingly normal and good, and it allowed more gainful time for his studies than he had had before. Not that he recommended the condition for anyone else—or even for himself. If he were lecturing on the sub-

[272]

ject, he would explain: *There are, of course, different kinds of living in sin, and they are usually found at the extremes of economic conditions—the man with too much wealth who feels that he can afford to flout convention with a kept mistress; and the poor man who flouts convention only in the sense that he cannot afford to observe it with the price of a wedding ring and a minister's fee. There is such a thing as living in sin with honorable intentions—* That was the condition in which he and Hope temporarily found themselves.

It troubled him more than it did Hope, who thought that other people should mind their own business, although she knew that they never did. He could not dismiss it that way. The need for secrecy and subterfuge galled him, and there were moments when he felt an unreasonable resentment against his mother for being forgetful about his check. Not that she had been under any obligation to send him to college, but having offered to do so, she could be more prompt. Willard didn't have Hope's gift of being able to live calmly and fully in the imperfect present.

He started up at the postman's knock on the downstairs door; his check, at last!

"Let's finish breakfast first," Hope said. "The mail can wait."

"It's probably my check," he reminded her. "If it is, we can be married at once!"

"We're living now, too, Willard!"

The postman knocked again, instead of slipping the mail under the door and going away as he usually did. Willard thundered down the wooden stairs to open the door.

"A registered letter for you, Mr. Pearson," the postman said. "Sign here, please." A registered letter from his mother meant cash, and he wouldn't even have to wait until the bank opened. . . .

On the way upstairs he tore open the envelope to make

sure, and found the gold-backed bills folded in the letter—a fifty and two tens!

He burst into the room, waving the bills. "Victory!"

Hope waved back from the table. "Good! Now you don't have to worry about that. Sit down and I'll warm up your coffee. What does your mother say?"

Willard unfolded the letter and read slowly:

My dear Son: You must have heard by now that the Revenue cutters have given up their search for the HUNTRESS. *They found no trace of her and there has been no news except for the mistaken report last week when someone mistook the* AMPHITRITE *for her and reported her arrival at the bar.*

It is not easy to write, but we must face the fact that Roger is probably lost. One would expect your Aunt Rita to go on hoping longer than anyone else, but curiously she became convinced that he was lost on the third day of the gale, before there was any reason to believe that he was in danger.

I don't have to tell you what a good brother and uncle and friend Roger has been to us. However, there are details which Roger did not want you children to worry over because he wanted you to grow up with a feeling of confidence and security. Of course, you knew that your father left us very little. Actually, you never knew how little. Such comfort as we have enjoyed has been due to Roger's help.

It was Roger who paid your expenses at college, and he left the money for your present semester shortly before this last fateful trip. I am sending it with this letter; make good use of it.

From our own standpoint, we can be thankful that Roger had already piloted us so far across the bar. Emily will soon be married to her fine young man;

Barry has a Saturday job at Hill's Grocery Store and can go on with his schooling. April and Louise are old enough for responsibilities at home while I find employment. As for yourself, I know that you won't be dismayed by adversity, and that by the time this money is gone you will have found the means of supporting yourself while finishing your work at the University.

Your loving

MOTHER.

After he had finished, Willard continued to stare at the letter, with its message echoing in his mind like thunder that grew louder instead of dying away. "This is terrible!" he said at last.

"It could have been much worse." Hope was standing beside his chair, with her arm comfortingly around his shoulder. "Roger Collins loved the sea, and he will never be away from it now."

Willard had not been thinking about his uncle at the moment. "It isn't going to be easy for any of us," he said.

"Does it have to be easy?" Hope asked him. "We are able and healthy, and it's only a question of where we are going to begin."

He said, "We'll begin by getting married."

"That won't solve many problems," Hope said. "The thing for me to do is to get a job." It was a practical suggestion, but it seemed to take the color and comfort out of life.

"I don't want you to do that," Willard said. "We wouldn't have any comfort, and it wouldn't help my studies any. We'd be better off if I got half-time work. We could manage."

"We could—if I didn't have a baby."

"You—you're not going to have a baby, are you?"

Her smile was reassuring. "Not so far as I know, Willard. But it will be surprising if it doesn't happen."

[275]

He looked down at the table, ashamed and frightened. "I'll drop out of the University and go to work."

"Never!" Hope said. "Your family and so many others are counting on your being a great lawyer; you can't disappoint them!"

Even while he was hating love that might have already trapped them, he found comfort in Hope's steady arm around his shoulder and in her buoyant voice. "You are important, too," he told her; "and there are other careers. I could succeed at something else."

She took her arm from his shoulders, and her voice sounded farther away and a little disappointed. "No, Willard, that would be too great a sacrifice—giving up what you've worked so hard for."

"Everyone makes sacrifices," he reminded her. "It happens every day."

"But it's wrong. People should do things only because they want to."

That was quibbling, he thought, but he let it go. "The first thing we're going to do is get married; I can't feel easy until we do. Would you rather have a minister, or a justice of the peace?"

"What about the president of your college?" Hope asked. "He's a clergyman, isn't he?"

"I don't think he would do." Hope wouldn't either if she knew the six-foot-seven New Englander, fanatical and gaunt, thundering imprecations at any young man and woman whom he caught walking together on the campus, or even discussing their lessons in a classroom. Nothing Willard had told her could make him as terrifying as he was.

"Maybe a justice of the peace would be better, since you are going to be a lawyer—"

From the street below came the sound of horses' hoofs on cobblestones, and the roll of iron wheels on iron rails. Hope

[276]

dashed to the bed and began picking up books. "You've time to make it!"

"But, Hope, we haven't decided—"

She pushed the books into his arms. "I think that's everything." She was breathless and sweet and capable, bringing him his hat and picking a white thread off his coat in the moment of kissing him. He freed an arm and held her close, feeling the living warmth of her body—warmth that was never oppressive heat; there as always a brightness about it, like warmth at the moment of changing into dazzling light. While he had her he would never be altogether lost or defenseless or unfortunate. "Hope, I don't want to leave you now!" He wanted to take her in his arms, but he was already committed to his books.

In the street below the iron wheels stopped, a bell clanged, and a voice called, *"Halloo, Willard!"*

Hope slipped from his embrace, flushed and bright. "Hurry!" she said.

"Coming!" Willard called and went dashing down the stairs.

He had planned to hurry home immediately after his three-o'clock class, but it was dusk when he finally reached Front Street. Everything had taken so much longer than he had expected and nearly everything had been so much more inconclusive than he had hoped. His only positive success had been to find a friendly justice of the peace who would marry him and Hope any time they were ready that evening— "any time up to bedtime," which seemed a reasonable qualification.

Finding a well-paying position was another matter. He had set as his goal something that paid five dollars a week and allowed time for morning classes—and the nearest approach had been a job in a bakery at three-fifty a week, beginning at noon and ending at eight in the evening. More hopeful for the future, he had discussed part of his problem with Doctor Hawley, who had guaranteed offhand that Willard would neither starve nor have to leave the University. He even thought, in view of Willard's legal knowledge and the brilliant showing he had made in his studies, he might secure a paying position in a law office. But such things were not managed overnight.

When he reached Front Street his tired feet hurried faster, and then forgot to be tired as he turned in toward the side door of the harness shop. He turned in quickly and collided with a tall black shadow in the doorway. "Excuse me," he said, recoiling from the shadow, which had broadcloth and bony substance.

"Mr. Pearson, I have been waiting for you."

Willard started at the familiar voice in the unexpected place, and he looked up to the gaunt heights of Doctor Mather's face. "How do you do, Doctor Mather?" His mind explained the improbable call by telling him that the president of the college had heard about Uncle Roger and was there to voice his sympathy or offer help. "I wish I had known you were coming," he said.

"I don't doubt that." Doctor Mather's voice was definitely unfriendly. "Will you open this door?"

It wasn't a call; it was a hostile invasion that bewildered the young man before he had time to feel guilty. "I don't understand," he said. "Has anything happened?"

"Open the door," Doctor Mather ordered. "The key is in your hand."

Willard could not deny it; he must have taken out the key automatically as he hurried his last steps to the harness shop. And there would be no use pretending that he didn't have the upstairs door key, which was on the same cord. He unlocked the door.

"I am here to inspect your living quarters," the doctor explained. "I trust I shall find them in good order."

The young man found himself being conducted up the wooden stairs, with no time for stratagem or the preparation of a defense. Hope! If Doctor Mather knew they were going to be married; if he knew that Willard had already made arrangements with the justice of the peace—

He stopped halfway up the stairs. "Doctor Mather, I ought to explain—"

With surprising facility the Doctor's long legs reversed themselves until his feet were on the same step as Willard's, and his hand was firm and harsh on the young man's upper arm. "The facts can explain themselves."

At the head of the stairs, when Willard deliberately tried the wrong key in the lock, the doctor struck an evil-smelling sulphur match, which he broke from a little block, and held it near the keyhole. When that failed to help, he discovered and lit the gas jet. Willard unlocked the door and started to go in, but his hostile companion brushed past him and went in first.

The room was quiet and dark; apparently Hope was out, opportunely, and she would be spared the thunders of damnation.

Doctor Mather struck another sulphur match and lit the gas jet in the room, which he turned up until it hissed its loudest, illuminating the living quarters of Willard Pearson, law student, with a hitherto unmarred record.

Hope was away, and even to Willard's frightened gaze there was nothing immediately incriminating about his well-ordered room. Apparently his visitor did not see anything, either, and he was now hunting with his other senses—standing in the middle of the room sniffing intently for the perfume of harlotry. There never had been any, and the room smelled only of clean-scrubbed woodwork and books and the last few apples in the barrel.

The gaunt sin-hunter now approached the bed. With a loathing finger and thumb he took hold of the covers and stripped them back. The bed was made up with freshly laundered sheets that had been drying that morning, and there was only one pillow.

With less revulsion President Mather put the covers back in place, and continued his inspection. His eyes lighted on the tall, polished wardrobe—tall enough for a person to stand in. He strode over and opened its door with a vigorous gesture. Nothing there but Willard's winter overcoat, his other suit, his dressing gown, and an old pair of jeans he kept for rough work.

The sin-hunter closed the door and went back to look under the bed. Nothing there. He then looked in the apple barrel without finding a hidden Eve. With less hostility he went to the kitchen end of the room and looked about sharply. "I never saw such cleanliness in a bachelor's quarters," he said at last.

"It's next to godliness," Willard said.

"No joking, Mr. Pearson." The doctor was now standing over the kitchen table, which was set for one: knife, fork and spoon, a freshly washed, unironed napkin, and a clean cup and saucer.

It was not until then that Willard realized the perfection of his alibi. Hope must have been aware of danger, and while Doctor Mather waited in the shadows of the doorway, she had cleared the room of every vestige of herself. She must be hiding in the dusty storeroom, a few yards away; there was no means of escape, except by the stairs and the shadowed doorway.

Doctor Mather had decided to give up the room as a bad job, or one above reproach. "We shall inspect the hall again," he decided.

Willard's spirits fell, then suddenly he felt pugnacious. If he wants to get into the storeroom, he thought, he'll have to break down the door, and he'll be guilty of unlawful entry.

Standing at the first door in the hall, the doctor asked, "Where does this door lead?"

"The water closet."

Doctor Mather knocked at the door, with a certain delicacy, and asked, "Is anyone there?" There was no answer and he opened the door vigorously. No one there. He closed the door again. His inspection seemed over when he noticed the last door in the hall, almost out of the gas jet's illumination. "What is in there?"

"A storeroom," Willard told him. "It belongs to the harness shop downstairs."

The Doctor held out a big, bony hand. "The key?"

"I have no key for it." Willard took out his keys to show that there were only two. "You would have to get that from Mr. Boyd."

Doctor Mather tried the door and found it locked. Then, dusting his hands, he seemed to lose interest in it. "Mr. Pearson," he said, "I have either done you a wrong, or you are a very clever dissembler."

"I haven't done any dissembling," Willard assured him. That was technically true—Hope had done it for him.

The doctor looked at him searchingly. "Mr. Pearson, I heard it whispered that you were living in sin and it was my duty to investigate. I have found no evidence of it. On the contrary, I congratulate you on keeping remarkably neat quarters." He looked at Willard more and more intently, until his eyes blazed with fanatical fire. "But if I find that you have deceived me—" He made a gesture of annihilation with a gaunt black arm.

When Willard was sure that his visitor was gone, he locked the downstairs door and dashed up to the storeroom. He knocked cautiously at the door and said, "Hope, it is I, Willard!"

There was no answer. He tried again and then took out the upstairs key, which Hope had discovered would fit both locks. He was in a panic now, thinking of improbable things that might have happened to her, and when he got the door open he went in fearfully.

The gaslight down the hall made a dusty twilight in the room, enough for him to see that she wasn't there; nothing but discarded harness, tarnished sleigh bells that had been found out of tune with the mild Salem winters, and ponderous ox yokes, resting forever after their labors on the Oregon Trail. She wasn't there, alive or dead, among the dusty relics of the past.

He went out and locked the door, relieved and puzzled, and went back to his room. She had gone, but how, and when? It could only have been down the stairs, and that meant she had left before Doctor Mather was standing guard at the door. Then she couldn't have known about him—yet she had prepared everything so perfectly!

He walked about the empty room, puzzled and annoyed. This wasn't like Hope. The justice of the peace would be expecting them any time, now; he would have to remember to take enough money for the fee. This morning he had dashed out with only sixteen cents in his pocket. He hoped the justice wouldn't charge more than two dollars, but he had better take five, just to make sure. He had left the money and the letters on the table among the breakfast things, and since then the dishes had been washed and the table set again for supper.

He found the money in the top drawer of the dresser. One of the tens had been broken and there were eight silver dollars in its place. The other ten and the fifty were there. Under them were his mother's letter and a note written in pencil:

Dear Willard:
   You must know how much I wanted to help you and make you happy, but with all that has happened you can see for yourself that it won't work.

Third thoughts are said to revert to first, and it seems to happen that way however much you want it to be otherwise. I came here because I had made up my mind that Father and Mother would never force me to anything, and before I did whatever that left me, I was going to do what I wanted to do. I hadn't expected that I would stay, or you would want me to, and it has turned out that way in spite of the brief appearance of permanence.

If you want to look at it so, I am leaving at the first sign of trouble. That may not be brave, but I think it is wise when my staying would mean expenses and responsibilities that would almost certainly pull you out of the University. This way, you still have your career, and I have my pride.

You will see that I took $2. I didn't want to, but I needed it for a ticket.

Your supper is on the stove; it only needs heating. Don't worry about me. Take good care of yourself, and don't neglect your studies.

Love,

HOPE.

Love, Hope—those were some of the things she had given him; now she was gone without any warning, without even saying where! It couldn't be far on two dollars. She hadn't even given him the chance to marry her. She shouldn't have come at all if she was going to leave him so much lonelier than he had been before.

Her note said it wouldn't work. It wouldn't work without her! The ticket agent would be sure to remember her—and remember where her ticket was for. She might even be at the station now, waiting for the evening train south. He began putting money in his pockets. He would find her wherever she was, and bring her back and marry her! He wouldn't be living until he did. She said she wanted to help him and make him happy. She had until today, when she left him. And she made it sound as if she were doing him a favor by going!

He paused with a sudden realization of the favor she had done him. If she hadn't gone, he thought, Doctor Mather would have trapped us here! I would have been expelled from the University in disgrace. It would have been another blow to the family and a black mark against me politically as long as I live. He took off his hat and sat down, sweating and weak with the realization of how he had grazed disaster —unhurt—not through any skill or wisdom of his own.

He put his hat away and started a fire in the cold stove with the kindling and newspaper Hope had left ready for him. It was nonsense, Hope's saying that their marriage wouldn't work, but this was no time for reckless, unplanned action. He had just come through a great crisis—the world had toppled about him, without hurting one root or branch of his budding legal career. He didn't believe in Providence, but it seemed to him that more than blind chance had controlled events, and he mustn't do anything foolish now. Hope had been an instrument of Providence; he would get in touch with her, and as soon as he found a job that would support them both without endangering his studies, they would be married.

The fire began to roar, and while the young man waited for the stew to heat and the coffee to boil, he began studying for tomorrow's examination. Standing at the stove with an open book in one hand and a wooden stirring spoon in the other, he might have been mistaken for an earnest cook following a recipe. But Hope had made the stew, and it had no relation to Hall's *Elements of Political Science* except that they were both ingredients of a lawyer in the making.

20

CHRISTMAS had come, inopportunely, and followed eighteen-hundred-odd other Christmases that extended through time like lonely mileposts, back to a baby in a manger and a star over Bethlehem. Behind the stable and the star there was only pagan darkness; and at the near end of the row of Christmases there had not been the warmth and light Mrs. Fortune dreamed of. The boys had not returned and Marjorie was in bed with influenza. Even then they might have gone through the motions, but Marjorie had been at her worst on Christmas Eve when her father should have lit the candles on the tree. In the morning they had taken her presents up to her, but she pushed them away. "Save them until Jack and Tom are here." She turned her face toward the window and began to cry. Christmas could be celebrated with only a baby boy, but not with an unwilling girl.

So Christmas still waited after the calendar had gone on to the next year's business. The door to the parlor was slid half open. Through it, from her place at the supper table, the woman saw one side of the waiting tree—still-green branches holding up spiraled white and green and red candles, erect in their neat tin holders. . . . Remember the thrashing Thomas had received the first Christmas of the patent holders? He had begged for permission to snap just one candleholder on a branch, and had been refused. It was a ritual that the parents dressed the tree; the children were not to come into the room until it was ready and perfect for their enjoyment. The boy had overstepped bounds to be there at all, and his clamor only hastened his being ordered from the room. He went, with grumblings that would have brought a whipping on a less generous day.

Half an hour later, with the stepladder and litter cleared away, the children were allowed to come in and admire the tree, and the incident was forgotten until later when the parents went to the door with Christmas Eve callers. From the carpeted hall they saw Thomas holding a lighted candle. He had the holder in both hands, with his thumbs pressing down the lever, and the toothed clasp, like the open jaws of a snake, was about to bite on a chosen branch. John was standing by anxiously, and Marjorie had an arm around Fido for comfort and one hand over her mouth to stifle any cry of fear which might betray her brother's disobedience. Then Marjorie saw her parents at the door and gave the alarm with a quick intake of breath.

"Don't put that on the tree!" the father warned.

Thomas looked up with startled defiance, afraid to disobey and unwilling to be balked. For a moment everyone and everything was still except for the lightning of warning and the small lightning of defiance meeting in the middle of the parlor. Then, quicker than thought, Thomas turned and let the toothed jaws of the holder snap on the nearest object of suitable size and shape—the end of Fido's tail.

The still picture erupted into noise and action: the dog's yelp, the man's roar, the woman's shriek, and the little girl's cry as she was bowled over by the frantic dog. For a blurred instant the candle was upright, with its flame blowing back in Fido's wake as he dashed toward the hall. Then the candle fell, extinguished and smoking, on the carpet, to be snatched up by the mother who had grabbed for the dog when it was already passed. The father had Thomas by the collar.

It was the epic beating of the boy's life—almost fit punishment for his epic naughtiness; like young Samson tying lighted torches to the tails of foxes and turning them loose to fire the grain of the Philistines. But Samson's had been a useful act of war. Thomas acted in wanton naughtiness against those who loved him, and the firebrand he turned loose might have burned down the house. . . .

Now you could not tell which candle holder had set its

teeth in Fido's tail. They sat unobtrusively among the green branches, holding up candles that were waiting to shine out their message of peace on earth and good will toward men. The candle-bearing branches were festooned with strings of white popcorn, red strings of cranberries, and many-colored paper chains, and they were hung with gold nuts, red apples from the Willamette Valley, oranges from California, and a spiraled candy cane. The white oblong package on the near branch was a copy of *Pilgrim's Progress* for Marjorie; the small, solid package below and to the left was a watch for young John; to the right, hidden by the door, there was a bicycle for Thomas; and that slender red package near the top of the tree—

"Will you pass me the cream, Dehlia?" her husband said.

She passed the cream, which he poured generously over his dessert, enjoying good things which had gone untasted half his life. But he was thinking of more than his own enjoyment. When she had refilled his coffee cup, he told her, "I talked to Alsop at lunch. He's sure that even if the boys don't get home for a month they can make up their work for the school year."

"They can; they're bright boys."

"Alsop says there isn't anything they can't do if they set their minds to it. It's only a matter of their applying themselves."

"I'm sure they will do that, John."

"They won't be allowed outdoors until they have given a good account of themselves for the day; there won't be any spending money for them unless we're satisfied with their work for the week. If it is necessary, we'll use sterner measures."

"We shall do everything necessary."

"We aren't to blame," he said, "but we must contribute, too. The boys will not have any chores until they have finished their lessons for the day."

She agreed, as she almost always did.

When she and her husband had finished, Dehlia went to the kitchen and made up Marjorie's supper tray for the second time that evening. Going upstairs with it, she saw John alone in the parlor, and even from a distance she knew his thoughts and feelings, and shared with him the pride and loneliness of parenthood. John was standing by the parlor fireplace with a schoolbook in his hand—a steady, solid figure of a man in good broadcloth and linen, with a gold watch chain making a festoon of approval across his front— his head bent over the open book and his neatly trimmed black beard covering his immaculate collar and silk cravat. The stairs took her up out of the sight of the parlor and of John, but she carried the picture with her—a vigorous and successful man, standing by the fireside in his own parlor, not at ease enough to sit in one of his comfortable chairs— going on from struggling for his own success to struggling for the welfare of his children; keeping the lonely vigil of parenthood.

When she turned up the gaslight in Marjorie's room, the girl was awake, staring at the ceiling with her velvety dark eyes which seemed to have grown larger with the wasting of her face. It would have been easy to imagine the child going into consumption, but Doctor Knight assured them she had a perfectly good pair of lungs, and she was suffering from nothing worse than influenza, which was epidemic that winter. Not that influenza was a joke; it didn't kill many people, but it could do more damage in two days than more serious ills could in a month. A good thing it wasn't a larger devil, the way it ripped at the body; the mind, too. Mrs. Fortune had heard about Gregory Rice.

"I brought your supper up earlier," her mother said, "but you were asleep and I didn't disturb you."

"I have noticed that."

The mother propped extra pillows against the dark walnut head of the bed. "Now sit up like a good girl and I'll give you your supper." Then she asked, "What was it you noticed?"

"That I'm usually either awake or asleep."

"Now sit up like a good girl," the mother repeated.

She sat up, like a good girl, but an untidy one. She had started as a neat child and become less neat as she approached adolescence, and now, while she was ill, she made no effort at all. At some time when she had been too warm she had unbuttoned the front of her nightgown, and later she had refastened one button, askew. "You'll catch your death of cold," her mother said, rebuttoning the nightgown. Then she added, "People usually are either awake or asleep."

"I never notice being asleep," Marjorie said, "except when I have dreams, and then I'm always sure I'm awake."

Her mother said, "Dreams can be very interesting."

"I hate them!"

The mother offered her the bowl of chicken broth from the tray, and when Marjorie only stared at it listlessly, she took up the spoon and began feeding her. "I've heard of people having pleasant dreams."

"I don't; it's always the same, and I hate it!"

After another reluctant spoonful, she asked, "What is it that you always dream?"

"The black box of measuring things; it's standing on a funny table in the parlor."

Feeding her, the mother confided, "I sometimes dream about the same thing several times, but that makes it more interesting."

"I didn't know you had dreams," Marjorie said.

The mother had never talked to her daughter this way before, but she felt hurt to think that Marjorie didn't even know she had dreams. "Of course, I have dreams! I'm a woman."

"Don't men have dreams?"

"Everyone has; I meant that I'm human."

"Oh." After another reluctant spoonful, Marjorie asked, "What are the same things you dream about?"

"Let me see. . . . I remember dreaming several times about an eel."

"Ugh! I hate eels!"

"I don't like eels, myself," the mother admitted. "We never have it in this house."

"What kind of eel was it, Mother?"

"A big, determined one, as I remember. I had gone down to the Columbia to bathe—"

"I didn't know you ever went bathing in the Columbia."

"I never thought of doing such a thing, but in my dream I went down to the river to bathe. It wasn't the way it is; there was no city there; I was alone. While I was on the bank the eel came out of the water directly toward me. I had that same dream several times."

"What happened?"

"I don't remember," her mother said.

"You must have run as hard as you could!"

"Very possibly."

"I thought you were going to tell me about a dream you liked."

"I told you the first one I thought of. Things are different in dreams; it didn't seem unpleasant at the time. Now, another spoonful."

"I don't want any more," Marjorie said; "I won't take it!" She had always been timid and obedient; but now, with illness for an ally, she was almost insolent.

The mother put the unfinished broth aside and took up the next dish. "Here's some custard; I made it with vanilla, the way you like it."

"I hate custard, mustard—yellow things," but she reluctantly accepted a spoonful.

"You hate a lot of things."

"Yes. Custard, mustard, bustard—what's a bustard?"

"A large bird," her mother said. "How can you hate it if you don't know what it is?"

"—and a black box with measuring things."

"I wish you could dream about something else."

"It's in the parlor on a funny table. I hate the table, too. It's the table you and your husband borrowed from the parsonage when you were too poor to have furniture of your own."

"Another spoonful, like a good girl." Then she said, very quietly, "That's an odd way to speak of your father."

The girl was sullen from the reproof. "That's what he is."

"He is your father. Why shouldn't you call him that?"

"Because I hate him."

The spoon clashed against the custard cup. "*Marjorie!*" If one of the boys had said that, or if Marjorie had said it when she wasn't helpless and sick—but the mother controlled herself. Doctor Knight had talked earnestly about the depressing effect of influenza, and there had been the shocking headline in the morning's *Astorian:* GREGORY RICE BLOWS OUT HIS BRAINS. And below it, next to an advertisement for Doctor Flint's Fabulous Discovery, guaranteed to cure coughs, colds, catarrh, influenza, and consumption, there were the unsparing details of how Gregory had blown out his brains in a fit of depression while suffering from influenza. This was not the time to punish Marjorie for her sacrilege, but it couldn't go unnoticed. "You shouldn't have said that terrible thing; when you are well again, you will take it back of your own accord. Now, another spoonful of custard."

"No." Marjorie closed her mouth and kept it closed until the spoonful was taken away. Then she said, "It tastes indecent! I hate custard, mustard, bustard—Father's an old bustard, and I hate him!"

Remonstrance only made it more flagrant. The best her mother could do was to ignore the mountainous offense and pretend they were on a level plain. "Would you like your milk, now?" she asked.

"No. A drink of water."

The mother filled a glass from the carafe and put in a fresh wheat straw. Marjorie sucked thirstily for a few seconds, then more slowly, until it became a listless game of pulling the water up in the straw and letting it fall back into the glass. Presently she let go the straw and pushed the glass abruptly toward her mother. "I want to lie down."

Marjorie had been shockingly bad, but it was clear that she got no pleasure from it. When she was lying down again, lonely and flushed and sullen, with her too-large eyes watching the ceiling, her mother felt only pity for her. She put her hands around the girl's thin shoulders with unaccustomed tenderness and touched her cheek against the too-warm face. "When you're sick, nothing seems right; but you'll feel better tomorrow. Don't fret about things now."

The girl reached up her hand and touched her mother's hair awkwardly. "You aren't really bad, are you?"

Bad? Dehlia straightened up and looked at the girl with wonder. "I never thought of myself as particularly bad. I'm just a mother who loves her children."

Marjorie looked at her, part suspicious and part confiding. "You can be almost nice," she decided. "I think you would have been a nice mother if it hadn't been for your husband. You could be nice to us now, if you got rid of him."

The mother was profoundly shocked, but it was worse than useless to remonstrate, and there was a certain satisfaction in having some merit in the child's stern judgment. "You won't think that when you are well. By next week you'll be going to school with Barry. And soon John and Tom will be home. We'll have good times!"

Marjorie looked at the ceiling wearily. "Why? Has this family changed?"

"Why should it change?"

"If it hasn't, they shouldn't come home."

This didn't sound like Marjorie, the timid and obedient child. "Marjorie! Don't you want your brothers home? Where else should they be?"

"Where they're happy," she answered, sullen and matter-of-fact. "Anywhere."

The mother drew a chair up beside the bed and sat down to hide her weakness, as much from herself as from her daughter. The boys had been trouble enough, but there had never been rebellion like this—that shook the foundations of life! . . . But remember the depressing effect of influenza; control yourself and make the child as comfortable as you can. . . . "Marjorie, dear, you want your brothers home, too. It was your idea that we keep Christmas for them."

"I know." The girl gave a long sigh. "But it's no good."

The mother took her hand. "It is good," she insisted. "We shall have a happy Christmas."

"No, we never will."

"Why shouldn't we?"

"Because we are we," she said. "It will start all right, and I'll be happy because everyone else is. Then Tom will want to change a candleholder on the tree—and your husband will beat him."

The mother was startled to realize that the child remembered so far back. "That was a long time ago; Tom is nearly sixteen now and he can be trusted with candles."

"Then he'll want to do something that a boy wants to do when he's nearly sixteen, and your husband won't let him, and everything will be dreadful." Marjorie wouldn't speak of him that way if she knew how little the man had been a husband, and how much a father, making sacrifices for his children.

"The boys are older now," her mother said gently; "they will have more liberties because they are growing up, and we have missed them so much. I thought you missed them, too."

Marjorie answered by clutching her mother's hand convulsively and holding it against her face, crying hot tears onto it. "I miss them," she cried; "I miss them so! I miss them and love them, and I want them to be happy; I want us all to be happy, you and Tom and Jack—"

The woman wanted to add, "—and your father," but she only said, "We will be happy, and you can help by getting well. Now it is time for your sleeping powder."

She sat by the bed while Marjorie quieted and dozed, stirred restlessly and half opened her dark eyes to look at her mother in the dimmed light, and dozed again. Once she heard the doorbell and her mind leaped to the idea that it might be her sons coming home. But there was only one discreet peal, rung by someone who knew Marjorie was sick. Her husband went to the door, and the caller did not come in. She tiptoed to the window and saw Barry Pearson walking thoughtfully down the street.

Dehlia Fortune didn't have much use for the Pearson tribe: the smiling, tolerant-appearing mother, who was really as stubborn and opinionated as a mule; Willard, the long-legged prig, full of bright ideas that had come from everywhere except his own head; Emily, the prude of the approved brand, who knew how to get what she wanted by being all the proper and self-sacrificing things that were expected of her; calculating April, who had observed an unused corner to plant her selfishness where the others didn't even notice it; and the brattish Louise, who was still too young to matter much. With one exception, Dehlia didn't have much use for the Pearson tribe. The exception was the boy, who went back and forth through the barricades of family feuds trustingly, without knowing they existed. It had been sweet of him to call and inquire after Marjorie's health; without making too much of a point of it, Dehlia would tell Marjorie the first time she was thoroughly awake.

She heard her husband coming up the stairs and tiptoed out to the hall to meet him, with her finger on her lips, telling him she was not yet sure of the lasting quality of Marjorie's sleep.

"I'll sit by her," he whispered.

She shook her head.

He accepted the decision, bowing ever so slightly, and turned and went downstairs; the mother returned to the bedside.

She told herself it was best not to change nurses in midstream, between the shores of waking and sleeping. She also felt guilty of a necessary disloyalty. She had denied a father the right to watch beside his child; but she had also saved the child from waking and finding herself in the company of "your husband," whom she suddenly professed to hate.

[294]

With the aid of the sleeping powder, Marjorie's breathing became regular, although it had an uneasy rhythm. She seemed comfortable and past the danger of immediate waking. Silently the mother put the half-eaten custard back on the tray with the unfinished broth and untouched milk, and moved the glass of water to a convenient place on the bedside table. . . .

"*Don't let them touch the glass!*" Marjorie cried.

The mother was startled; she had been so sure the girl was asleep. "Don't let what touch the glass?"

"The apple blossoms."

Her mother saw that she was struggling with some dream in the depths of sleep, with her eyes closed and her face piteous and bleak. She took one of the restless hands and said gently, "We won't let the apple blossoms touch the glass," although she did not know what it meant. The dream passed, like the shadow of a cloud, and Marjorie's face was calm again. It was strange that the girl was talking of apple blossoms, when she complained that she dreamed of nothing but a black box with measuring instruments.

The mother sat quietly until the girl's hand relaxed. Her face showed no change when the gas was turned out and there was only the night light in the red glass beside her bed. She would sleep until morning now, with everything still in the big house among the trees on the quiet street.

The town was quiet, too, except for distant bursts of sound toward Chinatown and the river front—sounds too far away to trouble the sleeping or the waking. Exasperatingly, one of the sounds was coming nearer, too near and too indecently loud; drunken sailors bawling a song in a residential street where sailors were not supposed to be. Dehlia went to the window; she could not see them because of the trees, but she heard them distinctly now, singing in reasonable tune— but too loud:

> *Shake out the topsails and roll along home;*
> *Roll along home;*
> *Roll along, roll along, roll along home!*

The front door opened and closed. She heard John's determined, hurrying tread on the porch, and then again the triumphal voices bellowing their song:

Shake out the royals and roll along home;
Roll along home;
Roll along, roll along, roll along home!

John was at the gate now, the square, dark figure of an aroused citizen, hatless to show the haste in which he had rushed out to quiet the disturbance. "Gentlemen," he shouted, "please! This is a residential section!"

Shake out the skysails and roll along home;
Roll along home;
Roll along, roll along, roll along home!

John was shouting impotent prose against the rolling chorus; then he was opening the gate, fearless in his anger, and stepping out to meet the troublemakers. In the dim light, a tall figure suddenly grappled with him, and the watching woman stifled a shriek as another figure seized him from the other side.

She stood at the window, paralyzed by fear, then puzzled. The shouting died, and there was no struggle. The tall figures released her husband and he responded by putting an arm around the shoulder of each. Then all three of them were coming through the gate.

"Marjorie!" her mother cried; "Marjorie, the boys have come home!"

Marjorie slept on.

21

FOR THE FIRST HALF HOUR the household was incoherent.
Everyone talked and acted, but little that was said or done
dovetailed with anything else. Mr. Fortune brought the step-
ladder and lighted the candles on the tree, and his wife
alternated between cautioning everyone to speak quietly, because of Marjorie who was asleep upstairs, and raising her
voice to exclaim over her big, swaggering sons. Jack went to
the kitchen for a bucket of water in case the tree caught fire,
and came back with a chunk of fruitcake, half of which Tom
devoured while assuring his mother that he wasn't hungry.
Mr. Fortune mounted the stepladder again to light a candle
which he had overlooked, and let the unused match burn out
in his hand while he announced that this would be Christmas
Eve—it being then the sixth of January. Christmas would be
tomorrow, and presents would not be distributed or opened
until then because of Marjorie, who must not be disturbed.
After that, Tom mounted his new bicycle, which was not
adjusted to his newly acquired long legs, pedaled a pre-
carious voyage across the parlor and disappeared into the
hall, where he brought up with a crash. Dehlia unwrapped
Jack's watch and chain, to see how it looked on him. Jack,
who did not seem to notice the watch, was telling her
about a suit of clothes he had ordered in Liverpool and
failed to get for some unexplained reason.

"If I took a deep breath in this waistcoat," Jack said, "all
the buttons would fly off." He expanded his newly developed chest—and two buttons flew off.

Tom, who was untangling his bicycle from the umbrella
stand, called to know if Jack had told his father about the
John Fortune who was a tugboat captain on the Mersey. The
father ordered everyone present to keep an eye on the

candles while he brought the forgotten fire buckets, and after a minute he hurried back with a decanter of claret and three glasses. Marjorie, who had several times been pronounced asleep, was calling for her mother. The mother answered that she would be up directly and went to the hall, where she embraced Tom and demanded that he assure her that he was sound and well, and tell her, without leaving anything out, all that had happened in the last more than a year.

Without prearrangement, the family's center of gravity shifted to the hall. While Tom and his mother cross-questioned each other about things at sea and at home, Jack sat on the second step eating apples; and while drinking a glass of claret that he had poured for his oldest son, Mr. Fortune raised his voice above Marjorie's calling to remind everyone that the child was sleeping and must not be disturbed. Jack went to tell his "little monkey-face" good night, and presently he came staggering downstairs, carrying her in a long cocoon of bedclothes. Dehlia insisted that he take her back immediately—and made a place for her on the sofa by clearing away half-unwrapped presents, the boys' pea jackets and crumbs of fruitcake.

The family shifted back to the parlor, with Marjorie for the still center of its center. The boys sat at her head and feet, exclaiming over how long their "little monkey-face" had grown, while their parents marveled at how they had grown.

Up to the time they had gone to sea, the boys had been healthy and well-formed, but small for their ages, and Mrs. Fortune had resigned herself to the fact that they would never be taller than their father, who was five feet six. A year of time and sea air and coarse food had upset that calculation. Tom was already a shade taller than his father; Jack admitted to being five feet ten, and by the looks of him he would be every inch of six feet when he attained his growth. Both of them were lean as rails, but big-chested, with muscular shoulders and arms. At moments they showed signs of falling asleep, but they were plainly in splendid health; and when they exchanged looks, reminding one another of something to tell or not to tell, there was a devil of determination in their hard-bitten young faces.

The parents were slow in adjusting their eyes and minds to the hulking boys, but Marjorie seemed to make no progress at all. She lay on the sofa, mouse-still, her too-large velvety eyes looking from one boy to the other, too shyly for brothers and too constantly for strangers. She neither asked nor answered questions, but her look suggested deep and solemn feelings that marched on in an endless, swelling procession.

Jack said, "Our little monkey-face has lost her tongue; she hasn't said a word to me since I came home!"

"Or to me, either," Tom said.

"She doesn't like us any more." Jack made the motion of pinching her toes through the bedclothes. "What do you say, Marjorie; shall we go away?"

Marjorie's look was like a solemn rebuke.

"Marjorie," her father said, "we're making allowances for your illness, but this isn't the place for temperament. If you are not well enough to speak to your brothers, you are not well enough to be downstairs."

Until that evening, the mother would have agreed wholeheartedly with the pronouncement. It was reasonable—except for the fact that things were not that simple. Marjorie had missed her brothers more, if possible, than her parents had—and she had been willing for them not to come home at all, because in her stern judgment they would be happier elsewhere. Now they were home where she wanted them to be, and in danger of everything she dreaded. The two balanced each other like a seesaw resting on her heart, and she could only speak with her eyes.

"Marjorie, speak to your brothers!" the father ordered.

"She'll talk when she's ready," the mother observed soothingly; "give her time."

Jack said, "She'll be talking our heads off before we know it, and we'll tell her that children should be seen and not heard!"

"Marjorie," the father said, "you heard me. Will you speak to your brothers, or go upstairs?"

The girl looked from one big, encouraging boy to the other and her lips moved as if she were rehearsing a whisper.

"That's better!" Jack said. "I knew you were glad to see us."

"We're glad to see you," Tom said.

"I couldn't hear you," the father said.

"You are farther away than the rest of us," the mother pointed out. Actually, there had been no sound, but the effort brought tears into the girl's eyes. She found her voice and began to sob.

"This is too much excitement for Marjorie," the father said; "I'll take her to her room."

"Let her stay a few minutes," the mother said, with indulgence that was new to her. "You've never been a girl, John. Tears are a legitimate expression of joy."

The man accepted it, partly because Marjorie was growing quieter, and partly because he had always been more indulgent with her than with his sons. She meant less to him, and he was less concerned with what she did, so long as it wasn't annoying. The near scene had come about because he felt that she had been disrespectful to his sons. It was over now and he was able to give them his full attention. Earnest and alert in the brocaded armchair, he said, "Well, sons, you haven't had much chance to tell your experiences. We got your two letters from England, and a third from Shanghai, and we've read them I don't know how many times; but you have to bring your own news about your voyage home."

The brothers looked at each other as if they had a story to tell and were arranging their teamwork. Jack grinned and said, "We got here."

"It must have been a rough voyage—in winter!" the mother said.

Tom was judicious. "Not everyone would have liked it, but we liked it all right."

"And we were lucky," Jack put in.

"You also had a good master," his father said. "I've known Captain Slade since you were little boys. I don't doubt he's severe, but he's one of the best shipmasters afloat."

"He was better after we got to know him," Tom said generously.

Jack said, "He got to know us, too."

"I'll see him in the morning and thank him for bringing you home safely."

"You'll find him in Saint Mary's," Jack explained. "We took him there before we came up here."

"Is he very sick?"

"Hurt," Jack told him; "some ribs broken."

"I am sorry to hear that." The father paused, struck by an uneasy thought. "You boys didn't—"

They were twin portraits of reassurance. "There were times when we would have liked to break his neck," Jack said; "but the ribs were his own idea."

"Ran too long before a gale," Tom said.

"It was blowing force ten, Beauforte, and the old man kept before it until it was too late to heave to."

Tom said, "It was roll and go, or the deep six for all of us."

"We were trying to outrun a sixty-mile gale, with the whole Pacific Ocean chasing us," Jack said. "At the height of the gale, we were pooped by a great-grandfather of a sea and swept from stern to stem."

The mother put her hand to her heart. "It's a mercy you weren't lost!"

Mr. Fortune asked, "How did Captain Slade get hurt?"

"He got knocked down the companion steps, trying to reach the deck."

[301]

Jack fumbled in the pocket of his coat. "The old man wrote you a note when we were towing up the river to quarantine." He brought out a crumpled paper and handed it to his father, who unfolded the sheet of foolscap and examined it with the alert stateliness of an official studying a report.

"John, do read it aloud!" Dehlia begged. He cleared his throat, and read:

Dear John:

When you receive this, I shall be in the hospital, to which I am looking forward with eagerness.

With this note, I am returning your boys, in reasonably good condition. As far as it was in my power to do so, I have whipped them into shape, but I have my limitations. You particularly requested me to put the fear of God into them. That was easy enough to promise, and it would have been easy to do if you had raised a different brand of boy. As it has fallen out, they do not take kindly to any fear of God or man or devil or the deep sea. I advise against beating them.

The father frowned with disfavor and slurred over the words.

They have their good points as they are, and I commend them for quick wits and cool heads in an emergency. I refer particularly to the occasion on which I received my present injuries. During the mate's watch on the afternoon of December second we were boarded by an unusually large sea in which four men, including the mate, were swept overboard and lost—"

"Lost!" Mrs. Fortune looked anxiously at her sons. "It might have been you!"

"It wasn't," Jack said, undeniably having the best of the argument.

Mr. Fortune cleared his throat and resumed:

[302]

—and two other members of the crew seriously injured. The accident swept the quarter-deck of officer, helmsmen and crew, and in all likelihood the unattended ship would have broached to and been overwhelmed if your boys had not taken charge of the damaged wheel and kept us before it until I was able to clap on preventer tackles.

"And you didn't even tell us!" Their mother looked wonderingly at her big sons. "You were heroes!"

"No, Mother," Tom said modestly.

Jack said, "We were rats who wanted to live, and we fought like rats in a corner."

"You gave a good account of yourselves," the father said, "and I congratulate you. Shall I go on with the letter?" He had looked ahead and found lines more to his taste.

When I signed on your sons, it was with the understanding that you wanted them permanently cured of the sea—a sentiment in which I more than ever concur. With the help of an unkind Providence, I have given them a bitter bellyful. If they are as smart as I judge them to be, they have had enough, and I have no reason to suppose that you have altered your opposition to a seafaring life.

The rest of the letter Mr. Fortune slurred over impatiently, as if it were a matter of no great importance, and one already settled.

However, if your sons are to again eat their bread and butter on the sea, I earnestly request that you have them sail with me. I have little to offer them except more hard knocks and the opportunity to learn what I know of the ways of ships and the sea.

> *Your Obedient Servant,*
> *Philip Slade,*
> *Master, Ship* CHRISTMAS MORNING.

[303]

"The idea of his suggesting that you would go to sea again!" The mother was indignant.

But the father put the thought aside with the letter. "That's over with," he said. "It was more than any of us bargained for; with Captain Slade going on around the world instead of returning from Liverpool, you've lost a year and a half of school; but you won't have to lose more than a year in work. Today I had lunch with Professor Alsop; I doubt if you boys properly appreciate him, but he has a high regard for your abilities. He said there was no doubt that you could make up this year's work; he said there isn't anything you two couldn't do if you set your minds to it."

The brothers exchanged a look which the mother tried to fathom, and could not.

Jack smiled reminiscently. "That was nice of old Alsop, after all the trouble we've given him."

"You've had practical experience now," the father said; "physical experience. You'll find that you can pitch into your books and study as never before."

"That remains to be seen," Jack told him cryptically.

Tom said, "I'd forgotten there were such things as books."

"They're still with us," his father assured him. "In fact, I have a surprise for you." He got up briskly, then paused. "Books," he said. "They'll be with us as long as the civilized world lasts! Ships, beautiful women, blooded horses, great buildings—you could throw them all into the discard and it wouldn't make much difference. Burn the books, and the light of civilization would go out!"

"Hear, hear!" Jack responded cheerfully. The mother could not tell whether it was ironic or admiring, but the English form of applause for an American speech brought misgivings.

"Books," the father said again. He knelt between the far wall and the Christmas tree, and backed out with two solid stacks of them. "These are yours, John, and these yours, Tom."

"Thank you, Father," the brothers said.

"The world's priceless gift!"

Tom brushed a sprinkling of evergreen needles from the top of his stack and read, "First Year Latin."

Jack gave his books a glance of puzzled recognition, then looked at his father. "They're not—"

"They're your textbooks for this year. I got them from Alsop the day we heard that you were on your way home from Shanghai; I had promised myself to have them ready so you wouldn't lose any time."

The boys exchanged another look.

"You'll have to work hardest on Latin," the father said. "You're both good at mathematics, and other things come naturally to you, but Latin is something you have to work for." He knelt beside Tom's stack of books and began unfastening the shiny brown strap. "You have to work for it, but later it will work for you." Walking about, with a brown volume in his hand, he illustrated: "You are going to be a doctor, John; you, Thomas, are going to be a lawyer. They seem very different professions, but Latin is the language of them both.

"English law is based on Roman law," the mother put in.

"Quite. Through English law, American stems back to the Roman in spirit and technical language. The medical profession makes still more use of Latin; you'll find that out, John. Remember, when you're studying Latin, you're already learning to write prescriptions. I don't expect it to be easy, with four months to make up. You'll sweat, but you won't sweat alone. I have been studying Latin, myself, so I could help you." He opened the brown volume and read:

> *Galba est agricola.*
> *Gallia est terra Eurōpae.*
> *Luna et stellae sunt pulchrae.*

"It helps both your English and your Latin when you note that *agricola* is one who engages in agriculture; *terra* is 'land' as in 'terrain'; *luna* is 'moon,' and from it we have 'lunar,' pertaining to the moon. *Stellae* are the companions of the moon—the stars; and from it we have the English word 'stellar.' I have found declensions simple enough, too, with a little application; simpler than English, which uses two words to Latin's one. Take the verb *to love*—correct me if I am wrong—*amo, amas, amat, amamus, ama*—"

"John, that candle!" Mrs. Fortune interrupted with a cry. But Jack had already leaped across the room and crushed out the flame that endangered the dry tree.

Mr. Fortune put down the Latin book, regretfully. "We'll put them all out; they're burning dangerously low."

The boys helped with alacrity, Tom bringing the step-ladder and dashing up like a careful monkey, while Jack crushed out the flames of lower candles with his calloused bare finger and thumb.

"I hate to see the lights go out," the father observed; "but there's a satisfaction in doing it in time, in an orderly manner." He looked profoundly content, as he had not looked for a year, working in harmony with his capable big sons. With the last candle safely out, he said again, "I hate to see them go, but it's better than having one of them mar the best Christmas Eve we ever had." He took a deep breath. "Notice how the lingering smell of candles blends with the smell of evergreens! It's the only perfume I ever cared for."

It was the happiest Christmas Eve Dehlia could remember, and her husband did not mar it by reading any more Latin. He returned the brown volume to his younger son, observing, "The real start can wait until tomorrow; this is an evening to celebrate."

"That's right," the mother said. "No studies on Christmas Eve!"

"It's a good Christmas," Jack said.

Tom agreed. "The best yet!"

The father's eyes went back to the new books; he was like a miser looking at a treasure which had to wait until tomorrow to be counted. When he was turning toward his armchair, he said, "There's one thing, though—" He squatted beside Jack's books and began unbuckling the new strap. "There's one thing that might be classed as a Christmas present. Geometry is one of your studies this year, John." While the boys watched, puzzled and ill at ease, he sorted down through the books. "Ah, here we are!" He produced a black leather case and handed it to his older son.

"For me?"

"Of course," his father said. "Open it!"

The boy released the swing hook with a work-coarsened thumb and raised the cover, revealing a gleaming array of brass and steel instruments—compass and dividers and ruler and square, and more complicated instruments, of finest workmanship.

Jack looked embarrassed. "It was good of you, Father. They certainly are fine!"

The father cleared his throat. "You may not find them all immediately necessary in your geometry, but a doctor's hands must be accustomed to fine instruments."

"They're beauties," Tom said.

Until Jack had lifted the cover, the mother hadn't an idea of what was in the black leather case. It had been kept a secret even from her. That meant that John considered it extravagant. It was a complete surprise; it was also strangely familiar: measuring instruments in a black box—the things that Marjorie was always seeing in her nightmares!

The mother had told her there had never been anything of the kind in the house. Now the thing suddenly materialized out of a Christmas package! It was nothing—and it made her terribly uneasy. But children sometimes never even see the thing you expect to frighten them most. . . . When she found courage to look, Marjorie's eyes were closed. It was a hopeful sign.

"I think we should go to bed," she announced. "Your room is ready, boys, and you look as if you hadn't slept for—"

Marjorie interrupted by crying, "Take me upstairs! Take me upstairs!"

The brothers were startled by the suddenness of the outburst, and Mr. Fortune looked pained. "She's overwrought," he said, getting up quickly. "I told you she wasn't well enough to be here."

Jack smoothed her rumpled dark hair. "Our little monkey-face has had too big a day," he told her. "I'll carry you up topside."

"I'm taking her," Mr. Fortune said.

Marjorie said, "Let Jack!" But the father was already gathering her up.

The mother feared another outburst, but the girl lay motionless in her father's arms, her face like the face of a child being carried away on a dark flood that she was not resisting any more. Following, she said reassuringly, "I'll have you tucked away in a minute."

Alone downstairs, the brothers looked at each other.

"The old man hasn't changed any," Jack said. "*Amo, amas, amat*—I wonder what he knows about *love!*"

Tom said hopefully, "Mother's better than I remembered her. Can people learn after they're grown up?"

His brother did not know, and he was preoccupied, gathering together his Christmas presents.

"What are we going to do?" Tom asked.

"Get some sleep," Jack said, "if the old man doesn't come in to hear our lessons. We'll think about the rest in the morning."

Tom was collecting his smaller presents to take upstairs. The bicycle could wait. It was a wonderful present, and somehow silly. When he had everything together, he nodded to his brother, who was waiting for him. Then he saw the black case of instruments left carelessly on the pile of new books. "Did you forget that?"

Jack's look was dry and wary. "No; let it stay. There are strings to it."

Tom agreed. Then he reminded his brother, "We were going to tell Captain Collins and Rita that we're back."

"There wasn't a chance," Jack said, "and it's late. We'll see them in the morning."

While they were talking, their father came downstairs and joined them at the fireplace. "I'm sorry Marjorie made a scene," he apologized. "She's had a bad case of influenza, and children get out of hand when they're sick."

"She doesn't look well," Jack said.

Tom said, "I hope she's better soon."

"She's much better," the father assured them. "Doctor Knight says she'll be back in school next week. She hasn't done well in her studies this year." When the boys did not comment, he looked at them, falling asleep on their feet. "I didn't mean to keep you up," he said. "Tomorrow will be another day. Good night, boys."

"Good night, Father."

"We'll have lots to talk about in the morning." His eyes traveled to the neat bundles of schoolbooks. "John, you're forgetting your present!"

The boy was embarrassed and mumbled that he hadn't really forgotten it, but when his father picked it up and offered it to him, he refused it. "I thought I would leave it there until morning."

His father looked hurt. "Don't you want it?"

"It's a wonderful present," Jack said, "but I have to think it over."

The man was nonplused. "Think what over, John?"

"I mean I wouldn't take it under false pretenses."

His father looked more nonplused. "What are you driving at?" he asked, not unkindly. "Geometry is one of your subjects this year."

The brothers exchanged a glance, and there was no sign of wavering in either face. "I'd like to talk about it in the morning," Jack said. "I don't know just what we'll be doing—"

"You'll be in school," his father reminded him. "To-morrow is a school day."

"We're just home," Jack said; "we haven't really left the ship; some of our things are still on board—"

"I'll send a man for them; you're not going to miss a day of school for that."

"And we want time to look around and make up our minds—"

The father gave an impatient sigh and looked at his younger son. "Thomas, what is this rigmarole? Do you know what your brother is trying to say?"

"Yes, sir," Thomas said helpfully. "Jack is trying to tell you that we might have plans of our own."

"Plans!" The father stared at him. "What plans could you have, except for getting back to your studies as fast as you can?"

Jack said, "For one thing, there's the *Christmas Morning*. Her charter calls for her being in Portland Monday, and with Captain Slade in the hospital—"

"I forbid that," the father said. "There are deck swabs enough to look after her hawsers while she's towing up the river. You're not going to miss school for that!"

"Things are in a mess on board," Jack explained. "Captain Slade has been good to us, considering, and we aren't going to leave him in the lurch—"

"You heard his note. Captain Slade said he was returning you to me. That ends your obligation."

Jack persisted, "But there are things to be done! We've had responsibilities since half the crew was put out of commission."

"You're both to be in school in the morning," the father said, "and I forbid you to go on board the ship again." He looked at his sons with quiet determination. "Do we under-stand each other?"

[310]

"It seems not," Tom said.

"And why not? Could I make myself any plainer?"

"Maybe we don't agree with you," Jack told him. "You want to make a doctor out of me, and a lawyer out of Tom. I don't want to be a doctor; I never did!"

"And I won't be a lawyer," Tom said.

The father looked stunned. "Boys, what's got into you? You have to have professions!" He thought it over, and began to feel hurt when the first shock had passed. "Next thing, I suppose you'll tell me you don't want to go back to school!"

"That is the next thing," Tom said. "We're not going back."

"Not until we've done a few things, and made up our minds," Jack told him.

"Really—" The father was interrupted by his wife calling from the head of the stairs:

"John, boys! Haven't you visited enough for tonight? It's time we were all in bed." She tried to put it in a friendly light, but there was no doubt that the angry sound of voices had carried upstairs.

The father answered, "We'll be up in a minute!" He closed the sliding doors to the hall and turned to his sons again. "So you plan to throw your opportunities away! And I was hoping you had learned something in a year!"

"We think we have," Jack told him.

Tom said, "We hoped that you had learned something."

The father's face reddened as if from a blow. "You cub!" He seized the younger boy by the collar. "You've been spoiling for trouble long enough!"

Jack touched him on the shoulder. "Not that. Take your hands off him!"

"You cub!" the father said again. He had paid less attention to Thomas because he was the younger, but now it came to him that the young sprout had been bolder and more insolent all along. "I'll teach you to be insolent to your father!" He began shaking him more violently as the feeling of outrage sank deeper.

The older boy struck, almost regretfully, but with neat efficiency. Only his forearm moved as his rigid open hand described an arc and chopped down on his father's wrist at the base of the thumb. It sounded and felt like the blow of a dull ax, and the man was no longer grasping his son's collar. He glanced at the wrist of his paralyzed hand, expecting a wound and blood, but there was no mark—only a trick blow on a nerve, and his right arm was still good. He swung fiercely at his older son, but his arm was caught in a double vise and wrenched behind his back, while young John secured his other arm. On one side, level with his own, there was Tom's unrelenting, tense face; and on the other, looking down at him, there was young John's face, regretful and hurt, as if he were the one who had been struck. Holding like iron, young John said, "Father, I'm ashamed. We're too old for this kind of thing. You'll have to learn to control yourself."

Control himself! That from an irresponsible boy who planned to throw his opportunities away and drag his younger brother with him to the slums of water fronts. "You let me go," the father said, "and I'll beat some control into both of you!"

Jack said, "You're going to keep your hands off both of us. That sort of thing is over."

"It was over before we came home." Tom's face was harder and less kind than his brother's. "It's finished. Understand?"

The father said, "All I understand is that you're planning to throw your opportunities away. I'll fight that as long as I have a breath in my body! Let me go!"

"When you promise to keep your hands off us," Jack said.

"I'm not taking orders from my children." The father continued to struggle.

The brothers exchanged a look and then Jack said,

"Then we'll go where you can't get your hands on us."

"I forbid you to go back to the ship!"

"We'll go where we please," Tom said.

"You're my sons and I'm not going to let you ruin your lives!"

"They're our lives," Tom reminded him.

Jack decided, "We'll let you go, anyway, but if you try anything, you'll get hurt! All right, Tom." They released him and stepped back warily. He stood where he was, panting.

"You boys don't know what you're doing!"

"That's what you think," Jack told him. "We have our own ideas. When you agree to keep your hands off us, we might be willing to talk things over."

At the moment, the father was not inclined to strike either son, only to save them both from a fatal mistake; but he was not in the habit of taking orders from his children. "Don't dictate to me!"

"Or you to us!" Tom said.

Jack gave his younger brother a quieting look. "Let's get back to the ship."

"I forbid that," the father told them, "for your own good!"

"Come on, Tom." He slid open the door.

"Wait!" the father ordered.

They did not wait, and he followed them into the hall, where they put on their pea jackets, standing warily between the parlor door and the door to freedom. Physically, they were more than a match for him, but he had no intention of giving up.

"Never mind your coats," he said. "You're not leaving this house!"

Even while he was saying it, the older boy opened the door. "All right, Tom."

They went out, and the door closed firmly in the father's outraged face.

[313]

22

It had rained earlier, but it was not raining now, and it was not cold. The night had the even, fresh texture of a world that would go on for a long time; a world in which violent decisions and human haste were out of place. The brothers had no doubts about being right in what they had done, but their rightness seemed of less importance when they considered it outdoors. Before they had gone a block, their hurrying feet changed to the amiable gait of sailors who are already where they want to be, and use their legs chiefly to steady themselves against the roll and pitch of the earth. When they reached the corner, they continued east instead of turning downhill.

They were going back to the ship, as much because their father had forbidden it as anything else; but there was no great hurry. The night was young, and probably Captain Collins and Rita would be up, ready to welcome them to a more peaceful homecoming.

Before they reached the end of the third block, there were footsteps growing louder out of the silence behind them. They looked back and saw the square, hatless figure of their father hurrying after them. Jack wanted to run, but pride slowed his footsteps. He sighed, "Oh, Lord!"

"Stop, boys!"

Pride kept them from running, and it also kept them from obeying the command. They loitered on, with the footsteps gaining rapidly.

"Wonder what he wants now?" Tom said.

"Probably the declension of a Latin noun. You'd think the old man was all bulldog, the way he keeps after things!" A little farther on, he stopped. "We'll heave to; it's as good a place as any." They were on a raised board sidewalk, with a fence at their backs. Below the fence, in the sunken vacant lot, an evergreen blackberry vine swelled up in a dark wave that almost touched the stringers of the walk. Tom approved the strategy as he saw it. "We'll throw him into the blackberries if he tries anything."

His brother had thought of it only as a place where they wouldn't be airing a family quarrel in someone's front yard. "Take it easy," he advised. "The old man doesn't learn fast." The footsteps changed to thunder on the hollow sidewalk. "Watch out for squalls from loo'ard!"

When their father came up to them, they were perched on the top rail, warily but at ease, with the fence giving them the advantage of height even while they were sitting. They saw their father's dark, displeased face before them, and heard him ask with unexpected mildness, "Where are you boys going?"

"Does it matter?" Tom asked.

His brother said more reasonably, "We were going to see Captain Collins for a few minutes."

"You can spare yourselves the embarrassment," the father told them. "Captain Collins is dead."

"Dead?" the older boy echoed.

Tom cried, "No, no!" as if he could never accept that.

Neither of them said anything for a minute, then Jack protested, "We had a letter from him at Shanghai! What happened?"

"He disappeared with the *Huntress* a month ago. He was going to bring her into the river, and the ship has been missing ever since."

"Maybe they were blown offshore!" Tom suggested. "That could happen—"

"It was a southwest gale; evidently they didn't weather it."

"What about Mrs. Collins?"

"She's still here. The house is up for sale."

[315]

Tom said unsteadily, "A month ago; it must have been the storm we were in!" As if there was some comfort in that.

"Captain Collins!" Jack said. "I can't believe it!"

"I had a good opinion of him," the father said, "but I see nothing unusual in his being lost. You ought to know that it happens at sea."

"If I had known he was lost in that storm," Tom said, "I wouldn't have fought so hard to stay alive!"

His brother agreed. "You don't feel the same way about it when you have friends like him among the dead."

"It's much better to look at it as a useful warning," the father told them. "Now I want you boys to come home. All in all, you're lucky to have a home to go to and a school waiting for you!"

"We've been through all that!" Tom answered impatiently.

"If it's the same to you," Jack said, "we're going to take our time and think things over."

"It's not the same to me; now come along!"

Tom looked at him belligerently in the damp twilight. "We're not going!"

"Then I must take you!" The father grabbed for Tom's ankles, catching one and missing the other. He tried to pull the boy from the fence, while dodging kicks from the other foot.

The older brother sidled quickly along the fence and struck with a heavy foot. The blow loosened the man's grasp and he dodged back from Tom's flying feet, nursing his arm.

"There are two of us," Jack warned, "and we can kick the daylights out of you!"

Panting, the father said, "All right, if I can't do it one way, I'll do it another!"

"Do what?" Tom jeered. He did not see the revolver in his father's hand.

Jack saw it and felt too disgusted to be afraid. He had said the old man would stop at nothing, but he hadn't quite believed himself.

[316]

"You'll do what?" Tom jeered again. He still did not see the revolver, or he was too reckless to pay any attention.

"He's got a gun," Jack warned. "Stand by for a squall!"

"I have a revolver," the man corrected, "and it's loaded. Don't provoke me any farther! Come down from that fence and march home!"

"You'll have to shoot us down," Tom said, "and carry us home!"

"We'll come down," Jack said, staying where he was. "We'll come down. But you're a fine father! Before we're born you decide to make a doctor and a lawyer out of us— and when we don't like the idea, you want to shoot us!"

"Boys," the father said, "I don't want to hurt you. I'm sorry I have to take extreme measures, but it's for your own good—"

"Everything is for our own good!" Tom interrupted bitterly. "When we don't die of beatings for our own good, you want to shoot us for our own good!"

"You don't look as if you had been hurt by beatings!" his father said. "If I'm taking extreme measures now, it's because I know how much is at stake, and you don't. You want to throw your opportunities away and ruin your lives; I won't stop at anything to prevent that!"

"Not even at killing us!" Tom said.

"I don't want to hurt you. If you meant less to me, I'd let you go to hell without another thought. Now get down from there and come home!"

"At the point of a gun?" Jack asked.

"If you won't go any other way, yes."

"Not even at the point of a gun!" Tom said.

"And you have one minute to get down!"

The brothers exchanged a look which doubly irritated their father.

"We'll go with you," Jack said, "because it's better than being shot; but that doesn't mean—*Don't, Tom!*"

The man looked swiftly toward his younger son, who was sitting relaxed on the fence, with no sign of a weapon or threatening gesture. A shadow descended from the other side as Jack launched himself from the fence and bore his father down. There was a burst of flame as they crashed, and the hollow sidewalk made a sounding board for the explosion of the revolver, and powder smoke fogged the darkness about the father and his sons. . . .

"Is anyone hurt?" Jack asked.

"I don't think so." In the dim light from the sky, and in the clearing smoke, Tom had one foot on his father's wrist, and he was wrenching the revolver from his stubborn grip.

"I'll take it," Jack said. He got up carefully and took the revolver from his brother. "The fool," he said, "he might have killed one of us." He opened the breech, and one after another the heavy cartridges plunked into the blackberry vine.

The father stirred and sat up on the sidewalk. "Is anyone hurt?"

"Not if you aren't."

"I'm glad of that!" He got up, with his hands brushing his suit of their own accord while he looked about on the sidewalk.

"If you're looking for your revolver—" Jack began.

"My hat."

"You didn't have one."

"Quite so," the father recalled. "I came away without it." He touched his forehead and brought his hand away with blood on it. Then he took his handkerchief from his pocket and patted it against his temple. The cut did not amount to much, and he did it with the air of wanting to protect his good suit of clothes.

"Let's get out of here before someone comes!" Jack was sensitive about airing quarrels; it seemed too much like displaying the family's nakedness in public. He and Tom started on, with their father walking beside them. "Better go home, Father; there's nothing to wait for."

[318]

"We're not finished," the father said.

"*We're* finished," Tom told him unsympathetically.

"You boys don't know what you're doing. You want to throw your opportunities away, but I won't let you!"

"How many times do we have to go over that?" Jack wanted to know.

"Until you understand what I'm talking about!" the father answered. "You two have never wanted for anything; I had a hard time when I was a boy. I know what it means to be hungry and cold and responsible for younger children when I didn't know where I was going to get food for them; when I didn't know if there was going to be a roof over their heads tomorrow; and all the time feeling helpless—helpless!"

Tom made an almost sympathetic sound, and Jack said, "You had a bad time!" But he didn't see what it had to do with him, and he brought the little procession to a halt at the next corner, to give his father an opportunity to go home.

"There are things I've never even told your mother. I got food out of garbage pails, and when I had to, I begged and stole—" When the boys started at the word, he corrected himself. "I didn't really steal. But I couldn't see younger children starve—"

"I'm sorry," Jack said. He was sorry for his father's starved youth, but he didn't see what it had to do with himself or Tom, and he wanted the old man to go home.

"You know the rest," the father said; but he had to tell it to them. "I studied nights and got into the custom house —almost lifted myself by my boot straps, with your mother's help. I promised myself that if I ever had sons, they would never go through what I did; I would see to it that they had professions that put men in a different world, where they don't know what it means to be in want and fear and to feel helpless!"

"You've done well by us," Jack told him generously. "But

[319]

we happen to have our own ideas. We know what we want to do, and we can take care of ourselves."

"You think that because you're not old enough to know any better!"

"We won't go over that again," Jack said. "We've made our plans. If you promise to keep your hands off us, we'll see you again; but we're going up the river with the ship, and we're going to make another voyage. If you talk Captain Slade out of it, we'll sign on some other ship. We want to look at the South Pacific."

"So you want to be deck swabs!"

Tom said, "We'll be captains while you're still poking around in an office!"

"We know what we want to do," Jack told his father, "and you ought to know that you can't stop us."

"I know that, now."

"Then we're all settled up. You might as well go home, and we'll go on to the ship."

"It isn't settled," the father insisted. "What about me?"

"You?"

"You don't understand me. Look, for seventeen years I've lived mostly for you boys. I've planned and worked and denied myself to provide for your educations—"

"You still have the money," Jack reminded him. "You can spend it on something else."

"There's nothing else I care about—and it isn't a matter of dollars. I had plans for you—"

"We have our own plans," Tom said.

"I had such plans—"

"It's no use," the older boy told him. "We know what we want to do. There's nothing more to say except—good night."

"There is," the father insisted; "we've just started."

"I'm not staying to hear any more," Jack told him.

Tom said, "I've heard enough." They started down the

hill toward the comfortable lights of the town and the scattered anchor lights of ships on the dark river.

"*Wait!*" the father called.

They waited, wearily, while he caught up with them. His power over them was broken, and a dark ribbon of blood was starting down the side of his face again; but he was unwilling to admit defeat. "You boys hurt me!"

"I'm sorry," Jack told him; "but when you pull a gun, you have to take your chances."

The father wasn't thinking of physical hurts, or even aware of them. "It hurts me for you to think that I'm ready to abandon you; that I can't or won't help you. I could send you to a navigation school where you would get the best training that money could buy. It would put you years ahead of where you would be otherwise—where you might never be with your own efforts—"

"You wouldn't do that!" Tom said.

"Would you?"

The father made a helpless gesture. "If you won't listen to reason, if you insist on making your own choice, I still can't abandon you. I'm ready to help you be the best of whatever you're going to be."

"Father," Tom said, "you'll really do that?"

Jack said, "I didn't expect it!"

The father couldn't see why not. "You boys are everything to me. Unless I can help you, everything I've done has been for nothing—and there wouldn't be anything ahead of me but a stone wall."

"You can help us," Jack said, "and we'll try not to disappoint you."

Tom said, "You don't know how we can work if it's something we've set our hearts on!"

"I still think you're making a mistake," the father told them; "but if you insist on going to sea, we can at least make captains of you."

"We'll do our best." Then Jack said, "Your forehead is

[321]

still bleeding; you'd better get some sticking plaster on it. We'll walk home with you."

"Thank you. But if it's only because of this scratch—it doesn't amount to anything."

"I want to go home," Tom said.

Jack said, "There's no hurry about the ship, and a real bed would look good."

The man walked back with them, contentedly. "I want you to want to come home." Then as if he were afraid they still had the wrong impression of him, he said, "You boys may think I've been severe at times, but I learned in a hard school and I know the importance of hewing to the line." When that did not seem adequate, he tried again. "It's supposed to take three generations to make a gentleman. That isn't so important any more, but there's something in the maxim. It takes three generations—two, anyway—to be comfortable in your mind. You don't understand how I grew up, because you never had to do it, but I tell you it was no joke!" He walked along in the cool, even night between his sons, with his hands in his trouser pockets, jingling silver and gold. "Men who started with better opportunities have done worse—"

"A lot worse!" Jack agreed earnestly.

Tom said, "You're one of the most successful men in town."

"I'm only one generation away from the slums," he told them. "In some respects, I've come a long way—in others, I'm still there; I've never been able to live down my boyhood, the misery and the fear—"

"No one would ever know that," Jack told him.

"Well, I haven't, and it isn't likely to happen now. That's why I can't give you boys up, even though you're bent on careers I don't approve of. I have to give you all the help I can. When you were still babies, I realized that I would never have much of a life of my own; I haven't had much. That's why I have to live through you, my sons."

Months ago, on the other side of the world, the brothers had vowed their declaration of independence. Now it appeared that their father was dependent on them, and they were embarrassed.

"We're not going to disappoint you, Father," Jack mumbled earnestly.

Tom said, "Watch how we make out at navigation school! How soon can we start?"

"That's out of my field," their father said. "I suppose when you're old enough and can meet the requirements. It probably means finishing high school."

"Oh!" Tom sounded as if he had expected a catch to the offer.

His brother felt no disappointment. This was victory; he recognized it by its responsibilities. He and Tom had got what they wanted, and like everything worth having, it meant hard work and planning. For the moment, at least, he was suddenly grown up, and the feeling of a carefree young sailor was shadowed by the responsibility of command. In the cool half-darkness, under the cobblestone sky cemented with moonlight, he called up perfect moments at sea: Tom and himself whooping along the main deck in tropical sunshine and the shadow of white sails, pouncing on glittering flying fish that had just thudded on board; Tom and himself riding the flying jibboom, with the wide, free sky at their backs, idly watching the porpoises romp about the bow of the *Christmas Morning*, watching the warm indigo sea burst into snow against the black cutwater of the ship that roared after them forever as it bore them on. Now the sea was his and Tom's as long as they lived; the sea shadowed by responsibility. It seemed to him that some of its color was already gone with the carefree moment of youth.

Walking on one side of his father in the damp and quiet dark, he said, "We're going to make a good job of it; we'll do whatever is necessary."

[323]

When they turned in at the gate, their mother was on the porch, with her hat and coat on. She met them on the walk and embraced them all. "I wanted to go and look for you," she sobbed, "but I was afraid Marjorie would wake again; I've had a dreadful time!"

Jack had never seen his mother so upset. "You shouldn't have worried about us," he protested. "We were just talking over plans with Father."

"Wait till you hear the plans!" Tom said.

The mother was still trembling. "I heard a shot—"

"The revolver went off by accident," the father said; "no one was hurt."

"You were! There's blood on your face—"

"It's only a scratch," he assured her. "I got it running my head into a stone wall. It was rough for a minute, but all in all it was the most satisfactory talk I ever had with my sons. We've learned to respect each other's opinions."

The mother did not give the momentous news as much attention as her husband expected. Instead, she went on about her lesser adventures at home.

"The sound of that shot nearly killed me!" she said. "Marjorie heard you rush upstairs and she was sure you had taken your revolver. I had to keep her in bed by force, and I gave her another sleeping powder—"

"Our poor little monkey-face," Jack said. "She always worries too much about us!"

"I had a terrible time quieting her," the mother went on. "I don't know what would have happened if she had been awake for the sound of that shot! As it was, she started in her sleep, and then she had a nightmare. It's a wonder you didn't hear her screaming that the blossoms had touched the glass!"

"What blossoms?" Mr. Fortune asked.

"Apple blossoms—in a dream."

23

THE WEDDING CAKE from Cleveland's Bakery was the gift of the Bethel choir. On top, a miniature bride and groom took refuge under a sugar wedding bell, and the five snow-white tiers on which they stood were more than enough cake for everyone. The boys were holding large chunks of it as they climbed to the seat beside Barry, who had borrowed the grocery wagon for the wedding presents.

On the way to the dock, behind the old roan horse, there wasn't much conversation because of mouths full of cake, but they all agreed it had been a great wedding. Jack and Tom had their secret pride in it, because if it hadn't been for them there wouldn't have been any wedding. It was also quite satisfactory that Albert hadn't recognized them as his res-cuers; if he had, they were prepared to deny any part in the affair in which Jack had shot a crimp.

The *Telephone* had been drowsing at her berth since her night trip down the river, but she was wide awake when they drove onto the dock. Passengers were scattered along the rails of her two white upper decks; Captain Tomlinson, in his splendid uniform, was standing outside the pilothouse with its gilded eagle. Wood smoke poured from the high stack overhead and struggled with the morning sun for pos-session of the broom at the masthead. It was an ordinary straw broom, but it could be carried only by the fastest steam-boat on the river; the boys looked up at it respectfully as they unloaded the wedding presents and passed them on to the deck hands and the purser. The last and largest present was from Rita Collins—the revolving table built on the *Ariel's* wheel. The boys were parting with it regretfully when the steamer blew her warning whistle, and a few minutes later the wedding party trooped down the street and onto the dock.

It had been an early wedding to allow the people who were going inland to catch the morning steamer: Emily and her new husband were stopping off in Portland; the other Hedges were going on by train to the Wheatland ferry, and from there to the Yamhill; and Willard Pearson was going back to Salem.

Everyone from the wedding was there: Rita Collins, who had sold her house and was leaving for San Francisco in the morning; Mrs. Pearson and the girls—April with a pink-cheeked English apprentice from the *Falls of Clyde*; Mr. McMillan of the Seamen's Bethel; classmates of Emily's, and young men and girls who had sung with her in the Bethel choir.

The Fortune boys' favorites in the crowd were the elder Hedges. To the eye they were just a tall, sunburned man uncomfortable in his Sunday clothes and a quiet, sweet-faced woman in her old-fashioned blue-green changeable silk dress. But the boys had heard of their long-ago adventure in the mountains, and in imagination they saw them as a dashing young cattle dealer and his bride, shooting their way out of a trap where travelers before them had been turned into hogs. As a tie with the glamorous past, there was the odd bulge under the hip of Mr. Hedges' clawhammer coat; he didn't trust the river towns and he was carrying a revolver in case he met crimps.

Jack reminded himself that he was growing up and he joined the crowd around the bride and groom to wish them good luck; but he was hindered by women who were embracing Emily and crying over her in a shower of rice. Some of them also embraced Albert, to show that there was nothing personal in their tears.

Jack was still waiting, hat in hand, when the *Telephone* shouted her impatient final whistle. There was a scramble on board under a dwindling fall of rice, the gangplank was drawn in with a sliding rumble, and the lines cast off. Through cries of "Good-bye!" and "Good luck!" and "God bless·you!" the mate shouted, *"All clear, sir!"* The engine-room gong clanged, and the stern wheel's thunder was answered by the screaming of sea gulls as they took to the air.

As the steamer drew away, Albert and Emily appeared on the upper deck, waving in answer to their cheering friends. After he could no longer recognize their faces, Jack could still make out the flutter of Emily's handkerchief and the waving black round of Albert's bowler hat.

He watched until the steamer became a thin black smoke-stack and a white waterfall off Tongue Point, going away up the river, followed by the twinkling of gulls. When he looked about, there were only three people left on the rice-whitened dock—himself and Tom and Barry Pearson.

Barry still had to return the wagon to the store, and all of them were due back at high school, but they strolled to their favorite corner of the dock, with rice crackling under the soles of their Sunday shoes. The stringpiece was warm in the morning sun and the river went sliding by—tan-green, darkening under dark anchored ships, blue-green in mid-channel—

Barry said, "I'd like to play hookey for the rest of the day; take the boat out and just sail—or land some place where we've never been before and look around."

It used to be Jack and Tom who suggested playing hookey, but now there wasn't time for all the things they wanted to do. Jack said, "I'd be with you, Barry, if I didn't have work to make up."

Tom said, "Let's make it a Sunday." With Barry working on Saturdays, that was the only time that suited them all.

"What about this Sunday?"

"We're going to Portland," Jack said. "It will have to be the next."

Barry asked quietly, "Are you going to see Marjorie?"

"Yes."

"Why don't you let me go with you? I wouldn't mind—anything—if it helped."

Jack had asked Barry to look after Marjorie while he and Tom were away, and now he had to help him not to think about her any more. "Thanks, Barry, but you wouldn't be allowed. Anyway, it wouldn't do any good. She isn't Marjorie." He heard Barry give a sigh that caught somewhere. "You have to look at it that way: she isn't Marjorie."

It was time to take the wagon back to the store, and time to go back to school, but they sat a while longer, watching the river. This was the first time in a week that Jack had been on the river front. Life was so full now, with work to make up in high school and the extra studying from the books that had belonged to Captain Collins—navigation and naval architecture. During summer vacation they would be making coastwise voyages in the schooner *Halcyon*, adding up sea experience for their second mates' papers. And the summer after they would be in navigation school in San Francisco. Life was increasingly full and rich, but it seemed to put a wall of glass between him and the river. . . .

From the beginning he and Tom had been fascinated by the river. They had gone to it through the nettles of innumerable whippings, and they had run away to it and lived with it for a few enchanting weeks of summer. The river had made sailors of them and given them the world—and now they were farther from it than at the beginning. He didn't know how it had happened unless it was the current of the river pressing toward the ocean.

He remembered *Tenas Illihee*, "Little Land," that had been their home for an afternoon. Their boat was hidden in the tule beds at the south end of the island; bulrushes like giant grass waving out of the river. Beyond the edge of the tule bed there were *wapatos*, and two wild white swans were swimming and feeding; and an old man in a skiff was rowing up the channel between Illihee and the Hunting Islands. That was all, and nothing special happened; but while he watched idly, what he saw changed into music that he heard through his eyes. The round tule stems were half in air and half in water, and the little waves that rippled past their waists became music, singing of the river.

He had heard somewhere that swans live almost forever.

The swans glided back and forth without taking any notice of the current; they were part of the river, and they would be there forever. The old man in the boat would tire after a while and the current would carry him downstream. But the river would always be there—the bend of the river and the tule beds and the wild white swans. He and Tom didn't notice at the time, but the current was pulling at the anchor of their boat, trying to carry them away.

They had been carried downstream and given the world, but they might never really find the river again because they would always be busy with other things, or hurrying to the sea.

The river would always be there, but who would have time to sound its depths and explore its mysteries? Who would enter the caves in its rocky shores, and who would follow its winding sloughs through the lowlands where the otter and beaver lived? Who would fish for its harvest trout? Who would camp on its islands and lie naked in the sun on its shores; who would swim in its dim green tide and see the multitudes of Chinook salmon driving upstream to spawn, and the great sturgeon drowsing on its sandy floor? Who would drift at the edge of its forested mountains, watching the silken-black eagles blast through the sky? Who would have time to lie in the tule beds, listening to the song of the river, watching its wild white swans?

He loved the river and he had tried passionately to know it. It was still there, but he sensed that it had already escaped him, forever, almost unknown and unexplored.

At the Wheatland station Willard helped the women to the platform and shook hands with Mr. Hedges in the warm afterglow of the wedding.

Gripping Willard's hand in a calloused vise, Mr. Hedges

said, "Don't forget you're in the family, boy! Aim to get your nose out of your books long enough to come up and see us."

Mrs. Hedges' motherly sunburned face shone upon him. "Make it the first holiday you're not going home! There'll always be a room for you at the farm, and some home cooking won't hurt you."

Nancy said, "Good-bye, Willard." The grip of her young hand was like a friendly warning. "If you stay away too long, we'll come down to Salem and fetch you."

"I'll be there," he promised.

"We have some good saddle horses," she reminded him. "We'll see if you Astorians can ride as well as you sail."

"Don't expect that," Willard told her. "I wouldn't even know where to find the tiller!"

The train bell was ringing and the conductor had already shouted, "All aboard!"

"Good-bye!" Willard said.

"Good-bye, good-bye!"

Mrs. Hedges called after him, "It was a pretty wedding!"

Willard took an empty seat in the coach and waved to them as the train pulled away. The last one of the family he saw was Nancy, with her vivid, calculating face. She was a new type of girl to him: healthy and frank, but with ambitious drive. It seemed to him that a lawyer with a wife like her would rise to be Governor, or even President.

When the family was out of sight, Willard got up and dusted the plush seat and blew the cinders from the window sill, where he liked to rest his arm. His good suit would have to last until he hung out his shingle and he had to take care of it.

He settled down again, with a sober feeling of contentment he had never known before. Emily had married a fine young man with a good future. She would never reform the world, but she would be happy as a farmer's wife. If only she hadn't embarrassed him at the wedding breakfast by wishing that Hope Morris were there and wondering where she had gone. Willard didn't know, and there was nothing useful that he could say. He was reconciled now to losing her, and at the same time he thought of her with gratitude. She had seen what he hadn't been willing to admit to himself, that it wouldn't work—a penniless student burdened with a wife, and perhaps with babies.

Hope had been a phase of his life—one of the ingredients. He saw now that the life of a successful man is more than one life; it is made up of parts of other lives: Uncle Roger's years of help that had given him confidence and a feeling of security; his mother's tireless courage; and Hope's love, brief and complete, changing him from a green youth to a thoughtful man who saw the road ahead of him clearly.

Half an hour after he had said good-bye to the Hedges, Willard was in Salem, hurrying along Front Street. Curiously, during the days when he had scoured the town for a job, it was waiting for him downstairs, where Mr. Boyd had been deciding to take life easier. Now, on his free afternoons and Saturdays, he worked in the harness shop. Horses and harness had never been a part of Willard's life, but he made up for that by having a good manner with customers and keeping the books efficiently.

When Willard hurried in, the proprietor had already changed to his good clothes and was brushing his hat, preparatory to going home.

"I thought you would get here," he said. "Was it a nice wedding?"

"Everything went beautifully." Then Willard asked, "Is there anything special for me to do?"

"A few entries to make in the books; it's been a quiet day. But here's something that came today. I telegraphed Portland for it last Monday." He indicated a set of new harness on the rack—light, soft harness with gleaming buckles and mountings.

To Willard, harness had been something for utility, but the new set was enchanting to look at and to touch. "It's beautiful, really beautiful!"

"Did you ever feel such leather?" Mr. Boyd felt it again for himself. "And those are silver mountings."

"I didn't know we had a millionaire customer."

"He's new in town," Mr. Boyd said. "A young man named Black; I think he's in the Legislature."

Willard thought, and shook his head. "There's no one in the House or Senate by the name of Black."

Mr. Boyd wasn't going to argue with an expert. "He mentioned the Legislature, and he paid in advance. I was expecting him to come in, but it doesn't look as if he'd be here today."

When his employer was gone, Willard took off his good coat and hung it in the office, and he pulled his overalls on over his good trousers. Then he dashed upstairs to his living quarters and rescued his book on property law from among the unwashed dishes on the kitchen table. The room was a mess and it smelled musty with the windows closed all day. It had been so perfect when Hope kept house for him.

Downstairs he put his feet on the desk, found his place in the book and began to read—a young Abraham Lincoln studying while he kept store.

He started at a vigorous "Whoa!" Through the office window he saw a young man jump out of a light buggy and tie his horse to the hitching post, a beautiful bay hambletonian—there wasn't any doubt that the millionaire had arrived. Willard put his book aside and removed his feet from the desk.

He opened the door respectfully and the customer strode in, bringing with him the smell of Florida water and expensive cigar smoke, with a diamond cravat pin flashing in the subdued light of the store. "Hello! I dropped by for that set of—" He stopped and his big, honest face beamed. "Willard Pearson! Of all places to meet you!"

Shaking hands, Willard said, "George! This is a surprise!" It was more than that; it was a mystery! George Black, who hadn't finished high school until he was twenty—

the poorest and most unlikely of his class; George who humbly looked up to Willard as a shining light. And now, seemingly, George was a millionaire! "Come into the office," Willard said, "and we'll catch up on things—if you have time."

"I've an appointment to take a senator driving," George said, "but he can wait!" Seated in the comfortable chair in the office, he held out a handful of cigars. "Smoke? They're good Havana—Prima Dora."

Willard couldn't afford the luxury of tobacco, but as an afterthought he accepted one of the cigars for Mr. Boyd.

Across the desk, George said, "You could have knocked me over with a feather when I recognized you! Have you given up being a lawyer?"

"No. I only work here in my spare time; I keep the books for Mr. Boyd."

"How is everybody—your mother and sisters?"

"They're all well. I just got back from Emily's wedding."

"Emily married!" George said through rich cigar smoke. "You give me her address and I'll send a present. Anybody I know?"

Willard shook his head. "Albert Hedges, a young wheat grower; he has a farm up toward Lafayette." He thought a while, and said, "Yes, you did see him once. Remember the night we were coming down the river on the *Thompson*—the night they had the shanghaied crew on board?"

"Will I ever forget that night, and the wonderful speech you made? Some of the men cried—"

"Albert was the young man the Dirks slugged when he tried to get away. Emily got acquainted with him after he came back; and now they're married."

"I'll be damned!" George's big, well-groomed face glowed with recollections. "That was an adventure, that night on the river! Seems like twenty years ago. I'll never forget how green I felt; I was asking your advice about a job; I'd just been fired from a livery stable—"

Willard finished it for him, "Now I'm working in a livery stable and you're a millionaire!"

George protested warmly, "I didn't mean that! You'll go on and be a great lawyer while I'm just a businessman." Then he said, "My luck began in a livery stable—it was on the way before I talked to you that night."

"Tell me about it!"

"I told you about the drunk customer who said my honest face would be my fortune?"

"You did—the one who said he had a mind to take you into partnership."

"That's the one! I never expected to hear from him. But he must have got drunk again—he sent for me and we went into business together. I'm worth a cool hundred thousand now."

"That's wonderful, George! What is the business?"

"Timber land—we take up claims and sell them to the big companies."

Willard felt blank. "But a man can take up only one claim!"

"That's what people think," George said. "We've taken up thousands. Mr.—my partner makes up the lists of names and I file them at the Land Office. That's where my honest face comes in; my partner likes to stay in the dark."

Willard didn't understand. "If you take up land for other people, how can you sell it?"

"They're just names. My partner gets them out of old directories and passenger lists, and off tombstones."

"So that's how it's done!"

The tone of Willard's voice made George faintly apologetic. "Maybe it's not too straight—but it don't hurt anybody. And the claims cost us enough: filing fee and patent fee; and we have to pay the Deputy Surveyor for attesting that our people are on the claims, and we have to keep a federal land agent oiled. It even costs something to make cabins and take them to the claims—"

Willard suspected his old friend was drunk, or insane.

"You take cabins through the woods, when there are building materials on the spot?"

"We used to," George said. "We had a cabin on runners and three witnesses who traveled with it and swore that they had seen a cabin on each claim; but that was too much overhead. Now we build wholesale lots of twelve-by-sixteen cabins, with fireplace and window, and send one to each claim."

"Impossible!" Willard said.

George was enjoying his dismay. "We do it, just the same. The law requires twelve-by-sixteen cabins—and we make them twelve by sixteen—inches; dolls' houses!"

Willard slumped on his side of the desk. "Good God!"

George was disappointed at the way his friend was taking his business secrets. "If we didn't do it, somebody else would. We have competitors who aren't honest, and we have to work fast. That's why I'm in Salem now. There's too much red tape on the public domain and we want some of it cut—" He looked at Willard and asked anxiously, "What's the matter?"

Willard felt nauseated. "I think you'd better take your harness and go."

George got up, his big face looking hurt and worried. "Guess I talk too much; but it took me by surprise, meeting an old friend this way. Forget what I told you."

"You'd better go," Willard said.

When he was gone, Willard sat at the desk, feeling ill. His old schoolmate, George Black, selling the birthright of his state for a set of silver-mounted harness! "Maybe it isn't too straight." Maybe he could put his friend's big, honest face behind the bars, but "Mr.—my partner" would go free, and so would the corrupt officials and "our competitors who aren't honest" and the syndicates that had bought the public domain from jackals for small change.

He opened his book because he couldn't think of anything else to do. At first, as he read, he was haunted by a feeling

[335]

of revolt against the corrupt world. Then it passed and he was at peace—following his lonely path through the intricacies of property law.

Most of the people they met were busy with their own affairs, but a few smiled with open amusement, or gently as if they were bestowing a blessing on some fragile moment of happiness.

Emily said, "Maybe we don't look as much like old married people as we thought!"

"We got the best of it either way; we've that to look forward to, and we have now."

She pressed Albert's big-muscled arm through his cheviot sleeve. "And no one is going to shanghai you away from me!"

His tanned, ruddy face smiled down at her. "I don't aim to let them; but if they hadn't done it the first time, where would we be now?"

Emily didn't know; they certainly wouldn't be strolling about Portland on their wedding day. "Once worked beautifully, but don't let it happen again!"

"They tried it twice," he reminded her; "but I got away the second time." After a few more steps, he asked, "Who were those young fellows standing in the hall at the wedding —the black-haired ones who looked like twins, only one was older?"

"They're the Fortune boys—special friends of Barry's."

"The ones who had such terrible battles with their Pa and Ma?"

"They used to, but they get along beautifully now—only their battles were too much for their sister, who was always trying to make peace; she is up here in the asylum."

Albert surprised her by going back to the earlier subject. Putting his free hand over hers as it rested on his arm, he said, "Nobody's going to shanghai me the second time, Emily! It's like getting married: once is enough; I mean getting married to you!"

She smiled up at him happily. "Do you know where we are walking?"

"Together," he said.

"That's a nice way to walk!"

"If you are getting tired, we can go to our hotel."

"No, Albert; I feel as if I could walk forever with you!"

"Would you like to stop for a bite to eat?"

They were in a residential part of town, in a street of mansions, with a church down the block. It didn't look like a neighborhood for refreshments, and she didn't want any.

"Maybe you would like to see the stores," Albert said.

"I would, Albert! Mrs. Fortune gave us ten dollars to buy a wedding present; we could get a parlor lamp!"

"We'll go to Meier and Frank's," Albert said; "they had some beauties when I was there last week: china lamps with roses painted on the shades."

"That's the kind I want," Emily told him; "we can pick one out together."

Albert said, "I want to buy something for you, too; but you'll have to help me pick it out."

They walked back along the pleasant street that was lined with elm trees brought around the Horn by the New England fathers of the city; the afternoon sun showered down light and shadows on the broad street and on a carriage drawn by white horses—milk-white horses that walked with slow, prancing steps; a uniformed coachman with a top hat was perched high on the front of the gleaming carriage.

"Some day you can buy me a carriage and horses like that," Emily said.

"Not like that, Emily!" Albert's tone was shocked.

"I was only joking, Albert. I would never want anything so expensive."

He was looking down at her tenderly and ruefully. "It isn't the expense—it's what the rig is used for."

"What is it used for, Albert?"

"It belongs to Madam DeVore."

"Madam DeVore?" The name had a half-familiar sound. "Not—the bagnio keeper?"

"That's who, Emily."

It seemed impossible that the ancient evil was alive after all these years. "Aunt Rita told us about her! When the *Great Republic* was wrecked, Madam DeVore was on board, posing as the friend of homeless girls. She rounded up the prettiest ones and might have trapped them all if Uncle Roger hadn't got them into his boat and left her hanging onto a ladder—"

The carriage was almost abreast of them: the milk-white horses, in black harness that shone like patent leather, raising their polished hoofs in their slow prancing walk; the liveried coachman with a face like a withered mask; and the low-cut open carriage with its gleam and pomp of suave evil—like a glimpse of the streets of Babylon. Emily took one glance and turned her face away and held tighter to Albert's reassuring strong arm. I won't look until they're past, she thought. Probably Madam DeVore was there, the clever, cruel old woman who almost trapped Aunt Rita. What was she like? How did the face of evil look? Overwhelming curiosity made her turn.

The carriage was almost close enough for Emily to touch. Madam DeVore was not there—only four beautifully dressed girls no older than herself. They were sitting two and two, facing each other, holding silk parasols. One of the girls facing her looked like someone she knew—only more beautiful; delicate oval face and upward-looking blue eyes, like a radiant angel— *Hope!* The carriage rolled by and left Emily stock-still on the pavement. *Hope*—

"Emily, what is it?" Albert was beside her, looking tenderly anxious. "Don't you feel right?"

"That was Hope Morris! And I wanted her to be my bridesmaid!"

"It's a mercy she wasn't!"

"She left home last winter—no one knew where she was."

"You know now," he said mournfully. "It's too bad; she was pretty."

Emily was struggling like a swimmer under water. "And I didn't even speak to her!"

"I guess you wouldn't want to speak to a girl like that."

Albert was right; a respectable married woman didn't speak to a courtesan. But Emily thought, I would have spoken to her if I hadn't been too startled. It couldn't have been easy for Hope, flaunting her shame in Madam DeVore's carriage, meeting Emily on her wedding day. Maybe she hadn't noticed, but Emily was almost certain she had.

As she and Albert walked on, she continued to see Hope's delicate oval face and upward-looking eyes saluting her with a look of angelic dismay at the exigencies of this life.

When people in Astoria asked Rita why she was going back to San Francisco, she told them, "It was my home; I have friends and relations there."

She did not know of any relations besides Aunt Dolores, and she had not heard from her for years. But she did have friends. Since the newspaper stories about the disappearance of the *Huntress*, she had received a letter from Mary O'Malley, who was now the wife of a prosperous building contractor and the mother of six children. Mary's warm-hearted invitation had decided her—and the visit would have a kind of tardy honesty. When Rita had embarked on the *Great Republic*, it was with the pretense of spending the week with Mary O'Malley. Now that she was on the deck of a steamship again it didn't seem so long ago. She felt undamaged by time and strangely young—still young enough to have as many children as Mary O'Malley.

Steaming smoothly down the great river, the *Oregon* gave a questioning tremble and lifted to a profound swell that rose out of the quiet water in the sunrise light. The steamer lifted and settled deliberately, and lifted on a greater swell. To the north there was a mountainous cape with a lighthouse

[339]

on it, but ahead there was nothing between the ship and the limitless horizon. They were already crossing the bar. She looked anxiously at the box at her feet and decided that the mate had forgotten his promise; not that she couldn't manage by herself, if she only knew where. But, for the widow of a pilot, she was woefully ignorant of the river.

She was still fighting her chagrin over being forgotten when the young mate turned the corner of the deckhouse and came toward her briskly. "Good morning, Mrs. Collins." He touched his gold-braided cap as the ship sank in a valley where the light of the early sun did not reach. "We're having a peaceful crossing." He stopped beside her at the rail. "We'll be there in a few minutes."

"I thought you had forgotten."

"I should hardly be likely to forget, ma'am." He looked professionally toward the headland to the north, where the lighthouse went on flashing its spark, although it was already morning on the upper slopes of the great swells coming in over the bar.

He lifted the heavy box to the rail and balanced it as the *Oregon* rose to another swell. "The *Vandalia* was found over there, in Dead Man's Hollow—on this side of Cape Disappointment. Captain Beard washed ashore in the cove north of the lighthouse, the one known as Beard's Hollow."

The morning sun gleamed warmly on the wooden box and on lettering Rita hadn't noticed when she selected it: *Gail Borden's Eagle Brand Condensed Milk*, an incongruous touch that the mate didn't notice. His eyes were on the Cape.

"We're abreast now," he said; "shall I let it go?"

"Please."

Even then he waited until the ship rose out of the hollow and lifted into the sunlight, rolling outward a little. He tipped the box smartly from the rail; it fell clear of the ship's side, crashing a hole in the sea as it disappeared.

The mate started to dust his hands, then stopped as if it might be a disrespectful gesture. "That was as close as I could make it."

"Yes." She accepted his word for it. "Thank you."

With his cap in his hand, he said, "If I can be of any further help to you, please let me know, Mrs. Collins."

"Thank you," she said; "it was very kind of you."

He looked as if he would like to stay longer, but he bowed and went away with honest delicacy.

Rita stayed where she was, while the great swells of the bar sank into the lesser swells of the Pacific and Cape Disappointment bore astern. Bells clanged and the *Oregon* slowed and stopped. They were dropping the pilot—sour old Joe Ball. She would have liked to go around to the other side of the deck and see him clamber stiffly down the ladder into the small boat, but lonely professional loyalty kept her where she was.

Gongs clanged and the hungry sighing of the engines began again. Gathering weight, the *Oregon* raised her voice in two deep bellows. The whistle blasts were answered by a cocky, lesser whistle, and a tug appeared suddenly as the steamer turned more to the south. Astern of the tug a tall, low-hulled ship was walking over the sea, with the sunrise on white sails and on gray weathered sails patched with white. Men were going aloft in the black spider web of rigging and one of the sails crumpled as it was clewed up.

Through wild, dreaming seconds, Rita imagined it to be the *Huntress*, coming into the river at last. It could happen, even now! When the vessel came abreast, Rita saw that it was a bark; the *Huntress* was full-rigged.

On board the inbound ship the crew were aware of no disappointment. Men aloft on the footropes of yards waved recklessly from the dangerous heights, and men on deck, hauling on clew lines, found arms to wave. Rita could not grudge them their moment of triumph—making their landfall in the morning, coming safely to the mouth of the great river in the springtime. She waved her handkerchief in return, and it wasn't till then that she knew they were waving to her—men who had been months at sea waving to the one woman in sight on the passing ship. Sailors! Rita continued to wave; it was a part of the generous early morning and the renewed discovery of America. By night the triumph and the newness would be dulled in the saloons and brothels ashore; but now the faces of the sailors were bright in the sunrise and their dream of the land was golden. Rita waved until the vessels passed and drew away from each other.

She wondered how the mate would take it if he saw her waving to the homeward-bound crew—the mate who tiptoed away, cap in hand, from what he took to be a sentimental rite for a dead pilot.

Returning the *Vandalia's* bell to the Columbia had nothing to do with Roger Collins except to break her last dim bond with him. It seemed to her that she could never hear the bell without imagining Roger's jaunty step, without calling up his amused face and searching eyes with the prophetic blue of the sea in them. She would never be able to hear the deep tone of the bell without thrilling to the thought that Roger was coming home—to disappoint and torment her. Roger whom she had loved, and still loved. She thought: It isn't so different from the way it was when he was alive; even when he was in the same bed with me, he was sleeping with the sea!

Roger would never come home to her, and there was no good in keeping the bell snatched by a dead man from the earlier dead. It had been only right to return it to the rolling bar of the Columbia and the *Vandalia's* crew—ready to clang through their long sleep and bid them rise and shine on Judgment Day.